Henry Miller's *Tropic of Capricorn:*
The great companion volume to *Tropic of Cancer.*

This is an astonishing account of what it means to grow to manhood in modern America. Nothing like it, nothing even remotely approaching it, has ever been published in this country. Long banned because of its unprecedented frankness about sex, it gives complete expression to its author's determination to face everything in life without evasion, and to accept everything without reservation.

First published in Paris in 1939, five years after *Tropic of Cancer, Capricorn* takes the fictional autobiography of one of America's greatest writers back to earlier days, before the Paris vagabondage that produced *Cancer.* Here Henry Miller writes about the youthful years in Brooklyn, the job as employment manager for the "Cosmodemonic Telegraph Company," the first loves and the riotous sex episodes of the twenties. He gives us the New York he knew before he went to Paris to become a writer, and peoples it with those fabulous Miller characters, riotously funny, shockingly coarse, totally different from all the characters of polite literature and thus amazingly true and real.

But most of all he writes about himself. No other book by Henry Miller tells us so much about what went on within him that turned him into one of the most remarkable people and writers of this or any age.

TROPIC OF CAPRICORN

Henry Miller

BALLANTINE BOOKS • NEW YORK

ISBN 0-345-24499-0-195

This edition published by arrangement with Grove Press, Inc.

Manufactured in the United States of America

First Ballantine Books Edition: August 1973
Third Printing: December 1976

TO HER

FOREWORD

to

HISTORIA CALAMITATUM

(the story of my misfortunes)

Often the hearts of men and women are stirred, as likewise they are soothed in their sorrows, more by example than by words. And therefore, because I too have known some consolation from speech had with one who was a witness thereof, am I now minded to write of the sufferings which have sprung out of my misfortunes, for the eyes of one who, though absent, is of himself ever a consoler. This I do so that, in comparing your sorrows with mine, you may discover that yours are in truth nought, or at the most but of small account, and so shall you come to bear them more easily.

PETER ABELARD

ON THE OVARIAN TROLLEY

Once you have given up the ghost, everything follows with dead certainty, even in the midst of chaos. From the beginning it was never anything but chaos: it was a fluid which enveloped me, which I breathed in through the gills. In the substrata, where the moon shone steady and opaque, it was smooth and fecundating; above it was a jangle and a discord. In everything I quickly saw the opposite, the contradiction, and between the real and the unreal the irony, the paradox. I was my own worst enemy. There was nothing I wished to do which I could just as well not do. Even as a child, when I lacked for nothing, I wanted to die: I wanted to surrender because I saw no sense in struggling. I felt that nothing would be proved, substantiated, added or subtracted by continuing an existence which I had not asked for. Everybody around me was a failure, or if not a failure, ridiculous. Especially the successful ones. The successful ones bored me to tears. I was sympathetic to a fault, but it was not sympathy that made me so. It was a purely negative quality, a weakness which blossomed at the mere sight of human misery. I never helped any one expecting that it would do any good; I helped because I was helpless to do otherwise. To want to change the condition of affairs seemed futile to me; nothing would be altered, I was convinced, except by a change of heart, and who could change the hearts of men? Now and then a friend was converted: it was something to make me puke. I had no more need of God than He had of me, and if there were one, I often said to myself, I would meet Him calmly and spit in His face.

What was most annoying was that at first blush people

usually took me to be good, to be kind, generous, loyal, faithful. Perhaps I did possess these virtues but if so it was because I was indifferent: I could afford to be good, kind, generous, loyal, and so forth, since I was free of envy. Envy was the one thing I was never a victim of. I have never envied anybody or anything. On the contrary, I have only felt pity for everybody and everything.

From the very beginning I must have trained myself not to want anything too badly. From the very beginning I was independent, in a false way. I had need of nobody because I wanted to be free, free to do and to give only as my whims dictated. The moment anything was expected or demanded of me I balked. That was the form my independence took. I was corrupt, in other words, corrupt from the start. It's as though my mother fed me a poison, and though I was weaned young the poison never left my system. Even when she weaned me it seemed that I was completely indifferent; most children rebel, or make a pretense of rebelling, but I didn't give a damn. I was a philosopher when still in swaddling clothes. I was against life, on principle. What principle? The principle of futility. Everybody around me was struggling. I myself never made an effort. If I appeared to be making an effort it was only to please someone else; at bottom I didn't give a rap. And if you can tell me why this should have been so I will deny it, because I was born with a cussed streak in me and nothing can eliminate it. I heard later, when I had grown up, that they had a hell of a time bringing me out of the womb. I can understand that perfectly. Why budge? Why come out of a nice warm place, a cosy retreat in which everything is offered you gratis? The earliest remembrance I have is of the cold, the snow and ice in the gutter, the frost on the window panes, the chill of the sweaty green walls in the kitchen. Why do people live in outlandish climates in the *temperate* zones, as they are miscalled? Because people are naturally idiots, naturally sluggards, naturally cowards. Until I was about ten years old I never realized that there were "warm" countries, places where you didn't have to sweat for a living, nor shiver and pretend that it was tonic and exhilarating. Wherever there is cold there are people who work themselves to the bone and when they produce young they preach to the young the gospel of work—which is nothing, at bottom, but the doctrine of inertia. My people were entirely Nordic, which is to say *idiots*. Every wrong idea which has ever been expounded was theirs. Among them was the doctrine of cleanliness, to say nothing of righteousness. They were painfully clean. But inwardly they stank. Never once had they opened the door which leads to the soul; never once did they dream of taking a blind leap into the dark. After dinner the dishes were promptly washed and put in the closet; after the paper was read it was neatly folded and laid away on a shelf; after the clothes were washed they were ironed and folded and then tucked away in the drawers. Everything was for tomorrow, but tomorrow never came. The present was only a bridge and on this bridge they are still groaning, as the world groans, and not one idiot ever thinks of blowing up the bridge.

In my bitterness I often search for reasons to condemn them, the better to condemn myself. For I am like them too, in many ways. For a long while I thought I had escaped, but as time goes on I see that I am no better, that I am even a little worse, because I saw more clearly than they ever did and yet remained powerless to alter my life. As I look back on my life it seems to me that I never did anything of my own volition but always through the pressure of others. People often think of me as an adventurous fellow; nothing could be farther from the truth. My adventures were always adventitious, always thrust on me, always endured rather than undertaken. I am of the very essence of that proud, boastful Nordic people who have never had the least sense of adventure but who nevertheless have scoured the earth, turned it upside down, scattering relics and ruins everywhere. Restless spirits, but not adventurous ones. Agonizing spirits, incapable of living in the present. Disgraceful cowards, all of them, myself included. For there is only one great adventure and that is inward toward the self, and for that, time nor space nor even deeds matter.

Once every few years I was on the verge of making this discovery, but in characteristic fashion I always managed to dodge the issue. If I try to think of a good excuse I can think only of the environment, of the streets I knew and the people who inhabited them. I can think of no street in America, or of people inhabiting such a street, capable of leading one on toward the discovery of the self. I have walked the streets in many countries of the world but nowhere have I felt so degraded and humiliated as in America. I think of all the streets in America combined as forming a huge cesspool, a cesspool of the spirit in which everything is sucked down and drained away to everlasting shit. Over this cesspool the spirit of work weaves a magic wand; palaces and factories spring up side by side, and munition plants and chemical works and steel mills and sanatoriums and prisons and insane asylums. The whole continent is a nightmare producing the greatest misery of the greatest number. I was one, a single entity in the midst of the greatest jamboree of wealth and happiness (statistical wealth, statistical happiness) but I never met a man who was truly wealthy or truly happy. At least I knew that I was unhappy, unwealthy, out of whack and out of step. That was my only solace, my only joy. But it was hardly enough. It would have been better for my peace of mind, for my soul, if I had expressed my rebellion openly, if I had gone to jail for it, if I had rotted there and died. It would have been better if, like the mad Czolgosz, I had shot some good President McKinley, some gentle, insignificant soul like that who had never done anyone the least harm. Because in the bottom of my heart there was murder: I wanted to see America destroyed, razed from top to bottom. I wanted to see this happen purely out of vengeance, as atonement for the crimes that were committed against me and against others like me who have never been able to lift their voices and express their hatred, their rebellion, their legitimate blood lust.

I was the evil product of an evil soil. If the self were not imperishable, the "I" I write about would have been destroyed long ago. To some this may seem like an invention, but whatever I imagine to have happened did actually happen, *at least to me*. History may deny it, since I have played no part in the history of my people, but even if everything I say is wrong, is prejudiced, spiteful, malevolent, even if I am a liar and a poisoner, it is nevertheless the truth and it will have to be swallowed.

As to what happened . . .

Everything that happens, when it has significance, is in the nature of a contradiction. Until the one for whom this is written came along I imagined that somewhere outside, in life, as they say, lay the solution to all things. I thought, when I came upon her, that I was seizing hold of life, seizing hold of something which I could bite into. Instead I lost hold of life completely. I reached out for something to attach myself to—and I found nothing. But in reaching out, in the effort to grasp, to attach myself, left high and dry as I was, I nevertheless found something I had not looked for—*myself*. I found that what I had desired all my life was not to live—if what others are doing is called living—but to express myself. I realized that I had never the least interest in living, but only in this which I am doing now, something which is parallel to life, of it at the same time, and beyond it. What is true interests me scarcely at all, nor even what is real; only that interests me which I imagine to be, that which I had stifled every day in order to live. Whether I die today or tomorrow is of no importance to me, never has been, but that today even, after years of effort, I cannot say what I think and feel—that bothers me, that rankles. From childhood on I can see myself on the track of this specter, en-

joying nothing, desiring nothing but this power, this ability. Everything else is a lie—everything I ever did or
said which did not bear upon this. And that is pretty
much the greater part of my life.

I was a contradiction in essence, as they say. People
took me to be serious and high-minded, or to be gay and
reckless, or to be sincere and earnest, or to be negligent
and carefree. I was all these things at once—and beyond
that I was something else, something which no one suspected, least of all myself. As a boy of six or seven I used
to sit at my grandfather's workbench and read to him
while he sewed. I remember him vividly in those moments
when, pressing the hot iron against the seam of a coat, he
would stand with one hand over the other and look out
of the window dreamily. I remember the expression on
his face, as he stood there dreaming, better than the
contents of the books I read, better than the conversations
we had or the games which I played in the street. I used
to wonder what he was dreaming of, what it was that
drew him out of himself. I hadn't learned yet how to
dream wide-awake. I was always lucid, in the moment,
and all of a piece. His daydreaming fascinated me. I
knew that he had no connection with what he was doing,
not the least thought for any of us, that he was alone and
being alone he was free. I was never alone, least of all
when I was by myself. Always, it seems to me, I was
accompanied: I was like a little crumb of a big cheese,
which was the world, I suppose, though I never stopped
to think about it. But I know I never existed separately,
never thought myself the big cheese, as it were. So that
even when I had reason to be miserable, to complain, to
weep, I had the illusion of participating in a common, a
universal misery. When I wept the whole world was
weeping—so I imagined. I wept very seldom. Mostly I
was happy, I was laughing, I was having a good time.
I had a good time because, as I said before, I really
didn't give a fuck about anything. If things were wrong

with me they were wrong everywhere, I was convinced of it. And things were wrong usually only when one cared too much. That impressed itself on me very early in life. For example, I remember the case of my young friend Jack Lawson. For a whole year he lay in bed, suffering the worst agonies. He was my best friend, so people said at any rate. Well, at first I was probably sorry for him and perhaps now and then I called at his house to inquire about him; but after a month or two had elapsed I grew quite callous about his suffering. I said to myself he ought to die and the sooner he dies the better it will be, and having thought thus I acted accordingly: that is to say, I promptly forgot about him, abandoned him to his fate. I was only about twelve years old at the time and I remember being proud of my decision. I remember the funeral too—what a disgraceful affair it was. There they were, friends and relatives all congregated about the bier and all of them bawling like sick monkeys. The mother especially gave me a pain in the ass. She was such a rare, spiritual creature, a Christian Scientist, I believe, and though she didn't believe in disease and didn't believe in death either, she raised such a stink that Christ himself would have risen from the grave. But not her beloved Jack! No, Jack lay there cold as ice and rigid and unbeckonable. He was dead and there were no two ways about it. I knew it and I was glad of it. I didn't waste any tears over it. I couldn't say that he was better off because after all the "he" had vanished. *He* was gone and with him the sufferings he had endured and the suffering he had unwittingly inflicted on others. Amen!, I said to myself, and with that, being slightly hysterical, I let a loud fart—right beside the coffin.

This caring too much—I remember that it only developed with me about the time I first fell in love. And even then I didn't care enough. If I had really cared I wouldn't be here now writing about it: I'd have died of a broken heart, or I'd have swung for it. It was a bad experience because it taught me how to live a lie. It taught me to smile when I didn't want to smile, to work when I didn't believe in work, to live when I had no reason to go on living. Even when I had forgotten her I still retained the trick of doing what I didn't believe in.

It was all chaos from the beginning, as I have said. But sometimes I got so close to the center, to the very heart of the confusion, that it's a wonder things didn't explode around me.

It is customary to blame everything on the war. I say the war had nothing to do with me, with my life. At a time when others were getting themselves comfortable berths I was taking one miserable job after another, and never enough in it to keep body and soul together. Almost as quickly as I was hired I was fired. I had plenty of intelligence but I inspired distrust. Wherever I went I fomented discord—not because I was idealistic but because I was like a searchlight exposing the stupidity and futility of everything. Besides, I wasn't a good ass licker. That marked me, no doubt. People could tell at once when I asked for a job that I really didn't give a damn whether I got it or not. And of course I generally didn't get it. But after a time the mere looking for a job became an activity, a pastime, so to speak. I would go in and ask for most anything. It was a way of killing time—no worse, as far as I could see, than work itself. I was my own boss and I had my own hours, but unlike other bosses I entrained only my own ruin, my own bankruptcy. I was not a corporation or a trust or a state or a federation or a polity of nations—I was more like God, if anything.

This went on from about the middle of the war until . . . well, until one day I was trapped. Finally the day came when I did desperately want a job. I needed it. Not having another minute to lose, I decided that I would take the last job on earth, that of messenger boy. I walked into the employment bureau of the telegraph company—the Cosmodemonic Telegraph Company of North America—toward the close of the day, prepared to go through with it. I had just come from the public library and I had under my arm some fat books on economics and meta-physics. To my great amazement I was refused the job.

The guy who turned me down was a little runt who ran the switchboard. He seemed to take me for a college student, though it was clear enough from my application that I had long left school. I had even honored myself on the application with a Ph.D. degree from Columbia University. Apparently that passed unnoticed, or else was suspiciously regarded by this runt who had turned me down. I was furious, the more so because for once in my life I was in earnest. Not only that, but I had swallowed my pride, which in certain peculiar ways is rather large. My wife of course gave me the usual leer and sneer. I had done it as a gesture, she said. I went to bed thinking about it, still smarting, getting angrier and angrier as the night wore on. The fact that I had a wife and child to support didn't bother me so much; people didn't offer you jobs because you had a family to support, that much I understood only too well. No, what rankled was that they had rejected *me*, Henry V. Miller, a competent, superior individual who had asked for the lowest job in the world. That burned me up. I couldn't get over it. In the morning I was up bright and early, shaved, put on my best clothes and hotfooted it to the subway. I went immediately to the main offices of the telegraph company . . . up to the twenty-fifth floor or wherever it was that the president and the vice-presidents had their cubicles. I asked to see the president. Of course the president was either out of town or too busy to see me, but wouldn't I care to see the vice-president, or his secretary rather. I saw the vice-president's secretary, an intelligent, considerate sort of chap, and I gave him an earful. I did it adroitly, without too much heat, but letting him understand all the while that I wasn't to be put out of the way so easily.

When he picked up the telephone and demanded the general manager I thought it was just a gag, that they were going to pass me around like that from one to the other until I'd get fed up. But the moment I heard him talk I changed my opinion. When I got to the general manager's office, which was in another building uptown, they were waiting for me. I sat down in a comfortable leather chair and accepted one of the big cigars that were thrust forward. This individual seemed at once to be vitally concerned about the matter. He wanted me to tell him all about it, down to the last detail, his big hairy ears cocked to catch the least crumb of information which would justify something or other which was formulating itself inside his dome. I realized that by some accident I had really been instrumental in doing him a service. I let him wheedle it out of me to suit his fancy, observing all the time which way the wind was blowing. And as the talk progressed I noticed that he was warming up to me more and more. At last some one was showing a little confidence in me! That was all I required to get started on one of my favorite lines. For, after years of job hunting I had naturally become quite adept: I knew not only what *not* to say, but I knew also what to imply, what to insinuate. Soon the assistant general manager was called in and asked to listen to my story. By this time I knew what the story was. I understood that Hymie—"that little kike," as the general manager called him—had no business pretending that he was the employment manager. Hymie had usurped his prerogative, that much was clear. It was also clear that Hymie was a Jew and that Jews were not in good odor with the general manager, nor with Mr. Twilliger, the vice-president, who was a thorn in the general manager's side.

Perhaps it was Hymie, "the dirty little kike," who was responsible for the high percentage of Jews on the messenger force. Perhaps Hymie was really the one who was doing the hiring at the employment office—at Sunset Place, they called it. It was an excellent opportunity, I gathered, for Mr. Clancy, the general manager, to take down a certain Mr. Burns who, he informed me, had been the employment manager for some thirty years now and who was evidently getting lazy on the job.

The conference lasted several hours. Before it was terminated Mr. Clancy took me aside and informed me that he was going to make *me* the boss of the works. Before putting me into office, however, he was going to ask me as a special favor, and also as a sort of apprenticeship which would stand me in good stead, to work as a special messenger. I would receive the salary of employment manager, but it would be paid me out of a separate account. In short I was to float from office to office and observe the way affairs were conducted by all and sundry. I was to make a little report from time to time as to how things were going. And once in a while, so he suggested, I was to visit him at his home on the q.t. and have a little chat about the conditions in the hundred and one branches of the Cosmodemonic Telegraph Company in New York City. In other words I was to be a spy for a few months and after that I was to have the run of the joint. Maybe they'd make me a general manager too one day, or a vice-president. It was a tempting offer, even if it was wrapped up in a lot of horseshit. I said Yes.

In a few months I was sitting at Sunset Place hiring and firing like a demon. It was a slaughterhouse, so help me God. The thing was senseless from the bottom up. A waste of men, material and effort. A hideous farce against a backdrop of sweat and misery. But just as I had accepted the spying so I accepted the hiring and firing and all that went with it. I said Yes to everything. If the vice-president decreed that no cripples were to be hired I hired no cripples. If the vice-president said that all messengers over forty-five were to be fired without notice I fired them without notice. I did everything they instructed me to do, but in such a way that they had to pay for it. When there was a strike I folded my arms and waited for it to blow over. But I first saw to it that it cost them a good penny. The whole system was so rotten, so inhuman, so lousy, so hopelessly corrupt and

complicated, that it would have taken a genius to put
any sense or order into it, to say nothing of human kindness or consideration. I was up against the whole system
of American labor, which is rotten at both ends. I was
the fifth wheel on the wagon and neither side had any
use for me, except to exploit me. In fact, everybody was
being exploited—the president and his gang by the unseen powers, the employees by the officials, and so on and
around, in and out and through the whole works. From
my little perch at Sunset Place I had a bird's eye view
of the whole American society. It was like a page out
of the telephone book. Alphabetically, numerically, statistically, it made sense. But when you looked at it up
close, when you examined the pages separately, or the
parts separately, when you examined one lone individual
and what constituted him, examined the air he breathed,
the life he led, the chances he risked, you saw something
so foul and degrading, so low, so miserable, so utterly
hopeless and senseless, that it was worse than looking
into a volcano. You could see the whole American life—
economically, politically, morally, spiritually, artistically,
statistically, pathologically. It looked like a grand chancre
on a worn-out cock. It looked worse than that, really, because you couldn't even see anything resembling a cock
any more. Maybe in the past this thing had life, did produce something, did at least give a moment's pleasure, a
moment's thrill. But looking at it from where I sat it
looked rottener than the wormiest cheese. The wonder
was that the stench of it didn't carry 'em off. . . . I'm using
the past tense all the time, but of course it's the same now,
maybe even a bit worse. At least now we're getting it full
stink.

By the time Valeska arrived on the scene I had hired
several army corps of messengers. My office at Sunset
Place was like an open sewer, and it stank like one. I
had dug myself into the first-line trench and I was getting
it from all directions at once. To begin with, the man
I had ousted died of a broken heart a few weeks after

my arrival. He held out just long enough to break me in and then he croaked. Things happened so fast that I didn't have a chance to feel guilty. From the moment I arrived at the office it was one long uninterrupted pandemonium. An hour before my arrival—I was always late —the place was already jammed with applicants. I had to elbow my way up the stairs and literally force my way in to get to my desk. Before I could take my hat off I had to answer a dozen telephone calls. There were three telephones on my desk and they all rang at once. They were bawling the piss out of me before I had even sat down to work. There wasn't even time to take a crap —until five or six in the afternoon. Hymie was worse off than I because he was tied to the switchboard. He sat there from eight in the morning until six, moving waybills around. A waybill was a messenger loaned by one office to another office for the day or a part of the day. None of the hundred and one offices ever had a full staff; Hymie had to play chess with the waybills while I worked like a madman to plug up the gaps. If by a miracle I succeeded of a day in filling all the vacancies, the next morning would find the situation exactly the same—or worse. Perhaps twenty per cent of the force was steady; the rest was driftwood. The steady ones drove the new ones away. The steady ones earned forty to fifty dollars a week, sometimes sixty or seventy-five, sometimes as much as a hundred dollars a week, which is to say that they earned far more than the clerks and often more than their own managers. As for the new ones, they found it difficult to earn ten dollars a week. Some of them worked an hour and quit, often throwing a batch of telegrams in the garbage can or down the sewer. And whenever they quit they wanted their pay immediately, which was impossible, because in the complicated bookkeeping which ruled no one could say what a messenger had earned until at least ten days later. In the beginning I invited the applicant to sit down beside me and I explained everything to him in detail. I did that until I lost my voice.

Soon I learned to save my strength for the grilling that was necessary. In the first place, every other boy was a born liar, if not a crook to boot. Many of them had already been hired and fired a number of times. Some found it an excellent way to find another job, because their duty brought them to hundreds of offices which normally they would never have set foot in. Fortunately McGovern, the old trusty who guarded the door and handed out the application blanks, had a camera eye. And then there were the big ledgers behind me, in which there was a record of every applicant who had ever passed through the mill. The ledgers were very much like a police record; they were full of red ink marks, signifying this or that delinquency. To judge from the evidence I was in a tough spot. Every other name involved a theft, a fraud, a brawl, or dementia or perversion or idiocy. "Be careful—so-and-so is an epileptic!" "Don't hire this man—he's a nigger!" "Watch out—X has been in Dannemora—or else in Sing Sing."

If I had been a stickler for etiquette nobody would ever have been hired. I had to learn quickly, and not from the records or from those about me, but from experience. There were a thousand and one details by which to judge an applicant: I had to take them all in at once, and quickly, because in one short day, even if you are as fast as Jack Robinson, you can only hire so many and no more. And no matter how many I hired it was never enough. The next day it would begin all over again. Some I knew would last only a day, but I had to hire them just the same. The system was wrong from start to finish, but it was not my place to criticize the system. It was mine to hire and fire. I was in the center of a revolving disk which was whirling so fast that nothing could stay put. What was needed was a mechanic, but according to the logic of the higher-ups there was nothing wrong with the mechanism, everything was fine and dandy except that things were temporarily out of order. And things being temporarily out of order brought on epilepsy, theft, van-

dalism, perversion, niggers, Jews, whores and whatnot—
sometimes strikes and lockouts. Whereupon, according
to this logic, you took a big broom and you swept the
stable clean, or you took clubs and guns and you beat
sense into the poor idiots who were suffering from the
illusion that things were fundamentally wrong. It was
good now and then to talk of God, or to have a little community sing—maybe even a bonus was justifiable now
and then, that is when things were getting too terribly
bad for words. But on the whole, the important thing was
to keep hiring and firing; as long as there were men and
ammunition we were to advance, to keep mopping up the
trenches. Meanwhile Hymie kept taking cathartic pills—
enough to blow out his rear end if he had had a rear
end, but he hadn't one any more, he only imagined he was
taking a crap, he only imagined he was shitting on his
can. Actually the poor bugger was in a trance. There were
a hundred and one offices to look after and each one had
a staff of messengers which was mythical, if not hypothetical, and whether the messengers were real or unreal,
tangible or intangible, Hymie had to shuffle them about
from morning to night while I plugged up the holes,
which was also imaginary because who could say when
a recruit had been dispatched to an office whether he
would arrive there today or tomorrow or never. Some of
them got lost in the subway or in the labyrinths under the
skyscrapers; some rode around on the elevated line all
day because with a uniform it was a free ride and perhaps
they had never enjoyed riding around all day on the
elevated lines. Some of them started for Staten Island and
ended up in Canarsie, or else were brought back in a
coma by a cop. Some forgot where they lived and disappeared completely. Some whom we hired for New York
turned up in Philadelphia a month later, as though it were
normal and according to Hoyle. Some would start for
their destination and on the way decide that it was easier
to sell newspapers and they would sell them, in the uniform we had given them, until they were picked up. Some

went straight to the observation ward, moved by some strange preservative instinct.

When he arrived in the morning Hymie first sharpened his pencils; he did this religiously no matter how many calls were coming in, because, as he explained to me later, if he didn't sharpen the pencils first thing off the bat they would never get sharpened. The next thing was to take a glance out the window and see what the weather was like. Then, with a freshly sharpened pencil he made a little box at the head of the slate which he kept beside him and in it he gave the weather report. This, he also informed me, often turned out to be a useful alibi. If the snow were a foot thick or the ground covered with sleet, even the devil himself might be excused for not shuffling the waybills around more speedily, and the employment manager might also be excused for not filling up the holes on such days, no? But why he didn't take a crap first instead of plugging in on the switchboard soon as his pencils were sharpened was a mystery to me. That too he explained to me later. Anyway, the day always broke with confusion, complaints, constipation and vacancies. It also began with loud smelly farts, with bad breaths, with ragged nerves, with epilepsy, with meningitis, with low wages, with back pay that was overdue, with worn-out shoes, with corns and bunions, with flat feet and broken arches, with pocketbooks missing and fountain pens lost or stolen, with telegrams floating in the sewer, with threats from the vice-president and advice from the managers, with wrangles and disputes, with cloudbursts and broken telegraph wires, with new methods of efficiency and old ones that had been discarded, with hope for better times and a prayer for the bonus which never came. The new messengers were going over the top and getting machine-gunned; the old ones were digging in deeper and deeper, like rats in a cheese. Nobody was satisfied, especially not the public. It took ten minutes to reach San Francisco over the wire, but it might take a year

to get the message to the man whom it was intended for—
or it might never reach him.

The Y. M. C. A., eager to improve the morale of working boys everywhere in America, was holding meetings at
noon hour and wouldn't I like to send a few spruce-look-
ing boys to hear William Carnegie Asterbilt Junior give
a five-minute talk on service. Mr. Mallory of the Welfare
League would like to know if I could spare a few minutes
some time to tell me about the model prisoners who were
on parole and who would be glad to serve in any capacity,
even as messengers. Mrs. Guggenhoffer of the Jewish
Charities would be very grateful if I would aid her in
maintaining some broken-down homes which had broken
down because everybody was either infirm, crippled or
disabled in the family. Mr. Haggerty of the Runaway
Home for Boys was sure he had just the right youngsters
for me, if only I would give them a chance; all of them
had been mistreated by their stepfathers or stepmothers.
The Mayor of New York would appreciate it if I would
give my personal attention to the bearer of said letter
whom he could vouch for in every way—but why the hell
he didn't give said bearer a job himself was a mystery.
Man leaning over my shoulder hands me a slip of paper
on which he has just written—"Me understand everything
but me no hear the voices." Luther Winifred is standing
beside him, his tattered coat fastened together with safety
pins. Luther is two-sevenths pure Indian and five-sevenths
German-American, so he explains. On the Indian side he
is a Crow, one of the Crows from Montana. His last job
was putting up window shades, but there is no ass in his
pants and he is ashamed to climb a ladder in front of a
lady. He got out of the hospital the other day and so he is
still a little weak, but he is not too weak to carry messages,
so he thinks.

And then there is Ferdinand Mish—how could I have
forgotten him? He has been waiting in line all morning
to get a word with me. I never answered the letters he
sent me. Was that just? he asks me blandly. Of course

not. I remember vaguely the last letter which he sent me from the Cat and Dog Hospital on the Grand Concourse, where he was an attendant. He said he repented that he had resigned his post "but it was on account of his father being too strick over him, not giving him any recreation or outside pleasure." "I'm twenty-five now," he wrote, "and I don't think I should ought to be sleeping no more with my father, do you? I know you are said to be a very fine gentleman and I am now self-dependent, so I hope . . ." McGovern, the old trusty, is standing by Ferdinand's side waiting for me to give him the sign. He wants to give Ferdinand the bum's rush—he remembers him from five years ago when Ferdinand lay down on the sidewalk in front of the main office in full uniform and threw an epileptic fit. No, shit, I can't do it! I'm going to give him a chance, the poor bastard. Maybe I'll send him to Chinatown where things are fairly quiet. Meanwhile, while Ferdinand is changing into a uniform in the back room, I'm getting an earful from an orphan boy who wants to "help make the company a success." He says that if I give him a chance he'll pray for me every Sunday when he goes to church, except the Sundays when he has to report to his parole officer. He didn't do nothing, it appears. He just pushed the fellow and the fellow fell on his head and got killed. *Next:* An ex-consul from Gibraltar. Writes a beautiful hand—too beautiful. I ask him to see me at the end of the day—something fishy about him. Meanwhile Ferdinand's thrown a fit in the dressing room. Lucky break! If it had happened in the subway, with a number on his hat and everything, I'd have been canned. *Next:* A guy with one arm and mad as hell because McGovern is showing him the door. "What the hell! I'm strong and healthy, ain't I?" he shouts, and to prove it he picks up a chair with his good arm and smashes it to bits. I get back to the desk and there's a telegram lying there for me. I open it. It's from George Blasini, ex-messenger No. 2459 of S.W. office. "I am sorry that I had to quit so soon, but the job was not fitted for my character idleness and I am a true lover of labor and frugality but many a time we be unable to control or subdue our personal pride." Shit!

In the beginning I was enthusiastic, despite the damper above and the clamps below. I had ideas and I executed them, whether it pleased the vice-president or not. Every ten days or so I was put on the carpet and lectured for having "too big a heart." I never had any money in my pocket but I used other people's money freely. As long as I was the boss I had credit. I gave money away right and left; I gave my clothes away and my linen, my books, everything that was superfluous. If I had had the power I would have given the company away to the poor buggers who pestered me. If I was asked for a dime I gave a half dollar, if I was asked for a dollar I gave five. I didn't give a fuck how much I gave away, because it was easier to borrow and give than to refuse the poor devils. I never saw such an aggregation of misery in my life, and I hope I'll never see it again. Men are poor everywhere—they always have been and they always will be. And beneath the terrible poverty there is a flame, usually so low that it is almost invisible. But it is there and if one has the courage to blow on it it can become a conflagration. I was constantly urged not to be too lenient, not to be too sentimental, not to be too charitable. Be firm! Be hard! they cautioned me. Fuck that! I said to myself, I'll be generous, pliant, forgiving, tolerant, tender. In the beginning I heard every man to the end; if I couldn't give him a job I gave him money, and if I had no money I gave him cigarettes or I gave him courage. But I gave! The effect was dizzying. Nobody can estimate the results of a good deed, of a kind word. I was swamped with gratitude, with good wishes, with invitations, with pathetic, tender little gifts. If I had had real power instead of being the fifth wheel on a wagon, God knows what I might not have accomplished. I could have used the Cosmodemonic Telegraph Company of North America as a base to bring all humanity to God; I could have transformed North and

South America alike, and the Dominion of Canada too. I had the secret in my hand: it was to be generous, to be kind, to be patient. I did the work of five men. I hardly slept for three years. I didn't own a whole shirt and often I was so ashamed of borrowing from my wife, or robbing the kid's bank, that to get the carfare to go to work in the morning I would swindle the blind newspaperman at the subway station. I owed so much money all around that if I were to work for twenty years I would not have been able to pay it back. I took from those who had and I gave to those who needed, and it was the right thing to do, and I would do it all over again if I were in the same position.

I even accomplished the miracle of stopping the crazy turnover, something that nobody had dared to hope for. Instead of supporting my efforts they undermined me. According to the logic of the higher-ups the turnover had ceased because the wages were too high. So they cut the wages. It was like kicking the bottom out of a bucket. The whole edifice tumbled, collapsed on my hands. And, just as though nothing had happened they insisted that the gaps be plugged up immediately. To soften the blow a bit they intimated that I might even increase the percentage of Jews, I might take on a cripple now and then, if he were capable, I might do this and that, all of which they had informed me previously was against the code. I was so furious that I took on anything and everything; I would have taken on broncos and gorillas if I could have imbued them with the modicum of intelligence which was necessary to deliver messages. A few days previously there had been only five or six vacancies at closing time. Now there were three hundred, four hundred, five hundred—they were running out like sand. It was marvelous. I sat there and without asking a question I took them on in carload lots—niggers, Jews, paralytics, cripples, ex-convicts, whores, maniacs, perverts, idiots, any fucking bastard who could stand on two legs and hold a telegram in his hand. The managers of the hundred and one offices were frightened to death. I laughed. I laughed all day long thinking what a fine stinking mess I was making of it. Complaints were pouring in from all parts of the city. The service was crippled, constipated, strangulated. A mule could have gotten there faster than some of the idiots I put into harness.

The best thing about the new day was the introduction of female messengers. It changed the whole atmosphere of the joint. For Hymie especially it was a godsend. He moved his switchboard around so that he could watch me while juggling the waybills back and forth. Despite the added work he had a permanent erection. He came to work with a smile and he smiled all day long. He was in heaven. At the end of the day I always had a list of five or six who were worth trying out. The game was to keep them on the string, to promise them a job but to get a free fuck first. Usually it was only necessary to throw a feed into them in order to bring them back to the office at night and lay them out on the zinc-covered table in the dressing room. If they had a cosy apartment, as they sometimes did, we took them home and finished it in bed. If they liked to drink Hymie would bring a bottle along. If they were any good and really needed some dough Hymie would flash his roll and peel off a five spot or a ten spot, as the case might be. It makes my mouth water when I think of that roll he carried about with him. Where he got it from I never knew, because he was the lowest-paid man in the joint. But it was always there, and no matter what I asked for I got. And once it happened that we did get a bonus and I paid Hymie back to the last penny—which so amazed him that he took me out that night to Delmonico's and spent a fortune on me. Not only that, but the next day he insisted on buying me a hat and shirts and gloves. He even insinuated that I might come home and fuck his wife, if I liked, though he warned me that she was having a little trouble at present with her ovaries.

In addition to Hymie and McGovern I had as assistants a pair of beautiful blondes who often accompanied us to dinner in the evening. And there was O'Mara, an old friend of mine who had just returned from the Philippines and whom I made my chief assistant. There was also Steve Romero, a prize bull whom I kept around in case of trouble. And O'Rourke, the company detective, who reported to me at the close of day when he began his work. Finally I added another man to the staff— Kronski, a young medical student, who was diabolically interested in the pathological cases of which we had plenty. We were a merry crew, united in our desire to fuck the company at all costs. And while fucking the company we fucked everything in sight that we could get hold of, O'Rourke excepted, as he had a certain dignity to maintain, and besides he had trouble with his prostate and had lost all interest in fucking. But O'Rourke was a prince of a man, and generous beyond words. It was O'Rourke who often invited us to dinner in the evening and it was O'Rourke we went to when we were in trouble.

That was how it stood at Sunset Place after a couple of years had rolled by. I was saturated with humanity, with experiences of one kind and another. In my sober moments I made notes which I intended to make use of later if ever I should have a chance to record my experiences. I was waiting for a breathing spell. And then by chance one day, when I had been put on the carpet for some wanton piece of negligence, the vice-president let drop a phrase which stuck in my crop. He had said that he would like to see some one write a sort of Horatio Alger book about the messengers; he hinted that perhaps I might be the one to do such a job. I was furious to think what a ninny he was and delighted at the same time because secretly I was itching to get the thing off my chest. I thought to myself—you poor old futzer, you, just wait until I get it off my chest. . . . I'll give you an Horatio Alger book . . . just you wait! My head was in a whirl leaving his office. I saw the army of men, women and children that had passed through my hands, saw them weeping, begging, beseeching, imploring, cursing, spitting, fuming, threatening. I saw the tracks they left on the highways, the freight trains lying on the floor, the parents in rags, the coal box empty, the sink running over, the walls sweating and between the cold beads of sweat the cockroaches running like mad; I saw them hobbling along like twisted gnomes or falling backwards in the epileptic frenzy, the mouth twitching, the slaver pouring from the lips, the limbs writhing; I saw the walls giving way and the pest pouring out like a winged fluid, and the men higher up with their ironclad logic, waiting for it to blow over, waiting for everything to be patched up, waiting contentedly, smugly, with big cigars in their mouths and their feet on the desk, saying things were temporarily out of order. I saw the Horatio Alger hero, the dream of a sick America, mounting higher and higher, first messenger, then operator, then manager, then chief, then superintendent, then vice-president, then president, then trust magnate, then beer baron, then Lord of all the Americas, the money god, the god of gods, the clay of clay, nullity on high, zero with ninety-seven thousand decimals fore and aft. You shits, I said to myself, I will give you the picture of twelve little men, zeros without decimals, ciphers, digits, the twelve uncrushable worms who are hollowing out the base of your rotten edifice. I will give you Horatio Alger as he looks the day after the Apocalypse, when all the stink has cleared away.

From all over the earth they had come to me to be succored. Except for the primitives there was scarcely a race which wasn't represented on the force. Except for the Ainus, the Maoris, the Papuans, the Veddas, the Lapps, the Zulus, the Patagonians, the Igorots, the Hottentots, the Tuaregs, except for the lost Tasmanians, the lost Grimaldi men, the lost Atlanteans, I had a representative of almost every species under the sun. I had two brothers who were still sun-worshipers, two Nestorians from the old Assyrian world; I had two Maltese twins from Malta and a descendant of the Mayas from Yucatan; I had a few of our little brown brothers from the Philippines and some Ethiopians from Abyssinia; I had men from the pampas of Argentina and stranded cowboys from Montana; I had Greeks, Letts, Poles, Croats, Slovenes, Ruthenians, Czechs, Spaniards, Welshmen, Finns, Swedes, Russians, Danes, Mexicans, Puerto Ricans, Cubans, Uruguayans, Brazilians, Australians, Persians, Japs, Chinese, Javanese, Egyptians, Africans from the Gold Coast and the Ivory Coast, Hindus, Armenians, Turks, Arabs, Germans, Irish, English, Canadians—and plenty of Italians and plenty of Jews. I had only one Frenchman that I can recall and he lasted about three hours. I had a few American Indians, Cherokees mostly, but no Tibetans, and no Eskimos: I saw names I could never have imagined and handwriting which ranged from cuneiform to the sophisticated and astoundingly beautiful calligraphy of the Chinese. I heard men beg for work who had been Egyptologists, botanists, surgeons, gold miners, professors of Oriental languages, musicians, engineers, physicians, astronomers, anthropologists, chemists, mathematicians, mayors of cities and governors of states, prison wardens, cowpunchers, lumberjacks, sailors, oyster pirates, stevedores, riveters, dentists, painters, sculptors, plumbers, architects, dope peddlers, abortionists, white slavers, sea divers, steeplejacks, farmers, cloak and suit salesmen, trappers, lighthouse keepers, pimps, aldermen, senators, every bloody thing under the sun, and all of them down and out, begging for work, for cigarettes, for carfare, *for a chance, Christ Almighty, just another chance!* I saw and got to know men who were saints, if there are saints in this world; I saw and spoke to savants, crapulous and uncrapulous ones; I listened to men who had the divine fire in their bowels, who could have convinced God Almighty that they were worthy of another chance, but not the vice-president of the Cosmococcic Telegraph Company. I sat riveted to my desk and I traveled around the world at lightning speed, and I learned that everywhere it is the same—hunger, humiliation, ignorance, vice, greed, extortion, chicanery, torture, despotism: the inhumanity of man to man: the fetters, the harness, the halter, the bridle, the whip, the spurs. The finer the caliber the worse off the man. Men were walking the streets of New York in that bloody, degrading outfit, the despised, the lowest of the low, walking around like auks, like penguins, like oxen, like trained seals, like patient donkeys, like big jackasses, like crazy gorillas, like docile maniacs nibbling at the dangling bait, like waltzing mice, like guinea pigs, like squirrels, like rabbits, and many and many a one was fit to govern the world, to write the greatest book ever written. When I think of some of the Persians, the Hindus, the Arabs I knew, when I think of the character they revealed, their grace, their tenderness, their intelligence, *their holiness,* I spit on the white conquerors of the world, the degenerate British, the pigheaded Germans, the smug, self-satisfied French. The earth is one great sentient being, a planet saturated through and through with man, a live planet expressing itself falteringly and stutteringly; it is not the home of the white race or the black race or the yellow race or the lost blue race, but the home of *man* and all men are equal before God and will have their chance, if not now then a million years hence. The little brown brothers of the Philippines may bloom again one day and the murdered Indians of America north and south may also come alive one day to ride the plains where now the cities stand belching fire and pestilence. Who has the last say? *Man!* The earth is his because he *is* the earth, its fire, its water, its air, its mineral and vegetable matter, its spirit which is cosmic, which is imperishable, which is the spirit of all the planets, which transforms itself through him, through endless signs and symbols, through endless manifestations. Wait, you cosmococcic telegraphic shits, you demons on high waiting for the plumbing to be repaired, wait, you dirty white conquerors who have sullied the earth with your cloven hoofs, your instruments, your weapons, your disease germs, wait, all you who are sitting in clover and counting your coppers, it is not the end. The last man will have his say before it is finished. Down to the last sentient molecule justice must be done—*and will be done!* Nobody is getting away with anything, least of all the cosmococcic shits of North America.

When it came time for my vacation—I hadn't taken one for three years, I was so eager to make the company a success!—I took three weeks instead of two and I wrote the book about the twelve little men. I wrote it straight off, five, seven, sometimes eight thousand words a day. I thought that a man, to be a writer, must do at least five thousand words a day. I thought he must say everything all at once—in one book—and collapse afterwards. I didn't know a thing about writing. I was scared shitless. But I was determined to wipe Horatio Alger out of the North American consciousness. I suppose it was the worst book any man has ever written. It was a colossal tome and faulty from start to finish. But it was my first book and I was in love with it. If I had had the money, as Gide had, I would have published it at my own expense. If I had had the courage that Whitman had, I would have peddled it from door to door. Everybody I showed it to said it was terrible. I was urged to give up the idea of writing. I had to learn, as Balzac did, that one must write volumes before signing one's own name. I had to learn, as I soon did, that one must give up everything and not do anything else but write, that one must write and write and write, even if everybody in the world advises you against it, even if nobody believes in you. Perhaps one does it just because nobody believes; perhaps the real secret lies in making people believe. That the book was inadequate, faulty, bad, *terrible*, as they said, was only natural. I was attempting at the start what a man of genius would have undertaken only at the end. I wanted to say the last word at the beginning. It was absurd and pathetic. It was a crushing defeat, but it put iron in my backbone and sulphur in my blood. I knew at least what it was to fail. I knew what it was to attempt something big. Today, when I think of the circumstances under which I wrote that book, when I think of the overwhelming material which I tried to put into form, when I think of what I hoped to encompass, I pat myself on the back, I give myself a double A. I am proud of the fact that I made such a miserable failure of it; had I succeeded I would have been a monster. Sometimes, when I look over my notebooks, when I look at the names alone of those whom I thought to write about, I am seized with vertigo. Each man came to me with a world of his own; he came to me and unloaded it on my desk; he expected me to pick it up and put in on my shoulders. I had no time to make a world of my own: I had to stay fixed like Atlas, my feet on the elephant's back and the elephant on the tortoise's back. To inquire on what the tortoise stood would be to go mad.

I didn't dare to think of anything then except the "facts." To get beneath the facts I would have had to be an artist, and one doesn't become an artist overnight. First you have to be crushed, to have your conflicting points of view annihilated. You have to be wiped out as a human being in order to be born again an individual. You have to be carbonized and mineralized in order to work upwards from the last common denominator of the self. You have to get beyond pity in order to feel from the very roots of your being. One can't make a new heaven and earth with "facts." There are no "facts"—there is only *the fact* that man, every man everywhere in the world, is on his way to ordination. Some men take the long route and some take the short route. Every man is working out his destiny in his own way and nobody can be of help except by being kind, generous and patient. In my enthusiasm certain things were then inexplicable to me which now are clear. I think, for example, of Carnahan, one of the twelve little men I had chosen to write about. He was what is called a model messenger. He was a graduate of a prominent university, had a sound intelligence and was of exemplary character. He worked eighteen and twenty hours a day and earned more than any messenger on the force. The clients whom he served wrote letters about him, praising him to the skies; he was offered good positions which he refused for one reason or another. He lived frugally, sending the best part of his wages to his wife and children who lived in another city. He had two vices—drink and the desire to succeed. He could go for a year without drinking, but if he took one drop he was off. He had cleaned up twice in Wall Street and yet, before coming to me for a job, he had gotten no further than to be a sexton of a church in some little town. He had been fired from that job because he had broken into the sacramental wine and rung the bells all night long. He was truthful, sincere, earnest. I had implicit confidence in him and my confidence was proven by the record of his service which was without a blemish. Nevertheless he shot his wife and children in cold blood and then he shot himself. Fortunately none of them died; they all lay in the hospital together and they all recovered. I went to see his wife, after they had transferred him to jail, to get her help. She refused categorically. She said he was the meanest, cruelest son of a bitch that ever walked on two legs—she wanted to see him hanged. I pleaded with her for two days, but she was adamant. I went to the jail and talked to him through the mesh. I found that he had already made himself popular with the authorities, had already been granted special privileges. He wasn't at all dejected. On the contrary, he was looking forward to making the best of his time in prison by "studying up" on salesmanship. He was going to be the best salesman in America after his release. I might almost say that he seemed happy. He said not to worry about him, he would get along all right. He said everybody was swell to him and that he had nothing to complain about. I left him somewhat in a daze. I went to a nearby beach and decided to take a swim. I saw everything with new eyes. I almost forgot to return home, so absorbed had I become in my speculations about this chap. Who could say that everything that happened to him had not happened for the best? Perhaps he might leave the prison a full-fledged evangelist instead of a salesman. Nobody could predict what he might do. And nobody could aid him because he was working out his destiny in his own private way.

There was another chap, a Hindu named Guptal. He was not only a model of good behavior—he was a saint. He had a passion for the flute which he played all by himself in his miserable little room. One day he was found naked, his throat slit from ear to ear, and beside him on the bed was his flute. At the funeral there were a dozen women who wept passionate tears, including the wife of the janitor who had murdered him. I could write a book about this young man who was the gentlest and the holiest man I ever met, who had never offended anybody and never taken anything from anybody, but who had made the cardinal mistake of coming to America to spread peace and love.

There was Dave Olinski, another faithful, industrious messenger who thought of nothing but work. He had one fatal weakness—he talked too much. When he came to me he had already been around the globe several times and what he hadn't done to make a living isn't worth telling about. He knew about twelve languages and he was rather proud of his linguistic ability. He was one of those men whose very willingness and enthusiasm is their undoing. He wanted to help everybody along, show everybody how to succeed. He wanted more work than we could give him—he was a glutton for work. Perhaps I should have warned him, when I sent him to his office on the East Side, that he was going to work in a tough neighborhood, but he pretended to know so much and he was so insistent on working in that locality (because of his linguistic ability) that I said nothing. I thought to myself—you'll find out quickly enough for yourself. And sure enough, he was only there a short time when he got into trouble. A tough Jewboy from the neighborhood walked in one day and asked for a blank. Dave, the messenger, was behind the desk. He didn't like the way the man asked for the blank. He told him he ought to be more polite. For that he got a box in the ears. That made him wag his tongue some more, whereupon he got such a wallop that his teeth flew down his throat and his jawbone was broken in three places. Still he didn't know enough to hold his trap. Like the damned fool that he was he goes to the police station and registers a complaint. A week later, while he's sitting on a bench snoozing, a gang of roughnecks break into the place and beat him to a pulp. His head was so battered that his brains looked like an omelette. For good measure they emptied the safe and turned it upside down. Dave died on the way to the hospital. They found five hundred dollars hidden away in the toe of his sock. . . . Then there was Clausen and his wife Lena. They came in together when he applied for the job. Lena had a baby in her arms and he had two little ones by the hand. They were sent to me by some relief agency. I put him on as a night messenger so that he'd have a fixed salary. In a few days I had a letter from him, a batty letter in which he asked me to excuse him for being absent as he had to report to his parole officer. Then another letter saying that his wife had refused to sleep with him because she didn't want any more babies and would I please come to see them and try to persuade her to sleep with him. I went to his home—a cellar in the Italian quarter. It looked like a bughouse. Lena was pregnant again, about seven months under way, and on the verge of idiocy. She had taken to sleeping on the roof because it was too hot in the cellar, also because she didn't want him to touch her any more. When I said it wouldn't make any difference now she just looked at me and grinned. Clausen had been in the war and maybe the gas had made him a bit goofy—at any rate he was foaming at the mouth. He said he would brain her if she didn't stay off that roof. He insinuated that she was sleeping up there in order to carry on with the coal man who lived in the attic. At this Lena smiled again with that

mirthless batrachian grin. Clausen lost his temper and
gave her a swift kick in the ass. She went out in a huff taking the brats with her. He told her to stay out for good.
Then he opened a drawer and pulled out a big Colt. He
was keeping it in case he needed it some time, he said. He
showed me a few knives, too, and a sort of blackjack
which he had made himself. Then he began to weep. He
said his wife was making a fool of him. He said he was
sick of working for her because she was sleeping with
everybody in the neighborhood. The kids weren't his
because he couldn't make a kid any more even if he
wanted to. The very next day, while Lena was out market-
ing, he took the kids up to the roof and with the blackjack he had shown me he beat their brains out. Then he
jumped off the roof head first. When Lena came home and
saw what happened she went off her nut. They had to
put her in a strait jacket and call for the ambulance.
. . . There was Schuldig, the rat who had spent twenty
years in prison for a crime he had never committed. He
had been beaten almost to death before he confessed;
then solitary confinement, starvation, torture, perversion,
dope. When they finally released him he was no longer a
human being. He described to me one night his last thirty
days in jail, the agony of waiting to be released. I have
never heard anything like it; I didn't think a human being
could survive such anguish. Freed, he was haunted by the
fear that he might be obliged to commit a crime and be
sent back to prison again. He complained of being followed, spied on, perpetually tracked. He said "they" were
tempting him to do things he had no desire to do. "They"
were the dicks who were on his trail, who were paid to
bring him back again. At night, when he was asleep, they
whispered in his ear. He was powerless against them because they mesmerized him first. Sometimes they placed
dope under his pillow, and with it a revolver or a knife.
They wanted him to kill some innocent person so that
they would have a solid case against him this time. He got
worse and worse. One night, after he had walked around

for hours with a batch of telegrams in his pocket, he went up to a cop and asked to be locked up. He couldn't remember his name or address or even the office he was working for. He had completely lost his identity. He repeated over and over—"I'm innocent. . . . I'm innocent." Again they gave him the third degree. Suddenly he jumped up and shouted like a madman—"I'll confess . . . I'll confess"—and with that he began to reel off one crime after another. He kept it up for three hours. Suddenly, in the midst of a harrowing confession, he stopped short, gave a quick look about, like a man who has suddenly come to, and then, with the rapidity and the force which only a madman can summon he made a tremendous leap across the room and crashed his skull against the stone wall. . . . I relate these incidents briefly and hurriedly as they flash through my mind; my memory is packed with thousands of such details, with a myriad faces, gestures, tales, confessions all entwined and interlaced like the stupendous reeling façade of some Hindu temple made not of stone but of the experience of human flesh, a monstrous dream edifice built entirely of reality and yet not reality itself but merely the vessel in which the mystery of the human being is contained. My mind wanders to the clinic where in ignorance and good will I brought some of the younger ones to be cured. I can think of no more evocative image to convey the atmosphere of this place than the painting by Hieronymus Bosch in which the magician, after the manner of a dentist extracting a live nerve, is represented as the deliverer of insanity. All the trumpery and quackery of our scientific practitioners came to apotheosis in the person of the suave sadist who operated this clinic with the full concurrence and connivance of the law. He was a ringer for Caligari, except that he was minus the dunce cap. Pretending that he understood the secret regulations of the glands, invested with the power of a medieval monarch, oblivious of the pain he inflicted, ignorant of everything but his medical knowledge, he went to work on the human organism like a plumber sets to work on the underground drainpipes. In addition to the poisons he threw into the patient's system he had recourse to his fists or his knees as the case might be. Anything justified a "reaction." If the victim were lethargic he shouted at him, slapped him in the face, pinched his arm, cuffed him, kicked him. If on the contrary the victim were too energetic he employed the same methods, only with redoubled zest. The feelings of his subject were of no importance to him; whatever reaction he succeeded in obtaining was merely a demonstration or manifestation of the laws regulating the operation of the internal glands of secretion. The purpose of his treatment was to render the subject fit for society. But no matter how fast he worked, no matter whether he was successful or not successful, society was turning out more and more misfits. Some of them were so marvelously maladapted that when, in order to get the proverbial reaction, he slapped them vigorously on the cheek they responded with an uppercut or a kick in the balls. It's true, most of his subjects were exactly what he described them to be—incipient criminals. The whole continent was on the slide—is still on the slide—and not only the glands need regulating but the ball bearings, the armature, the skeletal structure, the cerebrum, the cerebellum, the coccyx, the larynx, the pancreas, the liver, the upper intestine and the lower intestine, the heart, the kidneys, the testicles, the womb, the Fallopian tubes, the whole goddamned works. The whole country is lawless, violent, explosive, demoniacal. It's in the air, in the climate, in the ultra-grandiose landscape, in the stone forests that are lying horizontal, in the torrential rivers that bite through the rocky canyons, in the supra-normal distances, the supernal arid wastes, the over-lush crops, the monstrous fruits, the mixture of quixotic bloods, the fatras of cults, sects, beliefs, the opposition of laws and languages, the contradictoriness of temperaments, principles, needs, requirements. The continent is full of buried violence, of the bones of antediluvian monsters and of lost races of man, of mysteries which are wrapped in doom. The atmosphere is at times so electrical that the soul is summoned out of its body and runs amok. Like the rain everything comes in bucketsful —or not at all. The whole continent is a huge volcano whose crater is temporarily concealed by a moving panorama which is partly dream, partly fear, partly despair. From Alaska to Yucatan it's the same story. Nature dominates. Nature wins out. Everywhere the same fundamental urge to slay, to ravage, to plunder. Outwardly they seem like a fine, upstanding people—healthy, optimistic, courageous. Inwardly they are filled with worms. A tiny spark and they blow up.

Often it happens, as in Russia, that a man came in with a chip on his shoulder. He woke up that way, as if struck by a monsoon. Nine times out of ten he was a good fellow, a fellow whom everyone liked. But when the rage came on nothing could stop him. He was like a horse with the blind staggers and the best thing you could do for him was to shoot him on the spot. It always happens that way with peaceable people. One day they run amok. In America they're constantly running amok. What they need is an outlet for their energy, for their blood lust. Europe is bled regularly by war. America is pacifistic and cannibalistic. Outwardly it seems to be a beautiful honeycomb, with all the drones crawling over each other in a frenzy of work; inwardly it's a slaughterhouse, each man killing off his neighbor and sucking the juice from his bones. Superficially it looks like a bold, masculine world; actually it's a whorehouse run by women, with the native sons acting as pimps and the bloody foreigners selling their flesh. Nobody knows what it is to sit on his ass and be content. That happens only in the films where everything is faked, even the fires of hell. The whole continent is sound asleep and in that sleep a grand nightmare is taking place.

Nobody could have slept more soundly than I in the midst of this nightmare. The war, when it came along, made only a sort of faint rumble in my ears. Like my compatriots, I was pacifistic and cannibalistic. The millions who were put away in the carnage passed away in a cloud, much like the Aztecs passed away, and the Incas and the red Indians and the buffaloes. People pretended to be profoundly moved, but they weren't. They were simply tossing fitfully in their sleep. No one lost his appetite, no one got up and rang the fire alarm. The day I first realized that there had been a war was about six months or so after the armistice. It was in a street car on the 14th Street crosstown line. One of our heroes, a Texas lad with a string of medals across his chest, happened to see an officer passing on the sidewalk. The sight of the officer enraged him. He was a sergeant himself and he probably had good reason to be sore. Anyway, the sight of the officer enraged him so that he got up from his seat and began to bawl the shit out of the government, the army, the civilians, the passengers in the car, everybody and everything. He said if there was ever another war they couldn't drag him to it with a twenty-mule team. He said he'd see every son of a bitch killed before he'd go again himself; he said he didn't give a fuck about the medals they had decorated him with and to show that he meant it he ripped them off and threw them out the window; he said if he was ever in a trench with an officer again he'd shoot him in the back like a dirty dog, and that held good for General Pershing or any other general. He said a lot more, with some fancy cuss words that he'd picked up over there, and nobody opened his trap to gainsay him. And when he got through I felt for the first time that there had really been a war and that the man I was listening to had been in it and that despite his bravery the war had made him a coward and that if he did any more killing it would be wide-awake and in cold blood, and nobody would have the guts to send him to the electric chair because he had performed his duty toward his fellow men, which was to deny his own sacred instincts and so everything was just and fair because one crime washes away the other in the name of God, country and humanity,

peace be with you all. And the second time I experienced
the reality of war was when ex-sergeant Griswold, one of
our night messengers, flew off the handle one day
and smashed the office to bits at one of the railway
stations. They sent him to me to give him the gate,
but I didn't have the heart to fire him. He had performed such a beautiful piece of destruction that I felt
more like hugging and squeezing him; I was only hoping to
Christ he would go up to the twenty-fifth floor, or where-
ever it was that the president and the vice-presidents had
their offices, and mop up the whole bloody gang. But in the
name of discipline, and to uphold the bloody farce it was,
I had to do something to punish him or be punished for
it myself, and so not knowing what less I could do I took
him off the commission basis and put him back on a salary
basis. He took it pretty badly, not realizing exactly where
I stood, either for him or against him, and so I got a letter
from him pronto, saying that he was going to pay me a
visit in a day or two and that I'd better watch out because
he was going to take it out of my hide. He said he'd come
up after office hours and that if I was afraid I'd better
have some strong-arm men around to look after me. I
knew he meant every word he said and I felt pretty
damned quaky when I put the letter down. I waited in
for him alone, however, feeling that it would be even more
cowardly to ask for protection. It was a strange experience. He must have realized the moment he laid eyes on
me that I was a son of a bitch and a lying, stinking hypo-
crite, as he had called me in his letter. I was only that because he was what he was, which wasn't a hell of a lot
better. He must have realized immediately that we were
both in the same boat and that the bloody boat was
leaking pretty badly. I could see something like that
going on in him as he strode forward, outwardly still
furious, still foaming at the mouth, but inwardly all spent,
all soft and feathery. As for myself, what fear I had
vanished the moment I saw him enter. Just being there
quiet and alone, and being less strong, less capable of

defending myself, gave me the drop on him. Not that I
wanted to have the drop on him either. But it had turned
out that way and I took advantage of it, naturally. The
moment he sat down he went soft as putty. He wasn't a
man any more, but just a big child. There must have
been millions of them like him, big children with machine
guns who could wipe out whole regiments without batting
an eyelash; but back in the work trenches, without a
weapon, without a clear, visible enemy, they were helpless as ants. Everything revolved about the question of
food. The food and the rent—that was all there was to
fight about—but there was no way, no clear, visible way,
to fight for it. It was like seeing an army strong and well
equipped, capable of licking anything in sight, and yet
ordered to retreat every day, to retreat and retreat and
retreat because that was the strategic thing to do, even
though it meant losing ground, losing guns, losing ammunition, losing food, losing sleep, losing courage, losing
life itself finally. Wherever there were men fighting for
food and rent there was this retreat going on, in the fog,
in the night, for no earthly reason except that it was the
strategic thing to do. It was eating the heart out of him.
To fight was easy, but to fight for food and rent was like
fighting an army of ghosts. All you could do was to retreat, and while you retreated you watched your own
brothers getting popped off, one after the other, silently,
mysteriously, in the fog, in the dark, and not a thing to
do about it. He was so damned confused, so perplexed, so
hopelessly muddled and beaten, that he put his head in
his arms and wept on my desk. And while he's sobbing like
that suddenly the telephone rings and its the vice-president's office—never the vice-president himself, but always
his office—and they want this man Griswold fired immediately and I say Yes Sir! and I hang up. I don't say
anything to Griswold about it but I walk home with him
and I have dinner with him and his wife and kids. And
when I leave him I say to myself that if I have to fire that
guy somebody's going to pay for it—and anyway I want

to know first where the order comes from and why. And
hot and sullen I go right up to the vice-president's office in
the morning and I ask to see the vice-president himself
and did you give the order I ask—*and why?* And before
he has a chance to deny it, or to explain his reason for it,
I give him a little war stuff straight from the shoulder
and where he don't like it and can't take it—and if you
don't like it, Mr. Will Twilldilliger, you can take the job,
my job and his job and you can shove them up your ass—
and like that I walk out on him. I go back to the slaughterhouse and I go about my work as usual. I expect, of course,
that I'll get the sack before the day's over. But nothing of
the kind. No, to my amazement I get a telephone call from
the general manager saying to take it easy, to just calm
down a bit, yes, just go easy, don't do anything hasty,
we'll look into it, etc. I guess they're still looking into it
because Griswold went on working just as always—in
fact, they even promoted him to a clerkship, which was a
dirty deal, too, because as a clerk he earned less money
than as a messenger, but it saved his pride and it also took
a little more of the spunk out of him too, no doubt. But
that's what happens to a guy when he's just a hero in his
sleep. Unless the nightmare is strong enough to wake you
up you go right on retreating, and either you end up on a
bench or you end up as vice-president. It's all one and
the same, a bloody fucking mess, a farce, a fiasco from
start to finish. I know it as was in it, because I woke up.
And when I woke up I walked out on it. I walked out by
the same door that I had walked in—without as much as
a by-your-leave, sir!

Things take place instantaneously, but there's a long
process to be gone through first. What you get when
something happens is only the explosion, and the second
before that the spark. But everything happens according
to law—and with the full consent and collaboration of
the whole cosmos. Before I could get up and explode
the bomb had to be properly prepared, properly primed.
After putting things in order for the bastards up above

I had to be taken down from my high horse, had to be kicked around like a football, had to be stepped on, squelched, humiliated, fettered, manacled, made impotent as a jellyfish. All my life I have never wanted for friends, but at this particular period they seemed to spring up around me like mushrooms. I never had a moment to myself. If I went home of a night, hoping to take a rest, somebody would be there waiting to see me. Sometimes a gang of them would be there and it didn't seem to make much difference whether I came or not. Each set of friends I made despised the other set. Stanley, for example, despised the whole lot. Ulric too was rather scornful of the others. He had just come back from Europe after an absence of several years. We hadn't seen much of each other since boyhood and then one day, quite by accident, we met on the street. That day was an important day in my life because it opened up a new world to me, a world I had often dreamed about but never hoped to see. I remember vividly that we were standing on the corner of Sixth Avenue and 49th Street toward dusk. I remember it because it seemed utterly incongruous to be listening to a man talking about Mt. Aetna and Vesuvius and Capri and Pompeii and Morocco and Paris on the corner of Sixth Avenue and 49th Street, Manhattan. I remember the way he looked about as he talked, like a man who hadn't quite realized what he was in for but who vaguely sensed that he had made a horrible mistake in returning. His eyes seemed to be saying all the time—this has no value, no value whatever. He didn't say that, however, but just this over and over: "I'm sure you'd like it! I'm sure it's just the place for you." When he left me I was in a daze. I couldn't get hold of him again quickly enough. I wanted to hear it all over again, in minute detail. Nothing that I had read about Europe seemed to match this glowing account from my friend's own lips. It seemed all the more miraculous to me in that we had sprung out of the same environment. He had managed it because he had rich friends—and because he knew how to save his money. I had never known any one who was rich, who had traveled, who had money in the bank. All my friends were like myself, drifting from day to day, and never a thought for the future. O'Mara, yes, he had traveled a bit, almost all over the world—but as a bum, or else in the army, which was even worse than being a bum. My friend Ulric was the first fellow I had ever met who I could truly say had traveled. And he knew how to talk about his experiences.

As a result of that chance encounter on the street we met frequently thereafter, for a period of several months. He used to call for me in the evening after dinner and we would stroll through the park which was nearby. What a thirst I had! Every slightest detail about the other world fascinated me. Even now, years and years since, even now, when I know Paris like a book, his picture of Paris is still before my eyes, still vivid, still real. Sometimes, after a rain, riding swiftly through the city in a taxi, I catch fleeting glimpses of this Paris he described; just momentary snatches, as in passing the Tuileries, perhaps, or a glimpse of Montmartre, of the Sacré Cœur, through the Rue Laffitte, in the last flush of twilight. *Just a Brooklyn boy!* That was an expression he used sometimes when he felt ashamed of his inability to express himself more adequately. And I was just a Brooklyn boy, too, which is to say one of the last and the least of men. But as I wander about, rubbing elbows with the world, seldom it happens that I meet any one who can describe so lovingly and faithfully what he has seen and felt. Those nights in Prospect Park with my old friend Ulric are responsible, more than anything else, for my being here today. Most of the places he described for me I have still to see; some of them I shall perhaps never see. But they live inside me, warm and vivid, just as he created them in our rambles through the park.

Interwoven with this talk of the other world was the whole body and texture of Lawrence's work. Often, when the park had long been emptied, we were still sitting on a bench discussing the nature of Lawrence's ideas. Looking back on these discussions now I can see how confused I was, how pitifully ignorant of the true meaning of Lawrence's words. Had I really understood, my life could never have taken the course it did. Most of us live the greater part of our lives submerged. Certainly in my own case I can say that not until I left America did I emerge above the surface. Perhaps America had nothing to do with it, but the fact remains that I did not open my eyes wide and full and clear until I struck Paris. And perhaps that was only because I had renounced America, renounced my past.

My friend Kronski used to twit me about my "euphorias." It was a sly way he had of reminding me, when I was extraordinarily gay, that the morrow would find me depressed. It was true. I had nothing but ups and downs. Long stretches of gloom and melancholy followed by extravagant bursts of gaiety, of trancelike inspiration. Never a level in which I was myself. It sounds strange to say so, yet I was never myself. I was either anonymous or the person called Henry Miller raised to the *n*th degree. In the latter mood, for instance, I could spill out a whole book to Hymie while riding a trolley car. Hymie, who never suspected me of being anything but a good employment manager. I can see his eyes now as he looked at me one night when I was in one of my states of "euphoria." We had boarded the trolley at the Brooklyn Bridge to go to some flat in Greenpoint where a couple of trollops were waiting to receive us. Hymie had started to talk to me in his usual way about his wife's ovaries. In the first place he didn't know precisely what ovaries meant and so I was explaining it to him in crude and simple fashion. In the midst of my explanation it suddenly seemed so profoundly tragic and ridiculous that Hymie shouldn't know what ovaries were that I became drunk, as drunk I mean as if I had had a quart of whisky under my belt. From the idea of diseased ovaries there

germinated in one lightning-like flash a sort of tropical
growth made up of the most heterogeneous assortment
of odds and ends in the midst of which, securely lodged,
tenaciously lodged, I might say, were Dante and Shake-
speare. At the same instant I also suddenly recalled my
whole private train of thought which had begun about
the middle of the Brooklyn Bridge and which suddenly
the word "ovaries" had broken. I realized that everything
Hymie had said up till the word "ovaries" had sieved
through me like sand. What I had begun, in the middle
of the Brooklyn Bridge, was what I had begun time and
time again in the past, usually when walking to my
father's shop, a performance which was repeated day in
and day out as if in a trance. What I had begun, in brief,
was a book of the hours, of the tedium and monotony of
my life in the midst of a ferocious activity. Not for years
had I thought of this book which I used to write every
day on my way from Delancey Street to Murray Hill.
But going over the bridge, the sun setting, the skyscrapers gleaming like phosphorescent cadavers, the remembrance of the past set in . . . remembrance of going
back and forth over the bridge, going to a job which was
death, returning to a home which was a morgue, memo-
rizing *Faust* looking down into the cemetery, spitting
into the cemetery from the elevated train, the same guard
on the platform every morning, an imbecile, the other
imbeciles reading their newspapers, new skyscrapers going up, new tombs to work in and die in, the boats passing
below, the Fall River Line, the Albany Day Line, why
am I going to work, what will I do tonight, the warm
cunt beside me and can I work my knuckles into her
groin, run away and become a cowboy, try Alaska, the
gold mines, get off and turn around, don't die yet, wait
another day, a stroke of luck, river, end it, down, down,
like a corkscrew, head and shoulders in the mud, legs
free; fish will come and bite, tomorrow a new life, where,
anywhere, why begin again, the same thing everywhere,
death, death is the solution, but don't die yet, wait an-

other day, a stroke of luck, a new face, a new friend, millions of chances, you're too young yet, you're melancholy,
you don't die yet, wait another day, a stroke of luck, fuck
anyway, and so on over the bridge into the glass shed,
everybody glued together, worms, ants, crawling out of a
dead tree and their thoughts crawling out the same
way. . . . Maybe, being up high between the two shores,
suspended above the traffic, above life and death, on each
side the high tombs, tombs blazing with dying sunlight,
the river flowing heedlessly, flowing on like time itself,
maybe each time I passed up there, something was tugging away at me, urging me to take it in, to announce myself; anyway each time I passed on high I was truly alone
and whenever that happened the book commenced to
write itself, screaming the things which I never breathed,
the thoughts I never uttered, the conversations I never
held, the hopes, the dreams, the delusions I never admitted. If this then was the true self it was marvelous,
and what's more it seemed never to change but always to
pick up from the last stop, to continue in the same vein, a
vein I had struck when I was a child and went down in
the street for the first time alone and there frozen into the
dirty ice of the gutter lay a dead cat, the first time I had
looked at death and grasped it. From that moment I
knew what it was to be isolated: every object, every living thing and every dead thing led its independent existence. My thoughts too led an independent existence.
Suddenly, looking at Hymie and thinking of that strange
word "ovaries," now stranger than any word in my whole
vocabulary, this feeling of icy isolation came over me
and Hymie sitting beside me was a bullfrog, absolutely
a bullfrog and nothing more. I was jumping from the
bridge head first, down into the primeval ooze, the legs
clear and waiting for a bite; like that Satan had plunged
through the heavens, through the solid core of the earth,
head down and ramming through to the very hub of the
earth, the darkest, densest, hottest pit of hell. I was walking through the Mojave Desert and the man beside me

was waiting for nightfall in order to fall on me and slay
me. I was walking again in Dreamland and a man was
walking above me on a tightrope and above him a man
was sitting in an airplane spelling letters of smoke in the
sky. The woman hanging on my arm was pregnant and
in six or seven years the thing she was carrying inside
her would be able to read the letters in the sky and he
or she or it would know that it was a cigarette and later
would smoke the cigarette, perhaps a package a day. In
the womb nails formed on every finger, every toe; you
could stop right there, at a toenail, the tiniest toenail
imaginable, and you could break your head over it, trying
to figure it out. On one side of the ledger are the books
man has written, containing such a hodgepodge of wisdom and nonsense, of truth and falsehood, that if one
lived to be as old as Methuselah one couldn't disentangle
the mess; on the other side of the ledger things like toenails, hair, teeth, blood, *ovaries,* if you will, all incalculable and all written in another kind of ink, in another
script, an incomprehensible, undecipherable script. The
bullfrog eyes were trained on me like two collar buttons
stuck in cold fat; they were stuck in the cold sweat of the
primeval ooze. Each collar button was an ovary that had
come unglued, an illustration out of the dictionary without benefit of lucubration; lackluster in the cold yellow
fat of the eyeball each buttoned ovary produced a subterranean chill, the skating rink of hell where men stood
upside down in the ice, the legs free and waiting for a
bite. Here Dante walked unaccompanied, weighed down
by his vision, and through endless circles gradually moving heavenward to be enthroned in his work. Here Shake-
speare with smooth brow fell into the bottomless reverie
of rage to emerge in elegant quartos and innuendoes. A
glaucous frost of non-comprehension swept clear by gales
of laughter. From the hub of the bullfrog's eye radiated
clean white spokes of sheer lucidity not to be annotated
or categorized, not to be numbered or defined, but revolving sightless in kaleidoscopic change. Hymie the

bullfrog was an ovarian spud generated in the high passage between two shores: for him the skyscrapers had been built, the wilderness cleared, the Indians massacred, the buffaloes exterminated; for him the twin cities had been joined by the Brooklyn Bridge, the caissons sunk, the cables strung from tower to tower; for him men sat upside down in the sky writing words in fire and smoke; for him the anesthetic was invented and the high forceps and the Big Bertha which could destroy what the eye could not see; for him the molecule was broken down and the atom revealed to be without substance; for him each night the stars were swept with telescopes and worlds coming to birth photographed in the act of gestation; for him the barriers of time and space were set at nought and all movement, be it the flight of birds or the revolution of the planets, expounded irrefutably and incontestably by the high priests of the depossessed cosmos. Then, as in the middle of the bridge, in the middle of a walk, in the middle always, whether of a book, a conversation, or making love, it was borne in on me again that I had never done what I wanted and out of not doing what I wanted to do there grew up inside me this creation which was nothing but an obsessional plant, a sort of coral growth, which was expropriating everything, including life itself, until life itself became this which was denied but which constantly asserted itself, making life and killing life at the same time. I could see it going on after death, like hair growing on a corpse, people saying "death" but the hair still testifying to life, and finally no death but this life of hair and nails, the body gone, the spirit quenched, but in the death something still alive, expropriating space, causing time, creating endless movement. Through love this might happen, or sorrow, or being born with a club foot; the cause nothing, the event everything. *In the beginning was the Word. . . .* Whatever this was, *the Word,* disease or creation, it was still running rampant; it would run on and on, outstrip time and space, outlast the angels, unseat God, unhook the universe. Any word contained all words—for him who had become detached through love or sorrow or whatever the cause. In every word the current ran back to the beginning which was lost and which would never be found again since there was neither beginning nor end but only that which expressed itself in beginning and end. So, on the ovarian trolley there was this voyage of man and bullfrog composed of identical stuff, neither better nor less than Dante but infinitely different, the one not knowing precisely the meaning of anything, the other knowing too precisely the meaning of everything, hence both lost and confused through beginnings and endings, finally to be deposited at Java or India Street, Greenpoint, there to be carried back into the current of life, so-called, by a couple of sawdust molls with twitching ovaries of the well-known gastropod variety.

What strikes me now as the most wonderful proof of my fitness, or unfitness, for the times is the fact that nothing people were writing or talking about had any real interest for me. Only the object haunted me, the separate, detached, insignificant *thing*. It might be a part of the human body or a staircase in a vaudeville house; it might be a smokestack or a button I had found in the gutter. Whatever it was it enabled me to open up, to surrender, to attach my signature. To the life about me, to the people who made up the world I knew, I could not attach my signature. I was as definitely outside their world as a cannibal is outside the bounds of civilized society. I was filled with a perverse love of the thing-in-itself—not a philosophic attachment, but a passionate, desperately passionate hunger, as if in this discarded, worthless *thing* which everyone ignored there was contained the secret of my own regeneration.

Living in the midst of a world where there was a plethora of the new I attached myself to the old. In every object there was a minute particle which particularly claimed my attention. I had a microscopic eye for the blemish, for the grain of ugliness which to me constituted

the sole beauty of the object. Whatever set the object
apart, or made it unserviceable, or gave it a date, attracted and endeared it to me. If this was perverse it was
also healthy, considering that I was not destined to belong to this world which was springing up about me.
Soon I too would become like these objects which I
venerated, a thing apart, a non-useful member of society.
I was definitely dated, that was certain. And yet I was
able to amuse, to instruct, to nourish. But never to be
accepted, in a genuine way. When I wished to, when
I had the itch, I could single out any man, in any stratum
of society, and make him listen to me. I could hold him
spellbound, if I chose, but, like a magican, or a sorcerer,
only as long as the spirit was in me. At bottom I sensed
in others a distrust, an uneasiness, an antagonism which,
because it was instinctive, was irremediable. I should
have been a clown; it would have afforded me the widest
range of expression. But I underestimated the profession.
Had I become a clown, or even a vaudeville entertainer,
I would have been famous. People would have appreciated me precisely because they would not have understood; but they would have understood that I was not to
be understood. That would have been a relief, to say the
least.

It was always a source of amazement to me how easily
people could become riled just listening to me talk. Perhaps my speech was somewhat extravagant, though often
it happened when I was holding myself in with main
force. The turn of a phrase, the choice of an unfortunate
adjective, the facility with which the words came to my
lips, the allusions to subjects which were taboo—everything conspired to set me off as an outlaw, as an enemy
of society. No matter how well things began sooner or
later they smelled me out. If I were modest and humble,
for example, then I was too modest, too humble. If I
were gay and spontaneous, bold and reckless, then I was
too free, too gay. I could never get myself quite *au point*
with the individual I happened to be talking to. If it

were not a question of life and death—everything was life and death to me then—if it was merely a question of passing a pleasant evening at the home of some acquaintance, it was the same thing. There were vibrations emanating from me, overtones and undertones, which charged the atmosphere unpleasantly. Perhaps the whole evening they had been amused by my stories, perhaps I had them in stitches, as it often happened, and everything seemed to augur well. But sure as fate something was bound to happen before the evening came to a close, some vibration set loose which made the chandelier ring or which reminded some sensitive soul of the pisspot under the bed. Even while the laughter was still dying off the venom was beginning to make itself felt. "Hope to see you again some time," they would say, but the wet, limp hand which was extended would belie the words.

Persona non grata! Jesus, how clear it seems to me now! No pick and choice possible: I had to take what was to hand and learn to like it. I had to learn to live with the scum, to swim like a sewer rat or be drowned. If you elect to join the herd you are immune. To be accepted and appreciated you must nullify yourself, make yourself indistinguishable from the herd. You may dream, if you dream alike. But if you dream something different you are not in America, of America American, but a Hottentot in Africa, or a Kalmuck, or a chimpanzee. The moment you have a "different" thought you cease to be an American. And the moment you become something different you find yourself in Alaska or Easter Island or Iceland.

Am I saying this with rancor, with envy, with malice? Perhaps. Perhaps I regret not having been able to become an American. *Perhaps.* In my zeal now, which is again *American*, I am about to give birth to a monstrous edifice, a skyscraper, which will last undoubtedly long after the other skyscrapers have vanished, but which will vanish too when that which produced it disappears. Everything American will disappear one day, more completely than that which was Greek, or Roman, or Egyptian. This is *one* of the ideas which pushed me outside the warm, comfortable bloodstream where, buffaloes all, we once grazed in peace. An idea that has caused me infinite sorrow, for not to belong to something enduring is the last agony. But I am not a buffalo and I have no desire to be one, I am not even a *spiritual* buffalo. I have slipped away to rejoin an older stream of consciousness, a race antecedent to the buffaloes, a race that will survive the buffalo.

All things, all objects animate or inanimate that are *different*, are veined with ineradicable traits. What is me is ineradicable, because it is different. This is a skyscraper, as I said, but it is *different* from the usual skyscraper à l'américaine. In this skyscraper there are no elevators, no seventy-third-story windows to jump from. If you get tired of climbing you are shit out of luck. There is no slot directory in the main lobby. If you are searching for somebody you will have to search. If you want a drink you will have to go out and get it; there are no soda fountains in this building, and no cigar stores, and no telephone booths. All the other skyscrapers have what you want! this one contains nothing but what *I* want, what *I* like. And somewhere in this skyscraper Valeska has her being, and we're going to get to her when the spirit move me. For the time being she's all right, Valeska, seeing as how she's six feet under and by now perhaps picked clean by the worms. When she was in the flesh she was picked clean too, by the human worms who have no respect for anything which has a different tint, a different odor.

The sad thing about Valeska was the fact that she had nigger blood in her veins. It was depressing for everybody around her. She made you aware of it whether you wished to be or no. The nigger blood, as I say, and the fact that her mother was a trollop. The mother was white, of course. Who the father was nobody knew, not even Valeska herself.

Everything was going along smoothly until the day an officious little Jew from the vice-president's office happened to espy her. He was horrified, so he informed me confidentially, to think that I had employed a colored person as my secretary. He spoke as though she might contaminate the messengers. The next day I was put on the carpet. It was exactly as though I had committed sacrilege. Of course I pretended that I hadn't observed anything unusual about her, except that she was extremely intelligent and extremely capable. Finally the president himself stepped in. There was a short interview between him and Valeska during which he very diplomatically proposed to give her a better position in Havana. No talk of the blood taint. Simply that her services had been altogether remarkable and that they would like to promote her—to Havana. Valeska came back to the office in a rage. When she was angry she was magnificent. She said she wouldn't budge. Steve Romero and Hymie were there at the time and we all went out to dinner together. During the course of the evening we got a bit tight. Valeska's tongue was wagging. On the way home she told me that she was going to put up a fight; she wanted to know if it would endanger my job. I told her quietly that if she were fired I would quit too. She pretended not to believe it at first. I said I meant it, that I didn't care what happened. She seemed to be unduly impressed; she took me by the two hands and she held them very gently, the tears rolling down her cheeks.

That was the beginning of things. I think it was the very next day that I slipped her a note saying that I was crazy about her. She read the note sitting opposite me and when she was through she looked me square in the eye and said she didn't believe it. But we went to dinner again that night and we had more to drink and we danced and while we were dancing she pressed herself against me lasciviously. It was just the time, as luck would have it, that my wife was getting ready to have another abortion. I was telling Valeska about it as we danced. On the

way home she suddenly said—"Why don't you let me
lend you a hundred dollars?" The next night I brought
her home to dinner and I let her hand the wife the hundred dollars. I was amazed how well the two of them
got along. Before the evening was over it was agreed
upon that Valeska would come to the house the day of
the abortion and take care of the kid. The day came and I
gave Valeska the afternoon off. About an hour after she
had left I suddenly decided that I would take the afternoon off also. I started toward the burlesque on Fourteenth Street. When I was about a block from the theater
I suddenly changed my mind. It was just the thought that
if anything happened—if the wife were to kick off—I
wouldn't feel so damned good having spent the afternoon
at the burlesque. I walked around a bit, in and out
of the penny arcades, and then I started homeward.

It's strange how things turn out. Trying to amuse the
kid I suddenly remembered a trick my grandfather had
shown me when I was a child. You take the dominoes and
you make tall battleships out of them; then you gently
pull the tablecloth on which the battleships are floating
until they come to the edge of the table when suddenly
you give a brisk tug and they fall onto the floor. We tried
it over and over again, the three of us, until the kid got
so sleepy that she toddled off to the next room and fell
asleep. The dominoes were lying all over the floor and
the tablecloth was on the floor too. Suddenly Valeska was
leaning against the table, her tongue halfway down my
throat, my hand between her legs. As I laid her back on
the table she twined her legs around me. I could feel one
of the dominoes under my feet—part of the fleet that we
had destroyed a dozen times or more. I thought of my
grandfather sitting on the bench, the way he had warned
my mother one day that I was too young to be reading
so much, the pensive look in his eyes as he pressed the
hot iron against the wet seam of a coat; I thought of the
attack on San Juan Hill which the Rough Riders had
made, the picture of Teddy charging at the head of his

volunteers in the big book which I used to read beside
the workbench; I thought of the battleship "Maine" that
floated over my bed in the little room with the iron-
barred window, and of Admiral Dewey and of Schley and
Sampson; I thought of the trip to the Navy Yard which I
never made because on the way my father suddenly remembered that we had to call on the doctor that afternoon and when I left the doctor's office I didn't have any
more tonsils nor any more faith in human beings. . . . We
had hardly finished when the bell rang and it was my
wife coming home from the slaughterhouse. I was still
buttoning my fly as I went through the hall to open the
gate. She was as white as flour. She looked as though
she'd never be able to go through another one. We put
her to bed and then we gathered up the dominoes and
put the tablecloth back on the table. Just the other night
in a *bistro,* as I was going to the toilet, I happened to
pass two old fellows playing dominoes. I had to stop a
moment and pick up a domino. The feeling of it immediately brought back the battleships, the clatter they
made when they fell on the floor. And with the battleships my lost tonsils and my faith in human beings gone.
So that every time I walked over the Brooklyn Bridge
and looked down toward the Navy Yard I felt as though
my guts were dropping out. Way up there, suspended
between the two shores, I felt always as though I were
hanging over a void; up there everything that had ever
happened to me seemed unreal, and worse than unreal—
unnecessary. Instead of joining me to life, to men, to the
activity of men, the bridge seemed to break all connec-
tions. If I walked toward the one shore or the other it
made no difference: either way was hell. Somehow I had
managed to sever my connection with the world that human hands and human minds were creating. Perhaps my
grandfather was right, perhaps I was spoiled in the bud
by the books I read. But it is ages since books have claimed
me. For a long time now I have practically ceased to read.
But the taint is still there. Now people are books to me.

I read them from cover to cover and toss them aside. I devour them, one after the other. And the more I read, the more insatiable I become. There is no limit to it. There could be no end, and there was none, until inside me a bridge began to form which united me again with the current of life from which as a child I had been separated.

A terrible sense of desolation. It hung over me for years. If I were to believe in the stars I should have to believe that I was completely under the reign of Saturn. Everything that happened to me happened too late to mean much to me. It was even so with my birth. Slated for Christmas I was born a half hour too late. It always seemed to me that I was meant to be the sort of individual that one is destined to be by virtue of being born on the 25th day of December. Admiral Dewey was born on that day and so was Jesus Christ . . . perhaps Krishnamurti too, for all I know. Anyway that's the sort of guy I was intended to be. But due to the fact that my mother had a clutching womb, that she held me in her grip like an octopus, I came out under another configuration— with a bad setup in other words. They say—the astrologers, I mean—that it will get better and better for me as I go on; the future, in fact, is supposed to be quite glorious. But what do I care about the future? It would have been better if my mother had tripped on the stairs the morning of the 25th of December and broken her neck: that would have given me a fair start! When I try to think, therefore, of where the break occurred I keep putting it back further and further, until there is no other way of accounting for it than by the retarded hour of birth. Even my mother, with her caustic tongue, seemed to understand it somewhat. "Always dragging behind, like a cow's tail"—that's how she characterized me. But is it my fault that she held me locked inside her until the hour had passed? Destiny had prepared me to be such and such a person; the stars were in the right conjunction and I was right with the stars and kicking to get out. But I had no choice about the mother who was to deliver me. Perhaps I was lucky not to have been born an idiot, considering all the circumstances. One thing seems clear, however—and this is a hangover from the 25th—that I was born with a crucifixion complex. That is, to be more precise, I was born a fanatic. *Fanatic!* I remember that word being hurled at me from early childhood on. By my parents especially. What is a fanatic? One who believes passionately and acts desperately upon what he believes. I was always believing in something and so getting into trouble. The more my hands were slapped the more firmly I believed. *I believed*—and the rest of the world did not! If it were only a question of enduring punishment one could go on believing till the end; but the way of the world is more insidious than that. Instead of being punished you are undermined, hollowed out, the ground taken from under your feet. It isn't even treachery, what I have in mind. Treachery is understandable and combatable. No, it is something worse, something *less* than treachery. It's a negativism that causes you to overreach yourself. You are perpetually spending your energy in the act of balancing yourself. You are seized with a sort of spiritual vertigo, you totter on the brink, your hair stands on end, you can't believe that beneath your feet lies an immeasurable abyss. It comes about through excess of enthusiasm, through a passionate desire to embrace people, to show them your love. The more you reach out toward the world the more the world retreats. Nobody wants real love, real hatred. Nobody wants you to put your hand in his sacred entrails—that's only for the priest in the hour of sacrifice. While you live, while the blood's still warm, you are to pretend that there is no such thing as blood and no such thing as a skeleton beneath the covering of flesh. *Keep off the grass!* That's the motto by which people live.

If you continue this balancing at the edge of the abyss long enough you become very very adept: no matter which way you are pushed you always right yourself. Being in constant trim you develop a ferocious gaiety, an unnatural gaiety, I might say. There are only two peoples in the world today who understand the meaning of such a statement—the Jews and the Chinese. If it happens that you are neither of these you find yourself in a strange predicament. You are always laughing at the wrong moment; you are considered cruel and heartless when in reality you are only tough and durable. But if you would laugh when others laugh and weep when they weep then you must be prepared to die as they die and live as they live. That means to be right and to get the worst of it at the same time. It means to be dead while you are alive and alive only when you are dead. In this company the world always wears a normal aspect, even under the most abnormal conditions. Nothing is right or wrong but thinking makes it so. You no longer believe in reality but in thinking. And when you are pushed off the dead end your thoughts go with you and they are of no use to you.

In a way, in a profound way, I mean, Christ was never pushed off the dead end. At the moment when he was tottering and swaying, as if by a great recoil, this negative backwash rolled up and stayed his death. The whole negative impulse of humanity seemed to coil up into a monstrous inert mass to create the human integer, the figure one, one and indivisible. There was a resurrection which is inexplicable unless we accept the fact that men have always been willing and ready to deny their own destiny. The earth rolls on, the stars roll on, but men, the great body of men which makes up the world, are caught in the image of the one and only one.

If one isn't crucified, like Christ, if one manages to survive, to go on living above and beyond the sense of desperation and futility, then another curious thing happens. It's as though one had actually died and actually been resurrected again; one lives a supernormal life, like the Chinese. That is to say, one is unnaturally gay, unnaturally healthy, unnaturally indifferent. The tragic sense is gone: one lives on like a flower, a rock, a tree, one with Nature and against Nature at the same time. If your best friend dies you don't even bother to go to the funeral; if a man is run down by a streetcar right before your eyes you keep on walking just as though nothing had happened; if a war breaks out you let your friends go to the front but you yourself take no interest in the slaughter. And so on and so on. Life becomes a spectacle and, if you happen to be an artist, you record the passing show. Loneliness is abolished, because all values, your own included, are destroyed. Sympathy alone flourishes, but it is not a human sympathy, a limited sympathy —it is something monstrous and evil. You care so little that you can afford to sacrifice yourself for anybody or anything. At the same time your interest, your curiosity, develops at an outrageous pace. This too is suspect, since it is capable of attaching you to a collar button just as well as to a cause. There is no fundamental, unalterable difference between things: all is flux, all is perishable. The surface of your being is constantly crumbling; within however you grow hard as a diamond. And perhaps it is this hard, magnetic core inside you which attracts others to you willy-nilly. One thing is certain, that when you die and are resurrected you belong to the earth and whatever is of the earth is yours inalienably. You become an anomaly of nature, a being without shadow; you will never die again but only pass away like the phenomena about you.

Nothing of this which I am now recording was known to me at the time that I was going through the great change. Everything I endured was in the nature of a preparation for that moment when, putting on my hat one evening, I walked out of the office, out of my hitherto private life, and sought the woman who was to liberate me from a living death. In the light of this I look back now upon my nocturnal rambles through the streets of New York, the white nights when I walked in my sleep and saw the city in which I was born as one sees things in a mirage. Often it was O'Rourke, the company detective, whom I accompanied through the silent streets. Often

the snow was on the ground and the air chill and frosty.
And O'Rourke talking interminably about thefts, about
murders, about love, about human nature, about the
Golden Age. He had a habit, when he was well launched
upon a subject, of stopping suddenly in the middle of the
street and planting his heavy foot between mine so that
I couldn't budge. And then, seizing the lapel of my coat,
he would bring his face to mine and talk into my eyes,
each word boring in like the turn of a gimlet. I can see
again the two of us standing in the middle of a street at
four in the morning, the wind howling, the snow blowing
down, and O'Rourke oblivious of everything but the story
he had to get off his chest. Always as he talked I remember taking in the surroundings out of the corner
of my eye, being aware not of what he was saying but of
the two of us standing in Yorkville or on Allen Street or on
Broadway. Always it seemed a little crazy to me, the
earnestness with which he recounted his banal murder
stories in the midst of the greatest muddle of architecture
that man had ever created. While he was talking about
fingerprints I might be taking stock of a coping or a
cornice on a little red brick building just back of his black
hat; I would get to thinking of the day the cornice had
been installed, who might be the man who had designed
it and why had he made it so ugly, so like every other
lousy, rotten cornice which we had passed from the East
Side up to Harlem and beyond Harlem, if we wanted to
push on, beyond New York, beyond the Mississippi, beyond the Grand Canyon, beyond the Mojave Desert,
everywhere in America where there are buildings for
man and woman. It seemed absolutely crazy to me that
each day of my life I had to sit and listen to other people's
stories, the banal tragedies of poverty and distress, of
love and death, of yearning and disillusionment. If, as it
happened, there came to me each day at least fifty men,
each pouring out his tale of woe, and with each one I had
to be silent and "receive," it was only natural that at
some point along the line I had to close my ears, had to

harden my heart. The tiniest little morsel was sufficient for me; I could chew on it and digest it for days and weeks. Yet I was obliged to sit there and be inundated, to get out at night again and receive more, to sleep listening, to dream listening. They streamed in from all over the world, from every stratum of society, speaking a thousand different tongues, worshiping different gods, obeying different laws and customs. The tale of the poorest among them was a huge tome, and yet if each and every one were written out at length it might all be compressed to the size of the Ten Commandments, it might all be recorded on the back of a postage stamp, like the Lord's Prayer. Each day I was so stretched that my hide seemed to cover the whole world; and when I was alone, when I was no longer obliged to listen, I shrank to the size of a pinpoint. The greatest delight, and it was a rare one, was to walk the streets alone . . . to walk the streets at night when no one was abroad and to reflect on the silence that surrounded me. Millions lying on their backs, dead to the world, their mouths wide open and nothing but snores emanating from them. Walking amidst the craziest architecture ever invented, wondering why and to what end, if every day from these wretched hovels or magnificent palaces there had to stream forth an army of men itching to unravel their tale of misery. In a year, reckoning it modestly, I received twenty-five thousand tales; in two years fifty thousand; in four years it would be a hundred thousand; in ten years I would be stark mad. Already I knew enough people to populate a good-sized town. What a town it would be, if only they could be gathered together! Would they want skyscrapers? Would they want museums? Would they want libraries? Would they too build sewers and bridges and tracks and factories? Would they make the same little cornices of tin, one like another, on, on, ad infinitum, from Battery Park to the Golden Bay? I doubt it. Only the lash of hunger could stir them. The empty belly, the wild look in the eye, the fear, the fear of worse, driving them on. One after the other, all the same, all goaded to desperation, out of the goad and whip of hunger building the loftiest skyscrapers, the most redoutable dreadnoughts, making the finest steel, the flimsiest lace, the most delicate glassware. Walking with O'Rourke and hearing nothing but theft, arson, rape, homicide was like listening to a little motif out of a grand symphony. And just as one can whistle an air of Bach and be thinking of a woman he wants to sleep with, so, listening to O'Rourke, I would be thinking of the moment when he would stop talking and say "what'll you have to eat?" In the midst of the most gruesome murder I could think of the pork tenderloin which we would be sure to get at a certain place farther up the line, and wonder too what sort of vegetables they would have on the side to go with it, and whether I would order pie afterwards or a custard pudding. It was the same when I slept with my wife now and then; while she was moaning and gibbering I might be wondering if she had emptied the grounds in the coffee pot, because she had the bad habit of letting things slide—the *important* things, I mean. Fresh coffee was important—and fresh bacon with the eggs. If she were knocked up again that would be bad, serious in a way, but more important than that was fresh coffee in the morning and the smell of bacon and eggs. I could put up with heartbreaks and abortions and busted romances, but I had to have something under my belt to carry on, and I wanted something nourishing, something appetizing. I felt exactly like Jesus Christ would have felt if he had been taken down from the cross and not permitted to die in the flesh. I am sure that the shock of crucifixion would have been so great that he would have suffered a complete amnesia as regards humanity. I am certain that after his wounds had healed he wouldn't have given a damn about the tribulations of mankind but would have fallen with the greatest relish upon a fresh cup of coffee and a slice of toast, assuming he could have had it.

Whoever, through too great love, which is monstrous after all, dies of his misery, is born again to know neither love nor hate, but to enjoy. And this joy of living, because it is unnaturally acquired, is a poison which eventually vitiates the whole world. Whatever is created beyond the normal limits of human suffering, acts as a boomerang and brings about destruction. At night the streets of New York reflect the crucifixion and death of Christ. When the snow is on the ground and there is the utmost silence there comes out of the hideous buildings of New York a music of such sullen despair and bankruptcy as to make the flesh shrivel. No stone was laid upon another with love or reverence; no street was laid for dance or joy. One thing has been added to another in a mad scramble to fill the belly, and the streets smell of empty bellies and full bellies and bellies half full. The streets smell of a hunger which has nothing to do with love; they smell of the belly which is insatiable and of the creations of the empty belly which are null and void.

In this null and void, in this zero whiteness, I learned to enjoy a sandwich, or a collar button. I could study a cornice or a coping with the greatest curiosity while pretending to listen to a tale of human woe. I can remember the dates on certain buildings and the names of the architects who designed them. I can remember the temperature and the velocity of the wind, standing at a certain corner; the tale that accompanied it is gone. I can remember that I was even then remembering something else, and I can tell you what it was that I was then remembering, but of what use? There was one man in me which had died and all that was left were his remembrances; there was another man who was alive, and that man was supposed to be me, myself, but he was alive only as a tree is alive, or a rock, or a beast of the field. Just as the city itself had become a huge tomb in which men struggled to earn a decent death so my own life came to resemble a tomb which I was constructing out of my own death. I was walking around in a stone forest the center of which was chaos; sometimes in the dead center, in the very heart of chaos, I danced or drank myself silly, or I made love, or

I befriended some one, or I planned a new life, but it was
all chaos, all stone, and all hopeless and bewildering. Until
the time when I would encounter a force strong enough
to whirl me out of this mad stone forest no life would be
possible for me nor could one page be written which
would have meaning. Perhaps in reading this, one has
still the impression of chaos but this is written from a
live center and what is chaotic is merely peripheral, the
tangential shreds, as it were, of a world which no longer
concerns me. Only a few months ago I was standing in the
streets of New York looking about me as years ago I had
looked about me; again I found myself studying the architecture, studying the minute details which only the dis-
located eye takes in. But this time it was like coming down
from Mars. What race of men is this, I asked myself. What
does it mean? And there was no remembrance of suffering or of the life that was snuffed out in the gutter, only
that I was looking upon a strange and incomprehensible
world, a world so removed from me that I had the sensation of belonging to another planet. From the top of the
Empire State Building I looked down one night upon the
city which I knew from below: there they were, in true
perspective, the human ants with whom I had crawled,
the human lice with whom I had struggled. They were
moving along at a snail's pace, each one doubtless fulfilling his microcosmic destiny. In their fruitless desperation they had reared this colossal edifice which was their
pride and boast. And from the topmost ceiling of this
colossal edifice they had suspended a string of cages in
which the imprisoned canaries warbled their senseless
warble. At the very summit of their ambition
there were these little spots of beings warbling away for
dear life. In a hundred years, I thought to myself, perhaps
they would be caging live human beings, gay, demented
ones, who would sing about the world to come. Perhaps
they would breed a race of warblers who would warble
while the others worked. Perhaps in every cage there
would be a poet or a musician so that life below might

flow on unimpeded, one with the stone, one with the forest, a rippling creaking chaos of null and void. In a thousand years they might all be demented, workers and poets alike, and everything fall back to ruin as has happened again and again. Another thousand years, or five thousand, or ten thousand, exactly where I am standing now to survey the scene, a little boy may open a book in a tongue as yet unheard of and about this life now passing, a life which the man who wrote the book never experienced, a life with deducted form and rhythm, with beginning and end, and the boy on closing the book will think to himself what a great race the Americans were, what a marvelous life there had once been on this continent which he is now inhabiting. But no race to come, except perhaps the race of blind poets, will ever be able to imagine the seething chaos out of which this future history was composed.

Chaos! A howling chaos! No need to choose a particular day. Any day of my life—back there—would suit. Every day of my life, my tiny, microscosmic life, was a reflection of the outer chaos. Let me think back. . . . At seven-thirty the alarm went off. I didn't bounce out of bed. I lay there till eight-thirty, trying to gain a little more sleep. Sleep— how could I sleep? In the back of my mind was an image of the office where I was already due. I could see Hymie arriving at eight sharp, the switchboard already buzzing with demands for help, the applicants climbing up the wide wooden stairway, the strong smell of camphor from the dressing room. Why get up and repeat yesterday's song and dance? As fast as I hired them they dropped out. Working my balls off and not even a clean shirt to wear. Mondays I got my allowance from the wife—carfare and lunch money. I was always in debt to her and she was in debt to the grocer, the butcher, the landlord, and so on. I couldn't be bothered shaving—there wasn't time enough. I put on the torn shirt, gobble up the breakfast, and borrow a nickel for the subway. If she were in a bad mood I would swindle the money from the newsdealer at the subway. I get to the office out of breath, an hour behind time and a dozen calls to make before I even talk to an applicant. While I make one call there are three other calls waiting to be answered. I use two telephones at once. The switchboard is buzzing. Hymie is sharpening his pencils between calls. McGovern the doorman is standing at my elbow to give me a word of advice about one of the applicants, probably a crook, who is trying to sneak back under a false name. Behind me the cards and ledgers containing the name of every applicant who had ever passed through the machine. The bad ones are starred in red ink; some of them have six aliases after their names. Meanwhile the room is crawling like a hive. The room stinks with sweat, dirty feet, old uniforms, camphor, lysol, bad breaths. Half of them will have to be turned away—not that we don't need them, but that even under the worst conditions they just won't do. The man in front of my desk, standing at the rail with palsied hands and bleary eyes, is an ex-mayor of New York City. He's seventy now and would be glad to take anything. He has wonderful letters of recommendation, but we can't take any one over forty-five years of age. Forty-five in New York is the deadline. The telephone rings and it's a smooth secretary from the Y.M.C.A. Wouldn't I make an exception for a boy who has just walked into his office—a boy who was in the reformatory for a year or so. *What did he do?* He tried to rape his sister. An Italian, of course. O'Mara, my assistant, is putting an applicant through the third degree. He suspects him of being an epileptic. Finally he succeeds and for good measure the boy throws a fit right there in the office. One of the women faints. A beautiful looking young woman with a handsome fur around her neck is trying to persuade me to take her on. She's a whore clean through and I know if I put her on there'll be hell to pay. She wants to work in a certain building uptown—because it is near home, she says. Nearing lunch time and a few cronies are beginning to drop in. They sit around watch-

ing me work, as if it were a vaudeville performance.
Kronski, the medical student, arrives; he says one of the
boys I've just hired has Parkinson's disease. I've been so
busy I haven't had a chance to go to the toilet. All the
telegraph operators, all the managers, suffer from hemor-
rhoids, so O'Rourke tells me. He's been having electrical
massages for the last two years, but nothing works. Lunch
time and there are six of us at the table. Some one will
have to pay for me, as usual. We gulp it down and rush
back. More calls to make, more applicants to interview.
The vice-president is raising hell because we can't keep
the force up to normal. Every paper in New York and
for twenty miles outside New York carries long ads demanding help. All the schools have been canvassed for
part-time messengers. All the charity bureaus and relief
societies have been invoked. They drop out like flies.
Some of them don't even last an hour. It's a human flour
mill. And the saddest thing about it is that it's totally
unnecessary. But that's not my concern. Mine is to do
or die, as Kipling says. I plug on, through one victim
after another, the telephone ringing like mad, the place
smelling more and more vile, the holes getting bigger
and bigger. Each one is a human being asking for a crust
of bread; I have his height, weight, color, religion, education, experience, etc. All the data will go into a ledger
to be filed alphabetically and then chronologically.
Names and dates. Fingerprints too, if we had the time
for it. So that what? So that the American people may
enjoy the fastest form of communication known to man,
so that they may sell their wares more quickly, so that the
moment you drop dead in the street your next of kin may
be apprised immediately, that is to say, within an hour,
unless the messenger to whom the telegram is entrusted
decides to throw up the job and throw the whole batch
of telegrams in the garbage can. Twenty million Christmas blanks, all wishing you a Merry Christmas and a
Happy New Year, from the directors and president and
vice-president of the Cosmodemonic Telegraph Com-

pany, and maybe the telegram reads "Mother dying, come at once," but the clerk is too busy to notice the message and if you sue for damages, spiritual damages, there is a legal department trained expressly to meet such emergencies and so you can be sure that your mother will die and you will have a Merry Christmas and Happy New Year just the same. The clerk, of course, will be fired and after a month or so he will come back for a messenger's job and he will be taken on and put on the night shift near the docks where nobody will recognize him, and his wife will come with the brats to thank the general manager, or perhaps the vice-president himself, for the kindness and consideration shown. And then one day everybody will be heartily surprised that said messenger robbed the till and O'Rourke will be asked to take the night train for Cleveland or Detroit and to track him down even if it costs ten thousand dollars. And then the vice-president will issue an order that no more Jews are to be hired, but after three or four days he will let up a bit because there are nothing but Jews coming for the job. And because it's getting so very tough and the timber so damned scarce I'm on the point of hiring a midget from the circus and I probably would have hired him if he hadn't broken down and confessed that he was a she. And to make it worse Valeska takes "it" under her wing, takes "it" home that night and under pretense of sympathy gives "it" a thorough examination, including a vaginal exploration with the index finger of the right hand. And the midget becomes very amorous and finally very jealous. It's a trying day and on the way home I bump into the sister of one of my friends and she insists on taking me to dinner. After dinner we go to a movie and in the dark we begin to play with each other and finally it gets to such a point that we leave the movie and go back to the office where I lay her out on the zinc-covered table in the dressing room. And when I get home, a little after midnight, there's a telephone call from Valeska and she wants me to hop into the subway immediately and come to her house, it's very urgent. It's an hour's ride and I'm dead weary, but she said it was urgent and so I'm on the way. And when I get there I meet her cousin, a rather attractive young woman, who, according to her own story, had just had an affair with a strange man because she was tired of being a virgin. And what was all the fuss about? Why this, that in her eagerness she had forgotten to take the usual precautions, and maybe now she was pregnant and then what? They wanted to know what I thought should be done and I said: "*Nothing.*" And then Valeska takes me aside and she asks me if I wouldn't care to sleep with her cousin, to break her in, as it were, so that there wouldn't be a repetition of that sort of thing.

The whole thing was cockeyed and we were all laughing hysterically and then we began to drink—the only thing they had in the house was kümmel and it didn't take much to put us under. And then it got more cockeyed because the two of them began to paw me and neither one would let the other do anything. The result was I undressed them both and put them to bed and they fell asleep in each other's arms. And when I walked out, toward five A.M., I discovered I didn't have a cent in my pocket and I tried to bum a nickel from a taxi driver but nothing doing so finally I took off my fur-lined overcoat and I gave it to him—for a nickel. When I got home my wife was awake and sore as hell because I had stayed out so long. We had a hot discussion and finally I lost my temper and I clouted her and she fell on the floor and began to weep and sob and then the kid woke up and hearing the wife bawling she got frightened and began to scream at the top of her lungs. The girl upstairs came running down to see what was the matter. She was in her kimono and her hair was hanging down her back. In the excitement she got close to me and things happened without either of us intending anything to happen. We put the wife to bed with a wet towel around her forehead and while the girl upstairs was bending over her I stood behind her and lifting her kimono I got it into her and she stood there a long time talking a lot of foolish, soothing nonsense. Finally I climbed into bed with the wife and to my utter amazement she began to cuddle up to me and without saying a word we locked horns and we stayed that way until dawn. I should have been worn out, but instead I was wide-awake, and I lay there beside her planning to take the day off and look up the whore with the beautiful fur whom I was talking to earlier in the day. After that I began to think about another woman, the wife of one of my friends who always twitted me about my indifference. And then I began to think about one after the other—all those whom I had passed up for one reason or another—until finally I fell sound asleep and in the midst of it I had a wet dream. At seven-thirty the alarm went off as usual and as usual I looked at my torn shirt hanging over the chair and I said to myself what's the use and I turned over. At eight o'clock the telephone rang and it was Hymie. Better get over quickly, he said, because there's a strike on. And that's how it went, day after day, and there was no reason for it, except that the whole country was cockeyed and what I relate was going on everywhere, either on a smaller scale or a larger scale, but the same thing everywhere, because it was all chaos and all meaningless.

It went on and on that way, day in and day out for almost five solid years. The continent itself perpetually wracked by cyclones, tornadoes, tidal waves, floods, droughts, blizzards, heat waves, pests, strikes, hold-ups, assassinations, suicides . . . a continuous fever and torment, an eruption, a whirlpool. I was like a man sitting in a lighthouse: below me the wild waves, the rocks, the reefs, the debris of shipwrecked fleets. I could give the danger signal but I was powerless to avert catastrophe. I *breathed* danger and catastrophe. At times the sensation of it was so strong that it belched like fire from my nostrils. I longed to be free of it all and yet I was irresistibly attracted. I was violent and phlegmatic at the same time. I was like the lighthouse itself—secure in the midst of the most turbulent sea. Beneath me was solid rock, the same shelf of rock on which the towering skyscrapers were reared. My foundations went deep into the earth and the armature of my body was made of steel riveted with hot bolts. Above all I was an eye, a huge searchlight which scoured far and wide, which revolved ceaselessly, pitilessly. This eye so wide-awake seemed to have made all my other faculties dormant; all my powers were used up in the effort to see, to take in the drama of the world.

If I longed for destruction it was merely that this eye might be extinguished. I longed for an earthquake, for some cataclysm of nature which would plunge the lighthouse into the sea. I wanted a metamorphosis, a change to fish, to leviathan, to destroyer. I wanted the earth to open up, to swallow everything in one engulfing yawn. I wanted to see the city buried fathoms deep in the bosom of the sea. I wanted to sit in a cave and read by candlelight. I wanted that eye extinguished so that I might have a chance to know my own body, my own desires. I wanted to be alone for a thousand years in order to reflect on what I had seen and heard—*and in order to forget.* I wanted something of the earth which was not of man's doing, something absolutely divorced from the human of which I was surfeited. I wanted something purely terrestrial and absolutely divested of idea. I wanted to feel the blood running back into my veins, even at the cost of annihilation. I wanted to shake the stone and the light out of my system. I wanted the dark fecundity of nature, the deep well of the womb, silence, or else the lapping of the black waters of death. I wanted to be that night which the remorseless eye illuminated, a night diapered with stars and trailing comets. To be of night so frighteningly silent, so utterly incomprehensible and eloquent at the same time. Never more to speak or to listen or to think. To be englobed and encompassed and to encompass and to englobe at the same time. No more pity, no more tenderness. To be human only terrestrially, like a plant or a worm or a brook. To be decomposed, divested of light and stone, variable as the molecule, durable as the atom, heartless as the earth itself.

It was just about a week before Valeska committed suicide that I ran into Mara. The week or two preceding that event was a veritable nightmare. A series of sudden deaths and strange encounters with women. First of all there was Pauline Janowski, a little Jewess of sixteen or seventeen who was without a home and without friends or relatives. She came to the office looking for a job. It was toward closing time and I didn't have the heart to turn her down cold. For some reason or other I took it into my head to bring her home for dinner and if possible try to persuade the wife to put her up for a while. What attracted me to her was her passion for Balzac. All the way home she was talking to me about *Lost Illusions*. The car was packed and we were jammed so tight together that it didn't make any difference what we were talking about because we were both thinking of only one thing. My wife of course was stupefied to see me standing at the door with a beautiful young girl. She was polite and courteous in her frigid way but I could see immediately that it was no use asking her to put the girl up. It was about all she could do to sit through the dinner with us. As soon as we had finished she excused herself and went to the movies. The girl started to weep. We were still sitting at the table, the dishes piled up in front of us. I went over to her and I put my arms around her. I felt genuinely sorry for her and I was perplexed as to what to do for her. Suddenly she threw her arms around my neck and she kissed me passionately. We stood there a long while embracing each other and then I thought to myself no, it's a crime, and besides maybe the wife didn't go to the movies at all, maybe she'll be ducking back any minute. I told the kid to pull herself together, that we'd take a trolley ride somewhere. I saw the child's

78

bank lying on the mantelpiece and I took it to the toilet
and emptied it silently. There was only about seventy-five
cents in it. We got on a trolley and went to the beach.
Finally we found a deserted spot and we lay down in
the sand. She was hysterically passionate and there was
nothing to do but to do it. I thought she would reproach
me afterwards, but she didn't. We lay there a while and
she began talking about Balzac again. It seems she had
ambitions to be a writer herself. I asked her what she
was going to do. She said she hadn't the least idea.
When we got up to go she asked me to put her on the
highway. Said she thought she would go to Cleveland or
some place. It was after midnight when I left her standing in front of a gas station. She had about thirty-five
cents in her pocketbook. As I started homeward I began
cursing my wife for the mean bitch that she was.
I wished to Christ it was she whom I had left standing on
the highway with no place to go to. I knew that when I
got back she wouldn't even mention the girl's name.

I got back and she was waiting up for me. I thought
she was going to give me hell again. But no, she had
waited up because there was an important message from
O'Rourke. I was to telephone him soon as I got home.
However, I decided not to telephone. I decided to get
undressed and go to bed. Just when I had gotten comfortably settled the telephone rang. It was O'Rourke.
There was a telegram for me at the office—he wanted
to know if he should open it and read it to me. I said of
course. The telegram was signed Monica. It was from
Buffalo. Said she was arriving at the Grand Central in
the morning with her mother's body. I thanked him and
went back to bed. No questions from the wife. I lay there
wondering what to do. If I were to comply with the re-
quest that would mean starting things all over again. I
had just been thanking my stars that I had gotten rid
of Monica. And now she was coming back with her
mother's corpse. Tears and reconciliation. No, I didn't
like the prospect at all. Supposing I didn't show up?

What then? There was always somebody around to take
care of a corpse. Especially if the bereaved were an attractive young blonde with sparkling blue eyes. I wondered if she'd go back to her job in the restaurant. If she
hadn't known Greek and Latin I would never have been
mixed up with her. But my curiosity got the better of me.
And then she was so goddamned poor, that too got me.
Maybe it wouldn't have been so bad if her hands hadn't
smelled greasy. That was the fly in the ointment—the
greasy hands. I remember the first night I met her and we
strolled through the park. She was ravishing to look at,
and she was alert and intelligent. It was just the time
when women were wearing short skirts and she wore
them to advantage. I used to go to the restaurant night
after night just to watch her moving around, watch her
bending over to serve or stooping down to pick up a fork.
And with the beautiful legs and the bewitching eyes a
marvelous line about Homer, with the pork and sauer-
kraut a verse of Sappho's, the Latin conjugations, the
odes of Pindar, with the dessert perhaps *The Rubaiyat*
or *Cynara*. But the greasy hands and the frowsy bed in
the boarding house opposite the marketplace—Whew! I
couldn't stomach it. The more I shunned her the more
clinging she became. Ten-page letters about love with
footnotes on *Thus Spake Zarathustra*. And then suddenly
silence and me congratulating myself heartily. No, I
couldn't bring myself to go to the Grand Central Station
in the morning. I rolled over and I fell sound asleep. In
the morning I would get the wife to telephone the office
and say I was ill. I hadn't been ill now for over a week—
it was coming to me.

At noon I find Kronski waiting for me outside the office.
He wants me to have lunch with him . . . there's an
Egyptian girl he wants me to meet. The girl turns out to
be a Jewess, but she came from Egypt and she looks like
an Egyptian. She's hot stuff and the two of us are working
on her at once. As I was supposed to be ill I decided not
to return to the office but to take a stroll through the East

Side. Kronski was going back to cover me up. We shook
hands with the girl and we each went our separate ways.
I headed toward the river where it was cool, having forgotten about the girl almost immediately. I sat on the
edge of the pier with my legs dangling over the stringpiece. A scow passed with a load of red bricks. Suddenly
Monica came to my mind. Monica arriving at the Grand
Central Station with a corpse. A corpse f. o. b. New York!
It seemed so incongruous and ridiculous that I burst out
laughing. What had she done with it? Had she checked it
or had she left it on a siding? No doubt she was cursing
me out roundly. I wondered what she would really think
if she could have imagined me sitting there at the dock
with my legs dangling over the stringpiece. It was warm
and sultry despite the breeze that was blowing off the
river. I began to snooze. As I dozed off Pauline came to
my mind. I imagined her walking along the highway with
her hand up. She was a brave kid, no doubt about it.
Funny that she didn't seem to worry about getting
knocked up. Maybe she was so desperate she didn't care.
And Balzac! That too was highly incongruous. Why Balzac? Well, that was her affair. Anyway she'd have enough
to eat with, until she met another guy. But a kid like that
thinking about becoming a writer! Well, why not? Everybody had illusions of one sort or another. Monica too
wanted to be a writer. Everybody was becoming a writer.
A writer! Jesus, how futile it seemed!

I dozed off . . . When I woke up I had an erection. The
sun seemed to be burning right into my fly. I got up and
I washed my face at the drinking fountain. It was still as
hot and sultry as ever. The asphalt was soft as mush, the
flies were biting, the garbage was rotting in the gutter.
I walked about between the pushcarts and looked at
things with an empty eye. I had a sort of lingering hard
on all the while, but no definite object in mind. It was
only when I got back to Second Avenue that I suddenly
remembered the Egyptian Jewess from lunch time. I

remembered her saying that she lived over the Russian restaurant near Twelfth Street. Still I hadn't any definite idea of what I was going to do. Just browsing about, killing time. My feet nevertheless were dragging me northward, toward Fourteenth Street. When I got abreast of the Russian restaurant I paused a moment and then I ran up the stairs three at a time. The hall door was open. I climbed up a couple of flights scanning the names on the doors. She was on the top floor and there was a man's name under hers. I knocked softly. No answer. I knocked again, a little harder. This time I heard some one moving about. Then a voice close to the door, asking who is it and at the same time the knob turning. I pushed the door open and stumbled into the darkened room. Stumbled right into her arms and felt her naked under the half-opened kimono. She must have come out of a sound sleep and only half realized who was holding her in his arms. When she realized it was me she tried to break away but I had her tight and I began kissing her passionately and at the same time backing her up toward the couch near the window. She mumbled something about the door being open but I wasn't taking any chance on letting her slip out of my arms. So I made a slight detour and little by little I edged her toward the door and made her shove it to with her ass. I locked it with my one free hand and then I moved her into the center of the room and with the free hand I unbuttoned my fly and got my pecker out and into position. She was so drugged with sleep that it was almost like working on an automaton. I could see too that she was enjoying the idea of being fucked half asleep. The only thing was that every time I made a lunge she grew more wide-awake. And as she grew more conscious she became more frightened. It was difficult to know how to put her to sleep again without losing a good fuck. I managed to tumble her on to the couch without losing ground and she was hot as hell now, twisting and squirming like an eel. From the time I had started to maul her I don't think she had opened her eyes once. I kept saying to myself—"an Egyptian fuck . . . an Egyptian fuck"—and so as not to shoot off immediately I deliberately began thinking about the corpse that Monica had dragged to the Grand Central Station and about the thirty-five cents that I had left with Pauline on the highway. Then bango! A loud knock on the door and with that she opens her eyes wide and looks at me in utmost terror. I started to pull away quickly but to my surprise she held me tight "Don't move," she whispered in my ear. "Wait!" There was another loud knock and then I heard Kronski's voice saying "It's me, Thelma . . . it's me, *Izzy*." At that I almost burst out laughing. We slumped back again into a natural position and as her eyes softly closed I moved it around inside her, gently, so as not to wake her up again. It was one of the most wonderful fucks I ever had in my life. I thought it was going to last forever. Whenever I felt in danger of going off I would stop moving and think—think for example of where I would like to spend my vacation, if I got one, or think of the shirts lying in the bureau drawer, or the patch in the bedroom carpet just at the foot of the bed. Kronksi was still standing at the door—I could hear him changing about from one position to another. Every time I became aware of him standing there I jibbed her a little for good measure and in her half sleep she answered back, humorously, as though she understood what I meant by this put-and-take language. I didn't dare to think what she might be thinking or I'd have come immediately. Sometimes I skirted dangerously close to it, but the saving trick was always Monica and the corpse at the Grand Central Station. The thought of that, the humorousness of it, I mean, acted like a cold douche.

When it was all over she opened her eyes wide and stared at me, as though she were taking me in for the first time. I hadn't a word to say to her; the only thought in my head was to get out as quickly as possible. As we were washing up I noticed a note on the floor near the door.

It was from Kronski. His wife had just been taken to the hospital—he wanted her to meet him at the hospital. I felt relieved! It meant that I could break away without wasting any words.

The next day I had a telephone call from Kronski. His wife had died on the operating table. That evening I went home for dinner; we were still at the table when the bell rang. There was Kronski standing at the gate looking absolutely sunk. It was always difficult for me to offer words of condolence; with him it was absolutely impossible. I listened to my wife uttering her trite words of sympathy and I felt more than ever disgusted with her. "Let's get out of here," I said.

We walked along in absolute silence for a while. At the park we turned in and headed for the meadows. There was a heavy mist which made it impossible to see a yard ahead. Suddenly, as we were swimming along, he began to sob. I stopped and turned my head away. When I thought he had finished I looked around and there he was staring at me with a strange smile. "It's funny," he said, "how hard it is to accept death." I smiled too now and put my hand on his shoulder. "Go on," I said, "talk your head off. Get it off your chest." We started walking again, up and down over the meadows, as though we were walking under the sea. The mist had become so thick that I could just barely discern his features. He was talking quietly and madly. "I knew it would happen," he said. "It was too beautiful to last." The night before she was taken ill he had had a dream. He dreamt that he had lost his identity. "I was stumbling around in the dark calling my own name. I remember coming to a bridge, and looking down into the water I saw myself drowning. I jumped off the bridge head first and when I came up I saw Yetta floating under the bridge. She was dead." And then suddenly he added: "You were there yesterday when I knocked at the door, weren't you? I knew you were there and I couldn't go away. I knew too that Yetta was dying and I wanted to be with her, but I was afraid to go alone." I said nothing and he rambled on. "The first girl I ever loved died in the same way. I was only a kid and I couldn't get over it. Every night I used to go to the cemetery and sit by her grave. People thought I was out of my mind. I guess I was out of my mind. Yesterday, when I was standing at the door, it all came back to me. I was back in Trenton, at the grave, and the sister of the girl I loved was sitting beside me. She said it couldn't go on that way much longer, that I would go mad. I thought to myself that I really was mad and to prove it to myself I decided to do something mad and so I said to her it isn't *her* I love, it's *you*, and I pulled her over me and we lay there kissing each other and finally I screwed her, right beside the grave. And I think that cured me because I never went back there again and I never thought about her any more—until yesterday when I was standing at the door. If I could have gotten hold of you yesterday I would have strangled you. I don't know why I felt that way but it seemed to me that you had opened up a tomb, that you were violating the dead body of the girl I loved. That's crazy, isn't it? And why did I come to see you tonight? Maybe it's because you're absolutely indifferent to me . . . because you're not a Jew and I can talk to you . . . because you don't give a damn, and you're right. . . . Did you ever read *The Revolt of the Angels?*"

We had just arrived at the bicycle path which encircles the park. The lights of the boulevard were swimming in the mist. I took a good look at him and I saw that he was out of his head. I wondered if I could make him laugh. I was afraid, too, that if he once got started laughing he would never stop. So I began to talk at random, about Anatole France at first, and then about other writers, and finally, when I felt that I was losing him, I suddenly switched to General Ivolgin, and with that he began to laugh, not a laugh either, but a cackle, a hideous cackle, like a rooster with its head on the block. It got him so badly that he had to stop and hold his guts; the tears were streaming down his eyes and between the cackles he let out the most terrible, heartrending sobs. "I knew you would do me good," he blurted out, as the last outbreak died away. "I always said you were a crazy son of a bitch. . . . You're a Jew bastard yourself, only you don't know it. . . . Now tell me, you bastard, how was it yesterday? Did you get your end in? Didn't I tell you she was a good lay? And do you know who she's living with? Jesus, you were lucky you didn't get caught. She's living with a Russian poet—you know the guy, too. I introduced you to him once at the Café Royal. Better not let him get wind of it. He'll beat your brains out . . . and then he'll write a beautiful poem about it and send it to her with a bunch of roses. Sure, I knew him out in Stelton, in the anarchist colony. His old man was a Nihilist. The whole family's crazy. By the way, you'd better take care of yourself. I meant to tell you that the other day, but I didn't think you would act so quickly. You know she may have syphilis. I'm not trying to scare you. I'm just telling you for your own good. . . ."

This outburst seemed to really assuage him. He was trying to tell me in his twisted Jewish way that he liked me. To do so he had to first destroy everything around me—the wife, the job, my friends, the "nigger wench," as he called Valeska, and so on. "I think some day you're going to be a great writer," he said. *"But,"* he added maliciously, "first you'll have to suffer a bit. I mean *really* suffer, because you don't know what the word means yet. You only *think* you've suffered. You've got to fall in love first. That nigger wench now . . . you don't really suppose that you're in love with her, do you? Did you ever take a good look at her ass . . . how it's spreading, I mean? In five years she'll look like Aunt Jemima. You'll make a swell couple walking down the avenue with a string of pickaninnies trailing behind you. Jesus, I'd rather see you marry a Jewish girl. You wouldn't appreciate her, of course, but she'd be good for you. You need something to steady yourself. You're scattering your energies. Listen, why do you run around with all these

dumb bastards you pick up? You seem to have a genius
for picking up the wrong people. Why don't you throw
yourself into something useful? You don't belong in that
job—you could be a big guy somewhere. Maybe a labor
leader . . . I don't know what exactly. But first you've
got to get rid of that hatchet-faced wife of yours. Ugh!
when I look at her I could spit in her face. I don't see
how a guy like you could ever have married a bitch like
that. What was it—just a pair of steaming ovaries? Listen,
that's what's the matter with you—you've got nothing
but sex on the brain. . . . No, I don't mean that either.
You've got a mind and you've got passion and enthusiasm
. . . but you don't seem to give a damn what you do or
what happens to you. If you weren't such a romantic
bastard I'd almost swear that you were a Jew. It's different with me—I never had anything to look forward to.
But you've got something in you—only you're too
damned lazy to bring it out. Listen, when I hear you talk
sometimes I think to myself—if only that guy would put
it down on paper! Why you could write a book that
would make a guy like Dreiser hang his head. You're
different from the Americans I know; somehow you don't
belong, and it's a damned good thing you don't. You're
a little cracked, too—I suppose you know that. But in a
good way. Listen, a little while ago, if it had been anybody else who talked to me that way I'd have murdered
him. I think I like you better because you didn't try to
give me any sympathy. I know better than to expect
sympathy from you. If you had said one false word tonight I'd have really gone mad. I know it. I was on the
very edge. When you started in about General Ivolgin I
thought for a minute it was all up with me. That's what
makes me think you've got something in you . . . that
was real cunning! And now let me tell *you* something . . .
if you don't pull yourself together soon you're going to
be screwy. You've got something inside you that's eating
you up. I don't know what it is, but you can't put it over
on me. I know you from the bottom up. I know there's

something griping you—and it's not just your wife, nor your job, nor even that nigger wench whom you think you're in love with. Sometimes I think you were born in the wrong time. Listen, I don't want you to think I'm making an idol of you but there's something to what I say . . . if you had just a little more confidence in yourself you could be the biggest man in the world today. You wouldn't even have to be a writer. You might become another Jesus Christ for all I know. Don't laugh—I mean it. You haven't the slightest idea of your own possibilities . . . you're absolutely blind to everything except your own desires. You don't know what you want. You don't know because you never stop to think. You're letting people use you up. You're a damned fool, an idiot. If I had a tenth of what you've got I could turn the world upside down. You think that's crazy, eh? Well, listen to me . . . I was never more sane in my life. When I came to see you to-night I thought I was about ready to commit suicide. It doesn't make much difference whether I do it or not. But anyway, I don't see much point in doing it now. That won't bring her back to me. I was born unlucky. Wherever I go I seem to bring disaster. But I don't want to kick off yet . . . I want to do some good in the world first. That may sound silly to you, but it's true. I'd like to do something for others. . . ."

He stopped abruptly and looked at me again with that strange wan smile. It was the look of a hopeless Jew in whom, as with all his race, the life instinct was so strong that, even though there was absolutely nothing to hope for, he was powerless to kill himself. That hopelessness was something quite alien to me. I thought to myself—if only we could change skins! Why, I could kill myself for a bagatelle! And what got me more than anything was the thought that he wouldn't even enjoy the funeral—his own wife's funeral! God knows, the funerals we had were sorry enough affairs, but there was always a bit of food and drink afterwards, and some good obscene jokes and some hearty belly laughs. Maybe I was too young to appreciate the sorrowful aspects, though I saw plainly enough how they howled and wept. But that never meant much to me because after the funeral, sitting in the beer garden next to the cemetery, there was always an atmosphere of good cheer despite the black garments and the crepes and the wreaths. It seemed to me, as a kid then, that they were really trying to establish some sort of communion with the dead person. Something almost Egyptian-like, when I think back on it. Once upon a time I thought they were just a bunch of hypocrites. But they weren't. They were just stupid, healthy Germans with a lust for life. Death was something outside their ken, strange to say, because if you went only by what they said you would imagine that it occupied a good deal of their thoughts. But they really didn't grasp it at all—not the way the Jew does, for example. They talked about the life hereafter but they never really believed in it. And if any one were so bereaved as to pine away they looked upon that person suspiciously, as you would look upon an insane person. There were limits to sorrow as there were limits to joy, that was the impression they gave me. And at the extreme limits there was always the stomach which had to be filled—with limburger sandwiches and beer and kümmel and turkey legs if there were any about. They wept in their beer, like children. And the next minute they were laughing, laughing over some curious quirk in the dead person's character. Even the way they used the past tense had a curious effect upon me. An hour after he was shoveled under they were saying of the defunct—"he was always so good-natured"—as though the person in mind were dead a thousand years, a character in history, or a personage out of the *Nibelungenlied*. The thing was that he was dead, definitely dead for all time, and they, the living, were cut off from him now and forever, and today as well as tomorrow must be lived through, the clothes washed, the dinner prepared, and when the next one was struck down there would be a coffin to select and a squabble about the will, but it would be all in the daily routine and to take time off to grieve and sorrow was sinful because God, if there was a God, had ordained it that way and we on earth had nothing to say about it. To go beyond the ordained limits of joy or grief was wicked. To threaten madness was the high sin. They had a terrific animal sense of adjustment, marvelous to behold if it had been truly animal, horrible to witness when you realized that it was nothing more than dull German torpor, insensitivity. And yet, somehow, I preferred these animated stomachs to the hydra-headed sorrow of the Jew. At bottom I couldn't feel sorry for Kronski—I would have to feel sorry for his whole tribe. The death of his wife was only an item, a trifle, in the history of his calamities. As he himself had said, he was born unlucky. He was born to see things go wrong—because for five thousand years things had been going wrong in the blood of the race. They came into the world with that sunken, hopeless leer on their faces and they would go out of the world the same way. They left a bad smell behind them—a poison, a vomit of sorrow. The stink they were trying to take out of the world was the stink they themselves had brought into the world. I reflected on all this as I listened to him. I felt so well and clean inside that when we parted, after I had turned down a side street, I began to whistle and hum. And then a terrible thirst came upon me and I says to meself in me best Irish brogue—shure and it's a bit of a drink ye should be having now, me lad—and saying it I stumbled into a hole in the wall and I ordered a big foaming stein of beer and a thick hamburger sandwich with plenty of onions. I had another mug of beer and then a drop of brandy and I thought to myself in my callous way—if the poor bastard hasn't got brains enough to enjoy his own wife's funeral then I'll enjoy it for him. And the more I thought about it, the happier I grew, and if there was the least bit of grief or envy it was only for the fact that I couldn't change places with her, the poor dead Jewish soul, because death was something absolutely beyond the grip and comprehension of a dumb goy like myself and it was a pity to waste it on the likes of them as knew all about it and didn't need it anyway. I got so damned intoxicated with the idea of dying that in my drunken stupor I was mumbling to the God above to kill me this night, kill me, God, and let me know what it's all about. I tried my stinking best to imagine what it was like, giving up the ghost, but it was no go. The best I could do was to imitate a death rattle, but on that I nearly choked, and then I got so damned frightened that I almost shit in my pants. That wasn't death, anyway. That was just choking. Death was more like what we went through in the park: two people walking side by side in the mist, rubbing against trees and bushes, and not a word between them. It was something emptier than the name itself and yet right and peaceful, dignified, if you like. It was not a continuation of life, but a leap in the dark and no possibility of ever coming back, not even as a grain of dust. And that was right and beautiful, I said to myself, because why would one want to come back. To taste it once is to taste it forever—life *or* death. Whichever way the coin flips is right, so long as you hold no stakes. Sure, it's tough to choke on your own spittle—it's disagreeable more than anything else. And besides, one doesn't always die choking to death. Sometimes one goes off in his sleep, peaceful and quiet as a lamb. The Lord comes and gathers you up into the fold, as they say. Anyway, you stop breathing. And why the hell should one want to go on breathing forever? Anything that would have to be done interminably would be torture. The poor human bastards that we are, we ought to be glad that somebody devised a way out. We don't quibble about going to sleep. A third of our lives we snore away like drunken rats. What about that? Is that tragic? Well then, say three-thirds of drunken ratlike sleep. Jesus, if we had any sense we'd be dancing with glee at the thought of it! We could all die in bed tomorrow, without pain, without suffering—if we had the sense to take advantage of our remedies. We don't

want to die, that's the trouble with us. That's why God
and the whole shooting match upstairs in our crazy dust-
bins. General Ivolgin! That got a cackle out of him . . .
and a few dry sobs. I might as well have said limburger
cheese. But General Ivolgin means something to him . . .
something crazy. Limburger cheese would be too sober,
too banal. It's all limburger cheese, however, including
General Ivolgin, the poor drunken sap. General Ivolgin
was evolved out of Dostoevski's limburger cheese, his
own private brand. That means a certain flavor, a certain
label. So people recognize it when they smell it, taste it.
But what made this General Ivolgin limburger cheese?
Why, whatever made limburger cheese, which is x and
therefore unknowable. And so therefore? Therefore
nothing . . . nothing at all. Full stop—or else a leap in the
dark and no coming back.

As I was taking my pants off I suddenly remembered
what the bastard had told me. I looked at my cock and it
looked just as innocent as ever. "Don't tell me you've got
the syph," I said, holding it in my hand and squeezing it
a bit as though I might see a bit of pus squirting out. No,
I didn't think there was much chance of having the syph.
I wasn't born under that kind of star. The clap, yes, that
was possible. Everybody had the clap sometime or other.
But not syph! I knew he'd wish it on me if he could, just
to make me realize what suffering was. But I couldn't be
bothered obliging him. I was born a dumb but lucky goy.
I yawned. It was all so much goddamned limburger
cheese that syph or no syph, I thought to myself, if she's
up to it I'll tear off another piece and call it a day. But
evidently she wasn't up to it. She was for turning her ass
on me. So I just lay there with a stiff prick up against her
ass and I gave it to her by mental telepathy. And by
Jesus, she must have gotten the message sound asleep
though she was, because it wasn't any trouble going in by the stable door and besides I didn't have to look
at her face which was one hell of a relief. I thought to
myself, as I gave her the last hook and whistle—"me lad,

it's limburger cheese and now you can turn over and snore. . . ."

It seemed as if it would go on forever, the sex and death chant. The very next afternoon at the office I received a telephone call from my wife saying that her friend Arline had just been taken to the insane asylum. They were friends from the convent school in Canada where they had both studied music and the art of masturbation. I had met the whole flock of them little by little, including Sister Antolina who wore a truss and who apparently was the high priestess of the cult of onanism. They had all had a crush on Sister Antolina at one time or another. And Arline with the chocolate eclair mug wasn't the first of the little group to go to the insane ayslum. I don't say it was masturbation that drove them there but certainly the atmosphere of the convent had something to do with it. They were all spoiled in the egg.

Before the afternoon was over my old friend Mac-Gregor walked in. He arrived looking glum as usual and complaining about the advent of old age, though he was hardly past thirty. When I told him about Arline he seemed to liven up a bit. He said he always knew there was something wrong with her. Why? Because when he tried to force her one night she began to weep hysterically. It wasn't the weeping as much as what she said. She said she had sinned against the Holy Ghost and for that she would have to lead a life of continence. Recalling the incident he began to laugh in his mirthless way. "I said to her—well you don't need to do it if you don't want . . . just hold it in your hand. Jesus, when I said that I thought she'd go clean off her nut. She said I was trying to soil her innocence—that's the way she put it. And at the same time she took it in her hand and she squeezed it so hard I damned near fainted. Weeping all the while, too. And still harping on the Holy Ghost and her 'innocence,' I remembered what you told me once and so I gave her a sound slap in the jaw. It worked like magic. She quieted down after a bit, enough to let me slip it in,

and then the real fun commenced. Listen, did you ever
fuck a crazy woman? It's something to experience. From
the instant I got it in she started talking a blue streak. I
can't describe it to you exactly, but it was almost as
though she didn't know I was fucking her. Listen, I don't
know whether you've ever had a woman eat an apple
while you were doing it . . . well, you can imagine how
that affects you. This one was a thousand times worse. It
got on my nerves so that I began to think I was a little
queer myself. . . . And now here's something you'll hardly
believe, but I'm telling you the truth. You know what
she did when we got through? She put her arms around
me and she thanked me. . . . Wait, that isn't all. Then she
got out of bed and she knelt down and offered up a prayer
for my soul. Jesus, I remember that so well. 'Please make
Mac a better Christian,' she said. And me lying there
with a limp cock listening to her. I didn't know whether
I was dreaming or what. 'Please make Mac a better
Christian!' Can you beat that?"

"What are you doing tonight?" he added cheerfully.

"Nothing special," I said.

"Then come along with me. I've got a gal I want you
to meet. . . . *Paula.* I picked her up at the Roseland a
few nights ago. She's not crazy—she's just a nymphomaniac. I want to see you dance with her. It'll be a treat
. . . just to watch you. Listen, if you don't shoot off in
your pants when she starts wiggling, well then I'm a
son of a bitch. Come on, close the joint. What's the use
of farting around in this place?"

There was a lot of time to kill before going to the Roseland so we went to a little hole in the wall over near
Seventh Avenue. Before the war it was a French joint;
now it was a speakeasy run by a couple of wops. There
was a tiny bar near the door and in the back a little room
with a sawdust floor and a slot machine for music. The
idea was that we were to have a couple of drinks and
then eat. That was the *idea.* Knowing him as I did, however, I wasn't at all sure that we would be going to the

Roseland together. If a woman should come along who pleased his fancy—and for that she didn't have to be either beautiful or sound of wind and limb—I knew he'd leave me in the lurch and beat it. The only thing that concerned me, when I was with him, was to make sure in advance that he had enough money to pay for the drinks we ordered. And, of course, never let him out of my sight until the drinks were paid for.

The first drink or two always plunged him into reminiscence. Reminiscences of cunt to be sure. His reminiscences were reminiscent of a story he had told me once and which made an indelible impression upon me. It was about a Scotchman on his deathbed. Just as he was about to pass away his wife, seeing him struggling to say something, bends over him tenderly and says—"What is it, Jock, what is it ye're trying to say?" And Jock, with a last effort, raises himself wearily and says: "Just cunt . . . cunt . . . cunt."

That was always the opening theme, and the ending theme, with MacGregor. It was his way of saying—*futility*. The leitmotif was disease, because between fucks, as it were, he worried his head off, or rather he worried the head off his cock. It was the most natural thing in the world, at the end of an evening, for him to say—"come on upstairs a minute, I want to show you my cock." From taking it out and looking at it and washing it and scrubbing it a dozen times a day naturally his cock was always swollen and inflamed. Every now and then he went to the doctor and he had it sounded. Or, just to relieve him, the doctor would give him a little box of salve and tell him not to drink so much. This would cause no end of debate, because as he would say to me, "if the salve is any good why do I have to stop drinking?" Or, "if I stopped drinking altogether do you think I would need to use the salve?" Of course, whatever I recommended went in one ear and out the other. He had to worry about something and the penis was certainly good food for worry. Sometimes he worried about his scalp. He had dandruff, as

most everybody has, and when his cock was in good
condition he forgot about that and he worried about
his scalp. Or else his chest. The moment he thought about
his chest he would start to cough. And such coughing!
As though he were in the last stages of consumption. And
when he was running after a woman he was as nervous
and irritable as a cat. He couldn't get her quickly enough.
The moment he had her he was worrying about how to
get rid of her. They all had something wrong with them,
some trivial little thing, usually, which took the edge off
his appetite.

He was rehearsing all this as we sat in the gloom of
the back room. After a couple of drinks he got up, as
usual, to go to the toilet, and on his way he dropped a
coin in the slot machine and the jiggers began to jiggle
and with that he perked up and pointing to the glasses
he said: "Order another round." He came back from the
toilet looking extraordinarily complacent, whether because he had relieved his bladder or because he had run
into a girl in the hallway, I don't know. Anyhow, as he
sat down, he started in on another tack—very composed
now and very serene, almost like a philosopher. "You
know, Henry, we're getting on in years. You and I
oughtn't to be frittering our time away like this. If we're
ever going to amount to anything it's high time we started
in. . . ." I had been hearing this line for years now and I
knew what the upshot would be. This was just a little
parenthesis while he calmly glanced about the room and
decided which bimbo was the least sottish-looking. While
he discoursed about the miserable failure of our lives his
feet were dancing and his eyes were getting brighter and
brighter. It would happen as it always happened that just
as he was saying—"Now you take Woodruff, for instance.
He'll never get ahead because he's just a natural mean
scrunging son of a bitch . . ."—just at such a moment, as
I say, it would happen that some drunken cow in passing
the table would catch his eye and without the slightest
pause he would interrupt his narrative to say "hello kid,

why don't you sit down and have a drink with us?" And
as a drunken bitch like that never travels alone, but always in pairs, why she'd respond with a "Certainly, can I
bring my friend over?" And MacGregor, as though he
were the most gallant chap in the world, would say "Why
sure, why not? What's her name?" And then, tugging at
my sleeve, he'd bend over and whisper: "Don't you beat
it on me, do you hear? We'll give 'em one drink and get
rid of them, see?"

And, as it always happened, one drink led to another
and the bill was getting too high and he couldn't see
why he should waste his money on a couple of bums so
you go out first, Henry, and pretend you're buying some
medicine and I'll follow in a few minutes . . . but wait for
me, you son of a bitch, don't leave me in the lurch like
you did the last time. And like I always did, when I got
outside I walked away as fast as my legs would carry me,
laughing to myself and thanking my lucky stars that I
had gotten away from him as easily as I had. With all
those drinks under my belt it didn't matter much where
my feet were dragging me. Broadway lit up just as
crazy as ever and the crowd thick as molasses. Just fling
yourself into it like an ant and let yourself get pushed
along. Everybody doing it, some for a good reason and
some for no reason at all. All this push and movement
representing action, success, get ahead. Stop and look at
shoes or fancy shirts, the new fall overcoat, wedding rings
at ninety-eight cents apiece. Every other joint a food
emporium.

Every time I hit that runway toward dinner hour a
fever of expectancy seized me. It's only a stretch of a few
blocks, from Times Square to Fiftieth Street, and when
one says Broadway that's all that's really meant and it's
really nothing, just a chicken run and a lousy one at that,
but at seven in the evening when everybody's rushing
for a table there's a sort of electrical crackle in the air
and your hair stands on end like antennae and if you're
receptive you not only get every flash and flicker but

you get the statistical itch, the *quid pro quo* of the in-
teractive, interstitial, ectoplasmatic quantum of bodies
jostling in space like the stars which compose the Milky
Way, only this is the Gay White Way, the top of the
world with no roof above and not even a crack or a hole
under your feet to fall through and say it's a lie. The
absolute impersonality of it brings you to a pitch of warm
human delirium which makes you run forward like a
blind nag and wag your delirious ears. Every one is so
utterly, confoundedly not himself that you become automatically the personification of the whole human race,
shaking hands with a thousand human hands, cackling
with a thousand different human tongues, cursing, ap-
plauding, whistling, crooning, soliloquizing, orating, ges-
ticulating, urinating, fecundating, wheedling, cajoling,
whimpering, bartering, pimping, caterwauling, and so on
and so forth. You are all the men who ever lived up to
Moses, and beyond that you are a woman buying a hat,
or a bird cage, or just a mouse trap. You can lie in wait in
a show window, like a fourteen-carat gold ring, or you can
climb the side of a building like a human fly, but nothing
will stop the procession, not even umbrellas flying at
lightning speed, nor double-decked walruses marching
calmly to the oyster banks. Broadway, such as I see it
now and have seen it for twenty-five years, is a ramp that
was conceived by St. Thomas Aquinas while he was yet
in the womb. It was meant originally to be used only by
snakes and lizards, by the horned toad and the red heron,
but when the great Spanish Armada was sunk the human
kind wriggled out of the ketch and slopped over, creating
by a sort of foul, ignominious squirm and wiggle the
cuntlike cleft that runs from the Battery south to the golf
links north through the dead and wormy center of Manhattan Island. From Times Square to Fiftieth Street all
that St. Thomas Aquinas forgot to include in his *mag-
num opus* is here included, which is to say, among other
things, hamburger sandwiches, collar buttons, poodle
dogs, slot machines, gray bowlers, typewriter ribbons,

orange sticks, free toilets, sanitary napkins, mint jujubes, billiard balls, chopped onions, crinkled doilies, manholes, chewing gum, sidecars and sourballs, cellophane, cord tires, magnetos, horse liniment, cough drops, feenamint, and that feline opacity of the hysterically endowed eunuch who marches to the soda fountain with a sawed-off shotgun between his legs. The before-dinner atmosphere, the blend of patchouli, warm pitchblende, iced electricity, sugared sweat and powdered urine drives one on to a fever of delirious expectancy. Christ will never more come down to earth nor will there be any lawgiver, nor will murder cease, nor theft, nor rape, and yet . . . and yet one expects something, something terrifyingly marvelous and absurd, perhaps a cold lobster with mayonnaise served gratis, perhaps an invention, like the electric light, like television, only more devastating, more soul-rending, an invention unthinkable that will bring a shattering calm and void, not the calm and void of death but of life such as the monks dreamed, such as is dreamed still in the Himalayas, in Tibet, in Lahore, in the Aleutian Islands, in Polynesia, in Easter Island, the dream of men before the flood, before the word was written, the dream of cave men and anthropophagists, of those with double sex and short tails, of those who are said to be crazy and have no way of defending themselves because they are outnumbered by those who are not crazy. Cold energy trapped by cunning brutes and then set free like explosive rockets, wheels intricately interwheeled to give the illusion of force and speed, some for light, some for power, some for motion, words wired by maniacs and mounted like false teeth, perfect, and repulsive as lepers, ingratiating, soft, slippery, nonsensical movement, vertical, horizontal, circular, between walls and through walls, for pleasure, for barter, for crime, for sex; all light, movement, power impersonally conceived, generated, and distributed throughout a choked, cuntlike cleft intended to dazzle and awe the savage, the yokel, the alien, but nobody dazzled or awed, this one hungry, that one lecherous, all one and the same and no different from the savage, the yokel, the alien, except for odds and ends, bric-à-brac, the soapsuds of thought, the sawdust of the mind. In the same cunty cleft, trapped and undazzled, millions have walked before me, among them one, Blaise Cendrars, who afterwards flew to the moon, thence back to earth and up the Orinoco impersonating a wild man but actually sound as a button, though no longer vulnerable, no longer mortal, a splendiferous hulk of a poem dedicated to the archipelago of insomnia. Of those with fever few hatched, among them myself still unhatched, but pervious and maculate, knowing with quiet ferocity the ennui of ceaseless drift and movement. Before dinner the slat and chink of sky light softly percolating through the bounded gray dome, the vagrant hemispheres spored with blue-egged nuclei coagulating, ramifying, in the one basket lobsters, in the other the germination of a world antiseptically personal and absolute. Out of the manholes, gray with the underground life, men of the future world saturated with shit, the iced electricity biting into them like rats, the day done in and darkness coming on like the cool, refreshing shadows of the sewers. Like a soft prick slipping out of an overheated cunt I, the still unhatched, making a few abortive wriggles, but either not dead and soft enough or else sperm-free and skating *ad astra,* for it is still not dinner and a peristaltic frenzy takes possession of the upper colon, the hypogastric region, the umbilical and the postpineal lobe. Boiled alive, the lobsters swim in ice, giving no quarter and asking no quarter, simply motionless and unmotivated in the ice-watered ennui of death, life drifting by the show window muffled in desolation, a sorrowful scurvy eaten away by ptomaine, the frozen glass of the window cutting like a jackknife, clean and no remainder.

Life drifting by the show window . . . I too as much a part of life as the lobster, the fourteen-carat ring, the horse liniment, but very difficult to establish the fact, the fact being that life is merchandise with a bill of lading attached, what I choose to eat being more important than I the eater, each one eating the other and consequently eating, *the verb*, ruler of the roost. In the act of eating the host is violated and justice defeated temporarily. The plate and what's on it, through the predatory power of the intestinal apparatus, commands attention and unifies the spirit, first hypnotizing it, then slowly swallowing it, then masticating it, then absorbing it. The spiritual part of the being passes off like a scum, leaves absolutely no evidence or trace of its passage, vanishes, vanishes even more completely than a point in space after a mathematical discourse. The fever, which may return tomorrow, bears the same relation to life as the mercury in a thermometer bears to heat. Fever will not make life heat, which is what was to have been proved and thus consecrates the meat balls and spaghetti. To chew while thousands chew, each chew an act of murder, gives the necessary social cast from which you look out the window and see that even human kind can be slaughtered justly, or maimed, or starved, or tortured because, while chewing, the mere advantage of sitting in a chair with clothes on, wiping the mouth with a napkin, enables you to comprehend what the wisest men have never been able to comprehend, namely that there is no other way of life possible, said wise men often disdaining to use chair, clothes or napkin. Thus men scurrying through a cunty cleft of a street called Broadway every day at regular hours, in search of this or that, tend to establish this and that, which is exactly the method of mathematicians, logicians, physicists, astronomers and such like. The proof is the fact and the fact has no meaning except what is given to it by those who establish the facts.

The meat balls devoured, the paper napkin carefully thrown on the floor, belching a trifle and not knowing why or whither, I step out into the twenty-four-carat sparkle and fall in with the theater pack. This time I wander through the side streets following a blind man with an accordion. Now and then I sit on a stoop and listen to an aria. At the opera, the music makes no sense; here in the street it has just the right demented touch to give it poignancy. The woman who accompanies the blind man holds a tin cup in her hands; he is a part of life too, like the tin cup, like the music of Verdi, like the Metropolitan Opera House. Everybody and everything is a part of life, but when they have all been added together, still somehow it is not life. *When is it life,* I ask myself, *and why not now?* The blind man wanders on and I remain sitting on the stoop. The meat balls were rotten, the coffee was lousy, the butter was rancid. Everything I look at is rotten, lousy, rancid. The street is like a bad breath; the next street is the same, and the next and the next. At the corner the blind man stops again and plays "Home to Our Mountains." I find a piece of chewing gum in my pocket —I chew it. I chew for the sake of chewing. There is absolutely nothing better to do unless it were to make a decision, which is impossible. The stoop is comfortable and nobody is bothering me. I am part of the world, of life, as they say, and I belong and I don't belong.

I sit on the stoop for an hour or so, mooning. I come to the same conclusions I always come to when I have a minute to think for myself. Either I must go home immediately and start to write or I must run away and start a wholly new life. The thought of beginning a book terrifies me: there is so much to tell that I don't know where or how to begin. The thought of running away and beginning all over again is equally terrifying: it means working like a nigger to keep body and soul together. For a man of my temperament, the world being what it is, there is absolutely no hope, no solution. Even if I *could* write the book I want to write nobody would take it—I know my compatriots only too well. Even if I *could* begin again it would be no use, because fundamentally I have no desire to work and no desire to become a useful member of society. I sit there staring at the house across the way. It seems not only ugly and senseless, like all the other houses on the street, but from staring at it so

intently, it has suddenly become absurd. The idea of constructing a place of shelter in that particular way strikes
me as absolutely insane. The city itself strikes me as a
piece of the highest insanity, everything about it, sewers,
elevated lines, slot machines, newspapers, telephones,
cops, doorknobs, flophouses, screens, toilet paper, everything. Everything could just as well not be and not only
nothing lost but a whole universe gained. I look at the
people brushing by me to see if by chance one of them
might agree with me. Supposing I intercepted one of
them and just asked him a simple question. Supposing I
just said to him suddenly: *"Why do you go on living the
way you do?"* He would probably call a cop. I ask myself
—does any one ever talk to himself the way I do? I ask
myself if there isn't something wrong with me. The only
conclusion I can come to is *that I am different.* And that's
a very grave matter, view it how you will. Henry, I say to
myself, rising slowly from the stoop, stretching myself,
brushing my trousers and spitting out the gum, Henry, I
say to myself, you are young yet, you are just a spring
chicken and if you let them get you by the balls you're an
idiot because you're a better man than any of them only
you need to get rid of your false notions about humanity.
You have to realize, Henry me boy, that you're dealing
with cutthroats, with cannibals, only they're dressed up,
shaved, perfumed, but that's all they are—cutthroats, cannibals. The best thing for you to do now, Henry, is to go
and get yourself a frosted chocolate and when you sit
at the soda fountain keep your eyes peeled and forget
about the destiny of man because you might still find
yourself a nice lay and a good lay will clean your ballbear-
ings out and leave a good taste in your mouth whereas this
only brings on dyspepsia, dandruff, halitosis, encephalitis.
And while I'm soothing myself thus a guy comes up to me
to bum a dime and I hand him a quarter for good measure
thinking to myself that if I had had a little more sense I'd
have had a juicy pork chop with that instead of the lousy
meat balls but what's the difference now it's all food and

food makes energy and energy is what makes the world go round. Instead of the frosted chocolate I keep walking and soon I'm exactly where I intended to be all the time, which is in front of the ticket window of the Roseland. And now, Henry, says I to myself, if you're lucky your old pal MacGregor will be here and first he'll bawl the shit out of you for running away and then he'll lend you a five spot, and if you just hold your breath while climbing the stairs maybe you'll see the nymphomaniac too and you'll get a dry fuck. Enter very calmly, Henry, and keep your eyes peeled! And I enter as per instructions on velvet toes, checking my hat and urinating a little as a matter of course, then slowly redescending the stairs and sizing up the taxi girls all diaphanously gowned, powdered, perfumed, looking fresh and alert but probably bored as hell and leg weary. Into each and every one of them, as I shuffle about, I throw an imaginary fuck. The place is just plastered with cunt and fuck and that's why I'm reasonably sure to find my old friend MacGregor here. The way I no longer think about the condition of the world is marvelous. I mention it because for a moment, just while I was studying a juicy ass, I had a relapse. I almost went into a trance again. I was thinking, Christ help me, that maybe I ought to beat it and go home and begin the book. A terrifying thought! Once I spent a whole evening sitting in a chair and saw nothing and heard nothing. I must have written a good-sized book before I woke up. Better not to sit down. Better to keep circulating. Henry, what you ought to do is to come here some time with a lot of dough and just see how far it'll take you. I mean a hundred or two hundred bucks, and spend it like water and say yes to everything. The haughty looking one with the statuesque figure, I bet she'd squirm like an eel if her palm were well greased. Supposing she said—*twenty bucks!* and you could say *Sure!* Supposing you could say—Listen, I've got a car downstairs . . . let's run down to Atlantic City for a few

days. Henry, there ain't no car and there ain't no twenty
bucks. *Don't sit down . . . keep moving.*

At the rail which fences off the floor I stand and watch
them sailing around. This is no harmless recreation . . .
this is serious business. At each end of the floor there is a
sign reading "No Improper Dancing Allowed." Well and
good. No harm in placing a sign at each end of the floor.
In Pompeii they probably hung a phallus up. This is the
American way. It means the same thing. I mustn't think
about Pompeii or I'll be sitting down and writing a book
again. *Keep moving, Henry. Keep your mind on the music.*
I keep struggling to imagine what a lovely time I would
have if I had the price of a string of tickets, but the more
I struggle the more I slip back. Finally I'm standing knee
deep in the lava beds and the gas is choking me. It wasn't
the lava that killed the Pompeians, it was the poison gas
that precipitated the eruption. That's how the lava caught
them in such queer poses, with their pants down, as it
were. If suddenly all New York were caught that way—
what a museum it would make! My friend MacGregor
standing at the sink scrubbing his cock . . . the abortionists
on the East Side caught red-handed . . . the nuns lying in
bed and masturbating one another . . . the auctioneer
with an alarm clock in his hand . . . the telephone girls at
the switchboard . . . J. P. Morganana sitting on the toilet
bowl placidly wiping his ass . . . dicks with rubber hoses
giving the third degree . . . strippers giving the last strip
and tease. . . .

Standing knee deep in the lava beds and my eyes
choked with sperm: J. P. Morganana is placidly wiping
his ass while the telephone girls plug the switchboards,
while dicks with rubber hoses practice the third degree,
while my old friend MacGregor scrubs the germs out
of his cock and sweetens it and examines it under the
microscope. Everybody caught with his pants down, including the strip teasers who wear no pants, no beards,
no mustaches, just a little patch to cover their twinkling
little cunts. Sister Antolina lying in the convent bed, her

guts trussed up, her arms akimbo and waiting for the
Resurrection, waiting, waiting for life without hernia,
without intercourse, without sin, without evil, meanwhile
nibbling a few animal crackers, a pimento, some fancy
olives, a little headcheese. The Jewboys on the East Side,
in Harlem, the Bronx, Canarsie, Brownsville, opening
and closing the trapdoors, pulling out arms and legs,
turning the sausage machine, clogging up the drains,
working like fury for cash down and if you let a peep
out of you out you go. With eleven hundred tickets in
my pocket and a Rolls Royce waiting for me downstairs
I could have the most excruciatingly marvelous time,
throwing a fuck into each and every one respectively re-
gardless of age, sex, race, religion, nationality, birth or
breeding. There is no solution for a man like myself, I
being what I am and the world being what it is. The
world is divided into three parts of which two parts are
meat balls and spaghetti and the other part a huge syphi-
litic chancre. The haughty one with the statuesque figure
is probably a cold turkey fuck, a sort of *con anonyme*
plastered with gold leaf and tin foil. Beyond despair and
disillusionment there is always the absence of worse
things and the emoluments of ennui. Nothing is lousier
and emptier than the midst of bright gaiety clicked by
the mechanical eye of the mechanical epoch, life matu-
rating in a black box, a negative tickled with acid and
yielding a momentaneous simulacrum of nothingness. At
the outermost limit of this momentaneous nothingness
my friend MacGregor arrives and is standing by my side
and with him is the one he was talking about, the nymphomaniac called Paula. She has the loose, jaunty swing
and perch of the double-barreled sex, all her movements
radiating from the groin, always in equilibrium, always
ready to flow, to wind and twist and clutch, the eyes going tic-toc, the toes twitching and twinkling, the flesh
rippling like a lake furrowed by a breeze. This is the incarnation of the hallucination of sex, the sea nymph
squirming in the maniac's arms. I watch the two of them

garbage pail, of fresh green snot and slimy unguents for the tender parts. The dance of the slot machine and the monsters who invent them. The dance of the gat and the slugs who use them. The dance of the blackjack and the pricks who batter brains to a polypous pulp. The dance of the magneto world, the spark that unsparks, the soft purr of the perfect mechanism, the velocity race on a turntable, the dollar at par and the forests dead and mutilated. The Saturday night of the soul's hollow dance, each jumping jigger a functional unit in the St. Vitus dance of the ringworm's dream. Laura the nympho brandishing her cunt, her sweet rose-petal lips toothed with ballbearing clutches, her ass balled and socketed. Inch by inch, millimeter by millimeter they shove the copulating corpse around. And then crash! Like pulling a switch the music suddenly stops and with the stoppage the dancers come apart, arms and legs intact, like tea leaves dropping to the bottom of the cup. Now the air is blue with words, a slow sizzle as of fish on the griddle. The chaff of the empty soul rising like monkey chatter in the topmost branches of the trees. The air blue with words passing out through the ventilators, coming back again in sleep through corrugated funnels and smoke-stacks, winged like the antelope, striped like the zebra, now lying quiet as the mollusk, now spitting flame. Laura the nympho cold as a statue, her parts eaten away, her hair musically enraptured. On the brink of sleep Laura stands with muted lips, her words falling like pollen through a fog. The Laura of Petrarch seated in a taxi, each word ringing through the cash register, then steri-lized, then cauterized. Laura the basilisk made entirely of asbestos, walking to the fiery stake with a mouth full of gum. Hunkydory is the word on her lips. The heavy fluted lips of the sea shell, Laura's lips, the lips of lost Uranian love. All floating shadowward through the slant-ing fog. Last murmuring dregs of shell-like lips slipping off the Labrador coast, oozing eastward with the mud easing starward in the iodine drift. Lost Laura, last of the Petrarchs, slowly fading on the brink of sleep. Not gray the world, but lackluster, the light bamboo sleep of spoon-backed innocence.

And this in the black frenzied nothingness of the hollow of absence leaves a gloomy feeling of saturated despondency not unlike the topmost tip of desperation which is only the gay juvenile maggot of death's exquisite rupture with life. From this inverted cone of ecstasy life will rise again into prosaic skyscraper eminence, dragging me by the hair and teeth, lousy with howling empty joy, the animated fetus of the unborn death maggot lying in wait for rot and putrefaction.

Sunday morning the telephone wakes me up. It's my friend Maxie Schnadig announcing the death of our friend Luke Ralston. Maxie has assumed a truly sorrowful tone of voice which rubs me the wrong way. He says Luke was such a swell guy. That too sounds the wrong note for me because while Luke was all right, he was only so-so, not precisely what you might call a swell guy. Luke was an ingrown fairy and finally, when I got to know him intimately, a big pain in the ass. I told Maxie that over the telephone; I could tell from the way he answered me that he didn't like it very much. He said Luke had always been a friend to me. It was true enough, but it wasn't enough. The truth was that I was really glad Luke had kicked off at the opportune moment: it meant that I could forget about the hundred and fifty dollars which I owed him. In fact, as I hung up the receiver I really felt joyous. It was a tremendous relief not to have to pay that debt. As for Luke's demise, that didn't disturb me in the least. On the contrary, it would enable me to pay a visit to his sister, Lottie, whom I always wanted to lay but never could for one reason or another. Now I could see myself going up there in the middle of the day and offering her my condolences. Her husband would be at the office and there would be nothing to interfere. I saw myself putting my arms around her and comforting her; nothing like tackling a woman when she is in sorrow. I could see her opening her eyes wide—she had beautiful, large gray eyes—as I moved her toward the couch. She was the sort of woman who would give you a fuck while pretending to be talking music or some such thing. She didn't like the naked reality, the bare facts, so to speak. At the same time she'd have enough presence of mind to slip a towel under her so as not to stain the couch. I knew her inside out. I knew that the best time to get her was now, now while she was running up a little fever of emotion over dear dead Luke—whom she didn't think much of, by the way. Unfortunately it was Sunday and the husband would be sure to be home. I went back to bed and I lay there thinking first about Luke and all that he had done for me and then about her, Lottie. Lottie Somers was her name—it always seemed a beautiful name to me. It matched her perfectly. Luke was stiff as a poker, with a sort of skull and bones face, and impeccable and just beyond words. She was just the opposite—soft, round, spoke with a drawl, caressed her words, moved languidly, used her eyes effectively. One would never take them for brother and sister. I got so worked up thinking about her that I tried to tackle the wife. But that poor bastard, with her Puritanical complex, pretended to be horrified. She liked Luke. She wouldn't say that he was a swell guy, because that wasn't like her, but she insisted that he was genuine, loyal, a true friend, etc. I had so many loyal, genuine, true friends that that was all horseshit to me. Finally we got into such an argument over Luke that she got an hysterical attack and began to weep and sob—in bed, mind you. That made me hungry. The idea of weeping before breakfast seemed monstrous to me. I went downstairs and I fixed myself a wonderful breakfast, and as I put it away I was laughing to myself, about Luke, about the hundred and fifty bucks that his sudden death had wiped off the slate, about Lottie and the way she would look at me when the moment came . . . and finally, the most absurd of all, I thought of Maxie, Maxie Schnadig, the faithful friend of Luke, standing at the grave with a big wreath and perhaps throwing a handful of earth on the coffin just as they were lowering it. Somehow that seemed just too stupid for words. I don't know why it should seem so ridiculous, but it did. Maxie was a simpleton. I tolerated him only because he was good for a touch now and then. And then too there was his sister Rita. I used to let him invite me to his home occasionally, pretending that I was interested in his brother who was deranged. It was always a good meal and the half-witted brother was real entertainment. He looked like a chimpanzee and he talked like one too. Maxie was too simple to suspect that I was merely enjoying myself; he thought I took a genuine interest in his brother.

It was a beautiful Sunday and I had as usual about a quarter in my pocket. I walked along wondering where to go to make a touch. Not that it was difficult to scrape up a little dough, no, but the thing was to get the dough and beat it without being bored stiff. I could think of a dozen guys right in the neighborhood, guys who would fork it out without a murmur, but it would mean a long conversation afterwards—about art, religion, politics. Another thing I could do, which I had done over and over again in a pinch, was to visit the telegraph offices, pretending to pay a friendly visit of inspection and then, at the last minute, suggest that they rifle the till for a buck or so until the morrow. That would involve time and even worse conversation. Thinking it over coldly and calculatingly I decided that the best bet was my little friend Curley up in Harlem. If Curley didn't have the money he would filch it from his mother's purse. I knew I could rely on him. He would want to accompany me, of course, but I could always find a way of ditching him before the evening was over. He was only a kid and I didn't have to be too delicate with him.

What I liked about Curley was that, although only a kid of seventeen, he had absolutely no moral sense, no scruples, no shame. He had come to me as a boy of four-

teen looking for a job as messenger. His parents, who
were then in South America, had shipped him to New
York in care of an aunt who seduced him almost immediately. He had never been to school because the
parents were always traveling; they were carnival people
who worked "the griffs and the grinds," as he put it. The
father had been in prison several times. He was not his
real father, by the way. Anyway, Curley came to me as
a mere lad who was in need of help, in need of a friend
more than anything. At first I thought I could do something for him. Everybody took a liking to him immediately, especially the women. He became the pet
of the office. Before long, however, I realized that
he was incorrigible, that at the best he had the
makings of a clever criminal. I liked him, however,
and I continued to do things for him, but I never trusted
him out of my sight. I think I liked him particularly because he had absolutely no sense of honor. He would do
anything in the world for me and at the same time betray
me. I couldn't reproach him for it . . . it was amusing to me.
The more so because he was frank about it. He just
couldn't help it. His Aunt Sophie, for instance. He said
she had seduced him. True enough, but the curious thing
was that he let himself be seduced while they were reading the Bible together. Young as he was he seemed to
realize that his Aunt Sophie had need of him in that way.
So he let himself be seduced, as he said, and then, after
I had known him a little while he offered to put me next
to his Aunt Sophie. He even went so far as to blackmail
her. When he needed money badly he would go to the
aunt and wheedle it out of her—with sly threats of ex-
posure. With an innocent face, to be sure. He looked
amazingly like an angel, with big liquid eyes that seemed
so frank and sincere. So ready to do things for you—almost like a faithful dog. And then cunning enough, once
he had gained your favor, to make you humor his little
whims. Withal extremely intelligent. The sly intelligence
of a fox and—the utter heartlessness of a jackal.

It wasn't at all surprising to me, consequently, to learn that afternoon that he had been tinkering with Valeska. After Valeska he tackled the cousin who had already been deflowered and who was in need of some male whom she could rely upon. And from her finally to the midget who had made herself a pretty little nest at Valeska's. The midget interested him because she had a perfectly normal cunt. He hadn't intended to do anything with her because, as he said, she was a repulsive little Lesbian, but one day he happened to walk in on her as she was taking a bath, and that started things off. It was getting to be too much for him, he confessed, because the three of them were hot on his trail. He liked the cousin best because she had some dough and she wasn't reluctant to part with it. Valeska was too cagey, and besides she smelled a little too strong. In fact, he was getting sick of women. He said it was his Aunt Sophie's fault. She gave him a bad start. While relating this he busies himself going through the bureau drawers. The father is a mean son of a bitch who ought to be hanged, he says, not finding anything immediately. He shows me a revolver with a pearl handle . . . what would it fetch? A gun was too good to use on the old man . . . he'd like to dynamite him. Trying to find out *why* he hated the old man so, it developed that the kid was really stuck on his mother. He couldn't bear the thought of the old man going to bed with her. You don't mean to say that you're jealous of your old man, I ask. Yes, he's jealous. If I wanted to know the truth it's that he wouldn't mind sleeping with his mother. Why not? That's why he had permitted his Aunt Sophie to seduce him . . . he was thinking of his mother all the time. But don't you feel bad when you go through her pocketbook, I asked. He laughed. It's not *her* money, he said, it's *his*. And what have they done for me? They were always farming me out. The first thing they taught me was how to cheat people. That's a hell of a way to raise a kid. . . .

There's not a red cent in the house. Curley's idea of a

way out is to go with me to the office where he works and while I engage the manager in conversation go through the wardrobe and clean out all the loose change. Or, if I'm not afraid of taking a chance, he will go through the cash drawer. They'll never suspect *us*, he says. Had he ever done that before, I ask. Of course . . . a dozen or more times, right under the manager's nose. And wasn't there any stink about it? To be sure . . . they had fired a few clerks. Why don't you borrow something from your Aunt Sophie, I suggest. That's easy enough, only it means a quick diddle and he doesn't want to diddle her any more. She stinks, Aunt Sophie. What do you mean, *she stinks?* Just that . . . she doesn't wash herself regularly. Why, what's the matter with her? Nothing, just religious. And getting fat and greasy at the same time. But she likes to be diddled just the same? *Does she?* She's crazier than ever about it. It's disgusting. It's like going to bed with a sow. What does your mother think about her? *Her?* She's sore as hell at her. She thinks Sophie's trying to seduce the old man. Well, maybe she is! No, the old man's got something else. I caught him red-handed one night, in the movies, mushing it up with a young girl. She's a manicurist from the Astor Hotel. He's probably trying to squeeze a little dough out of her. That's the only reason he ever makes a woman. He's a dirty, mean son of a bitch and I'd like to see him get the chair some day! You'll get the chair yourself some day if you don't watch out. *Who, me?* Not *me!* I'm too clever. You're clever enough but you've got a loose tongue. I'd be a little more tight-lipped if I were you. You know, I added, to give him an extra jolt, O'Rourke is wise to you; if you ever fall out with O'Rourke it's all up with you. . . . Well, why doesn't he say something if he's so wise? I don't believe you.

I explain to him at some length that O'Rourke is one of those people, and there are damned few in the world, who prefer *not* to make trouble for another person if they can help it. O'Rourke, I say, has the detective's instinct only in that he likes to *know* what's going on around him; people's characters are plotted out in his head, and filed there permanently, just as the enemy's terrain is fixed in the minds of army leaders. People think that O'Rourke goes around snooping and spying, that he derives a special pleasure in performing this dirty work for the company. Not so. O'Rourke is a born student of human nature. He picks things up without effort, due, to be sure, to his peculiar way of looking at the world. Now about you . . . I have no doubt that he knows everything about you. I never asked him, I admit, but I imagine so from the questions he poses now and then. Perhaps he's just giving you plenty of rope. Some night he'll run into you accidentally and perhaps he'll ask you to stop off somewhere and have a bite to eat with him. And out of a clear sky he'll suddenly say—you remember, Curley, when you were working up in SA office, the time that little Jewish clerk was fired for tapping the till? I think you were working overtime that night, weren't you? An interesting case, that. You know, they never discovered whether the clerk stole the money or not. They had to fire him, of course, for negligence, but we can't say for certain that he really stole the money. I've been thinking about that little affair now for quite some time. I have a hunch as to who took that money, but I'm not absolutely sure. . . . And then he'll probably give you a beady eye and abruptly change the conversation to something else. He'll probably tell you a little story about a crook he knew who thought he was very smart and getting away with it. He'll draw that story out for you until you feel as though you were sitting on hot coals. By that time you'll be wanting to beat it, but just when you're ready to go he'll suddenly be reminded of another very interesting little case and he'll ask you to wait just a little longer while he orders another dessert. And he'll go on like that for three or four hours at a stretch, never making the least overt insinuation, but studying you closely all the time, and finally, when you think you're free, just when you're shaking hands with him and breathing a sigh of relief, he'll step in front of you and, planting his big square feet between your legs, he'll grab you by the lapel and, looking straight through you, he'll say in a soft, winsome voice—*now look here, my lad, don't you think you had better come clean?* And if you think he's only trying to browbeat you and that you can pretend innocence and walk away, you're mistaken. Because at that point, when he asks you to come clean, he means business and nothing on earth is going to stop him. When it gets to that point I'd recommend you to make a clean sweep of it, down to the last penny. He won't ask me to fire you and he won't threaten you with jail—he'll just quietly suggest that you put aside a little bit each week and turn it over to him. Nobody will be the wiser. He probably won't even tell me. No, he's very delicate about these things, you'll see.

"And supposing," says Curley suddenly, "that I tell him I stole the money in order to help you out? What then?" He began to laugh hysterically.

"I don't think O'Rourke would believe that," I said calmly. "You can try it, of course, if you think it will help you to clear your own skirts. But I rather think it will have a bad effect. O'Rourke knows me . . . he knows I wouldn't let you do a thing like that."

"But you did let me do it!"

"I didn't tell you to do it. You did it without my knowledge. That's quite different. Besides, can you prove that I accepted money from you? Won't it seem a little ridiculous to accuse me, the one who befriended you, of putting you up to a job like that? Who's going to believe you? Not O'Rourke. Besides, he hasn't trapped you yet. Why worry about it in advance? Maybe you could begin to return the money little by little before he gets after you. Do it anonymously."

By this time Curley was quite used up. There was a little schnapps in the cupboard which his old man kept in reserve and I suggested that we take a little to brace us up. As we were drinking the schnapps it suddenly occurred to me that Maxie had said he would be at Luke's house to pay his respects. It was just the moment to get Maxie. He would be full of slobbering sentiments and I could give him any old kind of cock-and-bull story. I could say that the reason I had assumed such a hardboiled air on the phone was because I was harassed, because I didn't know where to turn for the ten dollars which I needed so badly. At the same time I might be able to make a date with Lottie. I began to smile thinking about it. If Luke could only see what a friend he had in me! The most difficult thing would be to go up to the bier and take a sorrowful look at Luke. *Not to laugh!*

I explained the idea to Curley. He laughed so heartily that the tears were rolling down his face. Which convinced me, by the way, that it would be safer to leave Curley downstairs while I made the touch. Anyway, it was decided on.

They were just sitting down to dinner when I walked in, looking as sad as I could possibly make myself look. Maxie was there and almost shocked by my sudden appearance. Lottie had gone already. That helped me to keep up the sad look. I asked to be alone with Luke a few minutes, but Maxie insisted on accompanying me. The others were relieved, I imagine, as they had been conducting the mourners to the bier all afternoon. And like the good Germans they were they didn't like having their dinner interrupted. As I was looking at Luke, still with that sorrowful expression I had mustered, I became aware of Maxie's eyes fixed on me inquisitively. I looked up and smiled at him in my usual way. He seemed absolutely nonplussed at this. "Listen, Maxie," I said, "are you sure they won't hear us?" He looked still more puzzled and grieved, but nodded reassuringly. "It's like this, Maxie . . . I came up here purposely to see you . . . to borrow a few bucks. I know it seems lousy but you can imagine how desperate I must be to do a thing like this." He was shaking his head solemnly as I spit this out, his

mouth forming a big O as if he were trying to frighten
the spirits away. "Listen, Maxie," I went on rapidly and
trying to keep my voice down sad and low, "this is no time
to give me a sermon. If you want to do something for me
lend me ten bucks now, right away . . . slip it to me right
here while I look at Luke. You know, I really liked Luke.
I didn't mean all that over the telephone. You got me at
a bad moment. The wife was tearing her hair out. We're
in a mess, Maxie, and I'm counting on you to do something. Come out with me if you can and I'll tell you more
about it. . . ." Maxie, as I had expected, couldn't come out
with me. He wouldn't think of deserting them at such a
moment. . . . "Well, give it to me now," I said, almost
savagely. "I'll explain the whole thing to you tomorrow.
I'll have lunch with you downtown."

"Listen, Henry," says Maxie, fishing around in his
pocket, embarrassed at the idea of being caught with a
wad in his hand at that moment, "listen," he said, "I don't
mind giving you the money, but couldn't you have found
another way of reaching me? It isn't because of Luke . . .
it's. . . ." He began to hem and haw, not knowing really
what he wanted to say.

"For Christ's sake," I muttered, bending over Luke
more closely so that if any one walked in on us they
would never suspect what I was up to . . . "for Christ's
sake, don't argue about it now . . . hand it over and be
done with it. . . . I'm desperate, do you hear me?" Maxie
was so confused and flustered that he couldn't disengage
a bill without pulling the wad out of his pocket. Leaning
over the coffin reverently I peeled off the topmost bill
from the wad which was peeping out of his pocket. I
couldn't tell whether it was a single or a ten spot. I didn't
stop to examine it but tucked it away as rapidly as possible and straightened myself up. Then I took Maxie by
the arm and returned to the kitchen where the family
were eating solemnly but heartily. They wanted me to
stay for a bite, and it was awkward to refuse, but I re-

fused as best I could and beat it, my face twitching now with hysterical laughter.

At the corner, by the lamppost, Curley was waiting for me. By this time I couldn't restrain myself any longer. I grabbed Curley by the arm and rushing him down the street I began to laugh, to laugh as I have seldom laughed in my life. I thought it would never stop. Every time I opened my mouth to start explaining the incident I had an attack. Finally I got frightened. I thought maybe I might laugh myself to death. After I had managed to quiet down a bit, in the midst of a long silence, Curley suddenly says: *"Did you get it?"* That precipitated another attack, even more violent than before. I had to lean against a rail and hold my guts. I had a terrific pain in the guts but a pleasurable pain.

What relieved me more than anything was the sight of the bill I had filched from Maxie's wad. It was a twenty-dollar bill! That sobered me up at once. And at the same time it enraged me a bit. It enraged me to think that in the pocket of that idiot, Maxie, there were still more bills, probably more twenties, more tens, more fives. If he had come out with me, as I suggested, and if I had taken a good look at that wad I would have felt no remorse in blackjacking him. I don't know why it should have made me feel so, but it enraged me. The most immediate thought was to get rid of Curley as quickly as possible—a five spot would fix him up—and then go on a little spree. What I particularly wanted was to meet some low-down, filthy cunt who hadn't a spark of decency in her. Where to meet one like that . . . *just like that?* Well, get rid of Curley first. Curley, of course, is hurt. He had expected to stick with me. He pretends not to want the five bucks, but when he sees that I'm willing to take it back, he quickly stows it away.

Again the night, the incalculably barren, cold, mechanical night of New York in which there is no peace, no refuge, no intimacy. The immense, frozen solitude of the million-footed mob, the cold, waste fire of the electrical display, the overwhelming meaninglessness of the perfection of the female who through perfection has crossed the frontier of sex and gone into the minus sign, gone into the red, like the electricity, like the neutral energy of the males, like planets without aspect, like peace programs, like love over the radio. To have money in the pocket in the midst of white, neutral energy, to walk meaningless and unfecundated through the bright glitter of the calcimined streets, to think aloud in full solitude on the edge of madness, to be of a city, a great city, to be of the last moment of time in the greatest city in the world and feel no part of it, is to become oneself a city, a world of dead stone, of waste light, of unintelligible motion, of imponderables and incalculables, of the secret perfection of all that is minus. To walk in money through the night crowd, protected by money, lulled by money, dulled by money, the crowd itself a money, the breath money, no least single object anywhere that is not money, money, money everywhere and still not enough, and then no money or a little money or less money or more money, but money, always money, and if you have money or you don't have money it is the money that counts and money makes money, *but what makes money make money?*

Again the dance hall, the money rhythm, the love that comes over the radio, the impersonal, wingless touch of the crowd. A despair that reaches down to the very soles of the boots, an ennui, a desperation. In the midst of the highest mechanical perfection to dance without joy, to be so desperately alone, to be almost inhuman because you are human. If there were life on the moon what more nearly perfect, joyless evidence of it could there be than this? If to travel away from the sun is to reach the chill idiocy of the moon, then we have arrived at our goal and life is but the cold, lunar incandescence of the sun. This is the dance of ice-cold life in the hollow of an atom, and the more we dance the colder it gets.

So we dance, to an ice-cold frenzied rhythm, to short waves and long waves, a dance on the inside of the cup of nothingness, each centimeter of lust running to dollars and cents. We taxi from one perfect female to another seeking the vulnerable defect, but they are flawless and impermeable in their impeccable lunar consistency. This is the icy white maidenhead of love's logic, the web of the ebbed tide, the fringe of absolute vacuity. And on this fringe of the virginal logic of perfection I am dancing the soul dance of white desperation, the last white man pulling the trigger on the last emotion, the gorilla of despair beating his breast with immaculate gloved paws. I am the gorilla who feels his wings growing, a giddy gorilla in the center of a satin-like emptiness; the night too grows like an electrical plant, shooting white-hot buds into velvet black space. I am the black space of the night in which the buds break with anguish, a starfish swimming on the frozen dew of the moon. I am the germ of a new insanity, a freak dressed in intelligible language, a sob that is buried like a splinter in the quick of the soul. I am dancing the very sane and lovely dance of the angelic gorilla. These are my brothers and sisters who are insane and unangelic. We are dancing in the hollow of the cup of nothingness. We are of one flesh, but separated like stars.

In the moment all is clear to me, clear that in this logic there is no redemption, the city itself being the highest form of madness and each and every part, organic or inorganic, an expression of this same madness. I feel absurdly and humbly great, not as megalomaniac, but as human spore, as the dead sponge of life swollen to saturation. I no longer look into the eyes of the woman I hold in my arms but I swim through, head and arms and legs, and I see that behind the sockets of the eyes there is a region unexplored, the world of futurity, and here there is no logic whatever, just the still germination of events unbroken by night and day, by yesterday and tomorrow. The eye, accustomed to concentration on points in space, now concentrates on points in time; the eye sees forward and backward at will. The eye which was the I of the self no longer exists; this selfless eye neither reveals nor illuminates. It travels along the line of the horizon, a ceaseless, uninformed voyager. Trying to retain the lost body I grew in logic as the city, a point digit in the anatomy of perfection. I grew beyond my own death, spiritually bright and hard. I was divided into endless yesterdays, endless tomorrows, resting only on the cusp of the event, a wall with many windows, but the house gone. I must shatter the walls and windows, the last shell of the lost body, if I am to rejoin the present. That is why I no longer look *into* the eyes or *through* the eyes, but by the legerdemain of will swim through the eyes, head and arms and legs, to explore the curve of vision. I see around myself as the mother who bore me once saw round the corners of time. I have broken the wall created by birth and the line of voyage is round and unbroken, even as the navel. No form, no image, no architecture, only concentric flights of sheer madness. I am the arrow of the dream's substantiality. I verify by flight. I nullify by dropping to earth.

Thus moments pass, veridic moments of time without space when I know all, and knowing all I collapse beneath the vault of the selfless dream.

Between these moments, in the interstices of the dream, life vainly tries to build up, but the scaffold of the city's mad logic is no support. As an individual, as flesh and blood, I am leveled down each day to make the fleshless, bloodless city whose perfection is the sum of all logic and death to the dream. I am struggling against an oceanic death in which my own death is but a drop of water evaporating. To raise my own individual life but a fraction of an inch above this sinking sea of death I must have a faith greater than Christ's, a wisdom deeper than that of the greatest seer. I must have the ability and the patience to formulate what is not contained in the language of our time, for what is now intelligible is meaningless. My eyes are useless, for they render back only the image of the known. My whole body must become a constant beam of light, moving with an ever greater rapidity, never arrested, never looking back, never dwindling. The city grows like a cancer; I must grow like a sun. The city eats deeper and deeper into the red; it is an insatiable white louse which must die eventually of inanition. I am going to starve the white louse which is eating me up. I am going to die as a city in order to become again a man. Therefore I close my ears, my eyes, my mouth.

Before I shall have become quite a man again I shall probably exist as a park, a sort of natural park in which people come to rest, to while away the time. What they say or do will be of little matter, for they will bring only their fatigue, their boredom, their hopelessness. I shall be a buffer between the white louse and the red corpuscle. I shall be a ventilator for removing the poisons accumulated through the effort to perfect that which is imperfectible. I shall be law and order as it exists in nature, as it is projected in dream. I shall be the wild park in the midst of the nightmare of perfection, the still, unshakeable dream in the midst of frenzied activity, the random shot on the white billiard table of logic. I shall know neither how to weep nor protest, but I shall be there always in absolute silence to receive and to restore. I shall say nothing until the time comes again to be a man. I shall make no effort to preserve, no effort to destroy. I shall make no judgments, no criticisms. Those who have had enough will come to me for reflection and meditation; those who have not had enough will die as they lived, in disorder, in desperation, in ignorance of the truth of redemption. If one says to me, you must be religious, I shall make no answer. If one says to me, I have no time now, there's a cunt waiting for me, I shall make no answer. Or even if there be a revolution brewing, I shall make no answer. There will always be a cunt or a revolution around the corner, but the mother who bore me turned many a corner and made no answer, and finally she turned herself inside out *and I am the answer*.

Out of such a wild mania for perfection naturally no one would have expected an evolution to a wild park, not even I myself, but it is infinitely better, while attending death, to live in a state of grace and natural bewilderment. Infinitely better, as life moves toward a deathly perfection, to be just a bit of breathing space, a stretch of green, a little fresh air, a pool of water. Better also to receive men silently and to enfold them, for there is no answer to make while they are still frantically rushing to turn the corner.

I'm thinking now about the rock fight one summer's afternoon long long ago when I was staying with my Aunt Caroline up near Hell Gate. My cousin Gene and I had been corralled by a gang of boys while we were playing in the park. We didn't know which side we were fighting for but we were fighting in dead earnest amidst the rock pile by the river bank. We had to show even more courage than the other boys because we were suspected of being sissies. That's how it happened that we killed one of the rival gang. Just as they were charging us my cousin Gene let go at the ringleader and caught him in the guts with a handsome-sized rock. I let go almost at the same instant and my rock caught him in the temple and when he went down he lay there for good and not a peep out of him. A few minutes later the cops came and the boy was found dead. He was eight or nine years old, about the same age as us. What they would have done to us if they had caught us I don't know. Anyway, so as not to arouse any suspicion we hurried home; we had cleaned up a bit on the way and had combed our hair. We walked in looking almost as immaculate as when we had left the house. Aunt Caroline gave us our usual two big slices of sour rye with fresh butter and a little sugar over it and we sat there at the kitchen table listening to her with an angelic smile. It was an extremely hot day and she thought we had better stay in the house, in the big front room where the blinds had been pulled down, and play marbles with our little friend Joey Kasselbaum. Joey had the reputation of being a little backward and ordinarily we would have trimmed him, but that afternoon, by a sort of mute understanding, Gene and I allowed him to win everything we had. Joey was so happy that he took us down to his cellar later and made his sister pull up her dress and show us what was underneath. Weesie, they called her, and I remember that she was stuck on me instantly. I came from another part of the city, so far away it seemed to them, that it was almost like coming from another country. They even seemed to think that I talked differently from them. Whereas the other urchins used to pay to make Weesie lift her dress up, for us it was done with love. After a while we persuaded her not to do it any more for the other boys—we were in love with her and we wanted her to go straight.

When I left my cousin the end of the summer I didn't see him again for twenty years or more. When we did meet what deeply impressed me was the look of innocence he wore—the same expression as the day of the rock fight. When I spoke to him about the fight I was still more amazed to discover that he had forgotten that it was we who had killed the boy; he remembered the boy's death but he spoke of it as though neither he nor I had any part in it. When I mentioned Weesie's name he had difficulty in placing her. Don't you remember the cellar next door . . . *Joey Kesselbaum?* At this a faint smile passed over his face. He thought it extraordinary that I should remember such things. He was already married, a father, and working in a factory making fancy pipe cases. He considered it extraordinary to remember events that had happened so far back in the past.

On leaving him that evening I felt terribly despondent. It was as though he had attempted to eradicate a precious part of my life, and himself with it. He seemed more attached to the tropical fish which he was collecting

than to the wonderful past. As for me I recollect everything, everything that happened that summer, and particularly the day of the rock fight. There are times, in fact,
when the taste of that big slice of sour rye which his
mother handed me that afternoon is stronger in my
mouth than the food I am actually tasting. And the sight
of Weesie's little bud almost stronger than the actual
feel of what is in my hand. The way the boy lay there
after we downed him, far far more impressive than the
history of the World War. The whole long summer, in
fact, seems like an idyll out of the Arthurian legends. I
often wonder what it was about this particular summer
which makes it so vivid in my memory. I have only to
close my eyes a moment in order to relive each day. The
death of the boy certainly caused me no anguish—it was
forgotten before a week had elapsed. The sight of Weesie
standing in the gloom of the cellar with her dress lifted
up, that too passed easily away. Strangely enough, the
thick slice of rye bread which his mother handed me each
day seems to possess more potency than any other image
of that period. I wonder about it . . . wonder deeply. Perhaps it is that whenever she handed me the slice of bread
it was with a tenderness and a sympathy that I had never
known before. She was a very homely woman, my Aunt
Caroline. Her face was marked by the pox, but it was a
kind, winsome face which no disfigurement could mar.
She was enormously stout and she had a very soft, a very
caressing voice. When she addressed me she seemed to
give me even more attention, more consideration, than
her own son. I would like to have stayed with her always: I would have chosen her for my own mother had
I been permitted. I remember distinctly how when my
mother arrived on a visit she seemed peeved that I was
so contented with my new life. She even remarked that
I was ungrateful, a remark I never forgot, because then
I realized for the first time that to be ungrateful was
perhaps necessary and good for one. If I close my eyes
now and I think about it, about the slice of bread, I

think almost at once that in this house I never knew what it was to be scolded. I think if I had told my Aunt Caroline that I had killed a boy in the lot, told her just how it happened, she would have put her arms around me and forgiven me—instantly. That's why perhaps that summer is so precious to me. It was a summer of tacit and complete absolution. That's why I can't forget Weesie either. She was full of a natural goodness, a child who was in love with me and who made no reproaches. She was the first of the other sex to admire me for being *different*. After Weesie it was the other way round. I was loved, but I was hated too for being what I was. Weesie made an effort to understand. The very fact that I came from a strange country, that I spoke another language, drew her closer to me. The way her eyes shone when she presented me to her little friends is something I will never forget. Her eyes seemed to be bursting with love and admiration. Sometimes the three of us would walk to the riverside in the evening and sitting on the bank we would talk as children talk when they are out of sight of their elders. We talked then, I know it now so well, more sanely and more profoundly than our parents. To give us that thick slice of bread each day the parents had to pay a heavy penalty. The worst penalty was that they became estranged from us. For, with each slice they fed us we became not only more indifferent to them, but we became more and more superior to them. In our ungratefulness was our strength and our beauty. Not being devoted we were innocent of all crime. The boy whom I saw drop dead, who lay there motionless, without making the slightest sound or whimper, the killing of that boy seems almost like a clean, healthy performance. The struggle for food, on the other hand, seems foul and degrading and when we stood in the presence of our parents we sensed that they had come to us unclean and for that we could never forgive them. The thick slice of bread in the afternoons, precisely because it was not earned, tasted delicious to us. Never again will bread taste this way. Never again will it be given this way. The day of the murder it was even tastier than ever. It had a slight taste of terror in it which has been lacking ever since. And it was received with Aunt Caroline's tacit but complete absolution.

There is something about the rye bread which I am trying to fathom—something vaguely delicious, terrifying and liberating, something associated with first discoveries. I am thinking of another slice of sour rye which was connected with a still earlier period, when my little friend Stanley and I used to rifle the icebox. That was *stolen* bread and consequently even more marvelous to the palate than the bread which was given with love. But it was in the act of eating the rye bread, the walking around with it and talking at the same time, that something in the nature of revelation occurred. It was like a state of grace, a state of complete ignorance, of self-abnegation. Whatever was imparted to me in these moments I seem to have retained intact and there is no fear that I shall ever lose the knowledge that was gained. It was just the fact perhaps that it was not knowledge as we ordinarily think of it. It was almost like receiving a truth, though truth is almost too precise a word for it. The important thing about the sour rye discussions is that they always took place away from home, away from the eyes of our parents whom we feared but never respected. Left to ourselves there were no limits to what we might imagine. Facts had little importance for us; what we demanded of a subject was that it allow us opportunity to expand. What amazes me, when I look back on it, is how well we understood one another, how well we penetrated to the essential character of each and every one, young or old. At seven years of age we knew with dead certainty, for example, that such a fellow would end up in prison, that another would be a drudge, and another a good for nothing, and so on. We were absolutely correct in our diagnoses, much more correct, for example, than our parents, or our teachers, more correct, indeed, than the so-called psychologists. Alfie Betcha turned out to be an absolute bum; Johnny Gerhardt went to the penitentiary; Bob Kunst became a work horse. Infallible predictions. The learning we received only tended to obscure our vision. From the day we went to school we learned nothing; on the contrary, we were made obtuse, we were wrapped in a fog of words and abstractions.

With the sour rye the world was what it is essentially, a primitive world ruled by magic, a world in which fear plays the most important role. The boy who could inspire the most fear was the leader and he was respected as long as he could maintain his power. There were other boys who were rebels, and they were admired, but they never became the leader. The majority were clay in the hands of the fearless ones; a few could be depended on, but the most not. The air was full of tension—nothing could be predicted for the morrow. This loose, primitive nucleus of a society created sharp appetites, sharp emotions, sharp curiosity. Nothing was taken for granted; each day demanded a new test of power, a new sense of strength or of failure. And so, up until the age of nine or ten, we had a real taste of life—we were on our own. That is, those of us who were fortunate enough not to have been spoiled by our parents, those of us who were free to roam the streets at night and to discover things with our own eyes.

What I am thinking of, with a certain amount of regret and longing, is that this thoroughly restricted life of early boyhood seems like a limitless universe and the life which followed upon it, the life of the adult, a constantly diminishing realm. From the moment when one is put in school one is lost; one has the feeling of having a halter put around his neck. The taste goes out of the bread as it goes out of life. Getting the bread becomes more important than the eating of it. Everything is calculated and everything has a price upon it.

My cousin Gene became an absolute nonentity; Stanley became a first-rate failure. Besides these two boys, for whom I had the greatest affection, there was another, Joey, who has since become a letter carrier. I could weep when I think of what life has made them. As boys they were perfect, Stanley least of all because Stanley was more temperamental. Stanley went into violent rages now and then and there was no telling how you stood with him from day to day. But Joey and Gene were the essence of goodness; they were friends in the old meaning of the word. I think of Joey often when I go out into the country because he was what is called a country boy. That meant, for one thing. that he was more loyal, more sincere, more tender, than the boys we knew. I can see Joey now coming to meet me; he was always running with arms wide open and ready to embrace me, always breathless with adventures that he was planning for my participation, always loaded with gifts which he had saved for my coming. Joey received me like the monarchs of old received their guests Everything I looked at was mine. We had innumerable things to tell each other and nothing was dull or boring. The difference between our respective worlds was enormous. Though I was of the city too, still, when I visited my cousin Gene, I became aware of an even greater city, a city of New York proper in which my sophistication was negligible. Stanley knew no excursions from his own neighborhood. but Stanley had come from a strange land over the sea. Poland, and there was always between us the mark of the voyage. The fact that he spoke another tongue also increased our admiration for him. Each one was surrounded by a distinguishing aura, by a well-defined identity which was preserved inviolate. With the entrance into life these traits of difference fell away and we all became more or less alike and, of course. most unlike our own selves. And it is this loss of the peculiar self, of the perhaps unimportant individuality, which saddens me and makes the rye bread stand out glowingly. The wonderful sour rye went into the making of our individual selves; it was like the communion loaf in which all participate but from which each one receives only according to his peculiar state of grace. Now we are eating of the same bread, but without benefit of communion, without grace. We are eating to fill our bellies and our hearts are cold and empty. We are separate but not individual.

There was another thing about the sour rye and that was that we often ate a raw onion with it. I remember standing with Stanley in the late afternoons, a sandwich in hand, in front of the veterinary's which was just opposite my home. It always seemed to be late afternoon when Dr. McKinney elected to castrate a stallion, an operation which was done in public and which always gathered a small crowd. I remember the smell of the hot iron and the quivering of the horse's legs, Dr. McKinney's goatee, the taste of the raw onion and the smell of the sewer gas just behind us where they were laying in a new gas main. It was an olfactory performance through and through and, as Abélard so well describes it, practically painless. Not knowing the reason for the operation we used to hold long discussions afterwards which usually ended in a brawl. Nobody liked Dr. McKinney either; there was a smell of iodoform about him and of stale horse piss. Sometimes the gutter in front of his office was filled with blood and in the wintertime the blood froze into the ice and gave a strange look to his sidewalk. Now and then the big two-wheeled cart came, an open cart which smelled like the devil, and they whisked a dead horse into it. Rather it was hoisted in, the carcass, by a long chain which made a creaking noise like the dropping of an anchor. The smell of a bloated dead horse is a foul smell and our street was full of foul smells. On the corner was Paul Sauer's place where raw hides and trimmed hides were stacked up in the street; they stank frightfully too. And then the acrid odor coming from the tin factory behind the house—like the smell of modern progress. The smell of a dead horse, which is almost unbearable, is still a thousand times better than the smell of burning chemicals. And the sight of a dead horse with a bullet hole in the temple, his head lying in a pool of blood and his asshole bursting with the last spasmic evacuation, is still a better

sight than that of a group of men in blue aprons coming
out of the arched doorway of the tin factory with a hand
truck loaded with bales of fresh-made tin. Fortunately for
us there was a bakery opposite the tin factory and from
the back door of the bakery, which was only a grill, we
could watch the bakers at work and get the sweet, ir-
resistible odor of bread and cake. And if, as I say, the gas
mains were being laid there was another strange medley
of smells—the smell of earth just turned up, of rotted
iron pipes, of sewer gas, and of the onion sandwiches
which the Italian laborers ate whilst reclining against
the mounds of upturned earth. There were other smells
too, of course, but less striking; such, for instance, as the
smell of Silverstein's tailor shop where there was always
a great deal of pressing going on. This was a hot, fetid
stench which can be best apprehended by imagining that
Silverstein, who was a lean, smelly Jew himself, was
cleaning out the farts which his customers had left behind
in their pants. Next door was the candy and stationery
shop owned by two daffy old maids who were religious;
here there was the almost sickeningly sweet smell of taffy,
of Spanish peanuts, of jujubes and Sen-Sen and of Sweet
Caporal cigarettes. The stationery store was like a beautiful cave, always cool, always full of intriguing objects;
where the soda fountain was, which gave off another
distinct odor, ran a thick marble slab which turned sour
in the summertime and yet mingled pleasantly, the sour-
ness, with the slightly ticklish, dry smell of the carbonated
water when it was fizzed into the glass of ice cream.

With the refinements that come with maturity the smells
faded out, to be replaced by only one other distinctly
memorable, distinctly pleasurable smell—the odor of the
cunt. More particularly the odor that lingers on the fingers
after playing with a woman, for, if it has not been noticed
before, this smell is even more enjoyable, perhaps because it already carries with it the perfume of the past
tense, than the odor of the cunt itself. But this odor,
which belongs to maturity, is but a faint odor compared

with the odors attaching to childhood. It is an odor which evaporates, almost as quickly in the mind's imagination, as in reality. One can remember many things about the woman one has loved but it is hard to remember the smell of her cunt—with anything like certitude. The smell of wet hair, on the other hand, a woman's wet hair, is much more powerful and lasting—why, I don't know. I can remember even now, after almost forty years, the smell of my Aunt Tillie's hair after she had taken a shampoo. This shampoo was performed in the kitchen which was always overheated. Usually it was a late Saturday afternoon, in preparation for a ball, which meant again another singular thing—that there would appear a cavalry sergeant with very beautiful yellow stripes, a singularly handsome sergeant who even to my eyes was far too gracious, manly and intelligent for an imbecile such as my Aunt Tillie. But anyway, there she sat on a little stool by the kitchen table drying her hair with a towel. Beside her was a little lamp with a smoked chimney and beside the lamp two curling irons the very sight of which filled me with an inexplicable loathing. Generally she had a little mirror propped up on the table; I can see her now making wry faces at herself as she squeezed the blackheads out of her nose. She was a stringy, ugly, imbecilic creature with two enormous buck teeth which gave her a horsey look whenever her lips drew back in a smile. She smelled sweaty, too, even after a bath. But the smell of her hair—that smell I can never forget, because somehow the smell is associated with my hatred and contempt for her. This smell, when the hair was just drying, was like the smell that comes up from the bottom of a marsh. There were two smells—one of the wet hair and another of the same hair when she threw it into the stove and it burst into flame. There were always curled knots of hair which came from her comb, and they were mixed with dandruff and the sweat of her scalp which was greasy and dirty. I used to stand by her side and watch her, wondering what the ball would be

like and wondering how she would behave at the ball.
When she was all primped up she would ask me if she
didn't look beautiful and if I didn't love her, and of
course I would tell her yes. But in the water closet later,
which was in the hall just next to the kitchen, I would
sit in the flickering light of the burning taper which was
placed on the window ledge, and I would say to myself
that she looked crazy. After she was gone I would pick
up the curling irons and smell them and squeeze them.
They were revolting and fascinating—like spiders.
Everything about this kitchen was fascinating to me.
Familiar as I was with it I never conquered it. It was at
once so public and so intimate. Here I was given my bath,
in the big tin tub, on Saturdays. Here the three sisters
washed themselves and primped themselves. Here my
grandfather stood at the sink and washed himself to the
waist and later handed me his shoes to be shined. Here
I stood at the window in the winter time and watched
the snow fall, watched it dully, vacantly, as if I were in
the womb and listening to the water running while my
mother sat on the toilet. It was in the kitchen where the
secret confabulations were held, frightening, odious sessions from which they always reappeared with long, grave
faces or eyes red with weeping. Why they ran to the
kitchen I don't know. But it was often while they stood
thus in secret conference, haggling about a will or deciding how to dispense with some poor relative, that the
door was suddenly opened and a visitor would arrive,
whereupon the atmosphere immediately changed.
Changed violently, I mean, as though they were relieved
that some outside force had intervened to spare them
the horrors of a protracted secret session. I remember
now that, seeing that door open and the face of an
unexpected visitor peering in, my heart would leap with
joy. Soon I would be given a big glass pitcher and asked
to run to the corner saloon where I would hand the
pitcher in, through the little window at the family entrance, and wait until it was returned brimming with

foamy suds. This little run to the corner for a pitcher of beer was an expedition of absolutely incalculable proportions. First of all there was the barber shop just below us, where Stanley's father practiced his profession. Time and again, just as I was dashing out for something, I would see the father giving Stanley a drubbing with the razor strop, a sight that made my blood boil. Stanley was my best friend and his father was nothing but a drunken Polack. One evening, however, as I was dashing out with the pitcher, I had the intense pleasure of seeing another Polack go for Stanley's old man with a razor. I saw his old man coming through the door backwards, the blood running down his neck, his face white as a sheet. He fell on the sidewalk in front of the shop, twitching and moaning, and I remember looking at him for a minute or two and walking on feeling absolutely contented and happy about it. Stanley had sneaked out during the scrimmage and was accompanying me to the saloon door. He was glad too, though he was a bit frightened. When we got back the ambulance was there in front of the door and they were lifting him in on the stretcher, his face and neck covered with a sheet. Sometimes it happened that Father Carroll's pet choirboy strolled by the house just as I was hitting the air. This was an event of primary importance. The boy was older than any of us and he was a sissy, a fairy in the making. His very walk used to enrage us. As soon as he was spotted the news went out in every direction and before he had reached the corner he was surrounded by a gang of boys all much smaller than himself who taunted him and mimicked him until he burst into tears. Then we would pounce on him, like a pack of wolves, pull him to the ground and tear the clothes off his back. It was a disgraceful performance but it made us feel good. Nobody knew yet what a fairy was, but whatever it was we were against it. In the same way we were against the Chinamen. There was one Chinaman, from the laundry up the street, who used to pass frequently and, like the sissy from Father Carroll's church, he too had to run the gantlet. He looked exactly like the picture of a coolie which one sees in the schoolbooks. He wore a sort of black alpaca coat with braided button holes, slippers without heels, and a pigtail. Usually he walked with his hands in his sleeves. It was his walk which I remember best, a sort of sly, mincing, feminine walk which was utterly foreign and menacing to us. We were in mortal dread of him and we hated him because he was absolutely indifferent to our gibes. We thought he was too ignorant to notice our insults. Then one day when we entered the laundry he gave us a little surprise. First he handed us the package of laundry; then he reached down below the counter and gathered a handful of lichee nuts from the big bag. He was smiling as he came from behind the counter to open the door. He was still smiling as he caught hold of Alfie Betcha and pulled his ears; he caught hold of each of us in turn and pulled our ears, still smiling. Then he made a ferocious grimace and, swift as a cat, he ran behind the counter and picked up a long, ugly-looking knife which he brandished at us. We fell over ourselves getting out of the place. When we got to the corner and looked around we saw him standing in the doorway with an iron in his hand looking very calm and peaceful. After this incident nobody would go to the laundry any more; we had to pay little Louis Pirossa a nickel each week to collect the laundry for us. Louis's father owned the fruit stand on the corner. He used to hand us the rotten bananas as a token of his affection. Stanley was especially fond of the rotten bananas as his aunt used to fry them for him. The fried bananas were considered a delicacy in Stanley's home. Once, on his birthday, there was a party given for Stanley and the whole neighborhood was invited. Everything went beautifully until it came to the fried bananas. Somehow nobody wanted to touch the bananas, as this was a dish known only to Polacks like Stanley's parents. It was considered disgusting to eat fried bananas. In the

midst of the embarrassment some bright youngster suggested that crazy Willie Maine should be given the
fried bananas. Willie Maine was older than any of us
but unable to talk. He said nothing but *Bjork! Bjork!* He
said this to everything. So when the bananas were passed
to him he said *Bjork!* and he reached for them with two
hands. But his brother George was there and George felt
insulted that they should have palmed off the rotten
bananas on his crazy brother. So George started a fight
and Willie, seeing his brother attacked, began to fight
also, screaming *Bjork! Bjork!* Not only did he strike
out at the other boys but at the girls too, which created
a pandemonium. Finally Stanley's old man, hearing the
noise, came up from the barber shop with a strop in his
hand. He took crazy Willie Maine by the scruff of the
neck and began to lambast him. Meanwhile his brother
George had sneaked off to call Mr. Maine senior. The
latter, who was also a bit of a drunkard, arrived in his
shirt sleeves and seeing poor Willie being beaten by
the drunken barber, he went for him with two stout fists
and beat him up unmercifully. Willie, who had gotten
free meanwhile, was on his hands and knees, gobbling up
the fried bananas which had fallen on the floor. He was
stuffing them away like a billy goat, fast as he could
find them. When the old man saw him there chewing
away like a goat he became furious and picking up the
strop he went after Willie with a vengeance. Now Willie
began to howl—*Bjork! Bjork!*—and suddenly everybody
began to laugh. That took the steam out of Mr. Maine
and he relented. Finally he sat down and Stanley's aunt
brought him a glass of wine. Hearing the racket some of
the other neighbors came in and there was more wine
and then beer and then schnapps and soon everybody
was happy and singing and whistling and even the kids
got drunk and then crazy Willie got drunk and again
he got down on the floor like a billy goat and he yelled
Bjork! Bjork! and Alfie Betcha, who was very drunk
though only eight years old, bit crazy Willie Maine in

the backside and then Willie bit him and then we all
started biting each other and the parents stood by
laughing and screaming with glee and it was very very
merry and there were more fried bananas and everybody ate them this time and then there were speeches
and more bumpers downed and crazy Willie Maine tried
to sing for us but could only sing *Bjork! Bjork!* It was a
stupendous success, the birthday party, and for a week
or more no one talked of anything but the party and what
good Polacks Stanley's people were. The fried bananas,
too, were a success and for a time it was hard to get any
rotten bananas from Louis Pirossa's old man because
they were so much in demand. And then an event occurred which cast a pall over the entire neighborhood—
the defeat of Joe Gerhardt at the hands of Joey Silverstein. The latter was the tailor's son; he was a lad of
fifteen or sixteen, rather quiet and studious looking, who
was shunned by the other older boys because he was a
Jew. One day as he was delivering a pair of pants to
Fillmore Place he was accosted by Joey Gerhardt who
was about the same age and who considered himself a
rather superior being. There was an exchange of words
and then Joe Gerhardt pulled the pants away from the
Silverstein boy and threw them in the gutter. Nobody
had ever imagined that young Silverstein would reply
to such an insult by recourse to his fists and so when he
struck out at Joe Gerhardt and cracked him square in
the jaw everybody was taken aback, most of all Joe
Gerhardt himself. There was a fight which lasted about
twenty minutes and at the end Joe Gerhardt lay on the
sidewalk unable to get up. Whereupon the Silverstein
boy gathered up the pair of pants and walked quietly
and proudly back to his father's shop. Nobody said a
word to him. The affair was regarded as a calamity.
Who had ever heard of a Jew beating up a Gentile? It
was something inconceivable, and yet it had happened,
right before everyone's eyes. Night after night, sitting on
the curb as we used to, the situation was discussed from

every angle, but without any solution until . . . well until Joe Gerhardt's younger brother, Johnny, became so wrought up about it that he decided to settle the matter himself. Johnny, though younger and smaller than his brother, was as tough and invincible as a young puma. He was typical of the shanty Irish who made up the neighborhood. His idea of getting even with young Silverstein was to lie in wait for him one evening as the latter was stepping out of the store and trip him up. When he tripped him up that evening he had provided himself in advance with two little rocks which he concealed in his fists and when poor Silverstein went down he pounced on him and then with the two handsome little rocks he pounded poor Silverstein's temples. To his amazement Silverstein offered no resistance; even when he got up and gave him a chance to get to his feet Silverstein never so much as budged. Then Johnny got frightened and ran away. He must have been thoroughly frightened because he never came back again; the next that was heard of him was that he had been picked up out West somewhere and sent to a reformatory. His mother, who was a slatternly, jolly Irish bitch, said that it served him right and she hoped to God she'd never lay eyes on him again. When the boy Silverstein recovered he was not the same any more; people said the beating had affected his brain, that he was a little daffy. Joe Gerhardt, on the other hand, rose to prominence again. It seems that he had gone to see the Silverstein boy while he lay in bed and had made a deep apology to him. This again was something that had never been heard of before. It was something so strange, so unusual, that Joe Gerhardt was looked upon almost as a knight errant. Nobody had approved of the way Johnny behaved, and yet nobody would have thought of going to young Silverstein and apologizing to him. That was an act of such delicacy, such elegance, that Joe Gerhardt was looked upon as a real gentleman—the first and only gentleman in the neighborhood. It was a word that had never been used among us and now it was on everybody's lips and it was considered a distinction to be a gentleman. This sudden transformation of the defeated Joe Gerhardt into a gentleman I remember made a deep impression upon me. A few years later, when I moved into another neighborhood and encountered Claude de Lorraine, a French boy, I was prepared to understand and accept "a gentleman." This Claude was a boy such as I had never laid eyes on before. In the old neighborhood he would have been regarded as a sissy; for one thing he spoke too well, too correctly, too politely, and for another thing he was too considerate, too gentle, too gallant. And then, while playing with him, to hear him suddenly break into French as his mother or father came along, provided us with something like a shock. German we had heard and German was a permissible transgression, but French! why to talk French, or even to understand it, was to be thoroughly alien, thoroughly aristocratic, rotten, distingué. And yet Claude was one of us, as good as us in every way, even a little bit better, we had to admit secretly. But there was a blemish—his French! It antagonized us. He had no right to be living in our neighborhood, no right to be as capable and manly as he was. Often, when his mother called him in and we had said good-by to him, we got together in the lot and we discussed the Lorraine family backwards and forwards. We wondered what they ate, for example, because being French they must have different customs than ours. No one had ever set foot in Claude de Lorraine's home either—that was another suspicious and repugnant fact. Why? What were they concealing? Yet when they passed us in the street they were always very cordial, always smiled, always spoke in English and a most excellent English it was. They used to make us feel rather ashamed of ourselves—they were superior, that's what it was. And there was still another baffling thing—with the other boys a direct question brought a direct answer, but with Claude de Lorraine there was

never any direct answer. He always smiled very charm-
ingly before replying and he was very cool, collected,
employing an irony and a mockery which was beyond
us. He was a thorn in our side, Claude de Lorraine, and
when finally he moved out of the neighborhood we all
breathed a sigh of relief. As for myself, it was only
maybe ten or fifteen years later that I thought about this
boy and his strange, elegant behavior. And it was then
that I felt I had made a bad blunder. For suddenly one
day it occurred to me that Claude de Lorraine had come
up to me on a certain occasion obviously to win my
friendship and I had treated him rather cavalierly. At
the time I thought of this incident it suddenly dawned
on me that Claude de Lorraine must have seen something
different in me and that he had meant to honor me by
extending the hand of friendship. But back in those days
I had a code of honor, such as it was, and that was to
run with the herd. Had I become a bosom friend of
Claude de Lorraine I would have been betraying the
other boys. No matter what advantages lay in the wake
of such a friendship they were not for me; I was one of
the gang and it was my duty to remain aloof from such
as Claude de Lorraine. I remembered this incident once
again, I must say, after a still greater interval—after I
had been in France a few months and the word *raison-
nable* had come to acquire a wholly new significance for
me. Suddenly one day, overhearing it, I thought of
Claude de Lorraine's overtures on the street in front of
his house. I recalled vividly that he had used the word
reasonable. He had probably asked me to be *reasonable*,
a word which then would never have crossed my lips as
there was no need for it in my vocabulary. It was a word,
like gentleman, which was rarely brought out and then
only with great discretion and circumspection. It was a
word which might cause others to laugh at you. There
were lots of words like that—*really*, for example. No one
I knew had ever used the word *really*—until Jack Lawson came along. He used it because his parents were

English and, though we made fun of him, we forgave him for it. *Really* was a word which reminded me immediately of little Carl Ragner from the old neighborhood. Carl Ragner was the only son of a politician who lived on the rather distinguished little street called Fillmore Place. He lived near the end of the street in a little red brick house which was always beautifully kept. I remember the house because passing it on my way to school I used to remark how beautifully the brass knobs on the door were polished. In fact, nobody else had brass knobs on their doors. Anyway, little Carl Ragner was one of those boys who was not allowed to associate with other boys. He was rarely seen, as a matter of fact. Usually it was a Sunday that we caught a glimpse of him walking with his father. Had his father not been a powerful figure in the neighborhood Carl would have been stoned to death. He was really impossible, in his Sunday garb. Not only did he wear long pants and patent leather shoes, but he sported a derby and a cane. At six years of age a boy who would allow himself to be dressed up in this fashion must be a ninny—that was the consensus of opinion. Some said he was sickly, as though that were an excuse for his eccentric dress. The strange thing is that I never once heard him speak. He was so elegant, so refined, that perhaps he had imagined it was bad manners to speak in public. At any rate, I used to lie in wait for him Sunday mornings just to see him pass with his old man. I watched him with the same avid curiosity that I would watch the firemen cleaning the engines in the firehouse. Sometimes on the way home he would be carrying a little box of ice cream, the smallest size they had, probably just enough for him, for his dessert. Dessert was another word which had somehow become familiar to us and which we used derogatorily when referring to the likes of little Carl Ragner and his family. We could spend hours wondering what these people ate for *dessert*, our pleasure consisting principally in bandying about this new-found word, *dessert*, which had probably been smuggled out of the Ragner household. It must also have been about this time that Santos Dumont came into fame. For us there was something grotesque about the name Santos Dumont. About his exploits we were not much concerned—just the name. For most of us it smelled of sugar, of Cuban plantations, of the strange Cuban flag which had a star in the corner and which was always highly regarded by those who saved the little cards which were given away with Sweet Caporal cigarettes and on which there were represented either the flags of the different nations or the leading soubrettes of the stage or the famous pugilists. Santos Dumont, then, was something delightfully foreign, in contradistinction to the usual foreign person or object, such as the Chinese laundry, or Claude de Lorraine's haughty French family. Santos Dumont was a magical word which suggested a beautiful flowing mustache, a sombrero, spurs, something airy, delicate, humorous, quixotic. Sometimes it brought up the aroma of coffee beans and of straw mats, or, because it was so thoroughly outlandish and quixotic, it would entail a digression concerning the life of the Hottentots. For there were among us, older boys who were beginning to read and who would entertain us by the hour with fantastic tales which they had gleaned from books such as *Ayesha* or Ouida's *Under Two Flags*. The real flavor of knowledge is most definitely associated in my mind with the vacant lot at the corner of the new neighborhood where I was transplanted at about the age of ten. Here, when the fall days came on and we stood about the bonfire roasting chippies and raw potatoes in the little cans which we carried, there ensued a new type of discussion which differed from the old discussions I had known in that the origins were always bookish. Some one had just read a book of adventure, or a book of science, and forthwith the whole street became animated by the introduction of a hitherto unknown subject. It might be that one of these boys had just discovered that there was such a thing as the

Japanese current and he would try to explain to us how the Japanese current came into existence and what the purpose of it was. This was the only way we learned things—against the fence, as it were, while roasting chippies and raw potatoes. These bits of knowledge sunk deep—so deep, in fact, that later, confronted with a more accurate knowledge it was often difficult to dislodge the older knowledge. In this way it was explained to us one day by an older boy that the Egyptians had known about the circulation of the blood, something which seemed so natural to us that it was hard later to swallow the story of the discovery of the circulation of the blood by an Englishman named Harvey. Nor does it seem strange to me now that in those days most of our conversation was about remote places, such as China, Peru, Egypt, Africa, Iceland, Greenland. We talked about ghosts, about God, about the transmigration of souls, about Hell, about astronomy, about strange birds and fish, about the formation of precious stones, about rubber plantations, about methods of torture, about the Aztecs and the Incas, about marine life, about volcanoes and earthquakes, about burial rites and wedding ceremonies in various parts of the earth, about languages, about the origin of the American Indian, about the buffaloes dying out, about strange diseases, about cannibalism, about wizardry, about trips to the moon and what it was like there, about murderers and highwaymen, about the miracles in the Bible, about the manufacture of pottery, about a thousand and one subjects which were never mentioned at home or in school and which were vital to us because we were starved and the world was full of wonder and mystery and it was only when we stood shivering in the vacant lot that we got to talking seriously and felt a need for communication which was at once pleasurable and terrifying.

The wonder and the mystery of life—which is throttled in us as we become responsible members of society! Until we were pushed out to work the world was very small and we were living on the fringe of it, on the frontier, as it were, of the unknown. A small Greek world which was nevertheless deep enough to provide all manner of variation, all manner of adventure and speculation. Not so very small either, since it held in reserve the most boundless potentialities. I have gained nothing by the enlargement of my world; on the contrary, I have lost. I want to become more and more childish and to pass beyond childhood in the opposite direction. I want to go exactly contrary to the normal line of development, pass into a superinfantile realm of being which will be absolutely crazy and chaotic but not crazy and chaotic as the world about me. I have been an adult and a father and a responsible member of society. I have earned my daily bread. I have adapted myself to a world which never was mine. I want to break through this enlarged world and stand again on the frontier of an unknown world which will throw this pale, unilateral world into shadow. I want to pass beyond the responsibility of fatherhood to the irresponsibility of the anarchic man who cannot be coerced nor wheedled nor cajoled nor bribed nor traduced. I want to take as my guide Oberon the nightrider who, under the spread of his black wings, eliminates both the beauty and the horror of the past; I want to flee toward a perpetual dawn with a swiftness and relentlessness that leaves no room for remorse, regret, or repentance. I want to outstrip the inventive man who is a curse to the earth in order to stand once again before an impassable deep which not even the strongest wings will enable me to traverse. Even if I must become a wild and natural park inhabited only by idle dreamers I must not stop to rest here in the ordered fatuity of responsible, adult life. I must do this in remembrance of a life beyond all comparison with the life which was promised me, in remembrance of the life of a child who was strangled and stifled by the mutual consent of those who had surrendered. Everything which the fathers and the mothers created I disown. I am going back to a world even smaller than the old Hellenic world, going back to a world which I can always touch with outstretched arms, the world of what I know and see and recognize from moment to moment. Any other world is meaningless to me, and alien and hostile. In retraversing the first bright world which I knew as a child I wish not to rest there but to muscle back to a still brighter world from which I must have escaped. What this world is like I do not know, nor am I even sure that I will find it, but it is my world and nothing else intrigues me.

The first glimpse, the first realization, of the bright new world came through my meeting Roy Hamilton. I was in my twenty-first year, probably the worst year of my whole life. I was in such a state of despair that I had decided to leave home. I thought and spoke only of California where I had planned to go to start a new life. So violently did I dream of this new promised land that later, when I had returned from California, I scarcely remembered the California I had seen but thought and spoke only of the California which I had known in my dreams. It was just prior to my leave-taking that I met Hamilton. He was a dubious half brother to my old friend MacGregor; they had only recently made each other's acquaintance, as Roy, who had lived most of his life in California, had been under the impression all along that his real father was Mr. Hamilton and not Mr. MacGregor. As a matter of fact it was in order to disentangle the mystery surrounding his parentage that he had come East. Living with the MacGregors had apparently brought him no nearer to a solution of the mystery. Indeed he seemed to be more perplexed than ever after getting acquainted with the man who he had concluded must be his legitimate father. He was perplexed, as he later admitted to me, because in neither man could he find any resemblance to the man he considered himself to be. It was probably this harassing problem of deciding whom to take for a father which had stimulated the development of his own character. I say this, because immediately upon being introduced to him, I felt that I was in the presence of a being such as I had never known before. I had been prepared, through MacGregor's description of him, to meet a rather "strange" individual, "strange" in MacGregor's mouth meaning slightly cracked. He was indeed strange, but so sharply sane that I at once felt exalted. For the first time I was talking to a man who got behind the meaning of words and went to the very essence of things. I felt that I was talking to a philosopher, not a philosopher such as I had encountered through books, but a man who philoso-phized constantly—*and who lived this philosophy which he expounded.* That is to say, he had no theory at all, except to penetrate to the very essence of things and, in the light of each fresh revelation to so live his life that there would be a minimum of discord between the truths which were revealed to him and the exemplification of these truths in action. Naturally his behavior was strange to those about him. It had not, however, been strange to those who knew him out on the Coast where, as he said, he was in his own element. There apparently he was regarded as a superior being and was listened to with the utmost respect, even with awe.

I came upon him in the midst of a struggle which I only appreciated many years later. At the time I couldn't see the importance which he attached to finding his real father; in fact, I used to joke about it because the role of the father meant little to me, or the role of the mother, for that matter. In Roy Hamilton I saw the ironic struggle of a man who had already emancipated himself and yet was seeking to establish a solid biological link for which he had absolutely no need. This conflict over the real father had, paradoxically, made him a superfather. He was a teacher and an exemplar; he had only to open his mouth for me to realize that I was listening to a wisdom which was utterly different from anything which I had heretofore associated with that word. It would be easy to dismiss him as a mystic, for a mystic he undoubtedly

was, but he was the first mystic I had ever encountered
who also knew how to keep his feet on the ground. He
was a mystic who knew how to invent practical things,
among them a drill such as was badly needed for the oil
industry and from which he later made a fortune. Because of his strange metaphysical talk, however, nobody
at the time gave much heed to his very practical invention. It was regarded as another one of his cracked ideas.

He was continually talking about himself and his relation to the world about, a quality which created the unfortunate impression that he was simply a blatant egotist.
It was even said, which was true enough as far as it
went, that he seemed more concerned about the truth
of Mr. MacGregor's fatherhood than about Mr. Mac-
Gregor, the father. The implication was that he had no
real love for his new-found father but was simply deriv-
ing a strong personal gratification from the truth of the
discovery, that he was exploiting his discovery in his
usual self-aggrandizing way. It was deeply true, of
course, because Mr. MacGregor in the flesh was infinitely less than Mr. MacGregor as symbol of the lost
father. But the MacGregors knew nothing about symbols
and would never have understood even had it been explained to them. They were making a contradictory
effort to at once embrace the long lost son and at the
same time reduce him to an understandable level on
which they could seize him not as the "long lost" but
simply as the son. Whereas it was obvious to any one
with the least intelligence that this son was not a son at
all but a sort of spiritual father, a sort of Christ, I might
say, who was making a most valiant effort to accept as
blood and flesh what he had already all too clearly freed
himself from.

I was surprised and flattered, therefore, that this
strange individual whom I looked upon with the warmest
admiration should elect to make me his confidant. By
comparison I was very bookish, intellectual, and worldly
in a wrong way. But almost immediately I discarded this

side of my nature and allowed myself to bask in the warm, immediate light which his profound and natural intuition of things created. To come into his presence gave me the sensation of being undressed, or rather peeled, for it was much more than mere nakedness which he demanded of the person he was talking to. In talking to me he addressed himself to a me whose existence I had only dimly suspected, the me, for example, which emerged when, suddenly, reading a book, I realized that I had been dreaming. Few books had this faculty of putting me into a trance, this trance of utter lucidity in which, unknown to oneself, one makes the deepest resolutions. Roy Hamilton's conversation partook of this quality. It made me more than ever alert, preternaturally alert, without at the same time crumbling the fabric of dream. He was appealing in other words, to the germ of the self, to the being who would eventually outgrow the naked personality, the synthetic individuality, and leave me truly alone and solitary in order to work out my own proper destiny.

Our talk was like a secret language in the midst of which the others went to sleep or faded away like ghosts. For my friend MacGregor it was baffling and irritating; he knew me more intimately than any of the other fellows but he had never found anything in me to correspond to the character which I now presented him with. He spoke of Roy Hamilton as a bad influence, which again was deeply true since this unexpected meeting with his half brother served more than anything else to alienate us. Hamilton opened my eyes and gave me new values, and though later I was to lose the vision which he had bequeathed me, nevertheless I could never again see the world, or my friends, as I had seen them prior to his coming. Hamilton altered me profoundly, as only a rare book, a rare personality, a rare experience, can alter one. For the first time in my life I understood what it was to experience a vital friendship and yet not to feel enslaved or attached because of the experience.

Never, after we parted, did I feel the need of his actual presence; he had given himself completely and I possessed him without being possessed. It was the first clean, whole experience of friendship, and it was never duplicated by any other friend. Hamilton was friendship itself, rather than a friend. He was the symbol personified and consequently entirely satisfactory, hence no longer necessary to me. He himself understood this thoroughly. Perhaps it was the fact of having no father that pushed him along the road toward the discovery of the self, which is the final process of identification with the world and the realization consequently of the uselessness of ties. Certainly, as he stood then, in the full plenitude of self-realization, no one was necessary to him, least of all the father of flesh and blood whom he vainly sought in Mr. MacGregor. It must have been in the nature of a last test for him, his coming East and seeking out his real father, for when he said good-by, when he renounced Mr. MacGregor and Mr. Hamilton also, he was like a man who had purified himself of all dross. Never have I seen a man look so single, so utterly alone and alive and confident of the future as Roy Hamilton looked when he said good-by. And never have I seen such confusion and misunderstanding as he left behind with the MacGregor family. It was as though he had died in their midst, had been resurrected, and was taking leave of them as an utterly new, unknown individual. I can see them now standing in the areaway, their hands sort of foolishly, helplessly empty, weeping they knew not why, unless it was because they were bereft of something they had never possessed. I like to think of it in just this way. They were bewildered and bereft, and vaguely, so very vaguely aware that somehow a great opportunity had been offered them which they had not the strength or the imagination to seize. It was this which the foolish, empty fluttering of the hands indicated to me; it was a gesture more painful to witness than anything I can imagine. It gave me the feeling of the horrible inadequacy of the world when brought face to face with truth. It gave me the feeling of the stupidity of the blood tie and of the love which is not spiritually imbued.

I look back rapidly and I see myself again in California. I am alone and I am working like a slave in the orange grove at Chula Vista. Am I coming into my own? I think not. I am a very wretched, forlorn, miserable person. I seem to have lost everything. In fact, I am hardly a person—I am more nearly an animal. All day long I am standing or walking behind the two jackasses which are hitched to my sledge. I have no thoughts, no dreams, no desires. I am thoroughly healthy and empty. I am a nonentity. I am so thoroughly alive and healthy that I am like the luscious deceptive fruit which hangs on the Californian trees. One more ray of sun and I will be rotten. *"Pourri avant d'être mûri!"*

Is it really *me* that is rotting in this bright California sunshine? Is there nothing left of me, of all that I was up to this moment? Let me think a bit. . . . There was Arizona. I remember now that it was already night when I first set foot on Arizona soil. Just light enough to catch the last glimpse of a fading mesa. I am walking through the main street of a little town whose name is lost. What am I doing here on this street, in this town? Why, I am in love with Arizona, an Arizona of the mind which I search for in vain with my two good eyes. In the train there was still with me the Arizona which I had brought from New York—even after we had crossed the state line. Was there not a bridge over a canyon which had startled me out of my reverie? A bridge such as I had never seen before, a natural bridge created by a cataclysmic eruption thousands of years ago? And over this bridge I had seen a man crossing, a man who looked like an Indian, and he was riding a horse and there was a long saddlebag hanging beside the stirrup. A natural millenary bridge which in the dying sun with air so clear looked like the youngest, newest bridge imaginable. And over that bridge so strong, so durable, there passed, praise be to God, just a man and a horse, nothing more. This then was Arizona, and Arizona was *not* a figment of the imagination but the imagination itself dressed as a horse and rider. And this was even more than the imagination itself because there was no aura of ambiguity but only sharp and dead isolate the thing itself which was the dream and the dreamer himself seated on horseback. And as the train stops I put my foot down and my foot has put a deep hole in the dream; I am in the Arizona town which is listed in the timetable and it is only the geographical Arizona which anybody can visit who has the money. I am walking along the main street with a valise and I see hamburger sandwiches and real estate offices. I feel so terribly deceived that I begin to weep. It is dark now and I stand at the end of a street, where the desert begins, and I weep like a fool. Which me is this weeping? Why it is the new little me which had begun to germinate back in Brooklyn and which is now in the midst of a vast desert and doomed to perish. *Now, Roy Hamilton, I need you!* I need you for one moment, just one little moment, while I am falling apart. I need you because I was not quite ready to do what I have done. And do I not remember your telling me that it was unnecessary to make the trip, but to do it if I must? Why didn't you persuade me not to go? Ah, to persuade was never his way. And to ask advice was never my way. So here I am, bankrupt in the desert, and the bridge which was real is behind me and what is unreal is before me and Christ only knows I am so puzzled and bewildered that if I could sink into the earth and disappear I would do so.

I look back rapidly and I see another man who was left to perish quietly in the bosom of his family—*my father*. I understand better what happened to him if I go back very, very far and think of such streets as Maujer, Conselyea, Humboldt . . . Humboldt particularly. These streets belonged to a neighborhood which was not far removed from our neighborhood but which was different, more glamorous, more mysterious. I had been on Humboldt Street only once as a child and I no longer remember the reason for that excursion unless it was to visit some sick relative languishing in a German hospital. But the street itself made a most lasting impression upon me; why I have not the faintest idea. It remains in my memory as the most mysterious and the most promising street that ever I have seen. Perhaps when we were making ready to go my mother had, as usual, promised something spectacular as a reward for accompanying her. I was always being promised things which never materialized. Perhaps then, when I got to Humboldt Street and looked upon this new world with astonishment, perhaps I forgot completely what had been promised me and the street itself became the reward. I remember that it was very wide and that there were high stoops, such as I had never seen before, on either side of the street. I remember too that in a dressmaker's shop on the first floor of one of these strange houses there was a bust in the window with a tape measure slung around the neck and I know that I was greatly moved by this sight. There was snow on the ground but the sun was out strong and I recall vividly how about the bottoms of the ash barrels which had been frozen into the ice there was then a little pool of water left by the melting snow. The whole street seemed to be melting in the radiant winter's sun. On the bannisters of the high stoops the mounds of snow which had formed such beautiful white pads were now beginning to slide, to disintegrate, leaving dark patches of the brownstone which was then much in vogue. The little glass signs of the dentists and physicians, tucked away in the corners of the windows, gleamed brilliantly in the noonday sun and gave me the feeling for the first time that these offices were perhaps not the torture chambers which I knew them to be. I imagined, in my childish way, that here in this neighborhood, in this street particularly, people were more friendly, more expansive, and of course infinitely more wealthy. I must have ex-panded greatly myself though only a tot, because for the first time I was looking upon a street which seemed de-void of terror. It was the sort of street, ample, luxurious, gleaming, melting which later, when I began reading Dostoevski, I associated with the thaws of St. Petersburg. Even the churches here were of a different style of architecture; there was something semi-Oriental about them, something grandiose and warm at the same time, which both frightened me and intrigued me. On this broad, spacious street I saw that the houses were set well back from the sidewalk, reposing in quiet and dignity, and unmarred by the intercalation of shops and factories and veterinary stables. I saw a street composed of nothing but residences and I was filled with awe and admiration. All this I remember and no doubt it influenced me greatly, yet none of this is sufficient to account for the strange power and attraction which the very mention of Humboldt Street still evokes in me. Some years later I went back in the night to look at this street again, and I was even more stirred than when I had looked upon it for the first time. The aspect of the street of course had changed, but it was night and the night is always less cruel than the day. Again I experienced the strange de-light of spaciousness, of that luxuriousness which was now somewhat faded but still redolent, still assertive in a patchy way as once the brownstone bannisters had asserted themselves through the melting snow. Most dis-tinct of all, however, was the almost voluptuous sensation of being on the verge of a discovery. Again I was strongly aware of my mother's presence, of the big puffy sleeves of her fur coat, of the cruel swiftness with which she had whisked me through the street years ago and of the stub-born tenacity with which I had feasted my eyes on all that was new and strange. On the occasion of this second visit I seemed to dimly recall another character out of my childhood, the old housekeeper whom they called by the outlandish name of Mrs. Kicking. I could not recall her being taken ill but I did seem to recall the fact that we were paying her a visit at the hospital where she was dying and that this hospital must have been near Humboldt Street which was not dying but which was radiant in the melting snow of a winter's noon. What then had my mother promised me that I have never since been able to recall? Capable as she was of promising anything, perhaps that day, in a fit of abstraction, she had promised something so preposterous that even I with all my childish credulity could not quite swallow it. And yet, if she had promised me the moon, though I knew it was out of the question, I would have struggled to invest her promise with a crumb of faith. I wanted desperately everything that was promised me, and if, upon reflection I realized that it was clearly impossible, I nevertheless tried in my own way to grope for a means of making these promises realizable. That people could make promises without ever having the least intention of fulfilling them was something unimaginable to me. Even when I was most cruelly deceived I still believed; I believed that something extraordinary and quite beyond the other person's power had intervened to make the promise null and void.

This question of belief, this old promise that was never fulfilled, is what makes me think of my father who was deserted at the moment of his greatest need. Up to the time of his illness neither my father nor my mother had ever shown any religious inclinations. Though always upholding the church to others, they themselves never set foot in a church from the time that they were married. Those who attended church too regularly they looked upon as being a bit daffy. The very way they said—"so and so is religious"—was enough to convey the scorn and contempt, or else the pity, which they felt for such individuals. If now and then, because of us children, the pastor called at the house unexpectedly, he was treated as one to whom they were obliged to defer out of ordinary politeness but whom they had nothing in common with, whom they were a little suspicious of, in fact, as representative of a species midway between a fool and a charlatan. To us, for example, they would say "a lovely man," but when their cronies came round and the gossip began to fly, then one would hear an entirely different brand of comment, accompanied usually by peals of scornful laughter and sly mimicry.

My father fell mortally ill as a result of swearing off too abruptly. All his life he had been a jolly hail fellow well met: he had put on a rather becoming paunch, his cheeks were well filled out and red as a beet, his manners were easy and indolent, and he seemed destined to live on into a ripe old age, sound and healthy as a nut. But beneath this smooth and jolly exterior things were not at all well. His affairs were in bad shape, the debts were piling up, and already some of his older friends were beginning to drop him. My mother's attitude was what worried him most. She saw things in a black light and she took no trouble to conceal it. Now and then she became hysterical and went at him hammer and tongs, swearing at him in the vilest language and smashing the dishes and threatening to run away for good. The upshot of it was that he arose one morning determined never to touch another drop. Nobody believed that he meant it seriously; there had been others in the family who swore off, who went on the water wagon, as they used to say, but who quickly tumbled off again. No one in the family, and they had all tried at different times, had ever become a successful teetotaler. But my old man was different. Where or how he got the strength to maintain his resolution, God only knows. It seems incredible to me, because had I been in his boots myself I would have drunk myself to death. Not the old man, however. This was the first time in his life he had ever shown any resolution about anything. My mother was so astounded that, idiot that she was, she began to make fun of him, to quip him about his strength of will which had heretofore been so lamentably weak. Still he stuck to his guns.

His drinking pals faded away rather quickly. In short, he soon found himself almost completely isolated. That must have cut him to the quick, for before very many weeks had passed, he became deathly ill and a consultation was held. He recovered a bit, enough to get out of bed and walk about, but still a very sick man. He was supposed to be suffering from ulcers of the stomach, though nobody was quite sure exactly what ailed him. Everybody understood, however, that he had made a mistake in swearing off so abruptly. It was too late, however, to return to a temperate mode of living. His stomach was so weak that it wouldn't even hold a plate of soup. In a couple of months he was almost a skeleton. And old. He looked like Lazarus raised from the grave.

One day my mother took me aside and with tears in her eyes begged me to go visit the family doctor and learn the truth about my father's condition. Dr. Rausch had been the family physician for years. He was a typical "Dutchman" of the old school, rather weary and crochety now after years of practicing and yet unable to tear himself completely away from his patients. In his stupid Teutonic way he tried to scare the less serious patients away, tried to argue them into health, as it were. When you walked into his office he didn't even bother to look up at you, but kept on writing or whatever it might be that he was doing while firing random questions at you in a perfunctory and insulting manner. He behaved so rudely, so suspiciously, that ridiculous as it may sound, it almost appeared as though he expected his patients to bring with them not only their ailments, but the *proof* of their ailments. He made one feel that there was not only something wrong physically but that there was also something wrong mentally. "You only imagine it" was his favorite phrase, which he flung out with a nasty, leering gibe. Knowing him as I did, and detesting him heartily, I came prepared, that is, with the laboratory analysis of my father's stool. I had also an analysis of his urine in my overcoat pocket, should he demand further proofs.

When I was a boy Dr. Rausch had shown some affection for me, but ever since the day I went to him with a dose of clap he had lost confidence in me and always showed a sour puss when I stuck my head through the door. Like father like son was his motto, and I was therefore not at all surprised when, instead of giving me the information which I demanded, he began to lecture me and the old man at the same time for our way of living. "You can't go against Nature," he said with a wry, solemn face, not looking at me as he uttered the words but making some useless notation in his big ledger. I walked quietly up to his desk, stood beside him a moment without making a sound, and then, when he looked up with his usual aggrieved, irritated expression, I said—"I didn't come here for moral instruction . . . I want to know what's the matter with my father." At this he jumped up and turning to me with his most severe look, he said, like the stupid, brutal Dutchman that he was: "Your father hasn't a chance of recovering; he'll be dead in less than six months." I said "Thank you, that's all I wanted to know," and I made for the door. Then, as though he felt that he had committed a blunder, he strode after me heavily and, putting his hand on my shoulder, he tried to modify the statement by hemming and hawing and saying I don't mean that it is absolutely certain he will die, etc., which I cut short by opening the door and yelling at him, at the top of my lungs, so that his patients in the anteroom would hear it—"I think you're a goddamned old fart and I hope you croak, good night!"

When I got home I modified the doctor's report somewhat by saying that my father's condition was very serious but that if he took good care of himself he would pull through all right. This seemed to cheer the old man up considerably. Of his own accord he took to a diet of milk and zwieback which, whether it was the best thing or not, certainly did him no harm. He remained a sort of semi-invalid for about a year, becoming more and more calm inwardly as time went on and apparently determined to let nothing disturb his peace of mind, nothing, no matter if everything went to hell. As he grew stronger he took to making a daily promenade to the cemetery which was nearby. There he would sit on a bench in the sun and watch the old people potter around the graves. The proximity to the grave, instead of rendering him morbid, seemed to cheer him up. He seemed, if anything, to have become reconciled to the idea of eventual death, a fact which no doubt he had heretofore refused to look in the face. Often he came home with flowers which he had picked in the cemetery, his face beaming with a quiet, serene joy, and seating himself in the armchair he would recount the conversation which he had had that morning with one of the other valetudinarians who frequented the cemetery. It was obvious after a time that he was really enjoying his sequestration, or rather not just enjoying it, but profiting deeply from the experience in a way that was beyond my mother's intelligence to fathom. He was getting lazy, was the way she expressed it. Sometimes she put it even more extremely, tapping her head with her forefinger as she spoke, but not saying anything overtly because of my sister who was without question a little wrong in the head.

And then one day, through the courtesy of an old widow who used to visit her son's grave every day and was, as my mother would say, "religious," he made the acquaintance of a minister belonging to one of the neighboring churches. This was a momentous event in the old man's life. Suddenly he blossomed forth and that little sponge of a soul which had almost atrophied through lack of nourishment took on such astounding proportions that he was almost unrecognizable. The man who was responsible for this extraordinary change in the old man was in no way unusual himself; he was a Congregationalist minister attached to a modest little parish which adjoined our neighborhood. His one virtue was that he kept his religion in the background. The old man quickly fell into a sort of boyish idolatry; he talked of nothing but this minister whom he considered his friend. As he had never looked at the Bible in his life, nor any other book for that matter, it was rather startling, to say the least, to hear him say a little prayer before eating. He performed this little ceremony in a strange way, much the way one takes a tonic, for example. If he recommended me to read a certain chapter of the Bible he would add very seriously—"it will do you good." It was a new medicine which he had discovered, a sort of quack remedy which was guaranteed to cure all ills and which one might take even if he had no ills, because in any case it could certainly do no harm. He attended all the services, all the functions which were held at the church, and between times, when out for a stroll, for example, he would stop off at the minister's home and have a little chat with him. If the minister said that the president was a good soul and should be re-elected the old man would repeat to every one exactly what the minister had said and urge them to vote for the president's re-election. Whatever the minister said was right and just and nobody could gainsay him. There's no doubt that it was an education for the old man. If the minister had mentioned the pyramids in the course of his sermon the old man immediately began to inform himself about the pyramids. He would talk about the pyramids as though every one owed it to himself to become acquainted with the subject. The minister had said that the pyramids were one of the crowning glories of man, ergo not to know about the pyramids was to be disgracefully ignorant, almost sinful. Fortunately the minister didn't dwell much on the subject of sin; he was of the modern type of preacher who prevailed on his flock more by arousing their curiosity than by appealing to their conscience. His sermons were more like a night-school ex-

tension course and for such as the old man, therefore,
highly entertaining and stimulating. Every now and then
the male members of the congregation were invited to a
little blowout which was intended to demonstrate that
the good pastor was just an ordinary man like themselves and could, on occasion, enjoy a hearty meal and
even a glass of beer. Moreover it was observed that he
even sang—not religious hymns, but jolly little songs of
the popular variety. Putting two and two together one
might even infer from such jolly behavior that now and
then he enjoyed getting a little piece of tail—always in
moderation, to be sure. That was the word that was
balsam to the old man's lacerated soul—"moderation." It
was like discovering a new sign in the zodiac. And though
he was still too ill to attempt a return to even a moderate
way of living, nevertheless it did his soul good. And so,
when Uncle Ned, who was continually going on the
water wagon and continually falling off it again, came
round to the house one evening the old man delivered
him a little lecture on the virtue of moderation. Uncle
Ned was, at that moment, *on* the water wagon and so,
when the old man, moved by his own words, suddenly
went to the sideboard to fetch a decanter of wine every
one was shocked. No one had ever dared invite Uncle
Ned to drink when he had sworn off; to venture such a
thing constituted a serious breach of loyalty. But the old
man did it with such conviction that no one could take
offense, and the result was that Uncle Ned took a small
glass of wine and went home that evening without stopping off at a saloon to quench his thirst. It was an extraordinary happening and there was much talk about it
for days after. In fact, Uncle Ned began to act a bit queer
from that day on. It seems that he went the next day to
the wine store and bought a bottle of sherry which he
emptied into the decanter. He placed the decanter on the
sideboard, just as he had seen the old man do, and, instead of polishing it off in one swoop, he contented himself with a glassful at a time—"just a thimbleful," as he

put it. His behavior was so remarkable that my aunt, who was unable to quite believe her eyes, came one day to the house and held a long conversation with the old man. She asked him, among other things, to invite the minister to the house some evening so that Uncle Ned might have the opportunity of falling under his beneficent influence. The long and short of it was that Ned was soon taken into the fold and, like the old man, seemed to be thriving under the experience. Things went fine until the day of the picnic. That day, unfortunately, was an unusually warm day and, what with the games, the excitement, the hilarity, Uncle Ned developed an extraordinary thirst. It was not until he was three sheets to the wind that some one observed the regularity and the frequency with which he was running to the beer keg. It was then too late. Once in that condition he was unmanageable. Even the minister could do nothing with him. Ned broke away from the picnic quietly and went on a little rampage which lasted for three days and nights. Perhaps it would have lasted longer had he not gotten into a fist fight down at the waterfront where he was found lying unconscious by the night watchman. He was taken to the hospital with a concussion of the brain from which he never recovered. Returning from the funeral the old man said with a dry eye—"Ned didn't know what it was to be temperate. It was his own fault. Anyway, he's better off now. . . ."

And as though to prove to the minister that he was not made of the same stuff as Uncle Ned he became even more assiduous in his churchly duties. He had gotten himself promoted to the position of "elder," an office of which he was extremely proud and by grace of which he was permitted during the Sunday services to aid in taking up the collection. To think of my old man marching up the aisle of a Congregational church with a collection box in his hand; to think of him standing reverently before the altar with this collection box while the minister blessed the offering, seems to me now something so

incredible that I scarcely know what to say of it. I like
to think, by contrast, of the man he was when I was just
a kid and I would meet him at the ferry house of a Saturday noon. Surrounding the entrance to the ferry house
there were then three saloons which of a Saturday noon
were filled with men who had stopped off for a little
bite at the free lunch counter and a schooner of beer. I
can see the old man, as he stood in his thirtieth year, a
healthy, genial soul with a smile for every one and a
pleasant quip to pass the time of day, see him with his
arm resting on the bar, his straw hat tipped on the back
of his head, his left hand raised to down the foaming
suds. My eye was then on about a level with his heavy
gold chain which was spread crosswise over his vest; I
remember the shepherd plaid suit which he wore in
midsummer and the distinction it gave him among the
other men at the bar who were not lucky enough to have
been born tailors. I remember the way he would dip his
hand into the big glass bowl on the free lunch counter
and hand me a few pretzels, saying at the same time that
I ought to go and have a look at the scoreboard in the
window of the *Brooklyn Times* nearby. And perhaps, as
I ran out of the saloon to see who was winning, a string
of cyclists would pass close to the curb, holding to the
little strip of asphalt which had been laid down expressly
for them. Perhaps the ferry boat was just coming into
the dock and I would stop a moment to watch the men
in uniform as they pulled away at the big wooden wheels
to which the chains were attached. As the gates were
thrown open and the planks laid down a mob would
rush through the shed and make for the saloons which
adorned the nearest corners. Those were the days when
the old man knew the meaning of "moderation," when
he drank because he was truly thirsty, and to down a
schooner of beer by the ferry house was a man's prerogative. Then it was as Melville has so well said: "Feed all
things with food convenient for them—that is, if the food
be procurable. The food of thy soul is light and space;

feed it then on light and space. But the food of the body is champagne and oysters; feed it then on champagne and oysters; and so shall it merit a joyful resurrection, if there is any to be." Yes, then it seems to me that the old man's soul had not yet shrivelled up, that it was endlessly bounded by light and space and that his body, heedless of the resurrection, was feeding on all that was convenient and procurable—if not champagne and oysters, at least good lager beer and pretzels. Then his body had not been condemned, nor his way of living, nor his absence of faith. Nor was he yet surrounded by vultures, but only by good comrades, ordinary mortals like himself who looked neither high nor low but straight ahead, the eye always fixed on the horizon and content with the sight thereof.

And now, as a battered wreck, he has made himself into an elder of the church and he stands before the altar, gray and bent and withered, while the minister gives his blessing to the measly collection which will go to make a new bowling alley. Perhaps it was necessary for him to experience the birth of the soul, to feed this spongelike growth with that light and space which the Congregational church offered. But what a poor substitute for a man who had known the joys of that food which the body craved and which, without the pangs of conscience, had flooded even his spongelike soul with a light and space that was ungodly but radiant and terrestrial. I think again of his seemly little "corporation" over which the thick gold chain was strung and I think that with that death of his paunch there was left to survive only the sponge of a soul, a sort of appendix to his own bodily death. I think of the minister who had swallowed him up as a sort of inhuman sponge eater, the keeper of a wigwam hung with spiritual scalps. I think of what subsequently ensued as a kind of tragedy in sponges, for though he promised light and space, no sooner had he passed out of my father's life than the whole airy edifice came tumbling down.

It all came about in the most ordinary lifelike way. One evening, after the customary men's meeting, the old man came home with a sorrowful countenance. They had been informed that evening that the minister was taking leave of them. He had been offered a more advantageous position in the township of New Rochelle and, despite his great reluctance to desert his flock, he had decided to accept the offer. He had of course accepted it only after much meditation—as a duty, in other words. It would mean a better income, to be sure, but that was nothing compared to the grave responsibilities which he was about to assume. They had need of him in New Rochelle and he was obeying the voice of his conscience. All this the old man related with the same unctuousness that the minister had given to his words. But it was immediately apparent that the old man was hurt. He couldn't see why New Rochelle could not find another minister. He said it wasn't fair to tempt the minister with a bigger salary. *We need him here*, he said ruefully, with such sadness that I almost felt like weeping. He added that he was going to have a heart-to-heart talk with the minister, that if anybody could persuade him to remain it was he. In the days that followed he certainly did his best, no doubt much to the minister's discomfiture. It was distressing to see the blank look on his face when he returned from these conferences. He had the expression of a man who was trying to grasp at a straw to keep from drowning. Naturally the minister remained adamant. Even when the old man broke down and wept before him he could not be moved to change his mind. That was the turning point. From that moment on the old man underwent a radical change. He seemed to grow bitter and querulous. He not only forgot to say grace at the table but he abstained from going to church. He resumed his old habit of going to the cemetery and basking on a bench. He became morose, then melancholy, and finally there grew into his face an expression of permanent sadness, a sadness encrusted with disillusionment, with despair, with futility. He never again mentioned the man's name, nor the church, nor any of the elders with whom he had once associated. If he happened to pass them in the street he bade them the time of day without stopping to shake hands. He read the newspapers diligently, from back to front, without comment. Even the ads he read, every one, as though trying to block up a huge hole which was constantly before his eyes. I never heard him laugh again. At the most he would give us a sort of weary, hopeless smile, a smile which faded instantly and left us with the spectacle of a life extinct. He was dead as a crater, dead beyond all hope of resurrection. And not even had he been given a new stomach, or a tough new intestinal tract, would it have been possible to restore him to life again. He had passed beyond the lure of champagne and oysters, beyond the need of light and space. He was like the dodo which buries its head in the sand and whistles out of its asshole. When he went to sleep in the Morris chair his lower jaw dropped like a hinge that has become unloosened; he had always been a good snorer but now he snored louder than ever, like a man who was in truth dead to the world. His snores, in fact, were very much like the death rattle, except that they were punctuated by an intermittent long drawn out whistling of the peanut stand variety. He seemed, when he snored, to be chopping the whole universe to bits so that we who succeeded him would have enough kindling wood to last a lifetime. It was the most horrible and fascinating snoring that I have ever listened to: it was stertorous and stentorian, morbid and grotesque; at times it was like an accordion collapsing, at other times like a frog croaking in the swamps; after a prolonged whistle there sometimes followed a frightful wheeze as if he were giving up the ghost, then it would settle back again into a regular rise and fall, a steady hollow chopping as though he stood stripped to the waist, with ax in hand, before the accumulated madness of all the bric-à-brac of this world. What gave these performances a slightly crazy quality was the mummy-like expression of the face in which the big blubber lips alone came to life; they were like the gills of a shark snoozing on the surface of the still ocean. Blissfully he snored away on the bosom of the deep, never disturbed by a dream or a draught, never fitful, never plagued by an unsatisfied desire; when he closed his eyes and collapsed, the light of the world went out and he was alone as before birth, a cosmos gnashing itself to bits. He sat there in his Morris chair as Jonah must have sat in the body of the whale, secure in the last refuge of a black hole, expecting nothing, desiring nothing, not dead but buried alive, swallowed whole and unscathed, the big blubber lips gently flapping with the flux and reflux of the white breath of emptiness. He was in the land of Nod searching for Cain and Abel but encountering no living soul, no word, no sign. He drove with the whale and scraped the icy black bottom; he covered furlongs at top speed, guided only by the fleecy manes of undersea beasts. He was the smoke that curled out of the chimney tops, the heavy layers of cloud that obscured the moon, the thick slime that made the slippery linoleum floor of the ocean depths. He was deader than dead because alive and empty, beyond all hope of resurrection in that he had traveled beyond the limits of light and space and securely nestled himself in the black hole of nothingness. He was more to be envied than pitied, for his sleep was not a lull or an interval but sleep itself which is the deep and hence sleeping ever deepening, deeper and deeper in sleep sleeping, the sleep of the deep in deepest sleep, at the nethermost depth full slept, the deepest and sleepest sleep of sleep's sweet sleep. He was asleep. He *is* asleep. He *will* be asleep. Sleep. Sleep. *Father, sleep, I beg you, for we who are awake are boiling in horror. . . .*

With the world fluttering away on the last wings of a hollow snore I see the door opening to admit Grover Watrous. "Christ be with you!" he says, dragging his clubfoot along. He is quite a young man now and he has found God. There is only one God and Grover Watrous

has found Him and so there is nothing more to say except
that everything has to be said over again in Grover
Watrous' new God-language. This bright new language
which God invented especially for Grover Watrous intrigues me enormously, first because I had always considered Grover to be a hopeless dunce, second because
I notice that there are no longer any tobacco stains on
his agile fingers. When we were boys Grover lived next
door to us. He would visit me from time to time in order to
practice a duet with me. Though he was only fourteen
or fifteen he smoked like a trooper. His mother could do
nothing against it because Grover was a genius and a
genius had to have a little liberty, particularly when he
was also unfortunate enough to have been born with a
clubfoot. Grover was the kind of genius who thrives on
dirt. He not only had nicotine stains on his fingers but he
had filthy black nails which would break under hours of
practicing, imposing upon young Grover the ravishing
obligation of tearing them off with his teeth. Grover used
to spit out broken nails along with the bits of tobacco
which got caught in his teeth. It was delightful and stimulating. The cigarettes burned holes into the piano and,
as my mother critically observed, also *tarnished* the keys.
When Grover took leave the parlor stank like the back-
room of an undertaker's establishment. It stank of dead
cigarettes, sweat, dirty linen, Grover's oaths and the
dry heat left by the dying notes of Weber, Berlioz, Liszt
and Co. It stank too of Grover's running ear and of his
decaying teeth. It stank of his mother's pampering and
whimpering. His own home was a stable divinely suited
to his genius, but the parlor of our home was like the
waiting room of a mortician's office and Grover was a
lout who didn't even know enough to wipe his feet. In
the wintertime his nose ran like a sewer and, Grover being
too engrossed in his music to bother wiping his nose, his
cold snot was left to trickle down until it reached his lips
where it was sucked in by a very long white tongue. To
the flatulent music of Weber, Berlioz, Liszt and Co. it

added a piquant sauce which made those empty devils palatable. Every other word from Grover's lips was an oath, his favorite expression being—"I can't get the fucking thing right!" Sometimes he grew so annoyed that he would take his fists and pound the piano like a madman. It was his genius coming out the wrong way. His mother, in fact, used to attach a great deal of importance to these fits of anger; they convinced her that he had something in him. Other people simply said that Grover was impossible. Much was forgiven, however, because of his clubfoot. Grover was sly enough to exploit this bad foot; whenever he wanted anything badly he developed pains in the foot. Only the piano seemed to have no respect for this maimed member. The piano therefore was an object to be cursed and kicked and pounded to bits. If he were in good form, on the other hand, Grover would remain at the piano for hours on end; in fact, you couldn't drag him away. On such occasions his mother would go stand in the grass plot in front of the house and waylay the neighbors in order to squeeze a few words of praise out of them. She would be so carried away by her son's "divine" playing that she would forget to cook the evening meal. The old man, who worked in the sewers, usually came home grumpy and famished. Sometimes he would march directly upstairs to the parlor and yank Grover off the piano stool. He had a rather foul vocabulary himself and when he let loose on his genius of a son there wasn't much left for Grover to say. In the old man's opinion Grover was just a lazy son of a bitch who could make a lot of noise. Now and then he threatened to chuck the fucking piano out of the window—and Grover with it. If the mother were rash enough to interfere during these scenes he would give her a clout and tell her to go piss up the end of a rope. He had his moments of weakness too, of course, and in such a mood he might ask Grover what the hell he was rattling away at, and if the latter said, for example, "why the Sonata *Pathétique*," the old buzzard would say—"What the hell does that mean? Why in

Christ's name don't they put it down in plain English?"
The old man's ignorance was even harder for Grover to
bear than his brutality. He was heartily ashamed of his
old man and when the latter was out of sight he would
ridicule him unmercifully. When he got a little older he
used to insinuate that he wouldn't have been born with a
clubfoot if the old man hadn't been such a mean bastard.
He said that the old man must have kicked his mother in
the belly when she was pregnant. This alleged kick in the
belly must have affected Grover in diverse ways, for when
he had grown up to be quite a young man, as I was saying, he suddenly took to God with such a passion that
there was no blowing your nose before him without first
asking God's permission.

Grover's conversion followed right upon the old man's
deflation, which is why I am reminded of it. Nobody had
seen the Watrouses for a number of years and then, right
in the midst of a bloody snore, you might say, in pranced
Grover scattering benedictions and calling upon God as
his witness as he rolled up his sleeves to deliver us from
evil. What I noted first in him was the change in his personal appearance; he had been washed clean in the blood
of the Lamb. He was so immaculate, indeed, that there
was almost a perfume emanating from him. His speech
too had been cleaned up; instead of wild oaths there were
now nothing but blessings and invocations. It was not a
conversation which he held with us but a monologue in
which, if there were any questions, he answered them himself. As he took the chair which was offered him he said
with the nimbleness of a jack rabbit that God had given
his only beloved Son in order that we might enjoy life
everlasting. Did we really want this life everlasting—or
were we simply going to wallow in the joys of the flesh
and die without knowing salvation? The incongruity of
mentioning the "joys of the flesh" to an aged couple, one
of whom was sound asleep and snoring, never struck him,
to be sure. He was so alive and jubilant in the first flush
of God's merciful grace that he must have forgotten that

my sister was dippy, for, without even inquiring how she had been, he began to harangue her in this new-found spiritual palaver to which she was entirely impervious because, as I say, she was minus so many buttons that if he had been talking about chopped spinach it would have been just as meaningful to her. A phrase like "the pleasures of the flesh" meant to her something like a beautiful day with a red parasol. I could see by the way she sat on the edge of her chair and bobbed her head that she was only waiting for him to catch his breath in order to inform him that the pastor—*her* pastor, who was an Episcopalian—had just returned from Europe and that they were going to have a fair in the basement of the church where she would have a little booth fitted up with doilies from the five-and-ten-cent store. In fact, no sooner had he paused a moment than she let loose—about the canals of Venice, the snow in the Alps, the dog carts in Brussels, the beautiful liverwurst in Munich. She was not only religious, my sister, but she was clean daffy. Grover had just slipped in something about having seen a new heaven and a new earth . . . *for the first heaven and the first earth were passed away,* he said, mumbling the words in a sort of hysterical glissando in order to unburden himself of an oracular message about the New Jerusalem which God had established on earth and in which he, Grover Watrous, once foul of speech and marred by a twisted foot, had found the peace and the calm of the righteous. *"There shall be no more death . . ."* he started to shout when my sister leaned forward and asked him very innocently if he liked to bowl because the pastor had just installed a beautiful new bowling alley in the basement of the church and she knew he would be pleased to see Grover because he was a lovely man and he was kind to the poor. Grover said that it was a sin to bowl and that he belonged to no church because the churches were godless; he had even given up playing the piano because God needed him for higher things. *"He that overcometh shall inherit all things,"* he added, *"and I will be his God,*

and he shall be my son." He paused again to blow his nose
in a beautiful white handkerchief, whereupon my sister
took the occasion to remind him that in the old days he
always had a running nose but that he never wiped it.
Grover listened to her very solemnly and then remarked
that he had been cured of many evil ways. At this point
the old man woke up and, seeing Grover sitting beside him
large as life, he was quite startled and for a moment
or two he was not sure, it seemed, whether Grover was a
morbid phenomenon of dream or an hallucination, but
the sight of the clean handkerchief brought him quickly
to his wits. "Oh, it's you!" he exclaimed. "The Watrous
boy, what? Well, what in the name of all that's holy
are you doing here?"

"I came in the name of the Holy of Holies," said Grover
unabashed. "I have been purified by the death of Calvary
and I am here in Christ's sweet name that ye may be re-
deemed and walk in light and power and glory."

The old man looked dazed. "Well, what's come over
you?" he said, giving Grover a feeble, consolatory smile.
My mother had just come in from the kitchen and had
taken a stand behind Grover's chair. By making a wry
grimace with her mouth she was trying to convey to the
old man that Grover was cracked. Even my sister seemed
to realize that there was something wrong with him,
especially when he had refused to visit the new bowling
alley which her lovely pastor had expressly installed for
young men such as Grover and his likes.

What was the matter with Grover? Nothing, except
that his feet were solidly planted on the fifth foundation
of the great wall of the Holy City of Jerusalem, the fifth
foundation made entirely of sardonyx, whence he commanded a view of a pure river of the water of life issuing
from the throne of God. And the sight of this river of life
was to Grover like the bite of a thousand fleas in his lower
colon. Not until he had run at least seven times around
the earth would he be able to sit quietly on his ass and
observe the blindness and the indifference of men with

something like equanimity. He was alive and purged, and though to the eyes of the sluggish, sluttish spirits who are sane he was "cracked," to me he seemed infinitely better off this way than before. He was a pest who could do you no harm. If you listened to him long enough you became somewhat purged yourself, though perhaps unconvinced. Grover's bright new language always caught me in the midriff and through inordinate laughter cleansed me of the dross accumulated by the sluggish sanity about me. He was alive as Ponce de Leon had hoped to be alive; alive as only a few men have ever been. And being unnaturally alive he didn't mind in the least if you laughed in his face, nor would he have minded if you had stolen the few possessions which were his. He was alive and empty, which is so close to Godhood that it is crazy.

With his feet solidly planted on the great wall of the New Jerusalem Grover knew a joy which is incommensurable. Perhaps if he had not been born with a clubfoot he would not have known this incredible joy. Perhaps it was well that his father had kicked the mother in the belly while Grover was still in the womb. Perhaps it was that kick in the belly which had sent Grover soaring, which made him so thoroughly alive and awake that even in his sleep he was delivering God's messages. The harder he labored the less he was fatigued. He had no more worries, no regrets, no clawing memories. He recognized no duties, no obligations, except to God. And what did God expect of him? Nothing, nothing . . . except to sing His praises. God only asked of Grover Watrous that he reveal himself alive in the flesh. He only asked of him to be more and more alive. And when fully alive Grover was a voice and this voice was a flood which made all dead things into chaos and this chaos in turn became the mouth of the world in the very center of which was the verb *to be. In the beginning there was the Word, and the Word was with God, and the word was God.* So God was this strange little infinitive which is all there is—and is it not enough? For Grover it was more than enough: it was everything. Starting from this Verb what difference did it make which road he traveled? To leave the Verb was to travel away from the center, to erect a Babel. Perhaps God had deliberately maimed Grover Watrous in order to hold him to the center, to the Verb. By an invisible cord God held Grover Watrous to his stake which ran through the heart of the world and Grover became the fat goose which laid a golden egg every day. . . .

Why do I write of Grover Watrous? Because I have met thousands of people and none of them were alive in the way that Grover was. Most of them were more intelligent, many of them were brilliant, some of them were even famous, but none were alive and empty as Grover was. Grover was inexhaustible. He was like a bit of radium which, even if buried under a mountain does not lose its power to give off energy. I had seen plenty of so-called *energetic* people before—is not America filled with them? —but never in the shape of a human being, a reservoir of energy. And what created this inexhaustible reservoir of energy? An illumination. Yes, it happened in the twinkling of an eye, which is the only way that anything important ever does happen. Overnight all Grover's preconceived values were thrown overboard. Suddenly, just like that, he ceased moving as other people move. He put the brakes on and he kept the motor running. If once, like other people, he had thought it was necessary to get somewhere now he knew that somewhere was anywhere and therefore right here and so why move? Why not park the car and keep the motor running? Meanwhile the earth itself is turning and Grover knew it was turning and knew that he was turning with it. Is the earth getting anywhere? Grover must undoubtedly have asked himself this question and must undoubtedly have satisfied himself that it was *not* getting anywhere. Who, then, had said that we must get somewhere? Grover would inquire of this one and that where they were heading for and the strange thing was that although they were all heading for their individual destinations none of them ever stopped to re-

flect that the one inevitable destination for all alike was
the grave. This puzzled Grover because nobody could
convince him that death was not a certainty, whereas anybody could convince anybody else that any other destination was an uncertainty. Convinced of the dead certainty of death Grover suddenly became tremendously
and overwhelmingly alive. For the first time in his life
he began to live, and at the same time the clubfoot
dropped completely out of his consciousness. This is a
strange thing, too, when you come to think of it, because
the clubfoot, just like death, was another ineluctable fact.
Yet the clubfoot dropped out of mind, or, what is more
important, all that had been attached to the clubfoot. In
the same way, having accepted death, death too dropped
out of Grover's mind. Having seized on the single certainty of death all the uncertainties vanished. The rest
of the world was now limping along with clubfooted uncertainties and Grover Watrous alone was free and unimpeded. Grover Watrous was the personification of certainty. He may have been wrong, but he was certain.
*And what good does it do to be right if one has to limp
along with a clubfoot?* Only a few men have ever realized
the truth of this and their names have become very great
names. Grover Watrous will probably never be known,
but he is very great just the same. This is probably the
reason why I write about him—just the fact that I had
enough sense to realize that Grover had achieved great-
ness even though nobody else will admit it. At the time
I simply thought that Grover was a harmless fanatic, yes,
a little "cracked," as my mother insinuated. But every man
who has caught the truth of certitude was a little cracked
and it is only these men who have accomplished anything
for the world. Other men, other *great* men, have destroyed
a little here and there, but these few whom I speak of,
and among whom I include Grover Watrous, were capable of destroying everything in order that the truth
might live. Usually these men were born with an impedi-
ment, with a clubfoot, so to speak, and by a strange irony

it is only the clubfoot which men remember. If a man like
Grover becomes depossessed of his clubfoot, the world
says that he has become "possessed." This is the logic
of incertitude and its fruit is misery. Grover was the only
truly joyous being I ever met in my life and this, therefore, is a little monument which I am erecting in his
memory, in the memory of his joyous certitude. It is a
pity that he had to use Christ for a crutch, but then what
does it matter how one comes by the truth so long as one
pounces upon it and lives by it?

AN INTERLUDE

Confusion is a word we have invented for an order
which is not understood. I like to dwell on this period
when things were taking shape because the order, if it
were understood, must have been dazzling. In the first
place there was Hymie, Hymie the bullfrog, and there
were also his wife's ovaries which had been rotting away
for a considerable time. Hymie was completely wrapped
up in his wife's rotting ovaries. It was the daily topic of
conversation; it took precedence now over the cathartic
pills and the coated tongue. Hymie dealt in "sexual prov-
erbs," as he called them. Everything he said began from
or led up to the ovaries. Despite everything he was still
nicking it off with the wife—prolonged snakelike copula-
tions in which he would smoke a cigarette or two before
uncunting. He would endeavor to explain to me how the
pus from the rotting ovaries put her in heat. She had
always been a good fuck, but now she was better than
ever. Once the ovaries were ripped out there'd be no
telling how she'd take it. She seemed to realize that too.
Ergo, fuck away! Every night, after the dishes were
cleared away, they'd strip down in their little birdlike
apartment and lie together like a couple of snakes. He
tried to describe it to me on a number of occasions—the
way she fucked. It was like an oyster inside, an oyster with

soft teeth that nibbled away at him. Sometimes it felt as
though he were right inside her womb, so soft and fluffy
it was, and those soft teeth biting away at his pecker and
making him delirious. They used to lie scissors-fashion
and look up at the ceiling. To keep from coming he would
think about the office, about the little worries which
plagued him and kept his bowels tied up in a knot. In
between orgasms he would let his mind dwell on someone
else, so that when she'd start working on him again he
might imagine he was having a brand new fuck with a
brand new cunt. He used to arrange it so that he could
look out the window while it was going on. He was getting
so adept at it that he could undress a woman on the
boulevard there under his window and transport her to
the bed; not only that, but he could actually make her
change places with his wife, all without un-cunting. Sometimes he'd fuck away like that for a couple of hours and
never even bother to shoot off. Why waste it! he would say.

Steve Romero, on the other hand, had a hell of a time
holding it in. Steve was built like a bull and he scattered
his seed freely. We used to compare notes sometimes
sitting in the chop suey joint around the corner from the
office. It was a strange atmosphere. Maybe it was because there was no wine. Maybe it was the funny little
black mushrooms they served us. Anyway it wasn't difficult to get started on the subject. By the time Steve met
us he would already have had his workout, a shower
and a rubdown. He was clean inside and out. Almost a
perfect specimen of a man. Not very bright, to be sure,
but a good egg, a companion. Hymie, on the other hand,
was like a toad. He seemed to come to the table direct
from the swamps where he had passed a mucky day. Filth
rolled off his lips like honey. In fact, you couldn't call it
filth, in his case, because there wasn't any other ingredient
with which you might compare it. It was all one fluid,
a slimy, sticky substance made entirely of sex. When he
looked at his food he saw it as potential sperm; if the
weather were warm he would say it was good for the

balls; if he took a trolley ride he knew in advance that
the rhythmic movement of the trolley would stimulate his
appetite, would give him a slow, "personal" hard on, as
he put it. Why "personal" I never found out, but that was
his expression. He liked to go out with us because we
were always reasonably sure of picking up something
decent. Left to himself he didn't always fare so well. With
us he got a change of meat—Gentile cunt, as he put it.
He liked Gentile cunt. Smelled sweeter, he said. Laughed
easier too. . . . Sometimes in the very midst of things.
The one thing he couldn't tolerate was dark meat. It
amazed and disgusted him to see me traveling around
with Valeska. Once he asked me if she didn't smell kind
of extra strong like. I told him I liked it that way—strong
and smelly, with lots of gravy around it. He almost blushed
at that. Amazing how delicate he could be about some
things. Food for example. Very finicky about his food.
Perhaps a racial trait. Immaculate about his person, too.
Couldn't stand the sight of a spot on his clean cuffs. Constantly brushing himself off, constantly taking his pocket
mirror out to see if there was any food between his teeth.
If he found a crumb he would hide his face behind the
napkin and extract it with his pearlhandled toothpick. The
ovaries of course he couldn't see. Nor could he smell
them either, because his wife too was an immaculate bitch.
Douching herself all day long in preparation for the evening nuptials. It was tragic, the importance she gave to
her ovaries.

Up until the day she was taken to the hospital she was
a regular fucking block. The thought of never being
able to fuck again frightened the wits out of her. Hymie of
course told her it wouldn't make any difference to him one
way or the other. Glued to her like a snake, a cigarette in
his mouth, the girls passing below on the boulevard, it
was hard for him to imagine a woman not being able to
fuck any more. He was sure the operation would be
successful. *Successful!* That's to say that she'd fuck even
better than before. He used to tell her that, lying on his

back looking up at the ceiling. "You know I'll always love you," he would say. "Move over just a little bit, will you. . . . there, like that. . . . that's it. What was I saying? Oh yes . . . why sure, why should you worry about things like that? Of course I'll be true to you. Listen, pull away just a little bit . . . yeah, that's it. . . . that's fine." He used to tell us about it in the chop suey joint. Steve would laugh like hell. Steve couldn't do a thing like that. He was too honest— especially with women. That's why he never had any luck. Little Curley, for example—Steve hated Curley—would always get what he wanted. . . . He was a born liar, a born deceiver. Hymie didn't like Curley much either. He said he was dishonest, meaning of course dishonest in money matters. About such things Hymie was scru- pulous. What he disliked especially was the way Curley talked about his aunt. It was bad enough, in Hymie's opinion, that he should be screwing the sister of his own mother, but to make her out to be nothing but a piece of stale cheese, that was too much for Hymie. One ought to have a bit of respect for a woman, provided she's not a whore. If she's a whore that's different. Whores are not women. Whores are whores. That was how Hymie looked at things.

The real reason for this dislike, however, was that when- ever they went out together Curley always got the best choice. And not only that, but it was usually with Hymie's money that Curley managed it. Even the way Curley asked for money irritated Hymie—it was like extortion, he said. He thought it was partly my fault, that I was too lenient with the kid. "He's got no moral character," Hymie would say. "And what about *you*, your moral character?" I would ask. "Oh *me!* Shit, I'm too old to have any moral character. But Curley's only a kid."

"You're jealous, that's what," Steve would say.

"*Me?* Me jealous of *him?*" And he'd try to smother the idea with a scornful little laugh. It made him wince, a jab like that. "Listen," he would say, turning to me, "did I ever act jealous toward you? Didn't I always turn a girl over to you if you asked me? What about that red-haired girl in SU office . . . you remember . . . the one with the big teats? Wasn't that a nice piece of ass to turn over to a friend? But I did it, didn't I? I did it because you said you liked big teats. But I wouldn't do it for Curley. He's a little crook. Let him do his own digging."

As a matter of fact, Curley was digging away very industriously. He must have had five or six on the string at one time, from what I could gather. There was Valeska, for example—he had made himself pretty solid with her. She was so damned pleased to have some one fuck her without blushing that when it came to sharing him with her cousin and then with the midget she didn't put up the least objection. What she liked best was to get in the tub and let him fuck her under water. It was fine until the midget got wise to it. Then there was a nice rumpus which was finally ironed out on the parlor floor. To listen to Curley talk he did everything but climb the chandeliers. And always plenty of pocket money to boot. Valeska was generous, but the cousin was a softy. If she came within a foot of a stiff prick she was like putty. An unbuttoned fly was enough to put her in a trance. It was almost shameful the things Curley made her do. He took pleasure in degrading her. I could scarcely blame him for it, she was such a prim, priggish bitch in her street clothes. You'd almost swear she didn't own a cunt, the way she carried herself in the street. Naturally, when he got her alone he made her pay for her highfalutin' ways. He went at it coldbloodedly. "Fish it out!" he'd say, opening his fly a little. "Fish it out with your tongue!" (He had it in for the whole bunch because, as he put it, they were sucking one another off behind his back.) Anyway, once she got the taste of it in her mouth you could do anything with her. Sometimes he'd stand her on her hands and push her around the room that way, like a wheelbarrow. Or else he'd do it dog fashion, and while she groaned and squirmed he'd nonchalantly light a cigarette and blow the smoke between her legs. Once he played her a dirty trick

doing it that way. He had worked her up to such a state
that she was beside herself. Anyway, after he had almost
polished the ass off her with his back-scuttling he pulled
out for a second, as though to cool his cock off, and then
very slowly and gently he shoved a big long carrot up her
twat. "That, Miss Abercrombie," he said, "is a sort of
Doppelgänger to my regular cock," and with that he un-
hitches himself and yanks up his pants. Cousin Abercrombie was so bewildered by it all that she let a tremendous fart and out tumbled the carrot. At least, that's how
Curley related it to me. He was an outrageous liar, to be
sure, and there may not be a grain of truth in the yarn, but
there's no denying that he had a flair for such tricks. As
for Miss Abercrombie and her high-tone Narragansett
ways, well, with a cunt like that one can always imagine
the worst. By comparison Hymie was a purist. Somehow
Hymie and his fat circumcised dick were two different
things. When he got a personal hard on, as he said, he
really meant that he was irresponsible. He meant that
Nature was asserting itself—through his, Hymie Laubscher's, fat circumcised dick. It was the same with his
wife's cunt. It was something she wore between her legs,
like an ornament. It was a part of Mrs. Laubscher but it
wasn't Mrs. Laubscher personally, if you get what I mean.

Well, all this is simply by way of leading up to the
general sexual confusion which prevailed at this time. It
was like taking a flat in the Land of Fuck. The girl upstairs, for instance . . . she used to come down now and
then, when the wife was giving a recital, to look after the
kid. She was so obviously a simpleton that I didn't give
her any notice at first. But like all the others she had a
cunt too, a sort of impersonal personal cunt which she was
unconsciously conscious of. The oftener she came down
the more conscious she got, in her unconscious way. One
night, when she was in the bathroom, after she had been
in there a suspiciously long while, she got me to thinking
of things. I decided to take a peep through the keyhole
and see for myself what was what. Lo and behold, if she

isn't standing in front of the mirror stroking and petting her little pussy. Almost talking to it, she was. I was so excited I didn't know what to do first. I went back into the big room, turned out the lights, and lay there on the couch waiting for her to come out. As I lay there I could still see that bushy cunt of hers and the fingers strumming it like. I opened my fly to let my pecker twitch about in the cool of the dark. I tried to mesmerize her from the couch, or at least I tried letting my pecker mesmerize her. "Come here, you bitch," I kept saying to myself, "come in here and spread that cunt over me." She must have caught the message immediately, for in a jiffy she had opened the door and was groping about in the dark to find the couch. I didn't say a word, I didn't make a move. I just kept my mind riveted on her cunt moving quietly in the dark like a crab. Finally she was standing beside the couch. She didn't say a word either. She just stood there quietly and as I slid my hand up her legs she moved one foot a little to open her crotch a bit more. I don't think I ever put my hand into such a juicy crotch in all my life. It was like paste running down her legs, and if there had been any billboards handy I could have plastered up a dozen or more. After a few moments, just as naturally as a cow lowering its head to graze, she bent over and put it in her mouth. I had my whole four fingers inside her, whipping it up to a froth. Her mouth was stuffed full and the juice pouring down her legs. Not a word out of us, as I say. Just a couple of quiet maniacs working away in the dark like gravediggers. It was a fucking Paradise and I knew it, and I was ready and willing to fuck my brains away if necessary. She was probably the best fuck I ever had. She never once opened her trap—not that night, nor the next night, nor any night. She'd steal down like that in the dark, soon as she smelled me there alone, and plaster her cunt all over me. It was an enormous cunt, too, when I think back on it. A dark, subterranean labyrinth fitted up with divans and cosy corners and rubber teeth and syringes and soft nestles and eiderdown and mulberry leaves. I used to nose in like the solitary worm and bury myself in a little cranny where it was absolutely silent, and so soft and restful that I lay like a dolphin on the oyster banks. A slight twitch and I'd be in the Pullman reading a newspaper or else up an impasse where there were mossy round cobblestones and little wicker gates which opened and shut automatically. Sometimes it was like riding the shoot-the-shoots, a steep plunge and then a spray of tingling sea crabs, the bulrushes swaying feverishly and the gills of tiny fishes lapping against me like harmonica stops. In the immense black grotto there was a silk-and-soap organ playing a predaceous black music. When she pitched herself high, when she turned the juice on full, it made a violaceous purple, a deep mulberry stain like twilight, a ventriloqual twilight such as dwarfs and cretins enjoy when they menstruate. It made me think of cannibals chewing flowers, of Bantus running amuck, of wild unicorns rutting in rhododendron beds. Everything was anonymous and unformulated, John Doe and his wife Emmy Doe; above us the gas tanks and below the marine life. Above the belt, as I say, she was batty. Yes, absolutely cuckoo, though still abroad and afloat. Perhaps that was what made her cunt so marvelously impersonal. It was one cunt out of a million, a regular Pearl of the Antilles, such as Dick Osborn discovered when reading Joseph Conrad. In the broad Pacific of sex she lay, a gleaming silver reef surrounded with human anemones, human starfish, human madrepores. Only an Osborn could have discovered her, given the proper latitude and longitude of cunt. Meeting her in the daytime, watching her slowly going daft, it was like trapping a weasel when night came on. All I had to do was to lie down in the dark with my fly open and wait. She was like Ophelia suddenly resurrected among the Kaffirs. Not a word of any language could she remember, especially not English. She was a deaf-mute who had lost her memory, and with the loss of memory she had lost her frigidaire, her curling irons, her tweezers and handbag. She was even more naked than a fish, except for the tuft of hair between her legs. And she was even slipperier than a fish because after all a fish has scales and she had none. It was dubious at times whether I was in her or she in me. It was open warfare, the newfangled Pancrace, with each one biting his own ass. Love among the newts and the cutout wide open. Love without gender and without lysol. Incubational love, such as the wolverines practice above the tree line. On the one side the Arctic Ocean, on the other the Gulf of Mexico. And though we never referred to it openly there was always with us King Kong, King Kong asleep in the wrecked hull of the Titanic among the phosphorescent bones of millionaires and lampreys. No logic could drive King Kong away. He was the giant truss that supports the soul's fleeting anguish. He was the wedding cake with hairy legs and arms a mile long. He was the revolving screen on which the news passes away. He was the muzzle of the revolver that never went off, the leper armed with sawed-off gonococci.

It was here in the void of hernia that I did all my quiet thinking via the penis. There was first of all the binomial theorem, a phrase which had always puzzled me: I put it under the magnifying glass and studied it from X to Z. There was Logos, which somehow I had always identified with breath: I found that on the contrary it was a sort of obsessional stasis, a machine which went on grinding corn long after the granaries had been filled and the Jews driven out of Egypt. There was Bucephalus, more fascinating to me perhaps than any word in my whole vocabulary: I would trot it out whenever I was in a quandary, and with it of course Alexander and his entire purple retinue. What a horse! Sired in the Indian Ocean, the last of the line, and never once mated, except to the Queen of the Amazons during the Mesopotamian adventure. There was the Scotch Gambit! An amazing expression which had nothing to do with chess. It came to me always in the shape of a man on stilts, page 2,498

of Funk and Wagnall's Unabridged Dictionary. A gambit
was a sort of leap in the dark with mechanical legs. A
leap for no purpose—*hence gambit!* Clear as a bell and
perfectly simple, once you grasped it. Then there was
Andromeda, and the Gorgon Medusa, and Castor and
Pollux of heavenly origin, mythological twins, eternally
fixed in the ephemeral stardust. There was lucubration, a
word distinctly sexual and yet suggesting such cerebral
connotations as to make me uneasy. Always "midnight
lucubrations," the midnight being ominously significant.
And then arras. Somebody some time or other had been
stabbed "behind the arras." I saw an altar cloth made of
asbestos and in it was a grievous rent such as Caesar himself might have made.

It was very quiet thinking, as I say, the kind that the
men of the Old Stone Age must have indulged in. Things
were neither absurd nor explicable. It was a jigsaw puz-
zle which, when you grew tired, you could push away
with two feet. Anything could be put aside with ease,
even the Himalaya mountains. It was just the opposite
kind of thinking from Mahomet's. It led absolutely nowhere and was hence enjoyable. The grand edifice
which you might construct throughout the course of a
long fuck could be toppled over in the twinkling of an
eye. It was the fuck that counted and not the construction
work. It was like living in the Ark during the Flood,
everything provided for down to a screwdriver. What
need to commit murder, rape or incest when all that was
demanded of you was to kill time? Rain, rain, rain, but
inside the Ark everything dry and toasty, a pair of every
kind and in the larder fine Westphalian hams, fresh eggs,
olives, pickled onions, Worcestershire sauce and other
delicacies. God had chosen me, Noah, to establish a new
heaven and a new earth. He had given me a stout boat
with all seams caulked and properly dried. He had given
me also the knowledge to sail the stormy seas. Maybe
when it stopped raining there would be other kinds of
knowledge to acquire, but for the present a nautical

knowledge sufficed. The rest was chess in the Café Royal, Second Avenue, except that I had to imagine a partner, a clever Jewish mind that would make the game last until the rains ceased. But, as I said before, I had no time to be bored; there were my old friends, Logos, Bucephalus, arras, lucubration and so on. Why play chess?

Locked up like that for days and nights on end I began to realize that thinking, when it is not masturbative, is lenitive, healing, pleasurable. The thinking that gets you nowhere takes you everywhere; all other thinking is done on tracks and no matter how long the stretch, in the end there is always the depot or the roundhouse. In the end there is always a red lantern which says STOP! But when the penis gets to thinking there is no stop or let: it is a perpetual holiday, the bait fresh and the fish always nibbling at the line. Which reminds me of another cunt, Veronica something or other, who always got me thinking the wrong way. With Veronica it was always a tussle in the vestibule. On the dance floor you'd think she was going to make you a permanent present of her ovaries, but as soon as she hit the air she'd start thinking, thinking of her hat, of her purse, of her aunt who was waiting up for her, of the letter she forgot to mail, of the job she was going to lose—all kinds of crazy, irrelevant thoughts which had nothing to do with the thing in hand. It was like she had suddenly switched her brain to her cunt— the most alert and canny cunt imaginable. It was almost a metaphysical cunt, so to speak. It was a cunt which thought out problems, and not only that, but a special kind of thinking it was, with a metronome going. For this species of displaced rhythmic lucubration a peculiar dim light was essential. It had to be just about dark enough for a bat and yet light enough to find a button if one happened to come undone and roll on the floor of the vestibule. You can see what I mean. A vague yet meticulous precision, a steely awareness that simulated absent-mindedness. And fluttery and fluky at the same time, so that you could never determine whether it was fish or fowl. *What is this I hold in my hand? Fine or superfine?* The answer was always duck soup. If you grabbed her by the boobies she would squawk like a parrot: if you got under her dress she would wriggle like an eel; if you held her too tight she would bite like a ferret. She lingered and lingered and lingered. Why? What was she after? Would she give in after an hour or two? Not a chance in a million. She was like a pigeon trying to fly with its legs caught in a steel trap. She pretended she had no legs. But if you made a move to set her free she would threaten to moult on you.

Because she had such a marvelous ass and because it was also so damned inaccessible I used to think of her as the Pons Asinorum. Every schoolboy knows that the Pons Asinorum is not to be crossed except by two white donkeys led by a blind man. I don't know why it is so, but that's the rule as it was laid down by old Euclid. He was so full of knowledge, the old buzzard, that one day —I suppose purely to amuse himself—he built a bridge which no living mortal could ever cross. He called it the Pons Asinorum because he was the owner of a pair of beautiful white donkeys, and so attached was he to these donkeys that he would let nobody take possession of them. And so he conjured a dream in which he, the blind man, would one day lead the donkeys over the bridge and into the happy hunting grounds for donkeys. Well, Veronica was very much in the same boat. She thought so much of her beautiful white ass that she wouldn't part with it for anything. She wanted to take it with her to Paradise when the time came. As for her cunt—which by the way she never referred to at all—as for her cunt, I say, well that was just an accessory to be brought along. In the dim light of the vestibule, without ever referring overtly to her two problems, she somehow made you uncomfortably aware of them. That is, she made you aware in the manner of a prestidigitator. You were to take a look or a feel only to be finally deceived, only to be shown that you had not seen and had not felt. It was a very subtle sexual algebra, the midnight lucubration which would earn you an A or a B next day, but nothing more. You passed your examinations, you got your diploma, and then you were turned loose. In the meantime you used your ass to sit down and your cunt to make water with. Between the textbook and the lavatory there was an intermediate zone which you were never to enter because it was labeled fuck. You might diddle and piddle, but you might not fuck. The light was never completely shut off, the sun never streamed in. Always just light or dark enough to distinguish a bat. And just that little eerie flicker of light was what kept the mind alert, on the lookout, as it were, for bags, pencils, buttons, keys, et cetera. You couldn't really think because your mind was already engaged. The mind was kept in readiness, like a vacant seat at the theater on which the owner has left his opera hat.

Veronica, as I say, had a talking cunt, which was bad because its sole function seemed to be to talk one out of a fuck. Evelyn, on the other hand, had a laughing cunt. She lived upstairs too, only in another house. She was always trotting in at mealtimes to tell us a new joke. A comedienne of the first water, the only really funny woman I ever met in my life. Everything was a joke, fuck included. She could even make a stiff prick laugh, which is saying a good deal. They say a stiff prick has no conscience, but a stiff prick that laughs too is phenomenal. The only way I can describe it is to say that when she got hot and bothered, Evelyn, she put on a ventriloqual act with her cunt. You'd be ready to slip it in when suddenly the dummy between her legs would let out a guffaw. At the same time it would reach out for you and give you a playful little tug and squeeze. It could sing too, this dummy of a cunt. In fact it behaved just like a trained seal.

Nothing is more difficult than to make love in a circus. Putting on the trained seal act all the time made her more inaccessible than if she had been trussed up with iron thongs. She could break down the most "personal" hard on in the world. Break it down with laughter. At the same time it wasn't quite as humiliating as one might be inclined to imagine. There was something sympathetic about this vaginal laughter. The whole world seemed to unroll like a pornographic film whose tragic theme is impotence. You could visualize yourself as a dog, or a weasel, or a white rabbit. Love was something on the side, a dish of caviar, say, or a wax heliotrope. You could see the ventriloquist in you talking about caviar or heliotropes, but the real person was always a weasel or a white rabbit. Evelyn was always lying in the cabbage patch with legs spread open offering a bright green leaf to the first comer. But if you made a move to nibble it the whole cabbage patch would explode with laughter, a bright, dewy, vaginal laughter such as Jesus H. Christ and Immanuel Pussyfoot Kant never dreamed of, because if they had the world would not be what it is today and besides there would have been no Kant and no Christ Almighty. The female seldom laughs, but when she does it's volcanic. When the female laughs the male had better scoot to the cyclone cellar. Nothing will stand up under that vaginating chortle, not even ferroconcrete. The female, when her risibility is once aroused, can laugh down the hyena or the jackal or the wildcat. Now and then one hears it at a lynching bee, for example. It means that the lid is off, that everything goes. It means that she will forage for herself—and watch out that you don't get your balls cut off! It means that if the pest is coming SHE is coming first, and with huge spiked thongs that will flay the living hide off you. It means that she will lay not only with Tom, Dick and Harry, but with Cholera, Meningitis, Leprosy; it means that she will lay herself down on the altar like a mare in rut and take on all comers, including the Holy Ghost. It means that what it took the poor male, with his logarithmic cunning, five thousand, ten thousand, twenty thousand years to build, she will pull down in a night. She will pull it down and pee on it, and nobody will stop her once she starts laughing in earnest. And when I said about Veronica that her laugh would break down the most "personal" hard on imaginable I meant it: she would break down the *personal* erection and hand you back an impersonal one that was like a red-hot ramrod. You might not get very far with Veronica herself, but with what she had to give you could travel far and no mistake about it. Once you came within earshot of her it was like you had gotten an overdose of Spanish fly. Nothing on earth could bring it down again, unless you put it under a sledge-hammer.

It was going on this way all the time, even though every word I say is a lie. It was a personal tour in the impersonal world, a man with a tiny trowel in his hand digging a tunnel through the earth to get to the other side. The idea was to tunnel through and find at last the Culebra Cut, the *ne plus ultra*, of the honeymoon of flesh. And of course there was no end to the digging. The best I might hope for was to get stuck in the dead center of the earth, where the pressure was strongest and most even all around, and stay stuck there forever. That would give me the feeling of Ixion on the wheel, which is one sort of salvation and not entirely to be sneezed at. On the other hand I was a metaphysician of the instinctivist sort: it was impossible for me to stay stuck anywhere, even in the dead center of the earth. It was most imperative to find and to enjoy the metaphysical fuck, and for that I would be obliged to come out on to a wholly new table-land, a mesa of sweet alfalfa and polished monoliths, where the eagles and the vultures flew at random.

Sometimes sitting in the park of an evening, especially a park littered with papers and bits of food, I would see one pass by, one that seemed to be going toward Tibet, and I would follow her with the round eye, hoping that suddenly she would begin to fly, for if she did that, if she would begin to fly, I knew I would be able to fly also, and that would mean an end to the digging and

the wallowing. Sometimes, probably because of twilight
or other disturbances, it seemed as though she actually
did fly on rounding a corner. That is, she would suddenly
be lifted from the ground for the space of a few feet, like
a plane too heavily loaded; but just that sudden involun-
tary lift, whether real or imaginary it didn't matter, gave
me hope, gave me courage to keep the still round eye
riveted on the spot.

There were megaphones inside which yelled "Go on,
keep going, stick it out," and all that nonsense. But why?
To what end? Whither? Whence? I would set the alarm
clock in order to be up and about at a certain hour, *but
why up and about?* Why get up at all? With that little
trowel in my hand I was working like a galley slave
and not the slightest hope of reward involved. Were I to
continue straight on I would dig the deepest hole any
man had ever dug. On the other hand, if I had truly
wanted to get to the other side of the earth, wouldn't it
have been much simpler to throw away the trowel and
just board an airplane for China? But the body follows
after the mind. The simplest thing for the body is not always easy for the mind. And when it gets particularly
difficult and embarrassing is that moment when the two
start going in opposite directions.

Laboring with the trowel was bliss: it left the mind
completely free and yet there was never the slightest
danger of the two being separated. If the she-animal
suddenly began groaning with pleasure, if the she-animal
suddenly began to throw a pleasurable conniption fit, the
jaws moving like old shoelaces, the chest wheezing and
the ribs creaking, if the she-bugger suddenly started to
fall apart on the floor, to the collapse of joy and over-
exasperation, just at the moment, not a second this side
or that, the promised tableland would heave in sight like
a ship coming up out of a fog and there would be nothing
to do but plant the stars and stripes on it and claim it in
the name of Uncle Sam and all that's holy. These mis-
adventures happened so frequently that it was impossible

not to believe in the reality of a realm which was called Fuck, because that was the only name which might be given to it, and yet it was more than fuck and by fucking one only began to approach it. Everybody had at one time or another planted the flag in this territory, and yet nobody was able to lay claim to it permanently. It disappeared overnight—sometimes in the twinkling of an eye. It was No Man's Land and it stank with the litter of invisible deaths. If a truce were declared you met in this terrain and shook hands or swapped tobacco. But the truces never lasted very long. The only thing that seemed to have permanency was the "zone between" idea. Here the bullets flew and the corpses piled up; then it would rain and finally there would be nothing left but a stench.

This is all a figurative way of speaking about what is unmentionable. What is unmentionable is pure fuck and pure cunt: it must be mentioned only in de luxe editions, otherwise the world will fall apart. What holds the world together, as I have learned from bitter experience, is sexual intercourse. But *fuck*, the real thing, *cunt*, the real thing, seems to contain some unidentified element which is far more dangerous than nitroglycerin. To get an idea of the real thing you must consult a Sears Roebuck catalogue endorsed by the Anglican Church. On page twenty-three you will find a picture of Priapus juggling a corkscrew on the end of his weeny; he is standing in the shadow of the Parthenon by mistake; he is naked except for a perforated jock-strap which was loaned for the occasion by the Holy Rollers of Oregon and Saskatchewan. Long distance is on the wire demanding to know if they should sell short or long. He says *go fuck yourself* and hangs up the receiver. In the background Rembrandt is studying the anatomy of our Lord Jesus Christ who, if you remember, was crucified by the Jews and then taken to Abyssinia to be pounded with quoits and other objects. The weather seems to be fair and warmer, as usual, except for a slight mist rising up out of the Ionian; this is the sweat of Neptune's balls which were castrated by the early monks, or perhaps it was by the Manicheans in the time of the Pentecostal plague. Long strips of horsemeat are hanging out to dry and the flies are everywhere, just as Homer describes it in ancient times. Hard by is a McCormick threshing machine, a reaper and binder with a thirty-six horsepower engine and no cutout. The harvest is in and the workers are counting their wages in the distant fields. This is the flush of dawn on the first day of sexual intercourse in the old Hellenistic world, now faithfully reproduced for us in color thanks to the Zeiss Brothers and other patient zealots of industry. But this is not the way it looked to the men of Homer's time who were on the spot. Nobody knows how the god Priapus looked when he was reduced to the ignominy of balancing a corkscrew on the end of his weeny. Standing that way in the shadow of the Parthenon he undoubtedly fell a-dreaming of far-off cunt; he must have lost consciousness of the corkscrew and the threshing and reaping machine; he must have grown very silent within himself and finally he must have lost even the desire to dream. It is my idea, and of course I am willing to be corrected if I am wrong, that standing thus in the rising mist he suddenly heard the Angelus peal and lo and behold there appeared before his very eyes a gorgeous green marshland in which the Choctaws were making merry with the Navajos; in the air above were the white condors, their ruffs festooned with marigolds. He saw also a huge slate on which was written the body of Christ, the body of Absalom and the evil which is lust. He saw the sponge soaked with frogs' blood, the eyes which Augustine had sewn into his skin, the vest which was not big enough to cover our iniquities. He saw these things in the whilomst moment when the Navajos were making merry with the Choctaws and he was so taken by surprise that suddenly a voice issued from between his legs, from the long thinking reed which he had lost in dreaming, and it was the most inspired, the most shrill and piercing, the most jubilant and ferocious cachinnating sort of voice that had ever wongled up from the depths. He began to sing through that long cock of his with such divine grace and elegance that the white condors came down out of the sky and shat huge purple eggs all over the green marshland. Our Lord Christ got up from his stone bed and, marked by the quoit though he was, he danced like a mountain goat. The fellaheen came out of Egypt in their chains, followed by the war-like Igorots and the snail-eating men of Zanzibar.

This is how things stood on the first day of sexual inter-course in the old Hellenistic world. Since then things have changed a great deal. It is no longer polite to sing through your weeny, nor is it permitted even to condors to shit purple eggs all over the place. All this is scato-logical, eschatological and ecumenical. It is forbidden. *Verboten.* And so the Land of Fuck becomes ever more re-ceding: it becomes mythological. Therefore am I con-strained to speak mythologically. I speak with extreme unction, and with precious unguents too. I put away the clashing cymbals, the tubas, the white marigolds, the ole-anders and the rhododendrons. Up with the thorns and the manacles! Christ is dead and mangled with quoits. The fellaheen are bleaching in the sands of Egypt, their wrists loosely shackled. The vultures have eaten away every de-composing crumb of flesh. All is quiet, a million golden mice nibbling at the unseen cheese. The moon is up and the Nile ruminates on her riparian ravages. The earth belches silently, the stars twitch and bleat, the rivers slip their banks. It's like this. . . . There are cunts which laugh and cunts which talk; there are crazy, hysterical cunts shaped like ocarinas and there are planturous, seismo-graphic cunts which register the rise and fall of sap; there are cannibalistic cunts which open wide like the jaws of the whale and swallow alive; there are also masochistic cunts which close up like the oyster and have hard shells and perhaps a pearl or two inside; there are dithyrambic cunts which dance at the very approach of the penis and go wet all over in ecstasy; there are the porcupine cunts which unleash their quills and wave little flags at Christmas time; there are telegraphic cunts which practice the Morse code and leave the mind full of dots and dashes; there are the political cunts which are saturated with ideology and which deny even the menopause; there are vegetative cunts which make no response unless you pull them up by the roots; there are the religious cunts which smell like Seventh Day Adventists and are full of beads, worms, clamshells, sheep droppings and now and then dried bread crumbs; there are the mammalian cunts which are lined with otter skin and hibernate during the long winter; there are cruising cunts fitted out like yachts, which are good for solitaries and epileptics; there are glacial cunts in which you can drop shooting stars without causing a flicker; there are miscellaneous cunts which defy category or description, which you stumble on once in a lifetime and which leave you seared and branded; there are cunts made of pure joy which have neither name nor antecedent and these are the best of all, but whither have they flown?

And then there is the one cunt which is all, and this we shall call the super-cunt, since it is not of this land at all but of that bright country to which we were long ago invited to fly. Here the dew is ever sparkling and the tall reeds bend with the wind. It is here that the great father of fornication dwells, Father Apis, the mantic bull who gored his way to heaven and dethroned the gelded deities of right and wrong. From Apis sprang the race of unicorns, that ridiculous beast of ancient writ whose learned brow lengthened into a gleaming phallus, and from the unicorn by gradual stages was derived the late-city man of which Oswald Spengler speaks. And from the dead cock of this sad specimen arose the giant skyscraper with its express elevators and observation towers. We are the last decimal point of sexual calculation; the world turns like a rotten egg in its crate of straw. Now for the aluminum wings with which to fly to that far-off place, the bright country where Apis, the father of fornication, dwells. Everything goes forward like oiled clocks; for each minute of the dial there are a million noiseless clocks which tick off the rinds of time. We are traveling faster than the lightning calculator, faster than starlight, faster than the magician can think. Each second is a universe of time. And each universe of time is but a wink of sleep in the cosmogony of speed. When speed comes to its end we shall be there, punctual as always and blissfully undenominated. We shall shed our wings, our clocks and our mantelpieces to lean on. We will rise up feathery and jubilant, like a column of blood, and there will be no memory to drag us down again. This time I call the realm of the super-cunt, for it defies speed, calculation or imagery. Nor has the penis itself a known size or weight. There is only the sustained feel of fuck, the fugitive in full flight, the nightmare smoking his quiet cigar. Little Nemo walks around with a seven-day hard on and a wonderful pair of blue balls bequeathed by Lady Bountiful. It is Sunday morning around the corner from Evergreen Cemetery.

It is Sunday morning and I am lying blissfully dead to the world on my bed of ferroconcrete. Around the corner is the cemetery, which is to say—the *world of sexual intercourse*. My balls ache with the fucking that is going on, but it is all going on beneath my window, on the boulevard where Hymie keeps his copulating nest. I am thinking of one woman and the rest is blotto. I say I am thinking of her, but the truth is I am dying a stellar death. I am lying there like a sick star waiting for the light to go out. Years ago I lay on this same bed and I waited and waited to be born. Nothing happened. Except that my mother, in her Lutheran rage, threw a bucket of water over me. My mother, poor imbecile that she was, thought I was lazy. She didn't know that I had gotten caught in the stellar drift, that I was being pulverized to a black extinction out there on the farthest rim of the universe. She thought it was sheer laziness that kept me riveted to the bed. She threw the bucket of water over me: I squirmed and shivered a bit, but I continued to lie there on my

ferroconcrete bed. I was immovable. I was a burned-out
meteor adrift somewhere in the neighborhood of Vega.

And now I'm on the same bed and the light that's in
me refuses to be extinguished. The world of men and
women are making merry in the cemetery grounds. They
are having sexual intercourse, God bless them, and I am
alone in the Land of Fuck. It seems to me that I hear the
clanking of a great machine, the linotype bracelets passing
through the wringer of sex. Hymie and his nymphomaniac of a wife are lying on the same level with me,
only they are across the river. The river is called Death
and it has a bitter taste. I have waded through it many
times, up to the hips, but somehow I have neither been
petrified nor immortalized. I am still burning brightly
inside, though outwardly dead as a planet. From this
bed I have gotten up to dance, not once but hundreds,
thousands of times. Each time I came away I had the
conviction that I had danced the skeleton dance on a
terrain vague. Perhaps I had wasted too much of my substance on suffering; perhaps I had the crazy idea that I
would be the first metallurgical bloom of the human
species; perhaps I was imbued with the notion that I was
both a sub-gorilla and a super-god. On this bed of ferroconcrete I remember everything and everything is in rock
crystal. There are never any animals, only thousands and
thousands of human beings all talking at once, and for
each word they utter I have an answer immediately, sometimes before the word is out of their mouths. There is
plenty of killing, but no blood. The murders are perpe-
trated with cleanliness, and always in silence. But even
if everyone were killed there would still be conversation,
and the conversation would be at once intricate and easy
to follow. Because it is I who create it! I know it, and
that is why it never drives me mad. I have conversations
which may take place only twenty years hence, when I
meet the right person, the one whom I shall create, let
us say, when the proper time comes. All these talks take
place in a vacant lot which is attached to my bed like a

mattress. Once I gave it a name, this *terrain vague*: I called it Ubiguchi, but somehow Ubiguchi never satisfied me, it was too intelligible, too full of meaning. It would be better to keep it just *terrain vague*, which is what I intend to do. People think that vacuity is nothingness, but it is not so. Vacuity is a discordant fullness, a crowded ghostly world in which the soul goes reconnoitering. As a boy I remember standing in the vacant lot as if I were a very lively soul standing naked in a pair of shoes. The body had been stolen from me because I had no particular need of it. I could exist with or without a body then. If I killed a little bird and roasted it over the fire and ate it, it was not because I was hungry but because I wanted to know about Timbuktu or Tierra del Fuego. I had to stand in the vacant lot and eat dead birds in order to create a desire for that bright land which later I would inhabit alone and people with nostalgia. I expected ultimate things of this place, but I was deplorably deceived. I went as far as one could go in a state of complete deadness, and then by a law, which must be the law of creation, I suppose, I suddenly flared up and began to live inexhaustibly, like a star whose light is unquenchable. Here began the real cannibalistic excursions which have meant so much to me: no more dead chippies picked from the bonfire, but live human meat, tender, succulent human flesh, secrets like fresh bloody livers, confidences like swollen tumors that have been kept on ice. I learned not to wait for my victim to die, but to eat into him while he was talking to me. Often when I walked away from an unfinished meal I discovered that it was nothing more than an old friend minus an arm or a leg. I sometimes left him standing there—a trunk full of stinking intestines.

Being of the city, of the only city in the world and no place like Broadway anywhere, I used to walk up and down staring at the floodlit hams and other delicacies. I was a schizerino from the sole of my boots to the tips of my hair. I lived exclusively in the gerundive, which I understood only in Latin. Long before I had read of her in the

Black Book I was cohabiting with Hilda, the giant cauli-
flower of my dreams. We traversed all the morganatic diseases together and a few which were *ex cathedra*. We
dwelt in the carcass of the instincts and were nourished by
ganglionic memories. There was never *a* universe, but millions and billions of universes, all of them put together no
bigger than a pinhead. It was a vegetal sleep in the wilderness of the mind. It was the past, which alone comprises
eternity. Amidst the fauna and flora of my dreams I would
hear long distance calling. Messages were dropped on
my table by the deformed and the epileptic. Hans Castorp
would call sometimes and together we would commit
innocent crimes. Or, if it were a bright freezing day, I
would do a turn in the velodrome with my Presto bike
from Chemnitz, Bohemia.

Best of all was the skeleton dance. I would first wash all
my parts at the sink, change my linen, shave, powder,
comb my hair, don my dancing pumps. Feeling abnor-
mally light inside and out I would wind in and out of the
crowd for a time to get the proper human rhythm, the
weight and substance of flesh. Then I would make a bee-
line for the dance floor, grab a hunk of giddy flesh and
begin the autumnal pirouette. It was like that I walked
into the hairy Greek's place one night and ran smack into
her. She seemed blue-black, white as chalk, ageless. There
was not just the flow to and from, but the endless chute,
the voluptuousness of intrinsic restlessness. She was
mercurial and at the same time of a savory weight. She
had the marmoreal stare of a faun embedded in lava. The
time has come, I thought, to wander back from the periphery. I made a move toward the center, only to find the
ground shifting from under my feet. The earth slid rapidly
beneath my bewildered feet. I moved again out of the
earth belt and behold, my hands were full of meteoric
flowers. I reached for her with two flaming hands but she
was more elusive than sand. I thought of my favorite
nightmares, but she was unlike anything which had made
me sweat and gibber. In my delirium I began to prance

and neigh. I bought frogs and mated them with toads. I thought of the easiest thing to do, which is to die, but I did nothing. I stood still and began to petrify at the extremities. That was so wonderful, so healing, so eminently sensible, that I began to laugh way down inside the viscera, like a hyena crazed with rut. Maybe I would turn into a rosetta stone! I just stood still and waited. Spring came, and fall, and then winter. I renewed my insurance policy automatically. I ate grass and the roots of deciduous trees. I sat for days on end looking at the same film. Now and then I brushed my teeth. If you fired an automatic at me the bullets glanced off and made a queer tat-a-tat ricocheting against the walls. Once up a dark street, felled by a thug, I felt a knife go clean through me. It felt like a spritz bath. Strange to say, the knife left no holes in my skin. The experience was so novel that I went home and stuck knives into all parts of my body. More needle baths. I sat down, pulled all the knives out, and again I marveled that there was no trace of blood, no holes, no pain. I was just about to bite into my arm when the telephone rang. It was long distance calling. I never knew who put in the calls because no one ever came to the phone. However, the skeleton dance. . . .

Life is drifting by the show window. I lie there like a floodlit ham waiting for the ax to fall. As a matter of fact, there is nothing to fear, because everything is cut neatly into fine little slices and wrapped in cellophane. Suddenly all the lights of the city are extinguished and the sirens sound their warning. The city is enveloped in poison gas, bombs are bursting, mangled bodies flying through the air. There is electricity everywhere, and blood and splinters and loudspeakers. The men in the air are full of glee; those below are screaming and bellowing. When the gas and the flames have eaten all the flesh away the skeleton dance begins. I watch from the show window which is now dark. It is better than the sack of Rome because there is more to destroy.

Why do the skeletons dance so ecstatically, I wonder.

Is it the fall of the world? Is it the dance of death which has been so often heralded? To see millions of skeletons dancing in the snow while the city founders is an awesome sight. Will anything ever grow again? Will babes come out of the womb? Will there be food and wine? There are men in the air, to be sure. They will come down to plunder. There will be cholera and dysentery and those who were above and triumphant will perish like the rest. I have the sure feeling that I will be the last man on earth. I will emerge from the show window when it is all over and walk calmly amidst the ruins. I will have the whole earth to myself.

Long distance calling! To inform me that I am not utterly alone. Then the destruction was not complete? It's discouraging. Man is not even able to destroy himself; he can only destroy others. I am disgusted. What a malicious cripple! What cruel delusions! So there are more of the species about and they will tidy up the mess and begin again. God will come down again in flesh and blood and take up the burden of guilt. They will make music and build things in stone and write it all down in little books. Pfui! What blind tenacity, what clumsy ambitions!

I am on the bed again. The old Greek world, the dawn of sexual intercourse—and Hymie! Hymie Laubscher always on the same level, looking down on the boulevard across the river. There is a lull in the nuptial feast and the clam fritters are brought in. *Move over just a little*, he says. *There, like that, that's it!* I hear frogs croaking in the swamp outside my window. Big cemetery frogs nourished by the dead. They are all huddled together in sexual intercourse; they are croaking with sexual glee.

I realize now how Hymie was conceived and brought into being. Hymie the bullfrog! His mother was at the bottom of the pack and Hymie, then an embryo, was hidden away in her sac. It was in the early days of sexual intercourse and there were no Marquis of Queensbury rules to hinder. It was fuck and be fucked—and the devil take the hindmost. It has been that way ever since the

Greeks—a blind fuck in the mud and then a quick spawn and then death. People are fucking on different levels but it's always in a swamp and the litter is always destined for the same end. When the house is torn down the bed is left standing: the cosmosexual altar.

I was polluting the bed with dreams. Stretched out taut on the ferroconcrete my soul would leave its body and roam from place to place on a little trolley such as is used in department stores for making change. I made ideological changes and excursions; I was a vagabond in the country of the brain. Everything was absolutely clear to me because done in rock crystal; at every egress there was written in big letters ANNIHILATION. The fright of extinction solidified me; the body became itself a piece of ferroconcrete. It was ornamented by a permanent erection in the best taste. I had achieved that state of vacuity so earnestly desired by certain devout members of esoteric cults. I was no more. *I was not even a personal hard on.*

It was about this time, adopting the pseudonym Samson Lackawanna, that I began my depredations. The criminal instinct in me had gotten the upper hand. Whereas heretofore I had been only an errant soul, a sort of Gentile Dybbuk, now I became a flesh-filled ghost. I had taken the name which pleased me and I had only to act instinctively. In Hong Kong, for instance, I made my entry as a book agent. I carried a leather purse filled with Mexican dollars and I visited religiously all those Chinese who were in need of further education. At the hotel I rang for women like you would ring for whisky and soda. Mornings I studied Tibetan in order to prepare for the journey to Lhasa. I already spoke Yiddish fluently, and Hebrew too. I could count two rows of figures at once. It was so easy to swindle the Chinese that I went back to Manila in disgust. There I took a Mr. Rico in hand and taught him the art of selling books with no handling charges. All the profit came from ocean freight rates, but it was sufficient to keep me in luxury while it lasted.

The breath had become as much a trick as breathing. Things were not dual merely, but multiple. I had became a cage of mirrors reflecting vacuity. But vacuity once stoutly posited I was at home and what is called creation was merely a job of filling up holes. The trolley conveniently carried me about from place to place and in each little side pocket of the great vacuum I dropped a ton of poems to wipe out the idea of annihilation. I had ever before me boundless vistas. I began to live in the vista, like a microscopic speck on the lens of a giant telescope. There was no night in which to rest. It was perpetual starlight on the arid surface of dead planets. Now and then a lake black as marble in which I saw myself walking amidst brilliant orbs of light. So low hung the stars and so dazzling was the light they shed, that it seemed as if the universe were only about to be born. What rendered the impression stronger was that I was alone; not only were there no animals, no trees, no other beings, but there was not even a blade of grass, not even a dead root. In that violet incandescent light without even the suggestion of a shadow, motion itself seemed to be absent. It was like a blaze of pure consciousness, thought become God. And God, for the first time in my knowledge, was clean-shaven. I was also clean-shaven, flawless, deadly accurate. I saw my image in the marble black lakes and it was diapered with stars. Stars, stars . . . like a clout between the eyes and all remembrance fast run out. I was Samson and I was Lackawanna and I was dying as one being in the ecstasy of full consciousness.

And now here I am, sailing down the river in my little canoe. Anything you would like to have me do I will do for you—gratis. This is the Land of Fuck, in which there are no animals, no trees, no stars, no problems. Here the spermatazoon reigns supreme. Nothing is determined in advance, the future is absolutely uncertain, the past is non-existent. For every million born 999,999 are doomed to die and never again be born. But the one that makes a home run is assured of life eternal. Life is squeezed into a seed, which is a soul. Everything has soul, including minerals, plants, lakes, mountains, rocks. Everything is sentient, even at the lowest stage of consciousness.

Once this fact is grasped there can be no more despair. At the very bottom of the ladder, *chez* the spermatozoa, there is the same condition of bliss as at the top, *chez* God. God is the summation of all the spermatozoa come to full consciousness. Between the bottom and the top there is no stop, no halfway station. The river starts somewhere in the mountains and flows on into the sea. On this river that leads to God the canoe is as serviceable as the dreadnought. From the very start the journey is homeward.

Sailing down the river. . . . Slow as the hookworm, but tiny enough to make every bend. And slippery as an eel withal. What is your name? shouts someone. *My name? Why just call me God—God the embryo.* I go sailing on. Somebody would like to buy me a hat. What size do you wear, imbecile! he shouts. *What size? Why size X!* (And why do they always shout at me? Am I supposed to be deaf?) The hat is lost at the next cataract. *Tant pis*—for the hat. Does God need a hat? God needs only to become God, more and more God. All this voyaging, all these pitfalls, the time that passes, the scenery, and against the scenery *man*, trillions and trillions of things called man, like mustard seeds. Even in embryo God has no memory. The backdrop of consciousness is made up of infinitesimally minute ganglia, a coat of hair soft as wool. The mountain goat stands alone amidst the Himalayas; he doesn't question how he got to the summit. He grazes quietly amidst the *décor;* when the time comes he will travel down again. He keeps his muzzle to the ground, grubbing for the sparse nourishment which the mountain peaks afford. In this strange Capricornian condition of embryosis God the he-goat ruminates in stolid bliss among the mountain peaks. The high altitudes nourish the germ of separation which will one day estrange him completely from the soul of man, which will make him a desolate, rocklike father dwelling forever apart in a void which is unthinkable. But first come the morganatic diseases, of which we must now speak. . . .

There is a condition of misery which is irremediable—because its origin is lost in obscurity. Bloomingdale's, for example, can bring about this condition. All department stores are symbols of sickness and emptiness, but Bloomingdale's is my special sickness, my incurable obscure malady. In the chaos of Bloomingdale's there is an order, but this order is absolutely crazy to me: it is the order which I would find on the head of a pin if I were to put it under the miscroscope. It is the order of an accidental series of accidents accidentally conceived. This order has, above all, an odor—and it is the odor of Bloomingdale's which strikes terror into my heart. In Bloomingdale's I fall apart completely: I dribble onto the floor, a helpless mess of guts and bones and cartilage. There is the smell, not of decomposition, but of misalliance. Man, the miserable alchemist, has welded together, in a million forms and shapes, substances and essences which have nothing in common. Because in his mind there is a tumor which is eating him away insatiably; he has left the little canoe which was taking him blissfully down the river in order to construct a bigger, safer boat in which there may be room for everyone. His labors take him so far afield that he has lost all remembrance of why he left the little canoe. The ark is so full of bric-à-brac that it has become a stationary building above a subway in which the smell of linoleum prevails and predominates. Gather together all the significance hidden away in the interstitial miscellany of Bloomingdale's and put it on the head of a pin and you will have left a universe in which the grand constellations move without the slightest danger of collision. It is this microscopic chaos which brings on my morganatic ailments. In the street I began to stab horses at random, or I lift a skirt here and there looking for a letter box, or I put a postage stamp across a mouth, an eye, a vagina. Or

I suddenly decide to climb a tall building, like a fly, and once having reached the roof I do fly with real wings and I fly and fly and fly, covering towns like Weehawken, Hoboken, Hackensack, Canarsie, Bergen Beach in the twinkling of an eye. Once you become a real schizerino flying is the easiest thing in the world; the trick is to fly with the etheric body, to leave behind in Bloomingdale's your sack of bones, guts, blood and cartilage; to fly only with your immutable self which, if you stop a moment to reflect, is always equipped with wings. Flying this way, in full daylight, has advantages over the ordinary night-flying which everybody indulges in. You can leave off from moment to moment, as quick and decisive as stepping on a brake; there is no difficulty in finding your other self, because the moment you leave off you *are* your other self, which is to say, the so-called whole self. Only, as the Bloomingdale experience goes to prove, this whole self, about which so much boasting has been done, falls apart very easily. The smell of linoleum, for some strange reason, will always make me fall apart and collapse on the floor. It is the smell of all the unnatural things which were glued together in me, which were assembled, so to say, by negative consent.

It is only after the third meal that the morning gifts, bequeathed by the phony alliance of the ancestors, begin to drop away and the true rock of the self, the happy rock sheers up out of the muck of the soul. With nightfall the pinhead universe begins to expand. It expands organically, from an infinitesimal nuclear speck, in the way that minerals or star clusters form. It eats into the surrounding chaos like a rat boring through store cheese. All chaos could be gathered together on a pinhead, but the self, microscopical at the start, works up to a universe from any point in space. This is not the self about which books are written, but the ageless self which has been farmed out through millenary ages to men with names and dates, the self which begins and ends as a worm, which *is* the worm in the cheese called the world. Just as the slightest

breeze can set a vast forest in motion so, by some unfathomable impulse from within, the rocklike self can
begin to grow, and in this growth nothing can prevail
against it. It's like Jack Frost at work, and the whole
world a windowpane. No hint of labor, no sound, no
struggle, no rest; relentless, remorseless, unremitting, the
growth of the self goes on. Only two items on the bill of
fare: the self and the not-self. And an eternity in which to
work it out. In this eternity, which has nothing to do with
time or space, there are interludes in which something like
a thaw sets in. The form of the self breaks down, but the
self, like climate, remains. In the night the amorphous
matter of the self assumes the most fugitive forms; error
seeps in through the portholes and the wanderer is un-
latched from his door. This door which the body wears,
if opened out onto the world, leads to annihilation. It is
the door in every fable out of which the magician steps;
nobody has ever read of him returning home through the
selfsame door. If opened inward there are infinite doors,
all resembling trapdoors: no horizons are visible, no air-
lines, no rivers, no maps, no tickets. Each *couche* is a
halt for the night only, be it five minutes or ten thousand
years. The doors have no handles and they never wear
out. Most important to note—there is no end in sight.
All these halts for the night, so to speak, are like abortive
explorations of a myth. One can feel his way about, take
bearings, observe passing phenomena; one can even feel
at home. But there is no taking root. Just at the moment
when one begins to feel "established" the whole terrain
founders, the soil underfoot is afloat, the constellations
are shaken loose from their moorings, the whole known
universe, including the imperishable self, starts moving
silently, ominously, shudderingly serene and unconcerned,
toward an unknown, unseen destination. All the doors
seem to be opening at once; the pressure is so great that
an implosion occurs and in the swift plunge the skeleton
bursts asunder. It was some such gigantic collapse which
Dante must have experienced when he situated himself in

Hell; it was not a bottom which he touched, but a core, a dead center from which time itself is reckoned. Here the comedy begins, from here it is seen to be divine.

All this by way of saying that in going through the revolving door of the Amarillo Dance Hall one night, some twelve or fourteen years ago, the great event took place. The interlude which I think of as the Land of Fuck, a realm of time more than of space, is for me the equivalent of that Purgatory which Dante has described in nice detail. As I put my hand on the brass rail of the revolving door to leave the Amarillo Dance Hall, all that I had previously been, was, and about to be foundered. There was nothing unreal about it; the very time in which I was born passed away, carried off by a mightier stream. Just as I had previously been bundled out of the womb, so now I was shunted back to some timeless vector where the process of growth is kept in abeyance. I passed into the world of effects. There was no fear, only a feeling of fatality. My spine was socketed to the node; I was up against the coccyx of an implacable new world. In the plunge the skeleton blew apart, leaving the immutable ego as helpless as a squashed louse.

If from this point I do not begin, it is because there is no beginning. If I do not fly at once to the bright land it is because wings are of no avail. It is zero hour and the moon is at nadir. . . .

Why I think of Maxie Schnadig I don't know, unless it is because of Dostoevski. The night I sat down to read Dostoevski for the first time was a most important event in my life, even more important than my first love. It was the first deliberate, conscious act which had significance for me; it changed the whole face of the world. Whether it is true that the clock stopped that moment when I looked up after the first deep gulp I don't know any more. But the world stopped dead for a moment, that I know. It was my first glimpse into the soul of a man, or shall I say simply that Dostoevski was the first man to reveal his soul to me? Maybe I had been a bit queer before that, without realizing it, but from the moment that I dipped into Dostoevski I was definitely, irrevocably, contentedly queer. The ordinary, waking, workaday world was finished for me. Any ambition or desire I had to write was also killed—for a long time to come. I was like those men who have been too long in the trenches, too long under fire. Ordinary human suffering, ordinary human jealousy, ordinary human ambitions—it was just so much shit to me.

I can visualize best my condition when I think of my relations with Maxie and his sister Rita. At the time Maxie and I used to go swimming together a great deal, that I remember well. Often we passed the whole day and night at the beach. I had only met Maxie's sister once or twice; whenever I brought up her name Maxie would rather frantically begin to talk about something else. That annoyed me because I was really bored to death with Maxie's company, tolerating him only because he loaned me money readily and bought me things which I needed. Every time we started for the beach I was in hopes his sister would turn up unexpectedly. But no, he always managed to keep her out of reach. Well, one day as we were undressing in the bathhouse and he was showing me what a fine tight scrotum he had, I said to him right out of the blue—"Listen, Maxie, that's all right about your nuts, they're fine and dandy, and there's nothing to worry about but where in hell is Rita all the time, why don't you bring her along some time and let me take a good look at her quim . . . yes, *quim*, you know what I mean." Maxie, being a Jew from Odessa, had never heard the word quim before. He was deeply shocked by my words and yet at the same time intrigued by this new word. In a sort of daze he said to me— "Jesus, Henry, you oughtn't to say a thing like that to me!" "Why not?" I answered. "She's got a cunt, your sister, hasn't she?" I was about to add something else when he broke into a terrific fit of laughter. That saved the situation, for the time being. But Maxie didn't like the idea at all deep down. All day long it bothered him, though he never referred to our conversation again. No, he was very silent that day. The only form of revenge he could think of was to urge me to swim far beyond the safety zone in the hope of tiring me out and letting me drown. I could see so clearly what was in his mind that I was possessed with the strength of ten men. Damned if I would go drown myself just because his sister like all other women happened to have a cunt.

It was at Far Rockaway where this took place. After we had dressed and eaten a meal I suddenly decided that I wanted to be alone and so, very abruptly, at the corner of a street, I shook hands and said good-by. And there I was! Almost instantaneously I felt alone in the world, alone as one feels only in moments of extreme anguish. I think I was picking my teeth absentmindedly when this wave of loneliness hit me full on, like a tornado. I stood there on the street corner and sort of felt myself all over to see if I had been hit by something. It was inexplicable, and at the same time it was very wonderful, very exhilarating, like a double tonic, I might say. When I say that I was at Far Rockaway I mean that I was standing at the end of the earth, at a place called Xanthos, if there be such a place, and surely there ought to be a word like this to express no place at all. If Rita had come along then I don't think I would have recognized her. I had become an absolute stranger standing in the very midst of my own people. They looked crazy to me, my people, with their newly sunburned faces and their flannel trousers and their clockwork stockings. They had been bathing like myself because it was a pleasant, healthy recreation and now like myself they were full of sun and food and a little heavy with fatigue. Up until this loneliness hit me I too was a bit weary, but suddenly, standing there completely shut off from the world, I woke up with a start. I became so electrified that I didn't dare move for fear I would charge like a bull or start to climb the wall of a building or else dance and scream. Suddenly I realized that all this was because I was really a brother to Dostoevski, that perhaps I was the only man in all America who knew what he meant in writing those books. Not only that, but I felt all the books I would one day write myself germinating inside me: they were bursting inside like ripe cocoons. And since up to this time I had written nothing but fiendishly long letters about everything and nothing, it was difficult for me to realize that there must come a time when I should begin, when I should put down the first word, *the first real word*. And this time was now! That was what dawned on me.

I used the word Xanthos a moment ago. I don't know whether there is a Xanthos or not, and I really don't care one way or another, but there must be a place in the world, perhaps in the Grecian islands, where you come to the end of the known world and you are thoroughly alone and yet you are not frightened of it but rejoice, because at this dropping off place you can feel the old ancestral world which is eternally young and new and fecundating. You stand there, wherever the place is, like a newly hatched chick beside its eggshell. This place is Xanthos, or as it happened in my case, Far Rockaway.

There I was! It grew dark, a wind came up, the streets became deserted, and finally it began to pour cats and dogs. Jesus, that finished me! When the rain came down, and I got it smack in the face staring at the sky, I suddenly began to bellow with joy. I laughed and laughed and laughed, exactly like an insane man. Nor did I know what I was laughing about. I wasn't thinking of a thing. I was just overwhelmed with joy, just crazy with delight in finding myself absolutely alone. If then and there a nice juicy quim had been handed me on a platter, if all the quims in the world had been offered me for to make my choice, I wouldn't have batted an eyelash. I had what no quim could give me. And just about at that point, thoroughly drenched but still exultant, I thought of the most irrelevant thing in the world—*carfare!* Jesus, the bastard Maxie had walked off without leaving me a sou. There I was with my fine budding antique world and not a penny in my jeans. Herr Dostoevski Junior had now to begin to walk here and there peering into friendly and unfriendly faces to see if he could pry loose a dime. He walked from one end of Far Rockaway to the other but nobody seemed to give a fuck about handing out carfare in the rain. Walking about in that heavy animal stupor which comes with begging I got to thinking of Maxie the window trimmer and how the first time I spied him he was standing in the show window dressing a mannikin. And from that in a few minutes to Dostoevski, then the world stopped dead, and then, like a great rosebush opening in the night, his sister Rita's warm, velvety flesh.

Now this is what is rather strange. . . . A few minutes after I thought of Rita, her private and extraordinary quim, I was in the train, bound for New York and dozing off with a marvelous languid erection. And stranger still, when I got out of the train, when I had walked but a block or two from the station, whom should I bump into rounding a corner but Rita herself. And as though she had been informed telepathically of what was going on in my brain, Rita too was hot under the whiskers. Soon we were sitting in a chop suey joint, seated side by side in a little booth, behaving exactly like a pair of rabbits in rut. On the dance floor we hardly moved. We were wedged in tightly and we stayed that way, letting them jog and jostle us about as they might. I could have taken her home to my place, as I was alone at the time, but no, I had a notion to bring her back to her own home, stand her up in the vestibule and give her a fuck right under Maxie's nose—which I did. In the midst of it I thought again of the mannikin in the show window and of the way he had laughed that afternoon when I let drop the word quim. I was on the point of laughing aloud when suddenly I felt that she was coming, one of those long drawn out orgasms such as you get now and then in a Jewish cunt. I had my hands under her buttocks, the tips of my fingers just inside her cunt, in the lining, as it were; as she began to shudder I lifted her from the ground and raised her gently up and down on the end of my cock. I thought she would go off her nut completely, the way she began to carry on. She must have had four or five orgasms like that in the air, before I put her feet down on the ground. I took it out without spilling a drop and made her lie down in the vestibule. Her hat had rolled off into a corner and her handbag had spilled open and a few coins had tumbled out. I note this because just before I gave it to her good and proper I made a mental note to pocket a few coins for my carfare home. Anyway, it was only a few hours since I had said to Maxie in the bathhouse that I would like to take a look at his sister's quim, and here it was now smack up against me, sopping wet and throwing out one squirt after another. If she had been fucked before she had never been fucked properly, that's a cinch. And I myself was never in such a fine cool collected scientific frame of mind as now lying on the floor of the vestibule right under Maxie's nose, pumping it into the private, sacred, and extraordinary quim of his sister Rita. I could have held it in indefinitely—it was incredible how detached I was and yet thoroughly aware of every quiver and jolt she made. But somebody had to pay for making me walk around in the rain grubbing a dime. Somebody had to pay for the ecstasy produced by the germination of all those unwritten books inside me. Somebody had to verify the authenticity of this private, concealed cunt which had been plaguing me for weeks and months. Who better qualified than I? I thought so hard and fast between orgasms that my cock must have grown another inch or two. Finally I decided to make an end of it by turning her over and back-scuttling her. She balked a bit at first, but when she felt the thing slipping out of her she nearly went crazy. "Oh yes, oh yes, do it, do it!" she gibbered, and with that I really got excited, I had hardly slipped it into her when I felt it coming, one of those long agonizing spurts from the tip of the spinal column. I shoved it in so deep that I felt as if something had given way. We fell over, exhausted, the both of us, and panted like dogs. At the same time, however, I had the presence of mind to feel around for a few coins. Not that it was necessary, because she had already loaned me a few dollars, but to make up for the carfare which I was lacking in Far Rockaway. Even then, by Jesus, it wasn't finished. Soon I felt her groping about, first with her hands, then with her mouth. I had still a sort of semi hard on. She got it into her mouth and she began to caress it with her tongue. I saw stars. The next thing I knew her feet were around my neck and my tongue up her twat. And then I had to get over her again and shove it in, up to the hilt. She squirmed around like an eel, so help me God. And then she began to come again, long, drawn out, agonizing orgasms, with a whimpering and gibbering that was hallucinating. Finally I had to pull it out and tell her to stop. What a quim! And I had only asked to take a look at it!

Maxie with his talk of Odessa revived something which I had lost as a child. Though I had never a very clear picture of Odessa the aura of it was like the little neighborhood in Brooklyn which meant so much to me and from which I had been torn away too soon. I get a very definite feeling of it every time I see an Italian painting without perspective; if it is a picture of a funeral procession, for example, it is exactly the sort of experience which I knew as a child, one of intense immediacy. If it is a picture of the open street, the women sitting in the windows are sitting *on* the street and not above it and away from it. Everything that happens is known immediately by everybody, just as among primitive people. Murder is in the air, chance rules.

Just as in the Italian primitives this perspective is lacking, so in the little old neighborhood from which I was uprooted as a child there were these parallel vertical planes on which everything took place and through which, from layer to layer, everything was communicated, as if by osmosis. The frontiers were sharp, clearly defined, but they were not impassable. I lived then, as a boy, close to the boundary between the north and the south side. I was just a little bit over on the north side, just a few steps from a broad thoroughfare called North Second Street, which was for me the real boundary line between the north and the south side. The actual boundary was Grand Street, which led to Broadway Ferry, but this street meant nothing to me, except that it was already beginning to be filled with Jews. No, North Second Street was the mystery street, the frontier between two worlds. I was living, therefore, between two boundaries, the one real, the other imaginary—as I have lived all my life. There was a little street, just a block long, which lay between Grand Street and North Second Street, called Fillmore Place. This little street was obliquely opposite the house my grandfather owned and in which we lived. It was the most enchanting street I have ever seen in all my life. It was the ideal street—for a boy, a lover, a maniac, a drunkard, a crook, a lecher, a thug, an astronomer, a musician, a poet, a tailor, a shoemaker, a politician. In fact this was just the sort of street it was, containing just such representatives of the human race, each one a world unto himself and all living together harmoniously and inharmoniously, *but together,* a solid corporation, a close knit human spore which could not disintegrate unless the street itself disintegrated.

So it seemed, at least. Until the Williamsburg Bridge was opened, whereupon there followed the invasion of the Jews from Delancey Street, New York. This brought about the disintegration of our little world, of the little street called Fillmore Place, which like the name itself was a street of value, of dignity, of light, of surprises. The Jews came, as I say, and like moths they began to eat into the fabric of our lives until there was nothing left but this mothlike presence which they brought with them everywhere. Soon the street began to smell bad, soon the real people moved away, soon the houses began to deteriorate and even the stoops fell away, like the paint. Soon the street looked like a dirty mouth with all the prominent teeth missing, with ugly charred stumps gaping here and there, the lips rotting, the palate gone. Soon the garbage was knee deep in the gutter and the fire escapes filled with bloated bedding, with cockroaches, with dried blood. Soon the kosher sign appeared on the shop windows and there was poultry everywhere and lox and sour pickles and enormous loaves of bread. Soon there were baby carriages in every areaway and on the stoops and in the little yards and before the shop fronts. And with the change the English language also disappeared; one heard nothing but Yiddish, nothing but this sputtering, choking, hissing tongue in which God and rotten vegetables sound alike and mean alike.

We were among the first families to move away, following the invasion. Two or three times a year I came back to the old neighborhood, for a birthday or for Christmas or Thanksgiving. With each visit I marked the loss of something I had loved and cherished. It was like a bad dream. It got worse and worse. The house in which my relatives still lived was like an old fortress going to ruin; they were stranded in one of the wings of the fortress, maintaining a forlorn, island life, beginning themselves to look sheepish, hunted, degraded. They even began to make distinctions between their Jewish neighbors, finding some of them quite human, quite decent, clean, kind, sympathetic, charitable, etc. etc. To me it was heartrending. I could have taken a machine gun and mowed the whole neighborhood down, Jew and Gentile together.

It was about the time of the invasion that the authorities decided to change the name of North Second Street to Metropolitan Avenue. This highway, which to the Gentiles had been the road to the cemeteries, now became what is called an artery of traffic, a link between two ghettos. On the New York side the river front was rapidly being transformed owing to the erection of the skyscrapers. On our side, the Brooklyn side, the ware-

houses were piling up and the approaches to the various
new bridges created plazas, comfort stations, poolrooms,
stationery shops, ice-cream parlors, restaurants, clothing
stores, hock shops, etc. In short everything was becoming
metropolitan, in the odious sense of the word.

As long as we lived in the old neighborhood we never
referred to Metropolitan Avenue: it was always North
Second Street, despite the official change of name. Perhaps it was eight or ten years later, when I stood one
winter's day at the corner of the street facing the river
and noticed for the first time the great tower of the
Metropolitan Life Insurance Building, that I realized
that North Second Street was no more. The imaginary
boundary of my world had changed. My glance traveled
now far beyond the cemeteries, far beyond the rivers, far
beyond the city of New York or the State of New York,
beyond the whole United States indeed. At Point Loma,
California, I had looked out upon the broad Pacific and
I had felt something there which kept my face permanently screwed in another direction. I came back to the
old neighborhood, I remember, one night with my old
friend Stanley who had just come out of the army, and
we walked the streets sadly and wistfully. A European
can scarcely know what this feeling is like. Even when
a town becomes modernized, in Europe, there are still
vestiges of the old. In America, though there are vestiges,
they are effaced, wiped out of the consciousness, trampled
upon, obliterated, nullified by the new. The new is, from
day to day, a moth which eats into the fabric of life,
leaving nothing finally but a great hole. Stanley and I,
we were walking through this terrifying hole. Even a war
does not bring this kind of desolation and destruction.
Through war a town may be reduced to ashes and the
entire population wiped out, but what springs up again
resembles the old. Death is fecundating, for the soil as
well as for the spirit. In America the destruction is complete, annihilating. There is no rebirth, only a cancerous

growth, layer upon layer of new, poisonous tissue, each one uglier than the previous one.

We were walking through this enormous hole, as I say, and it was a winter's night. clear, frosty sparkling and as we came through the south side toward the boundary line we saluted all the old relics or the spots where things had once stood and where there had been once something of ourselves. And as we approached North Second Street between Fillmore Place and North Second Street—a distance of only a few yards and yet such a rich, full area of the globe before Mrs. O'Melio's shanty I stopped and looked up at the house where I had known what it was to really have a being. Everything had shrunk now to diminutive proportions, including the world which lay beyond the boundary line, the world which had been so mysterious to me and so terrifyingly grand, so delimited. Standing there in a trance I suddenly recalled a dream which I have had over and over, which I still dream now and then and which I hope to dream as long as I live. It was the dream of passing the boundary line As in all dreams the remarkable thing is the vividness of the reality, the fact that *one is in reality* and not dreaming. Across the line I am unknown and absolutely alone Even the language has changed. In fact, I am always regarded as a stranger a foreigner. I have unlimited time on my hands and I am absolutely content in sauntering through the streets There is only *one* street. I must say —the continuation of the street on which I lived. I come finally to an iron bridge over the railroad yards. It is always nightfall when I reach the bridge though it is only a short distance from the boundary line Here I look down upon the webbed tracks, the freight stations. the tenders the storage sheds. and as I gaze down upon this cluster of strange moving substances a process of metamorphosis takes place *just as in a dream*. With the transformation and deformation I become aware that this is the old dream which I have dreamed so often. I have a wild fear that I shall wake up, and indeed I know that I will wake up shortly, just at the moment when in the midst of a great open space I am about to walk into the house which contains something of the greatest importance for me. Just as I go toward this house the lot on which I am standing begins to grow vague at the edges, to dissolve, to vanish. Space rolls in on me like a carpet and swallows me up, and with it of course the house which I never succeed in entering.

There is absolutely no transition from this, the most pleasurable dream I know, to the heart of a book called *Creative Evolution*. In this book by Henri Bergson, which I came to as naturally as to the dream of the land beyond the boundary, I am again quite alone, again a foreigner, again a man of indeterminate age standing on an iron bridge observing a peculiar metamorphosis without and within. If this book had not fallen into my hands at the precise moment it did, perhaps I would have gone mad. It came at a moment when another huge world was crumbling on my hands. If I had never understood a thing which was written in this book, if I have preserved only the memory of one word, *creative*, it is quite sufficient. This word was my talisman. With it I was able to defy the whole world, and especially my friends.

There are times when one must break with one's friends in order to understand the meaning of friendship. It may seem strange to say so, but the discovery of this book was equivalent to the discovery of a weapon, an implement, wherewith I might lop off all the friends who surrounded me and who no longer meant anything to me. This book became my friend because it taught me that I had no need of friends. It gave me the courage to stand alone, and it enabled me to appreciate loneliness. I have never understood the book; at times I thought I was on the point of understanding, but I never really did understand. It was more important for me not to understand. With this book in my hands, reading aloud to my friends, questioning them, explaining to them, I was made clearly to understand that I had no friends, that I was alone in the world. Because in not understanding the meaning of the words, neither I nor my friends, one thing became very clear and that was that there were ways of not understanding and that the difference between the non-understanding of one individual and the non-understanding of another created a world of terra firma even more solid than differences of understanding. Everything which once I thought I had understood crumbled, and I was left with a clean slate. My friends, on the other hand, entrenched themselves more solidly in the little ditch of understanding which they had dug for themselves. They died comfortably in their little bed of understanding, to become useful citizens of the world. I pitied them, and in short order I deserted them one by one, without the slightest regret.

What was there then in this book which could mean so much to me and yet remain obscure? I come back to the word *creative*. I am sure that the whole mystery lies in the realization of the meaning of this word. When I think of the book now, and the way I approached it, I think of a man going through the rites of initiation. The disorientation and reorientation which comes with the initiation into any mystery is the most wonderful experience which it is possible to have. Everything which the brain has labored for a lifetime to assimilate, categorize and synthesize has to be taken apart and reordered. Moving day for the soul! And of course it's not for a day, but for weeks and months that this goes on. You meet a friend on the street by chance, one whom you haven't seen for several weeks, and he has become an absolute stranger to you. You give him a few signals from your new perch and if he doesn't cotton you pass him up—*for good*. It's exactly like mopping up a battlefield: all those who are hopelessly disabled and agonizing you dispatch with one swift blow of your club. You move on, to new fields of battle, to new triumphs or defeats. But you move! And as you move the world moves with you, with terrifying exactitude. You seek out new fields of operation, new specimens of the human race whom you patiently instruct and equip with the new symbols. You choose sometimes those whom you would never have looked at before. You try everybody and everything within range, provided they are ignorant of the revelation.

It was in this fashion that I found myself sitting in the busheling room of my father's establishment, reading aloud to the Jews who were working there. Reading to them from this new Bible in the way that Paul must have talked to the disciples. With the added disadvantage, to be sure, that these poor Jew bastards could not read the English language. Primarily I was directing myself toward Bunchek the cutter, who had a rabbinical mind. Opening the book I would pick a passage at random and read it to them in a transposed English almost as primitive as pidgin English. Then I would attempt to explain, choosing for example and analogy the things they were familiar with. It was amazing to me how well they understood, how much better they understood, let me say, than a college professor or a literary man or any educated man. Naturally what they understood had nothing to do finally with Bergson's book, as a book, but was not that the purpose of such a book as this? My understanding of the meaning of a book is that the book itself disappears from sight, that it is chewed alive, digested and incorporated into the system as flesh and blood which in turn creates new spirit and reshapes the world. It was a great communion feast which we shared in the reading of this book and the outstanding feature of it was the chapter on Disorder which, having penetrated me through and through, has endowed me with such a marvelous sense of order that if a comet suddenly struck the earth and jarred everything out of place, stood everything upside down, turned everything inside out, I could orient myself to the new order in the twinkling of an eye. I have no fear or illusions about disorder any more than I have of death. The labyrinth is my happy hunting ground and the deeper I burrow into the maze the more oriented I become.

With *Creative Evolution* under my arm I board the elevated line at the Brooklyn Bridge after work and I commence the journey homeward toward the cemetery. Sometimes I get on at Delancey Street, the very heart of the ghetto, after a long walk through the crowded streets. I enter the elevated line below the ground, like a worm being pushed through the intestines. I know each time I take my place in the crowd which mills about the platform that I am the most unique individual down there. I look upon everything which is happening about me like a spectator from another planet. My language, my world, is under my arm. I am the guardian of a great secret; if I were to open my mouth and talk I would tie up traffic. What I have to say, and what I am holding in every night of my life on this journey to and from the office, is absolute dynamite. I am not ready yet to throw my stick of dynamite. I nibble at it meditatively, ruminatively, cogently. Five more years, ten more years perhaps, and I will wipe these people out utterly. If the train in making a curve gives a violent lurch I say to myself *fine! jump the track, annihilate them!* I never think of myself as being endangered should the train jump the track. We're wedged in like sardines and all the hot flesh pressed against me diverts my thoughts. I become conscious of a pair of legs wrapped around mine. I look down at the girl sitting in front of me, I look her right in the eye, and I press my knees still further into her crotch. She grows uneasy, fidgets about in her seat, and finally she turns to the girl next to her and complains that I am molesting her. The people about look at me hostilely. I look out of the window blandly and pretend I have heard nothing. Even if I wished to I can't remove my legs. Little by little though, the girl, by a violent pushing and squiggling, manages to unwrap her legs from mine. I find myself almost in the same situation with the girl next to her, the one she was addressing her complaints to. Almost at once I feel a sympathetic touch and then, to my surprise, I hear her tell the other girl that one can't help these things, that it is really not the man's fault but the fault of the company for packing us in like sheep. And again I feel the quiver of her legs against mine, a warm, human pressure, like squeezing one's hand. With my one free hand I manage to open my book. My object is two-fold: first I want her to see the kind of book I read, second, I want to be able to carry on the leg language with-out attracting attention. It works beautifully. By the time the train empties a bit I am able to take a seat beside her and converse with her—about the book, naturally. She's a voluptuous Jewess with enormous liquid eyes and the frankness which comes from sensuality. When it comes time to get off we walk arm in arm through the streets, toward her home. I am almost on the confines of the old neighborhood. Everything is familiar to me and yet repulsively strange. I have not walked these streets for years and now I am walking with a Jew girl from the ghetto, a beautiful girl with a strong Jewish accent. I look incongruous walking beside her. I can sense that people are staring at us behind our backs. I am the in-truder, the goy who has come down into the neighbor-hood to pick off a nice ripe cunt. She on the other hand seems to be proud of her conquest; she's showing me off to her friends. This is what I picked up in the train, an educated goy, a refined goy! I can almost hear her think it. Walking slowly I'm getting the lay of the land, all the practical details which will decide whether I call for her after dinner or not. There's no thought of asking her to dinner. It's a question of what time and where to meet and how will we go about it, because, as she lets drop just before we reach the door, she's got a husband who's a traveling salesman and she's got to be careful. I agree to come back and to meet her at the corner in front of the candy store at a certain hour. If I want to bring a friend along she'll bring her girl friend. No, I decide to see her alone. It's agreed. She squeezes my hand

and darts off into a dirty hallway. I beat it quickly back to the elevated station and hasten home to gulp down the meal.

It's a summer's night and everything flung wide open. Riding back to meet her the whole past rushes up kaleidoscopically. This time I've left the book at home. It's cunt I'm out for now and no thought of the book is in my head. I am back again this side of the boundary line, each station whizzing past making my world grow more diminutive. I am almost a child by the time I reach the destination. I am a child who is horrified by the metamorphosis which has taken place. What has happened to me, a man of the Fourteenth Ward, to be jumping off at this station in search of a Jewish cunt? Supposing I do give her a fuck, what then? What have I got to say to a girl like that? What's a fuck when what I want is love? Yes, suddenly it comes over me like a tornado. . . . Una, the girl I loved, the girl who lived here in this neighborhood, Una with big blue eyes and flaxen hair, Una who made me tremble just to look at her, Una whom I was afraid to kiss or even to touch her hand. *Where is Una?* Yes, suddenly, that's the burning question: *where is Una?* In two seconds I am completely unnerved, completely lost, desolate, in the most horrible anguish and despair. How did I ever let her go? Why? What happened? *When* did it happen? I thought of her like a maniac night and day, year in and year out, and then, without even noticing it, she drops out of my mind, like that, like a penny falling through a hole in your pocket. Incredible, monstrous, mad. Why all I had to do was to ask her to marry me, ask her hand—that's all. If I had done that she would have said yes immediately. She loved me, she loved me desperately. Why yes, I remember now, I remember how she looked at me the last time we met. I was saying good-by because I was leaving that night for California, leaving everybody to begin a new life. And I never had any intention of leading a new life. I intended to ask her to marry me, but the story

I had framed like a dope came out of my lips so naturally that I believed it myself, and so I said good-by and I walked off, and she stood there looking after me and I felt her eyes pierce me through and through, I heard her howling inside, but like an automaton I kept on walking and finally I turned the corner and that was the end of it. Good-by! Like that. Like in a coma. And I meant to say *come to me! Come to me because I can't live any more without you!*

I am so weak, so rocky, that I can scarcely climb down the El steps. Now I know what's happened—I've crossed the boundary line! This Bible that I've been carrying around with me is to instruct me, initiate me into a new way of life. The world I knew is no more, it is dead, finished, cleaned up. And everything that I was is cleaned up with it. I am a carcass getting an injection of new life. I am bright and glittery, rabid with new discoveries, but in the center it is still leaden, still slag. I begin to weep—right there on the El stairs. I sob aloud, like a child. Now it dawns on me with full clarity: *you are alone in the world!* You are alone . . . alone . . . alone. It is bitter to be alone . . . bitter, bitter, bitter, bitter. There is no end to it, it is unfathomable, and it is the lot of every man on earth, but especially mine . . . especially mine. Again the metamorphosis. Again everything totters and careens. I am in the dream again, the painful, delirious, pleasurable, maddening dream of beyond the boundary. I am standing in the center of the vacant lot, but my home I do not see. I have no home. The dream was a mirage. There never was a house in the midst of the vacant lot. That's why I was never able to enter it. My home is not in this world, nor in the next. I am a man without a home, without a friend, without a wife. I am a monster who belongs to a reality which does not exist yet. Ah, but it does exist, it will exist, I am sure of it. I walk now rapidly, head down, muttering to myself. I've forgotten about my rendezvous so completely that I never even noticed whether I walked past her or not. Probably

I did. Probably I looked right at her and didn't recognize her. Probably she didn't recognize me either. I am mad, mad with pain, mad with anguish. I am desperate. But I am not lost. No, there *is* a reality to which I belong. It's far away, very far away. I may walk from now till doomsday with head down and never find it. But it is there, I am sure of it. I look at people murderously. If I could throw a bomb and blow the whole neighborhood to smithereens I would do it. I would be happy seeing them fly in the air, mangled, shrieking, torn apart, annihilated. I want to annihilate the whole earth. I am not a part of it. It's mad from start to finish. The whole shooting match. It's a huge piece of stale cheese with maggots festering inside it. Fuck it! Blow it to hell! Kill, kill, kill: Kill them all, Jews and Gentiles, young and old, good and bad. . . .

I grow light, light as a feather, and my pace becomes more steady, more calm, more even. What a beautiful night it is! The stars shining so brightly, so serenely, so remotely. Not mocking me precisely, but reminding me of the futility of it all. Who are you, young man, to be talking of the earth, of blowing things to smithereens? Young man, we have been hanging here for millions and billions of years. We have seen it all, everything, and still we shine peacefully every night, we light the way, we still the heart. Look around you, young man, see how still and beautiful everything is. Do you see, even the garbage lying in the gutter looks beautiful in this light. Pick up the little cabbage leaf, hold it gently in your hand. I bend down and pick up the cabbage leaf lying in the gutter. It looks absolutely new to me, a whole universe in itself. I break a little piece off and examine that. Still a universe. Still unspeakably beautiful and mysterious. I am almost ashamed to throw it back in the gutter. I bend down and deposit it gently with the other refuse. I become very thoughtful, very, very calm. I love everybody in the world. I know that somewhere at this very moment there is a woman waiting for me and if only I proceed very calmly, very gently, very slowly, I will come to her. She will be standing on a corner perhaps and when I come in sight she will recognize me—immediately. I believe this, so help me God! I believe that everything is just and ordained. My home? Why it is the world—the whole world! I am at home everywhere, only I did not know it before. But I know now. There is no boundary line any more. There never was a boundary line: it was I who made it. I walk slowly and blissfully through the streets. The beloved streets. Where everybody walks and everybody suffers without showing it. When I stand and lean against a lamppost to light my cigarette even the lamppost feels friendly. It is not a thing of iron—it is a creation of the human mind, shaped a certain way, twisted and formed by human hands, blown on with human breath, placed by human hands and feet. I turn round and rub my hand over the iron surface. It almost seems to speak to me. It is a human lamppost. It *belongs*, like the cabbage leaf, like the torn socks, like the mattress, like the kitchen sink. Everything stands in a certain way in a certain place, as our mind stands in relation to God. The world, in its visible, tangible substance, is a map of our love. Not God but *life* is love. Love, love, love. And in the midmost midst of it walks this young man, myself, who is none other than Gottlieb Leberecht Müller.

Gottlieb Leberecht Müller! This is the name of a man who lost his identity. Nobody could tell him who he was, where he came from or what had happened to him. In the movies, where I first made the acquaintance of this individual, it was assumed that he had met with an accident in the war. But when I recognized myself on the screen, knowing that I had never been to the war, I realized that the author had invented this little piece of fiction in order not to expose me. Often I forget which is the real me. Often in my dreams I take the draught of forgetfulness, as it is called, and I wander forlorn and desperate,

seeking the body and the name which is mine. And sometimes between the dream and reality there is only the
thinnest line. Sometimes while a person is talking to me
I step out of my shoes and, like a plant drifting with the
current, I begin the voyage of my rootless self. In this
condition I am quite capable of fulfilling the ordinary
demands of life—of finding a wife, of becoming a father,
of supporting the household, of entertaining friends, of
reading books, of paying taxes, of performing military
service, and so on and so forth. In this condition I am
capable, if needs be, of killing in cold blood, for the sake
of my family or to protect my country, or whatever it
may be. I am the ordinary, routine citizen who answers to
a name and who is given a number in his passport.
I am thoroughly irresponsible for my fate.

Then one day, without the slightest warning, I wake
up and looking about me I understand absolutely nothing
of what is going on about me, neither my own behavior
nor that of my neighbors, nor do I understand why the
governments are at war or at peace, whichever the case
may be. At such moments I am born anew, born and
baptized by my right name: Gottlieb Leberecht Müller!
Everything I do in my right name is looked upon as
crazy. People make furtive signs behind my back, sometimes to my face even. I am forced to break with friends
and family and loved ones. I am obliged to break camp.
And so, just as naturally as in dream, I find myself once
again drifting with the current, usually walking along a
highway, my face set toward the sinking sun. Now all my
faculties become alert. I am the most suave, silky, cunning animal—and I am at the same time what might
be called a holy man. I know how to fend for myself. I
know how to avoid work, how to avoid entangling rela-
tionships, how to avoid pity, sympathy, bravery, and all
the other pitfalls. I stay in place or with a person just
long enough to obtain what I need, and then I'm off
again. I have no goal: the aimless wandering is sufficient
unto itself. I am free as a bird, sure as an equilibrist.

Manna falls from the sky; I have only to hold out my hands and receive. And everywhere I leave the most pleasant feeling behind me, as though, in accepting the gifts that are showered upon me, I am doing a real favor to others. Even my dirty linen is taken care of by loving hands. Because everybody loves a right-living man! Gottlieb! What a beautiful name it is! Gottlieb! I say it to myself over and over. Gottlieb Leberecht Müller!

In this condition I have always fallen in with thieves and rogues and murderers, and how kind and gentle they have been with me! As though they were my brothers. And are they not, indeed? Have I not been guilty of every crime, and suffered for it? And is it not just because of my crimes that I am united so closely to my fellowman? Always, when I see a light of recognition in the other person's eyes, I am aware of this secret bond. It is only the just whose eyes never light up. It is the just who have never known the secret of human fellowship. It is the just who are committing the crimes against man, the just who are the real monsters. It is the just who demand our fingerprints, who prove to us that we have died even when we stand before them in the flesh. It is the just who impose upon us arbitrary names, false names, who put false dates in the register and bury us alive. I prefer the thieves, the rogues, the murderers, unless I can find a man of my own stature, my own quality.

I have never found such a man! I have never found a man as generous as myself, as forgiving, as tolerant, as carefree, as reckless, as clean at heart. I forgive myself for every crime I have committed. I do it in the name of humanity. I know what it means to be human, the weakness and the strength of it. I suffer from this knowledge and I revel in it also. If I had the chance to be God I would reject it. If I had the chance to be a star I would reject it. The most wonderful opportunity which life offers is to be human. It embraces the whole universe. It includes the knowledge of death, which not even God enjoys.

At the point from which this book is written I am the man who baptized himself anew. It is many years since this happened and so much has come in between that it is difficult to get back to that moment and retrace the journey of Gottlieb Leberecht Müller. However, perhaps I can give the clue if I say that the man which I now am was born out of a wound. That wound went to the heart. By all man-made logic I should have been dead. I was in fact given up for dead by all who once knew me; I walked about like a ghost in their midst. They used the past tense in referring to me, they pitied me, they shoveled me under deeper and deeper. Yet I remember how I used to laugh then, as always, how I made love to other women, how I enjoyed my food and drink, and the soft bed which I clung to like a fiend. Something had killed me, and yet I was alive. But I was alive without a memory, without a name; I was cut off from hope as well as from remorse or regret. I had no past and I would probably have no future; I was buried alive in a void which was the wound that had been dealt me. *I was the wound itself.*

I have a friend who talks to me from time to time about the Miracle of Golgotha of which I understand nothing. But I do know something about the miraculous wound which I received, the wound which killed me in the eyes of the world and out of which I was born anew and rebaptized. I know something of the miracle of this wound which I lived and which healed with my death. I tell it as of something long past, but it is with me always. Everything is long past and seemingly invisible, like a constellation which has sunk forever beneath the horizon.

What fascinates me is that anything so dead and buried as I was could be resuscitated, and not just once, but innumerable times. And not only that, but each time I faded out I plunged deeper than ever into the void, so that with each resuscitation the miracle becomes greater. And never any stigmata! The man who is reborn is always the same man, more and more himself with each rebirth. He is only shedding his skin each time, and with his skin his sins. The man whom God loves is truly a right-living man. The man whom God loves is the onion with a million skins. To shed the first layer is painful beyond words; the next layer is less painful, the next still less, until finally the pain becomes pleasurable, more and more pleasurable, a delight, an ecstasy. And then there is neither pleasure nor pain, but simply darkness yielding before the light. And as the darkness falls away the wound comes out of its hiding place: the wound which is man, man's love, is bathed in light. The identity which was lost is recovered. Man walks forth from his open wound, from the grave which he had carried about with him so long.

In the tomb which is my memory I see her buried now, the one I loved better than all else, better than the world, better than God, better than my own flesh and blood. I see her festering there in that bloody wound of love, so close to me that I could not distinguish her from the wound itself. I see her struggling to free herself, to make herself clean of love's pain, and with each struggle sinking back again into the wound, mired, suffocated, writhing in blood. I see the terrible look in her eyes, the mute piteous agony, the look of the beast that is trapped. I see her opening her legs for deliverance and each orgasm a groan of anguish. I hear the walls falling, the walls caving in on us and the house going up in flames. I hear them calling us from the street, the summons to work, the summons to arms, but we are nailed to the floor and the rats are biting into us. The grave and womb of love entombing us, the night filling our bowels and the stars shimmering over the black bottomless lake. I lose the memory of words, of her name even which I pronounce like a monomaniac. I forgot what she looked like, what she felt like, what she smelt like, what she fucked like, piercing deeper and deeper into the night of the fathomless cavern. I followed her to the deepest hole of her being, to the charnel house of her soul, to the breath which had not yet expired from her lips. I sought relentlessly for her whose name was not written anywhere, I penetrated to the very altar and found—nothing. I wrapped myself around this hollow shell of nothingness like a serpent with fiery coils; I lay still for six centuries without breathing as world events sieved through to the bottom forming a slimy bed of mucus. I saw the constellations wheeling about the huge hole in the ceiling of the universe; I saw the outer planets and the black star which was to deliver me. I saw the Dragon shaking itself free of dharma and karma, saw the new race of man stewing in the yolk of futurity. I saw through to the last sign and symbol, *but I could not read her face.* I could see only the eyes shining through, huge, fleshy-like luminous breasts, as though I were swimming behind them in the electric effluvia of her incandescent vision.

How had she come to expand thus beyond all grip of consciousness? By what monstrous law had she spread herself thus over the face of the world, revealing everything and yet concealing herself? She was hidden in the face of the sun, like the moon in eclipse; she was a mirror which had lost its quicksilver, the mirror which yields both the image and the horror. Looking into the backs of her eyes, into the pulpy translucent flesh, I saw the brain structure of all formations, all relations, all evanescence. I saw the brain within the brain, the endless machine endlessly turning, the word Hope revolving on a spit, roasting, dripping with fat, revolving ceaselessly in the cavity of the third eye. I heard her dreams mumbled in lost tongues, the stifled screams reverberating in minute crevices, the gasps, the groans, the pleasurable sighs, the swish of lashing whips. I heard her call my own name which I had not yet uttered, I heard her curse and shriek with rage. I heard everything magnified a thousand times, like a homunculus imprisoned in the belly of an organ. I caught the muffled breathing of the world, as if fixed in the very crossroads of sound.

Thus we walked and slept and ate together, the Siamese twins whom Love had joined and whom Death alone could separate.

We walked upside down, hand in hand, at the neck of the bottle. She dressed in black almost exclusively, except for patches of purple now and then. She wore no underclothes, just a simple sheath of black velvet saturated with a diabolical perfume. We went to bed at dawn and got up just as it was darkling. We lived in black holes with drawn curtains, we ate from black plates, we read from black books. We looked out of the black hole of our life into the black hole of the world. The sun was permanently blacked out, as though to aid us in our continuous internecine strife. For sun we had Mars, for moon Saturn; we lived permanently in the zenith of the underworld. The earth had ceased to revolve and through the hole in the sky above us there hung the black star which never twinkled. Now and then we had fits of laughter, crazy, batrachian laughter which made the neighbors shudder. Now and then we sang, delirious, off key, full tremolo. We were locked in throughout the long dark night of the soul, a period of incommensurable time which began and ended in the manner of an eclipse. We revolved about our own egos, like phantom satellites. We were drunk with our own image which we saw when we looked into each other's eyes. How then did we look to others? As the beast looks to the plant, as the stars look to the beast. Or as God would look to man if the devil had given him wings. And with it all, in the fixed, close intimacy of a night without end she was radiant, jubilant, an ultra-black jubilation streaming from her like a steady flow of sperm from the Mithraic Bull. She was double barreled, like a shotgun, a female bull with an acetylene torch in her womb. In heat she focused on the grand cosmocrator, her eyes rolled back to the whites, her lips a-slaver. In the blind hole of sex she waltzed like a trained mouse, her jaws unhinged like a snake's, her skin horripilating in barbed plumes. She had the insatiable lust of a unicorn, the itch that laid the Egyptians low. Even the hole in the sky through which the lackluster star shone down was swallowed up in her fury.

We lived glued to the ceiling, the hot rancid fumes of the everyday life steaming up and suffocating us. We lived at marble heat, the ascending glow of human flesh warming the snakelike coils in which we were locked. We lived riveted to the nethermost depths, our skins smoked to the color of a gray cigar by the fumes of worldly passion. Like two heads carried on the pikes of our executioners we circled slowly and fixedly over the heads and shoulders of the world below. What was life on the solid earth to us who were decapitated and forever joined at the genitals? We were the twin snakes of Paradise, lucid in heat and cool as chaos itself. Life was a perpetual black fuck about a fixed pole of insomnia. Life was Scorpio conjunction Mars, conjunction Mercury, conjunction Venus, conjunction Saturn, conjunction Pluto, conjunction Uranus, conjunction quicksilver, laudanum, radium, bismuth. The grand conjunction was every Saturday night, Leo fornicating with Draco in the house of brother and sister. The great *malheur* was a ray of sunlight stealing through the curtains. The great curse was Jupiter, king of the fishes, that he might flash a benevolent eye.

The reason why it is difficult to tell it is because I remember too much. I remember everything, but like a dummy sitting on the lap of a ventriloquist. It seems to me that throughout the long, uninterrupted connubial solstice I sat on her lap (even when she was standing) and spoke the lines she had taught me. It seems to me that she must have commanded God's chief plumber to keep the black star shining through the hole in the ceiling, must have bid him to rain down perpetual night and with it all the crawling torments that move noiselessly about in the dark so that the mind becomes a twirling awl burrowing frantically into black nothingness. Did I only imagine that she talked incessantly, or had I be-

come such a marvelously trained dummy that I intercepted the thought before it reached the lips? The lips
were finely parted, smoothed down with a thick paste of
dark blood; I watched them open and close with the
utmost fascination, whether they hissed a viper's hate
or cooed like a turtle dove. They were always close up,
as in the movie stills, so that I knew every crevice, every
pore, and when the hysterical slavering began I watched
the spittle fume and foam as though I were sitting in a
rocking chair under Niagara Falls. I learned what to do
just as though I were a part of her organism; I was better
than a ventriloquist's dummy because I could act without
being violently jerked by strings. Now and then I did
things impromptu like, which sometimes pleased her
enormously; she would pretend, of course, not to notice
these irruptions, but I could always tell when she was
pleased by the way she preened herself. She had the gift
for transformation; almost as quick and subtle she was as
the devil himself. Next to the panther and the jaguar
she did the bird stuff best: the wild heron, the ibis, the
flamingo, the swan in rut. She had a way of swooping
suddenly, as if she had spotted a ripe carcass, diving right
into the bowels, pouncing immediately on the tidbits—
the heart, the liver, or the ovaries—and making off again
in the twinkling of an eye. Did someone spot her, she
would lie stone quiet at the base of a tree, her eyes not
quite closed but immovable in that fixed stare of the
basilisk. Prod her a bit and she would become a rose, a
deep black rose with the most velvety petals and of a
fragrance that was overpowering. It was amazing how
marvelously I learned to take my cue; no matter how
swift the metamorphosis I was always there in her lap,
bird lap, beast lap, snake lap, rose lap, what matter: the
lap of laps, the lip of lips, tip to tip, feather to feather,
the yoke in the egg, the pearl in the oyster, a cancer
clutch, a tincture of sperm and cantharides. Life was
Scorpio conjunction Mars, conjunction Venus, Saturn,
Uranus, et cetera; love was conjunctivitis of the mandi-

bles, clutch this, clutch that, clutch, clutch, the mandibu-
lar clutch-clutch of the mandala wheel of lust. Come food
time I could already hear her peeling the eggs, and inside
the egg *cheep-cheep*, blessed omen of the next meal to
come. I ate like a monomaniac: the prolonged dreamlit
voracity of the man who is thrice breaking his fast. And
as I ate she purred, the rhythmic predatory wheeze of the
succubus devouring her young. What a blissful night of
love! Saliva, sperm, succubation, sphincteritis all in one:
the conjugal orgy in the Black Hole of Calcutta.

Out there where the black star hung, a Pan-Islamic
silence, as in the cavern world where even the wind is
stilled. Out there, did I dare to brood on it, the spectral
quietude of insanity, the world of men lulled, exhausted
by centuries of incessant slaughter. Out there one gory
encompassing membrane within which all activity took
place, the hero-world of lunatics and maniacs who had
quenched the light of the heavens with blood. How
peaceful our little dove-and-vulture life in the dark! Flesh
to bury in with teeth or penis, abundant odorous flesh
with no mark of knife or scissors, no scar of exploded
shrapnel, no mustard burns, no scalded lungs. Save for the
hallucinating hole in the ceiling, an almost perfect womb
life. But the hole was there—like a fissure in the bladder
—and no wadding could plug it permanently, no urina-
tion could pass off with a smile. Piss large and freely,
aye, but how forget the rent in the belfry, the silence
unnatural, the imminence, the terror, the doom of the
"other" world? Eat a bellyful, aye, and tomorrow another
bellyful, and tomorrow and tomorrow and tomorrow—but
finally, what then? *Finally? What was finally?* A change
of ventriloquist, a change of lap, a shift in the axis, another
rift in the vault . . . *what? what?* I'll tell you—sitting in her
lap, petrified by the still, pronged beams of the black
star, horned, snaffled, hitched and trepanned by the
telepathic acuity of our interacting agitation, I thought of
nothing at all, nothing that was outside the cell we inhabited, not even the thought of a crumb on a white

tablecloth. I thought purely within the walls of our amoebic life, the pure thought such as Immanuel Pussy-foot Kant gave us and which only a ventriloquist's dummy could reproduce. I thought out every theory of science, every theory of art, every grain of truth in every cock-eyed system of salvation. I calculated everything out to a pinpoint with gnostic decimals to boot, like *primes* which a drunk hands out at the finish of a six-day race. But everything was calculated for another life which somebody else would live some day—*perhaps.* We were at the very neck of the bottle, *her and I,* as they say, but the neck of the bottle had been broken off and the bottle was only a fiction.

I remember how the second time I met her she told me that she had never expected to see me again, and the next time I saw her she said she thought I was a dope fiend, and the next time she called me a god, and after that she tried to commit suicide and then I tried and then she tried again, and nothing worked except to bring us closer together, so close indeed that we interpenetrated, exchanged personalities, name, identity, religion, father, mother, brother. Even her body went through a radical change, not once but several times. At first she was big and velvety, like the jaguar, with that silky, deceptive strength of the feline species, the crouch, the spring, the pounce; then she grew emaciated, fragile, delicate, almost like a corn-flower, and with each change thereafter she went through the subtlest modulations—of skin, muscle, color, posture, odor, gait, gesture, et cetera. She changed like a chame-leon. Nobody could say what she really was like because with each one she was an entirely different person. After a time she didn't even know herself what she was like. She had begun this process of metamorphosis before I met her, as I later discovered. Like so many women who think themselves ugly she had willed to make herself beautiful, dazzlingly beautiful. To do this she first of all renounced her name, then her family, her friends, everything which might attach her to the past. With all

her wits and faculties she devoted herself to the cultiva-
tion of her beauty, of her charm, which she already
possessed to a high degree but which she had been made
to believe were nonexistent. She lived constantly before
the mirror, studying every movement, every gesture, every
slightest grimace. She changed her whole manner of
speech, her diction, her intonation, her accent, her phrase-
ology. She conducted herself so skilfully that it was impossible even to broach the subject of origins. She was
constantly on her guard, even in her sleep. And, like a
good general, she discovered quickly enough that the best
defense is attack. She never left a single position un-
occupied; her outposts, her scouts, her sentinels were
stationed everywhere. Her mind was a revolving searchlight which was never dimmed.

Blind to her own beauty, her own charm, her own
personality, to say nothing of her identity, she launched
her full powers toward the fabrication of a mythical
creature, a Helen, a Juno, whose charms neither man
nor woman would be able to resist. Automatically, without
the slightest knowledge of legend, she began to create
little by little the ontological background, the mythic
sequence of events preceeding the conscious birth. She
had no need to remember her lies, her fictions—she had
only to bear in mind her role. There was no lie too monstrous for her to utter, for in her adopted role she was
absolutely faithful to herself. She did not have to *invent* a
past: she *remembered* the past which belonged to her.
She was never outflanked by a direct question since she
never presented herself to an adversary except obliquely.
She presented only the angles of the ever-turning facets,
the blinding prisms of light which she kept constantly
revolving. She was never a being, such as might finally
be caught in repose, but the mechanism itself, relentlessly
operating the myriad mirrors which would reflect the
myth she had created. She had no poise whatsoever; she
was eternally poised above her multiple identities in
the vacuum of the self. She had not intended to make her-

self a legendary figure, she had merely wanted her beauty to be recognized. But in the pursuit of beauty, she soon forgot her quest entirely, became the victim of her own creation. She became so stunningly beautiful that at times she was frightening, at times positively uglier than the ugliest woman in the world. She could inspire horror and dread, especially when her charm was at its height. It was as though the will, blind and uncontrollable, shone through the creation, exposing the monster which it is.

In the dark, locked away in the black hole with no world looking on, no adversary, no rivals, the blinding dynamism of the will slowed down a bit, gave her a molten copperish glow, the words coming out of her mouth like lava, her flesh clutching ravenously for a hold, a perch on something solid and substantial, something in which to reintegrate and repose for a few moments. It was like a frantic long-distance message, an S O S from a sinking ship. At first I mistook it for passion, for the ecstasy produced by flesh rubbing against flesh. I thought I had found a living volcano, a female Vesuvius. I never thought of a human ship going down in an ocean of despair, in a Sargasso of impotence. Now I think of that black star gleaming through the hole in the ceiling, that fixed star which hung above our conjugal cell, more fixed, more remote than the Absolute, and I know it was her, emptied of all that was properly herself: a dead black sun without aspect. I know that we were conjugating the verb love like two maniacs trying to fuck through an iron grate. I said that in the frantic grappling in the dark I sometimes forgot her name, what she looked like, who she was. It's true. I overreached myself in the dark. I slid off the flesh rails into the endless space of sex, into the channel-orbits established by this one and that one: Georgiana, for instance, of only a brief afternoon, Thelma, the Egyptian whore, Carlotta, Alannah, Una, Mona, Magda, girls of six or seven; waifs, will-o'-the-wisps, faces, bodies, thighs, a subway brush, a dream, a memory, a desire, a longing. I could start with Georgiana of a Sunday afternoon near the railroad tracks, her dotted Swiss dress, her swaying haunch, her Southern drawl, her lascivious mouth, her molten breasts; I could start with Georgiana, the myriad branched candelabra of sex, and work outwards and upwards through the ramification of cunt into the nth dimension of sex, world without end. Georgiana was like the membrane of the tiny little ear of an unfinished monster called sex. She was transparently alive and breathing in the light of the memory of a brief afternoon on the avenue, the first tangible odor and substance of the world of fuck which is in itself a being limitless and undefinable, like our world the world. The whole world of fuck like unto the ever-increasing membrane of the animal we call sex, which is like another being growing into our own being and gradually displacing it, so that in time the human world will be only a dim memory of this new, all-inclusive, all-procreative being which is giving birth to itself.

It was precisely this snakelike copulation in the dark, this double-jointed, double-barreled hookup, which put me in the strait jacket of doubt, jealousy, fear, loneliness. If I began my hemstitching with Georgiana and the myriad-branched candelabra of sex I was certain that she too was at work building membrane, making ears, eyes, toes, scalp and whatnot of sex. She would begin with the monster who had raped her, assuming there was truth in the story; in any case she too began somewhere on a parallel track, working upwards and outwards through this multiform, uncreated being through whose body we were both striving desperately to meet. Knowing only a fraction of her life, possessing only a bag of lies, of inventions, of imaginings, of obsessions and delusions, putting together tag ends, coke dreams, reveries, unfinished sentences, jumbled dream talk, hysterical ravings, ill-disguised fantasies, morbid desires, meeting now and then a name become flesh, overhearing stray bits of conversation, observing smuggled glances, half-arrested gestures, I could well credit her with a pantheon of her own private fucking gods, of only too vivid flesh and blood creatures, men of perhaps that very afternoon, of perhaps only an hour ago, her cunt perhaps still choked with the sperm of the last fuck. The more submissive she was, the more passionately she behaved, the more abandoned she looked, the more uncertain I became. There was no beginning, no personal, individual starting point; we met like experienced swordsmen on the field of honor now crowded with the ghosts of victory and defeat. We were alert and responsive to the least thrust, as only the practiced can be.

We came together under cover of dark with our armies and from opposite sides we forced the gates of the citadel. There was no resisting our bloody work; we asked for no quarter and we gave none. We came together swimming in blood, a gory, glaucous reunion in the night with all the stars extinguished save the fixed black star hanging like a scalp above the hole in the ceiling. If she were properly coked she would vomit it forth like an oracle, everything that had happened to her during the day, yesterday, the day before, the year before last, *everything*, down to the day she was born. And not a word of it was true, not a single detail. Not a moment did she stop, for if she had, the vacuum she created in her flight would have brought about an explosion fit to sunder the world. She was the world's lying machine in microcosm, geared to the same unending, devastating fear which enables men to throw all their energies into creation of the death apparatus. To look at her one would think her fearless, one would think her the personification of courage and she *was*, so long as she was not obliged to turn in her traces. Behind her lay the calm fact of reality, a colossus which dogged her every step. Every day this colossal reality took on new proportions, every day it became more terrifying, more paralyzing. Every day she had to grow swifter wings, sharper jaws, more piercing, hypnotic eyes. It was a race to the outermost limits of the world, a race lost from the start, and no one to stop it. At the edge of the vacuum stood Truth, ready in one lightning-like sweep to recover the stolen ground. It was so simple and obvious that it drove her frantic. Marshal a thousand personalities, commandeer the biggest guns, deceive the greatest minds, make the longest detour—still the end would be defeat. In the final meeting everything was destined to fall apart —the cunning, the skill, the power, everything. She would be a grain of sand on the shore of the biggest ocean, and, worse than anything, she would resemble each and every other grain of sand on that ocean's shore. She would be condemned to rocognize her unique self everywhere until the end of time. What a fate she had chosen for herself! That her uniqueness should be engulfed in the universal! That her power should be reduced to the utmost node of passivity! It was maddening, hallucinating. It could not be! It *must* not be! Onward! Like the black legions. Onward! Through every degree of the ever-widening circle. Onward and away from the self, until the last substantial particle of the soul be stretched to infinity. In her panic-stricken flight she seemed to bear the whole world in her womb. We were being driven out of the confines of the universe toward a nebula which no instrument could visualize. We were being rushed to a pause so still, so prolonged, that death by comparison seems a mad witches' revel.

In the morning, gazing at the bloodless crater of her face. Not a line in it, not a wrinkle, not a single blemish! The look of an angel in the arms of the Creator. *Who killed Cock Robin? Who massacred the Iroquois?* Not I, my lovely angel could say, and by God, who, gazing at that pure, blameless face, could deny her? Who could see in that sleep of innocence that one half of the face belonged to God and the other half to Satan? The mask was smooth as death, cool, lovely to the touch, waxen, like a petal open to the faintest breeze. So alluringly still and guileless was it that one could drown in it, one could go down into it, body and all, like a diver, and nevermore return. Until the eyes opened upon the world she would lie like that, thoroughly extinguished and gleaming with a reflected light, like the moon itself. In her deathlike trance of innocence she fascinated even more; her crimes dissolved, exuded through the pores, she lay coiled like a sleeping serpent riveted to the earth. The body, strong, lithe, muscular, seemed possessed of a weight unnatural; she had a more than human gravity, the gravity, one might almost say, of a warm corpse. She was like one might imagine the beautiful Nefertiti to have been after the first thousand years of mummification, a marvel of mortuary perfection, a dream of flesh preserved from mortal decay. She lay coiled at the base of a hollow pyramid, enshrined in the vacuum of her own creation like a sacred relic of the past. Even her breathing seemed stopped, so profound was her slumber. She had dropped below the human sphere, below the animal sphere, below the vegetative sphere even: she had sunk down to the level of the mineral world where animation is just a notch above death. She had so mastered the art of deception that even the dream was powerless to betray her. She had learned how not to dream: when she coiled up in sleep she automatically switched off the current. If one could have caught her thus and opened up the skull one would have found it absolutely void. She kept no disturbing secrets; everything was killed off which could be humanly killed. She might live on endlessly, like the moon, like any dead planet, radiating an hypnotic effulgence, creating tides of passion, engulfing the world in madness, discoloring all earthly substances with her magnetic, metallic rays. Sowing her own death she brought everyone about her to fever pitch. In the heinous stillness of her sleep she renewed her own magnetic death by union with the cold magma of the lifeless planetary worlds. She was magically intact. Her gaze fell upon one with a transpiercing fixity: it was the moon-gaze through which the dead dragon of life gave off a cold fire. The one eye was a warm brown, the color of an autumn leaf; the other was hazel, the magnetic eye which flickered like a compass needle. Even in sleep this eye continued to flicker under the shutter of the lid; it was the only apparent sign of life in her.

The moment she opened her eyes she was wide awake. She awoke with a violent start, as if the sight of the world and its human paraphernalia were a shock. Instantly she was in full activity, lashing about like a great python. What annoyed her was the light! She awoke cursing the sun, cursing the glare of reality. The room had to be darkened, the candles lit, the windows tightly shut to prevent the noise of the street from penetrating the room. She moved about naked with a cigarette dangling from the corner of her mouth. Her toilet was an affair of great preoccupation; a thousand trifling details had to be attended to before she could so much as don a bathrobe. She was like an athlete preparing for the great event of the day. From the roots of her hair, which she studied with keen attention, to the shape and length of her toenails, every part of her anatomy was thoroughly inspected before sitting down to breakfast. Like an athlete I said she was, but in fact she was more like a mechanic overhauling a fast plane for a test flight. Once she slipped on her dress she was launched for the day, for the flight which might end perhaps in Irkutsk or Teheran. She would take on enough fuel at breakfast to last the entire trip. The breakfast was a prolonged affair: it was the one ceremony of the day over which she dawdled and lingered. It was exasperatingly prolonged, indeed. One wondered if she would ever take off, one wondered if she had forgotten the grand mission which she had sworn to accomplish each day. Perhaps she was dreaming of her itinerary, or perhaps she was not dreaming at all but simply allowing time for the functional processes of her marvelous machine so that once embarked there would be no turning back. She was very calm and self-possessed at this hour of the day; she was like a great bird of the air perched on a mountain crag, dreamily surveying the terrain below. It was not from the breakfast table that she would suddenly swoop and dive to pounce upon her prey. No, from the early morning perch she would take off slowly and majestically, synchronizing her every movement with the pulse of the motor. All space lay before her, her direction dictated only by caprice. She was almost the image of freedom, were it not for the Saturnian weight of her body and the abnormal span of her wings. However poised she seemed, especially at the take-off, one sensed the terror which motivated the daily flight. She was at once obedient to her destiny and at the same time frantically eager to overcome it. Each morning she soared aloft from her perch, as from some Himalayan peak; she seemed always to direct her flight toward some uncharted region into which, if all went well, she would disappear forever. Each morning she seemed to carry aloft with her this desperate, last-minute hope; she took leave with calm, grave dignity, like one about to go down into the grave. Never once did she circle about the flying field; never once did she cast a glance backward toward those whom she was abandoning. Nor did she leave the slightest crumb of personality behind her; she took to the air with all her belongings, with every slightest scrap of evidence which might testify to the fact of her existence. She didn't even leave the breath of a sigh behind, not even a toenail. A clean exit, such as the Devil himself might make for reasons of his own. One was left with a great void on his hands. One was deserted, and not only deserted, but betrayed, inhumanly betrayed. One had no desire to detain her nor to call her back; one was left with a curse on his lips, with a black hatred which darkened the whole day. Later, moving about the city, moving slowly in pedestrian fashion, crawling like the worm, one gathered rumors of her spectacular flight; she had been seen rounding a certain point, she had dipped here or there for what reason no one knew, she had done a tailspin elsewhere, she had passed like a comet, she had written letters of smoke in the sky, and so on and so forth. Everything she had done was enigmatic and exasperating, done apparently without purpose. It was like a symbolic and ironic commentary on human life, on the behavior of the antlike creature man, viewed from another dimension.

Between the time she took off and the time she returned I lived the life of a full-blooded schizerino. It was not an eternity which elapsed, because somehow eternity has to do with peace and with victory, it is something man made, something earned: no, I experienced an entr'acte in which every hair turns white to the roots, in which every millimeter of skin itches and burns until the whole body becomes a running sore. I see myself sitting before a table in the dark, my hands and feet growing enormous, as though elephantiasis were overtaking me at a gallop. I hear the blood rushing up to the brain and pounding at the eardrums like Himalayan devils with sledge-hammers; I hear her flapping her huge wings, even in Irkutsk, and I know she is pushing on and on, ever further away, ever further beyond reach. It is so quiet in the room and so frightfully empty that I shriek and howl just to make a little noise, a little human sound. I try to lift myself from the table but my feet are too heavy and my hands have become like the shapeless feet of the rhinoceros. The heavier my body becomes the lighter the atmosphere of the room; I am going to spread and spread until I fill the room with one solid mass of stiff jelly. I shall fill up even the cracks in the wall; I shall grow through the wall like a parasitic plant, spreading and spreading until the whole house is an indescribable mass of flesh and hair and nails. I know that this is death, but I am powerless to kill the knowledge of it, or the knower. Some tiny particle of me is alive, some speck of consciousness persists, and, as the inert carcass expands, this flicker of life becomes sharper and sharper and gleams inside me like the cold fire of a gem. It lights up the whole gluey mass of pulp so that I am like a diver with a torch in the body of a dead marine monster. By some slender hidden filament I am still connected with the life above the surface of the deep, but it is so far away, the upper world, and the weight of the corpse so great that, even if it were possible, it would take years to reach the surface. I move around in my own dead body, exploring every nook and cranny of its huge, shapeless mass. It is an endless exploration, for with the ceaseless growth the whole topography changes, slipping and drifting like the hot magma of the earth. Never for a minute is there terra firma, never for a minute does anything remain still and recognizable: it is a growth without landmarks, a voyage in which the destination changes with every least move or shudder. It is this interminable filling of space which kills all sense of space or time; the more the body expands the tinier becomes the world, until at last I feel that everything is concentrated on the head of a pin. Despite the floundering of this enormous dead mass which I have become, I feel that what sustains it, the world out of which it grows, is no bigger than a pinhead. In the midst of pollution, in the very heart and gizzard of death, as it were, I sense the seed, the miraculous, infinitesimal lever which balances the world. I have overspread the world like a syrup and the emptiness of it is terrifying, but there is no dislodging the seed; the seed has become a little knot of cold fire which roars like a sun in the vast hollow of the dead carcass.

When the great plunder-bird returns exhausted from her flight she will find me here in the midst of my nothingness, I, the imperishable schizerino, a blazing seed hidden in the heart of death. Every day she thinks to find another means of sustenance, but there is no other, only this eternal seed of light which by dying each day I rediscover for her. Fly, O devouring bird, fly to the limits of the universe! Here is your nourishment glowing in the sickening emptiness you have created! You will come back to perish once more in the black hole; you will come back again and again, for you have not the wings to carry you out of the world. This is the only world you can inhabit, this tomb of the snake where darkness reigns.

And suddenly for no reason at all, when I think of her returning to her nest, I remember Sunday mornings in the little old house near the cemetery. I remember sitting at the piano in my nightshirt, working away at the pedals with bare feet, and the folks lying in bed toasting themselves in the next room. The rooms opened one on the other, telescope fashion, as in the good old American railroad flats. Sunday mornings one lay in bed until one was ready to screech with well-being. Toward eleven or so the folks used to rap on the wall of my room for me to come and play for them. I would dance into the room like the Fratellini Brothers, so full of flame and feathers that I could hoist myself like a derrick to the topmost limb of the tree of heaven. I could do anything and everything singlehanded, being double-jointed at the same time. The old man called me "Sunny Jim," because I was full of "Force," full of vim and vigor. First I would do a few handsprings for them on the carpet before the bed; then I would sing falsetto, trying to imitate a ventriloquist's dummy; then I would dance a few light fantastic steps to show which way the wind lay, and zoom! like a breeze I was on the piano stool and doing a velocity exercise. I always began with Czerny, in order to limber up for the performance. The old man hated Czerny, and so did I, but Czerny was the *plat du jour* on the bill of fare then, and so Czerny it was until my joints were rubber. In some vague way Czerny reminds me of the great emptiness which came upon me later. What a velocity I would work up, riveted to the piano stool! It was like swallowing a bottle of tonic at one gulp and then having someone strap you to the bed. After I had played about ninety-eight exercises I was ready to do a little improvising. I used to take a fistful of chords and crash the piano from one end to the other, then sullenly modulate into "The Burning of Rome" or the "Ben Hur Chariot Race" which everybody liked because it was intelligible noise. Long before I read Wittgenstein's *Tractatus Logico-Philosophicus* I was composing the music to it, in the key of sassafras. I was learned then in science and philosophy, in the history of religions, in inductive and deductive logic, in liver mantic, in the shape and weight of skulls, in pharmacopeia and metallurgy, in all the useless branches of learning which give you indigestion and melancholia before your time. This vomit of learned truck was stewing in my guts the whole week long, waiting for it to come Sunday to be set to music. In between "The Midnight Fire Alarm" and "Marche Militaire" I would get my inspiration, which was to destroy all the existent forms of harmony and create my own cacophony. Imagine Uranus well aspected to Mars, to Mercury, to the Moon, to Jupiter, to Venus. It's hard to imagine because Uranus functions best when it is badly aspected, when it is "afflicted," so to speak. Yet that music which I gave off Sunday mornings, a music of well-being and of well-nourished desperation, was born of an illogically well-aspected Uranus firmly anchored in the Seventh House. I didn't know it then, I didn't know that Uranus existed, and lucky it was that I was ignorant. But I can see it now, because it was a fluky joy, a phony well-being, a destructive sort of fiery creation. The greater my euphoria the more tranquil the folks became. Even my sister who was dippy became calm and composed. The neighbors used to stand outside the window and listen, and now and then I would hear a burst of applause, and then bang, zip! like a rocket I was off again—Velocity Exercise No. 947½. If I happened to espy a cockroach crawling up the wall I was in bliss: that would lead me without the slightest modulation to Opus Izzit of my sadly corrugated clavichord. One Sunday, just like that, I composed one of the loveliest scherzos imaginable—to a louse. It was spring and we were all getting the sulphur treatment; I had been poring all week over Dante's *Inferno* in English. Sunday came like a thaw, the birds driven so crazy by the sudden heat that they flew in and out of the window, immune to the music. One of the German relatives had just arrived from Hamburg, or Bremen, a maiden aunt who looked like a bull-dyker. Just to be near her was sufficient to throw me into a fit of rage. She used to pat me on the head and tell me I would be another Mozart. I hated Mozart, and I hate him still, and so to get even with her I would play badly, play all the sour notes I knew. And then came the little louse, as I was saying, a real louse which had gotten buried in my winter underwear. I got him out and I put him tenderly on the tip of a black key. Then I began to do a little gigue around him with my right hand; the noise had probably deafened him. He was hypnotized, it seemed, by my nimble pyrotechnic. This trancelike immobility finally got on my nerves. I decided to introduce a chromatic scale, coming down on him full force with my third finger. I caught him fair and square, but with such force that he was glued to my fingertip. That put the St. Vitus Dance in me. From then on the scherzo commenced. It was a potpourri of forgotten melodies spiced with aloes and the juice of porcupines, played sometimes in three keys at once and pivoting always like a waltzing mouse around the immaculate conception. Later, when I went to hear Prokofiev, I understood what was happening to him; I understood Whitehead and Russell and Jeans and Eddington and Rudolf Eucken and Frobenius and Link Gillespie; I understood why, if there had never been a binominal theorem, man would have invented it; I understood why electricity and compressed air, to say nothing of Sprudel baths and fango packs. I understood very clearly, I must say, that man has a dead louse in his blood, and that when you're handed a symphony or a fresco or a high explosive you're really getting an ipecac reaction which was not included in the predestined bill of fare. I understood too why I had failed to become the musician I was. All the compositions I had created in my head, all these private and artistic auditions which were permitted me, thanks to St. Hildegarde or St. Bridget, or John of the Cross, or God knows whom, were written for an age to come, an age with less instruments and stronger antennae, stronger eardrums too. A different kind of suffering has to be experienced before such music can be appreciated. Beethoven staked out the new territory—one is aware of its presence when he erupts, when he breaks down in the very core of his stillness. It is a realm of new vibrations— to us only a misty nebula, for we have yet to pass beyond our own conception of suffering. We have yet to ingest this nebulous world, its travail, its orientation. I was permitted to hear an incredible music lying prone and indifferent to the sorrow about me. I heard the gestation of the new world, the sound of torrential rivers taking their course, the sound of stars grinding and chafing, of fountains clotted with blazing gems. All music is still governed by the old astronomy, is the product of the hothouse, a panacea for *Weltschmerz*. Music is still the antidote for the nameless, but this is not yet *music*. Music is planetary fire, an irreducible which is all sufficient; it is the slate-writing of the gods, the abracadabra which the learned and the ignorant alike muff because the axle has been unhooked. Look to the bowels, to the unconsolable and ineluctable! Nothing is determined, nothing is settled or solved. All this that is going on, all music, all architecture, all law, all government, all invention, all discovery—all this is velocity exercises in the dark, Czerny with a capital Zed riding a crazy white horse in a bottle of mucilage.

One of the reasons why I never got anywhere with the bloody music is that it was always mixed up with sex. As soon as I was able to play a song the cunts were around me like flies. To begin with, it was largely Lola's fault. Lola was my first piano teacher. Lola Niessen. It was a ridiculous name and typical of the neighborhood we were living in then. It sounded like a stinking bloater, or a wormy cunt. To tell the truth, Lola was not exactly a beauty. She looked somewhat like a Kalmuck or a Chinook, with sallow complexion and bilious-looking eyes. She had a few warts and wens, not to speak of the mustache. What excited me, however, was her hairiness; she had wonderful long fine black hair which she arranged in ascending and descending buns on her Mongolian skull. At the nape of the neck she curled it up in a serpentine knot. She was always late in coming, being a conscientious idiot, and by the time she arrived I was always a bit enervated from masturbating. As soon as she took the stool beside me, however, I became excited again, what with the stinking perfume she soused her armpits with. In the summer she wore loose sleeves and I could see the tufts of hair under her arms. The sight of it drove me wild. I imagined her as having hair all over, even in her navel. And what I wanted to do was to roll in it, bury my teeth in it. I could have eaten Lola's hair as a delicacy, if there had been a bit of flesh attached to it. Anyway she was hairy, that's what I want to say, and being hairy as a gorilla she got my mind off the music and on to her cunt. I was so damned eager to see that cunt of hers that finally one day I bribed her little brother to let me have a peep at her while she was in the bath. It was even more wonderful than I had imagined: she had a shag that reached from the navel to the crotch, an enormous thick tuft, a sporran, rich as a hand-woven rug. When she went over it with the powder puff I thought I would faint. The next time she came for the lesson I left a couple of buttons open on my fly. She didn't seem to notice anything amiss. The following time I left my whole fly open. This time she caught on. She said, "I think you've forgotten something, Henry." I looked at her, red as a beet, and I asked her blandly *what?* She pretended to look away while pointing to it with her left hand. Her hand came so close that I couldn't resist grabbing it and pushing it in my fly. She got up quickly, looking pale and frightened. By this time my prick was out of my fly and quivering with delight. I closed in on her and I reached up under her dress to get at that hand-woven rug I had seen through the keyhole. Suddenly I got a sound box on the ears, and then another and then she took me by the ear and leading me to a corner of the room she turned my face to the wall and said, "Now button up your fly, you silly boy!" We went back to the piano in a few moments—back to Czerny and the velocity exercises.

I couldn't see a sharp from a flat any more, but I continued to play because I was afraid she might tell my mother of the incident. Fortunately it was not an easy thing to tell one's mother.

The incident, embarrassing as it was, marked a decided change in our relations. I thought that the next time she came she would be severe with me, but on the contrary, she seemed to have dolled herself up, to have sprinkled more perfume over herself, and she was even a bit gay, which was unusual for Lola because she was a morose, withdrawn type. I didn't dare to open my fly again, but I would get an erection and hold it throughout the lesson, which she must have enjoyed because she was always stealing sidelong glances in that direction. I was only fifteen at the time, and she was easily twenty-five or twenty-eight. It was difficult for me to know what to do, unless it was to deliberately knock her down one day while my mother was out. For a time I actually shadowed her at night, when she went out alone. She had a habit of going out for long walks alone in the evening. I used to dog her steps; hoping she would get to some deserted spot near the cemetery where I might try some rough tactics. I had a feeling sometimes that she knew I was following her and that she enjoyed it. I think she was waiting for me to waylay her—I think that was what she wanted. Anyway, one night I was lying in the grass near the railroad tracks; it was a sweltering summer's night and people were lying about anywhere and everywhere, like panting dogs. I wasn't thinking of Lola at all—I was just mooning there, too hot to think about anything. Suddenly I see a woman coming along the narrow cinder-path. I'm lying sprawled out on the embankment and nobody around that I can notice. The woman is coming along slowly, head down, as though she were dreaming. As she gets close I recognize her. "Lola!" I call. "Lola!" She seems to be really astonished to see me there. "Why, what are you doing here?" she says, and with that she sits down beside me on the embankment. I didn't bother to answer her, I didn't say a word—I just crawled over her and flattened her. "Not here, please," she begged, but I paid no attention. I got my hand between her legs, all tangled up in that thick sporran of hers, and she was sopping wet, like a horse slavering. It was my first fuck, by Jesus, and it had to be that a train would come along and shower hot sparks over us. Lola was terrified. It was her first fuck too, I guess, and she probably needed it more than I, but when she felt the sparks she wanted to tear loose. It was like trying to hold down a wild mare. I couldn't keep her down, no matter how I wrestled with her. She got up, shook her clothes down, and adjusted the bun at the nape of her neck. "You must go home," she says. "I'm not going home," I said, and with that I took her by the arm and started walking. We walked along in dead silence for quite a distance. Neither of us seemed to be noticing where we were going. Finally we were out on the highway and up above us were the reservoirs and near the reservoirs was a pond. Instinctively I headed toward the pond. We had to pass under some low-hanging trees as we neared the pond. I was helping Lola to stoop down when suddenly she slipped, dragging me with her. She made no effort to get up; instead she caught hold of me and pressed me to her, and to my complete amazement I also felt her slip her hand in my fly. She caressed me so wonderfully that in a jiffy I came in her hand. Then she took my hand and put it between her legs. She lay back completely relaxed and opened her legs wide. I bent over and kissed every hair on her cunt; I put my tongue in her navel and licked it clean. Then I lay with my head between her legs and lapped up the drool that was pouring from her. She was moaning now and clutching wildly with her hands; her hair had come completely undone and was lying over her bare abdomen. To make it short, I got it in again, and I held it a long time, for which she must have been damned grateful because she came I don't know how many times —it was like a pack of firecrackers going off, and with it all she sunk her teeth into me, bruised my lips, clawed me, ripped my shirt and what the hell not. I was branded like a steer when I got home and took a look at myself in the mirror.

It was wonderful while it lasted, but it didn't last long. A month later the Niessens moved to another city, and I never saw Lola again. But I hung her sporran over the bed and I prayed to it every night. And whenever I began the Czerny stuff I would get an erection, thinking of Lola lying in the grass, thinking of her long black hair, the bun at the nape of her neck, the groans she vented and the juice that poured out of her. Playing the piano was just one long vicarious fuck for me. I had to wait another two years before I would get my end in again, as they say, and then it wasn't so good because I got a beautiful dose with it, and besides it wasn't in the grass and it wasn't summer, and there was no heat in it but just a cold mechanical fuck for a buck in a dirty little hotel room, the bastard trying to pretend she was coming and not coming any more than Christmas was coming. And maybe it wasn't her that gave me the clap, but her pal in the next room who was laying up with my friend Simmons. It was like this—I had finished so quick with my mechanical fuck that I thought I'd go in and see how it was going with my friend Simmons. Lo and behold, they were still at it, and they were going strong. She was a Czech, his girl, and a bit sappy; she hadn't been at it very long, apparently, and she used to forget herself and enjoy the act. Watching her hand it out, I decided to wait and have a go at her myself. And so I did. And before the week was out I had a discharge, and after that I figured it would be blueballs or rocks in the groin.

Another year or so and I was giving lessons myself, and as luck would have it, the mother of the girl I'm teaching is a slut, a tramp and a trollop if ever there was one. She was living with a nigger, as I later found out. Seems she couldn't get a prick big enough to satisfy her. Anyway, every time I started to go home she'd hold me up at the door and rub it up against me. I was afraid of starting in with her because rumor had it that she was full of syph, but what the hell are you going to do when a hot bitch like that plasters her cunt up against you and slips her tongue halfway down your throat. I used to fuck her standing up in the vestibule, which wasn't so difficult because she was light and l could hold her in my hands like a doll. And like that I'm holding her one night when suddenly I hear a key being fitted into the lock, and she hears it too and she's frightened stiff. There's nowhere to go. Fortunately there's a portiere hanging at the doorway and I hide behind that. Then I hear her black buck kissing her and saying *how are yer, honey?* and she's saying how she had been waiting up for him and better come right upstairs because she can't wait and so on. And when the stairs stop squeaking I gently open the door and sally out, and then by God I have a real fright because if that black buck ever finds out I'll have my throat slit and no mistake about it. And so I stop giving lessons at that joint, but soon the daughter is after me—just turning sixteen—and won't I come and give her lessons at a friend's house? We begin the Czerny exercises all over again, sparks and everything. It's the first smell of fresh cunt I've had, and it's wonderful, like newmown hay. We fuck our way through one lesson after another and in between lessons we do a little extra fucking. And then one day it's the sad story—she's knocked up and what to do about it? I have to get a Jewboy to help me out, and he wants twenty-five bucks for the job and I've never seen twenty-five bucks in my life. Besides, she's under age. Besides, she might have blood poisoning. I give him five bucks on account and beat it to the Adirondacks for a couple of weeks. In the Adirondacks I meet a schoolteacher who's dying to take lessons. More velocity exercises, more condoms and conundrums. Every time I touched the piano I seemed to shake a cunt loose.

If there was a party I had to bring the fucking music roll along; to me it was just like wrapping my penis in a handkerchief and slinging it under my arm. In vacation time, at a farmhouse or an inn, where there was always a surplus of cunt, the music had an extraordinary effect. Vacation time was a period I looked forward to the whole year, not because of the cunts so much as because it meant no work. Once out of harness I became a clown. I was so chock-full of energy that I wanted to jump out of my skin. I remember one summer in the Catskills meeting a girl named Francie. She was beautiful and lascivious, with strong Scotch teats and a row of white even teeth that was dazzling. It began in the river where we were swimming. We were holding on to the boat and one of her boobies had slipped out of bounds. I slipped the other one out for her and then I undid the shoulder straps. She ducked under the boat coyly and I followed and as she was coming up for air I wiggled the bloody bathing suit off her and there she was floating like a mermaid with her big strong teats bobbing up and down like bloated corks. I wriggled out of my tights and we began playing like dolphins under the side of the boat. In a little while her girl friend came along in a canoe. She was a rather hefty girl, a sort of strawberry blonde with agate-colored eyes and full of freckles. She was rather shocked to find us in the raw, but we soon tumbled her out of the canoe and stripped her. And then the three of us began to play tag under the water, but it was hard to get anywhere with them because they were slippery as eels. After we had had enough of it we ran to a little bathhouse which was standing in the field like an abandoned sentry box. We had brought our clothes along and we were going to get dressed, the three of us, in this little box. It was frightfully hot and sultry and the clouds were gathering for a storm. Agnes—that was Francie's friend—was in a hurry to get dressed. She was beginning to be ashamed of herself standing there naked in front of us. Francie, on the other hand, seemed to be perfectly at ease. She was sitting on the bench with her legs crossed and smoking a cigarette. Anyway, just as Agnes was pulling on her chemise there came a flash of lightning and a terrifying clap of thunder right on the heels of it. Agnes screamed and dropped her chemise. There came another flash in a few seconds and again a peal of thunder, dangerously close. The air got blue all around us and the flies began to bite and we felt nervous and itchy and a bit panicky too. Especially Agnes who was afraid of the lightning and even more afraid of being found dead and the three of us stark naked. She wanted to get her things on and run for the house, she said. And just as she got that off her chest the rain came down, in bucketsful. We thought it would stop in a few minutes and so we stood there naked looking out at the steaming river through the partly opened door. It seemed to be raining rocks and the lightning kept playing around us incessantly. We were all thoroughly frightened now and in a quandary as to what to do. Agnes was wringing her hands and praying out loud; she looked like a George Grosz idiot, one of those lopsided bitches with a rosary around the neck and yellow jaundice to boot. I thought she was going to faint on us or something. Suddenly I got the bright idea of doing a war dance in the rain—to distract them. Just as I jump out to commence my shindig a streak of lightning flashes and splits open a tree not far off. I'm so damned scared that I lose my wits. Always when I'm frightened I laugh. So I laughed, a wild, bloodcurdling laugh which made the girls scream. When I heard them scream, I don't know why, but I thought of the velocity exercises, and with that I felt that I was standing in the void and it was blue all around and the rain was beating a hot-and-cold tattoo on my tender flesh. All my sensations had gathered on the surface of the skin and underneath the outermost layer of skin I was empty, light as a feather, lighter than air or smoke or talcum or magnesium or any goddamned thing you want. Suddenly I was a Chippewa and it was the key of sassafras again and I didn't give a fuck whether the girls were screaming or fainting or shitting in their pants, which they were minus anyway. Looking at crazy Agnes with the rosary around her neck and her big breadbasket blue with fright I got the notion to do a sacrilegious dance, with one hand cupping my balls and the other hand thumbing my nose at the thunder and lightning. The rain was hot and cold and the grass seemed full of dragonflies. I hopped about like a kangaroo and I yelled at the top of my lungs—"O Father, you wormy old son of a bitch, pull in that fucking lightning or Agnes won't believe in you any more! Do you hear me, you old prick up there, stop the shenanigans . . . you're driving Agnes nutty. Hey you, are you deaf, you old futzer?" And with a continuous rattle of this defiant nonsense on my lips I danced around the bathhouse, leaping and bounding like a gazelle and using the most frightful oaths I could summon. When the lightning cracked I jumped higher and when the thunder clapped I roared like a lion and then I did a handspring and then I rolled in the grass like a cub and I chewed the grass and spit it out for them and I pounded my chest like a gorilla and all the time I could see the Czerny exercises resting on the piano, the white page full of sharps and flats, and the fucking idiot, think I to myself, imagining that that's the way to learn how to manipulate the well-tempered clavichord. And suddenly I thought that Czerny might be in heaven by now and looking down on me and so I spat up at him high as I could spit and when the thunder rolled again I yelled with all my might —"You bastard, Czerny, *you* up there, may the lightning twist your balls off . . . may you swallow your own crooked tail and strangle yourself . . . do you hear me, you crazy prick?"

But in spite of all my good efforts Agnes was getting more delirious. She was a dumb Irish Catholic and she had never heard God spoken to that way before. Suddenly, while I was dancing about in the rear of the bathhouse she bolted for the river. I heard Francie scream—"Bring her back, she'll drown herself! Bring her back!" I started after her, the rain still coming down like pitchforks, and yelling to her to come back, but she ran on blindly as though possessed of the devil, and when she got to the water's edge she dove straight in and made for the boat. I swam after her and as we got to the side of the boat, which I was afraid she would capsize, I got hold of her round the waist with my one hand and I started to talk to her calmly and soothingly, as though I was talking to a child. "Go away from me," she said, "you're an atheist!" Jesus, you could have knocked me over with a feather, so astonished I was to hear that. So that was it? All that hysteria because I was insulting the Lord Almighty. I felt like batting her one in the eye to bring her to her senses. But we were out over our heads and I had a fear that she would do some mad thing like pulling the boat over our heads if I didn't handle her right. So I pretended that I was terribly sorry and I said I didn't mean a word of it, that I had been scared to death, and so on and so forth, and as I talked to her gently, soothingly, I slipped my hand down from her waist and I gently stroked her ass. That was what she wanted all right. She was talking to me blubberingly about what a good Catholic she was and how she had tried not to sin, and maybe she was so wrapped up in what she was saying she didn't know what I was doing, but just the same when I got my hand in her crotch and said all the beautiful things I could think of, about God, about love, about going to church and confessing and all that crap, she must have felt something because I had a good three fingers inside her and working them around like drunken bobbins. "Put your arms around me, Agnes," I said softly, slipping my hand out and pulling her to me so that I could get my legs between hers. . . . "There, that's a girl . . . take it easy now . . . it'll stop soon." And still talking about the church, the confessional, God, love, and the whole bloody mess I managed to get it inside of her. "You're very good to me," she said, just as though she didn't know my prick was in her, "and I'm sorry I acted like a fool." "I know, Agnes," I said, "it's all right . . .

listen, grab me tighter . . . yeah, that's it." "I'm afraid the
boat's going to tip over," she says, trying her best to keep
her ass in position by paddling with her right hand. "Yes,
let's get back to the shore," I said, and I start to pull away
from her. "Oh don't leave me," she says, clutching me
tighter. "Don't leave me, I'll drown." Just then Francie
comes running down to the water. "Hurry," says Agnes,
"hurry . . . I'll drown."

Francie was a good sort, I must say. She certainly
wasn't a Catholic and if she had any morals they were
of the reptilian order. She was one of those girls who
are born to fuck. She had no aims, no great desires,
showed no jealousy, held no grievances, was constantly
cheerful and not at all unintelligent. At nights when we
were sitting on the porch in the dark talking to the guests
she would come over and sit on my lap with nothing on
underneath her dress and I would slip it into her as she
laughed and talked to the others. I think she would have
brazened it out before the Pope if she had been given a
chance. Back in the city, when I called on her at her
home, she pulled the same stunt off in front of her mother
whose sight, fortunately, was growing dim. If we went
dancing and she got too hot in the pants she would drag
me to a telephone booth and, queer girl that she was,
she'd actually talk to some one, some one like Agnes, for
example while pulling off the trick. She seemed to get a
special pleasure out of doing it under people's noses; she
said there was more fun in it if you didn't think about it
too hard. In the crowded subway, coming home from the
beach, say, she'd slip her dress around so that the slit
was in the middle and take my hand and put it right on
her cunt. If the train was tightly packed and we were
safely wedged in a corner she'd take my cock out of my
fly and hold it in her two hands, as though it were a bird.
Sometimes she'd get playful and hang her bag on it, as
though to prove that there wasn't the least danger. Another thing about her was that she didn't pretend that I
was the only guy she had on the string. Whether she told

me everything I don't know, but she certainly told me plenty. She told me about her affairs laughingly, while she was climbing over me or when I had it in her, or just when I was about to come. She would tell me how they went about it, how big they were or how small, what they said when they got excited and so on and so forth, giving me every possible detail, just as though I were going to write a textbook on the subject. She didn't seem to have the least feeling of sacredness about her own body or her feelings or anything connected with herself. "Francie, you bloody fucker," I used to say, "you've got the morals of a clam." "But you like me, don't you?" she'd answer. "Men like to fuck, and so do women. It doesn't harm anybody and it doesn't mean you have to love everyone you fuck, does it? I wouldn't want to be in love; it must be terrible to have to fuck the same man all the time, don't you think? Listen, if you didn't fuck anybody but me all the time you'd get tired of me quick, wouldn't you? Sometimes it's nice to be fucked by some one you don't know at all. Yes, I think that's the best of all," she added— "there's no complications, no telephone numbers, no love letters, no scraps, what? Listen, do you think this is very bad? Once I tried to get my brother to fuck me; you know what a sissy he is—he gives everybody a pain. I don't remember exactly how it was any more, but anyway we were in the house alone and I was passionate that day. He came into my bedroom to ask me for something. I was lying there with my dress up, thinking about it and wanting it terribly, and when he came in I didn't give a damn about his being my brother, I just thought of him as a man, and so I lay there with my skirt up and I told him I wasn't feeling well, that I had a pain in my stomach. He wanted to run right out and get something for me but I told him no, just to rub my stomach a bit, that would do it good. I opened my waist and made him rub my bare skin. He was trying to keep his eyes on the wall, the big idiot, and rubbing me as though I were a piece of wood. 'It's not there, you chump,' I said, 'it's lower down . . .

what are you afraid of?' And I pretended that I was in
agony. Finally he touched me accidentally. 'There! that's
it!' I shouted. 'Oh do rub it, it feels so good!' Do you know,
the big sap actually massaged me for five minutes without realizing that it was all a game? I was so exasperated
that I told him to get the hell out and leave me alone.
'You're a eunuch,' I said, but he was such a sap I don't
think he knew what the word meant." She laughed, thinking what a ninny her brother was. She said he probably
still had his maiden. What did I think about it—was it
so terribly bad? Of course she knew I wouldn't think
anything of the kind. "Listen, Francie," I said, "did you
ever tell that story to the cop you're going with?" She
guessed she hadn't. "I guess so too," I said. "He'd beat
the piss out of you if he ever heard that yarn." "He's
socked me already," she answered promptly. "*What?*" I
said, "you let him beat you up?" "I don't ask him to," she
said, "but you know how quick-tempered he is. I don't
let anybody else sock me but somehow coming from him
I don't mind it so much. Sometimes it makes me feel good
inside. . . . I don't know, maybe a woman ought to get
beaten up once in a while. It doesn't hurt so much, if you
really like a guy. And afterwards he's so damned gentle—
I almost feel ashamed of myself. . . ."

It isn't often you get a cunt who'll admit such things
—I mean a regular cunt and not a moron. There was Trix
Miranda, for example, and her sister, Mrs. Costello. A
fine pair of birds they were. Trix, who was going with
my friend MacGregor, tried to pretend to her own sister,
with whom she was living, that she had no sexual relations with MacGregor. And the sister was pretending to
all and sundry that she was frigid, that she couldn't
have any relations with a man even if she wanted to,
because she was "built too small." And meanwhile my
friend MacGregor was fucking them silly, both of them,
and they both knew about each other but still they lied
like that to each other. Why? I couldn't make it out. The
Costello bitch was hysterical; whenever she felt that she

wasn't getting a fair percentage of the lays that Mac-Gregor was handing out she'd throw a pseudo-epileptic fit. That meant throwing towels over her, patting her wrists, opening her bosom, chafing her legs and finally hoisting her upstairs to bed where my friend MacGregor would look after her as soon as he had put the other one to sleep. Sometimes the two sisters would lie down together to take a nap of an afternoon; if MacGregor were around he would go upstairs and lie between them. As he explained it to me laughingly, the trick was for him to pretend to go to sleep. He would lie there breathing heavily, opening now one eye, now the other, to see which one was really dozing off. As soon as he was convinced that one of them was asleep he'd tackle the other. On such occasions he seemed to prefer the hysterical sister, Mrs. Costello, whose husband visited her about once every six months. The more risk he ran, the more thrill he got out of it, he said. If it were with the other sister, Trix, whom he was supposed to be courting, he had to pretend that it would be terrible if the other one were to catch them like that, and at the same time, he admitted to me, he was always hoping that the other one would wake and catch them. But the married sister, the one who was "built too small," as she used to say, was a wily bitch and besides she felt guilty toward her sister and if her sister had ever caught her in the act she'd probably have pretended that she was having a fit and didn't know what she was doing. Nothing on earth could make her admit that she was actually permitting herself the pleasure of being fucked by a man.

I knew her quite well because I was giving her lessons for a time, and I used to do my damnedest to make her admit that she had a normal cunt and that she'd enjoy a good fuck if she could get it now and then. I used to tell her wild stories, which were really thinly disguised accounts of her own doings, and yet she remained adamant. I had even gotten her to the point one day—and this beats everything—where she let me put my finger inside her. I thought sure it was settled. It's true she was dry and a bit tight, but I put that down to her hysteria. But imagine getting that far with a cunt and then having her say to your face, as she yanks her dress down violently —"you see, I told you I wasn't built right!" "I don't see anything of the kind," I said angrily. "What do you expect me to do—use a microscope on you?"

"I like that," she said, pretending to get on her high horse. "What a way of talking to me!"

"You know damned well you're lying," I continued. "Why do you lie like that? Don't you think it's human to have a cunt and to use it once in a while? Do you want it to dry up on you?"

"Such language!" she said, biting her underlip and reddening like a beet. "I always thought you were a gentleman."

"Well, you're no lady," I retorted, "because even a lady admits to a fuck now and then, and besides ladies don't ask gentlemen to stick their fingers up inside them and see how small they're built."

"I never asked you to touch me," she said. "I wouldn't think of asking you to put your hand on me, on my private parts anyway."

"Maybe you thought I was going to swab your ear for you, is that it?"

"I thought of you like a doctor at that moment, that's all I can say," she said stiffly, trying to freeze me out.

"Listen," I said, taking a wild chance, "let's pretend that it was all a mistake, that nothing happened, nothing at all. I know you too well to think of insulting you like that. I wouldn't think of doing a thing like that to you— no, damned if I would. I was just wondering if maybe you weren't right in what you said, if maybe you aren't built rather small. You know, it all went so quick I couldn't tell what I felt . . . I don't think I even put my finger inside you. I must have just touched the outside— that's about all. Listen, sit down here on the couch . . . let's be friends again." I pulled her down beside me—

she was melting visibly—and I put my arm around her waist, as though to console her more tenderly. "Has it always been like that?" I asked innocently, and I almost laughed the next moment, realizing what an idiotic question it was. She hung her head coyly, as though we were touching on an unmentionable tragedy. "Listen, maybe if you sat on my lap . . ." and I hoisted her gently on to my lap, at the same time delicately putting my hand under her dress and resting it lightly on her knee . . . "maybe if you sat a moment like this, you'd feel better . . . there, that's it, just snuggle back in my arms . . . are you feeling better?" She didn't answer, but she didn't resist either; she just lay back limply and closed her eyes. Gradually and very gently and smoothly I moved my hand up her leg, talking to her in a low, soothing voice all the time. When I got my fingers into her crotch and parted the little lips she was as moist as a dishrag. I massaged it gently, opening it up more and more, and still handing out a telepathic line about women sometimes being mistaken about themselves and how sometimes they think they're very small when really they're quite normal, and the longer I kept it up the juicier she got and the more she opened up. I had four fingers inside her and there was room inside for more if I had had more to put in. She had an enormous cunt and it had been well reamed out, I could feel. I looked at her to see if she was still keeping her eyes shut. Her mouth was open and she was gasping but her eyes were tight shut, as though she were pretending to herself that it was all a dream. I could move her about roughly now—no danger of the slightest protest. And maliciously perhaps, I jostled her about unnecessarily, just to see if she would come to. She was as limp as a feather pillow and even when her head struck the arm of the sofa she showed no sign of irritation. It was as though she had anesthetized herself for a gratuitous fuck. I pulled all her clothes off and threw them on the floor, and after I had given her a bit of a workout on the sofa I slipped it out and laid her on the

floor, on her clothes; and then I slipped it in again and
she held it tight with that suction valve she used so skill-
fully, despite the outward appearance of coma.

It seems strange to me that the music always passed
off into sex. Nights, if I went out alone for a walk, I was
sure to pick up someone—a nurse, a girl coming out of a
dance hall, a salesgirl, anything with a skirt on. If I went
out with my friend MacGregor in his car—just a little
spin to the beach, he would say—I would find myself
by midnight sitting in some strange parlor in some queer
neighborhood with a girl on my lap, usually one I didn't
give a damn about because MacGregor was even less
selective than I. Often, stepping in his car I'd say to him
—"listen, no cunts tonight, what?" And he'd say—"Jesus,
no, I'm fed up . . . just a little drive somewhere . . . maybe
to Sheepshead Bay, what do you say?" We wouldn't have
gone more than a mile when suddenly he'd pull the car
up to the curb and nudge me. "Get a look at that," he'd
say, pointing to a girl strolling along the sidewalk. "Jesus,
what a leg!" Or else—"Listen, what do you say we ask
her to come along? Maybe she can dig up a friend." And
before I could say another word he'd be hailing her and
handing out his usual patter, which was the same for
everyone. And nine times out of ten the girl came along.
And before we'd gone very far, feeling her up with his
free hand, he'd ask her if she didn't have a friend she
could dig up to keep us company. And if she put up a
fuss, if she didn't like being pawed over that way too
quickly, he'd say—"All right, get the hell out then . . .
we can't waste any time on the likes of you!" And with
that he'd slow up and shove her out. "We can't be
bothered with cunts like that, can we Henry?" he'd say,
chuckling softly. "You wait, I promise you something
good before the night's over." And if I reminded him that
we were going to lay off for one night he'd answer: "Well,
just as you like. . . . I was only thinking it might make
it more pleasant for you." And then suddenly the brakes

would pull us up and he'd be saying to some silky silhouette looming out of the dark—"hello sister, what yer doing—taking a little stroll?" And maybe this time it would be something exciting, a dithery little bitch with nothing else to do but pull up her skirt and hand it to you. Maybe we wouldn't even have to buy her a drink, just haul up somewhere on a side road and go at it, one after the other, in the car. And if she was an emptyheaded bimbo, as they usually were, he wouldn't even bother to drive her home. "We're not going that way," he'd say, the bastard that he was. "You'd better jump out here," and with that he'd open the door and out with her. His next thought was, of course, was she clean? That would occupy his mind all the way back. "Jesus, we ought to be more careful," he'd say. "You don't know what you're getting yourself into picking them up like that. Ever since that last one—you remember, the one we picked up on the Drive—I've been itchy as hell. Maybe it's just nervousness . . . I think about it too much. Why can't a guy stick to one cunt, tell me that, Henry. You take Trix, now, she's a good kid, you know that. And I like her too, in a way, but . . . shit, what's the use of talking about it? You know me—I'm a glutton. You know, I'm getting so bad that sometimes when I'm on my way to a date—mind you, with a girl I want to fuck, and everything fixed too—as I say, sometimes I'm rolling along and maybe out of the corner of my eye I catch a flash of a leg crossing the street and before I know it I've got her in the car and the hell with the other girl. I must be cunt-struck, I guess . . . what do you think? Don't tell me," he would add quickly. " I know you, you bugger . . . you'll be sure to tell me the worst." And then, after a pause— "you're a funny guy, do you know that? I never notice you refusing anything, but somehow you don't seem to be worrying about it all the time. Sometimes you strike me as though you didn't give a damn one way or the other. And you're a steady bastard too—almost a monog- amist, I'd say. How you can keep it up so long with one

woman beats me. Don't you get bored with them? Jesus,
I know so well what they're going to say. Sometimes I
feel like saying . . . you know, just breeze in on 'em and
say: 'Listen, kid, don't say a word . . . just fish it out and
open your legs wide.' " He laughed heartily. "Can you
imagine the expression on Trix's face if I pulled a line
like that on her? I'll tell you, once I came pretty near
doing it. I kept my hat and coat on. *Was she sore!* She
didn't mind my keeping my coat on so much, but the hat!
I told her I was afraid of a draught . . . of course there
wasn't any draught. The truth is, I was so damned impa-
tient to get away that I thought if I kept my hat on I'd be
off quicker. Instead I was there all night with her. She put
up such a row that I couldn't get her quiet. . . . But listen,
that's nothing. Once I had a drunken Irish bitch and this
one had some queer ideas. In the first place, she never
wanted it in bed . . . always on the table. You know, that's
all right once in a while, but if you do it often it wears you
out. So one night—I was a little tight, I guess—I says to
her, no, nothing doing, you drunken bastard . . . you're
gonna go to bed with me tonight. I want a real fuck—*in
bed*. You know, I had to argue with that bitch for
an hour almost before I could persuade her to go to
bed with me, and then only on the agreement that I was
to keep my hat on. Listen, can you picture me getting
over that stupid bitch with my hat on? And stark naked
to boot! I asked her . . . I said, 'why do you want me to
keep my hat on?' You know what she said? She said it
seemed more genteel. Can you imagine what a mind that
cunt had? I used to hate myself for going with that bitch.
I never went to her sober, that's one thing. I'd have to
be tanked up first and kind of blind and batty—you
know how I get sometimes. . . ."

I knew very well what he meant. He was one of my
oldest friends and one of the most cantankerous bastards
I ever knew. Stubborn wasn't the word for it. He was
like a mule—a pigheaded Scotchman. And his old man
was even worse. When the two of them got into a rage it

was a pretty sight. The old man used to dance, positively *dance* with rage. If the old lady got between she'd get a sock in the eye. They used to put him out of the house regularly. Out he'd go, with all his belongings, including the furniture, including the piano too. In a month or so he'd be back again—because they always gave him credit at home. And then he'd come home drunk some night with a woman he'd picked up somewhere and the rumpus would start all over again. It seems they didn't mind so much his coming home with a girl and keeping her all night, but what they did object to was the cheek of him asking his mother to serve them breakfast in bed. If his mother tried to bawl him out he'd shut her up by saying —"What are you trying to tell me? You wouldn't have been married yet if you hadn't been knocked up." The old lády would wring her hands and say—"What a son! What a son! God help me, what have I done to deserve this?" To which he'd remark, "Aw forget it! You're just an old prune!" Often as not his sister would come up to try and smooth matters out. "Jesus, Wallie," she'd say, "it's none of my business what you do, but can't you talk to your mother more respectfully?" Whereupon MacGregor would make his sister sit on the bed and start coaxing her to bring up the breakfast. Usually he'd have to ask his bed-mate what her name was in order to present her to his sister. "She's not a bad kid," he'd say, referring to his sister. "She's the only decent one in the family. . . . Now listen, Sis, bring up some grub, will yer? Some nice bacon and eggs, eh, what do you say? Listen, is the old man around? What's his mood today? I'd like to borrow a couple of bucks. You try and worm it out of him, will you? I'll get you something nice for Christmas." Then, as though everything were settled, he'd pull back the covers to expose the wench beside him. "Look at her, Sis, ain't she beautiful? Look at that leg! Listen, you ought to get yourself a man . . . you're too skinny. Patsy here, I bet she doesn't go begging for it, eh Patsy?" and with that a sound slap on the rump for Patsy. "Now scram, Sis, I want some coffee . . . and don't forget, make the bacon crisp! Don't get any of that lousy store bacon . . . get something extra. And be quick about it!"

What I liked about him were his weaknesses; like all men who practice will power he was absolutely flabby inside. There wasn't a thing he wouldn't do—out of weakness. He was always very busy and he was never really doing anything. And always boning up on something, always trying to improve his mind. For example, he would take the unabridged dictionary and, tearing out a page each day, would read it through religiously on his way back and forth from the office. He was full of facts, and the more absurd and incongruous the facts, the more pleasure he derived from them. He seemed to be bent on proving to all and sundry that life was a farce, that it wasn't worth the game, that one thing canceled out another, and so on. He was brought up on the North Side, not very far from the neighborhood in which I had spent my childhood. He was very much a product of the North Side, too, and that was one of the reasons why I liked him. The way he talked, out of the corner of his mouth, for instance, the tough air he put on when talking to a cop, the way he spat in disgust, the peculiar curse words he used, the sentimentality, the limited horizon, the passion for playing pool or shooting craps, the staying up all night swapping yarns, the contempt for the rich, the hobnobbing with politicians, the curiosity about worthless things, the respect for learning, the fascination of the dance hall, the saloon, the burlesque, talking about seeing the world and never budging out of the city, idolizing no matter whom so long as the person showed "spunk," a thousand and one little traits or peculiarities of this sort endeared him to me because it was precisely such idiosyncrasies which marked the fellows I had known as a child. The neighborhood was composed of nothing, it seemed, but lovable failures. The grownups behaved like children and the children were incorrigible. Nobody could rise very far above his neighbor or he'd be lynched. It was amazing that any one ever became a doctor or a lawyer. Even so, he had to be a good fellow, had to pretend to talk like everyone else, and he had to vote the Democratic ticket. To hear MacGregor talk about Plato or Nietzsche, for instance, to his buddies was something to remember. In the first place, to even get permission to talk about such things as Plato or Nietzsche to his companions, he had to pretend that it was only by accident that he had run across their names; or perhaps he'd say that he had met an interesting drunk one night in the back room of a saloon and this drunk had started talking about these guys Nietzsche and Plato. He would even pretend he didn't quite know how the names were pronounced. Plato wasn't such a dumb bastard, he would say apologetically. Plato had an idea or two in his bean, yes sir, yes siree. He'd like to see one of those dumb politicians at Washington trying to lock horns with a guy like Plato. And he'd go on, in this roundabout, matter of fact fashion to explain to his crapshooting friends just what kind of a bright bird Plato was in his time and how he measured up against other men in other times. Of course, he was probably a eunuch, he would add, by way of throwing a little cold water on all this erudition. In those days, as he nimbly explained, the big guys, the philosophers, often had their nuts cut off—a fact!—so as to be out of all temptation. The other guy, Nietzsche, he was a real case, a case for the bughouse. He was supposed to be in love with his sister. Hypersensitive like. Had to live in a special climate—in Nice, he thought it was. As a rule he didn't care much for the Germans, but this guy Nietzsche was different. As a matter of fact, he hated the Germans, this Nietzsche. He claimed he was a Pole or something like that. He had them dead right, too. He said they were stupid and swinish, and by God, he knew what he was talking about. Anyway, he showed them up. He said they were full of shit, to make it brief, and by God, wasn't he right though? Did you see the way those bastards turned tail when they got a dose of their own medicine?

"Listen, I know a guy who cleaned out a nestful of them in the Argonne region—he said they were so goddamned low he wouldn't shit on them. He said he wouldn't even waste a bullet on them—he just bashed their brains in with a club. I forget this guy's name now, but anyway he told me he saw aplenty in the few months he was there. He said the best fun he got out of the whole fucking business was to pop off his own major. Not that he had any special grievance against him—he just didn't like his mug. He didn't like the way the guy gave orders. Most of the officers that were killed got it in the back, he said. Served them right, too, the pricks! He was just a lad from the North Side. I think he runs a poolroom now down near Wallabout Market. A quiet fellow, minds his own business. But if you start talking to him about the war he goes off the handle. He says he'd assassinate the President of the United States if they ever tried to start another war. Yeah, and he'd do it too, I'm telling you. . . . But shit, what was that I wanted to tell you about Plato? Oh yeah. . . ."

When the others were gone he'd suddenly shift gears. "You don't believe in talking like that, do you?," he'd begin. I had to admit I didn't. "You're wrong," he'd continue. "You've got to keep in with people, you don't know when you may need one of these guys. You act on the assumption that you're free, independent! You act as though you were superior to these people. Well, that's where you make a big mistake. How do you know where you'll be five years from now, or even six months from now? You might be blind, you might be run over by a truck, you might be put in the bughouse; you can't tell what's going to happen to you. Nobody can. You might be as helpless as a baby. . . ."

"So what?" I would say.

"Well, don't you think it would be good to have a friend when you need one? You might be so goddamned helpless you'd be glad to have some one help you across the street. You think these guys are worthless; you think I'm wasting my time with them. Listen, you never know what a man might do for you some day. Nobody gets anywhere alone. . . ."

He was touchy about my independence, what he called my indifference. If I was obliged to ask him for a little dough he was delighted. That gave him a chance to deliver a little sermon on friendship. "So you have to have money, too?" he'd say, with a big satisfied grin spreading all over his face. "So the poet has to eat too? Well, well. . . . It's lucky you came to me, Henry me boy, because I'm easy with you, I know you, you heartless son of a bitch. Sure, what do you want? I haven't got very much, but I'll split it with you. That's fair enough, isn't it? Or do you think, you bastard, that maybe I ought to give you it all and go out and borrow something for myself? I suppose you want a *good* meal, eh? Ham and eggs wouldn't be good enough, would it? I suppose you'd like me to drive you to the restaurant too, eh? Listen, get up from that chair a minute—I want to put a cushion under your ass. Well, well, so you're broke! Jesus, you're always broke—I never remember seeing you with money in your pocket. Listen, don't you ever feel ashamed of yourself? You talk about those bums I hang out with . . . well listen, mister, those guys never come and bum me for a dime like you do. They've got more pride— they'd rather steal it than come and grub it off me. But *you*, shit, you're full of highfalutin' ideas, you want to reform the world and all that crap—you don't want to work for money, no, not you . . . you expect somebody to hand it to you on a silver platter. Huh! Lucky there's guys like me around that understand you. You need to get wise to yourself, Henry. You're dreaming. Everybody wants to eat, don't you know that? Most people are willing to work for it—they don't lie in bed all day like you and then suddenly pull on their pants and run to the first friend at hand. Supposing I wasn't here, what would you have done? Don't answer . . . I know what you're going to say. But listen, you can't go on all your life like that. Sure, you talk fine—it's a pleasure to listen to you. You're the only guy I know that I really enjoy talking to, but where's it going to get you? One of these days they'll lock you up for vagrancy. You're just a bum, don't you know that? You're not even as good as those other bums you preach about. Where are you when I'm in a jam? You can't be found. You don't answer my letters, you don't answer the telephone, you even hide sometimes when I come to see you. Listen, I know—you don't have to explain to me. I know you don't want to hear my stories all the time. But shit, sometimes I really have to talk to you. A fucking lot you care though. So long as you're out of the rain and putting another meal under your belt you're happy. You don't think about your friends—until you're desperate. That's no way to behave, *is it?* Say no and I'll give you a buck. Goddamn it, Henry, you're the only real friend I've got, but you're a son of a bitch of a mucker if I know what I'm talking about. You're just a born good for nothing son of a bitch. You'd rather starve than turn your hand to something useful. . . ."

Naturally I'd laugh and hold my hand out for the buck he had promised me. That would irritate him afresh. "You're ready to say anything, aren't you, if only I give you the buck I promised you? What a guy! Talk about morals —Jesus, you've got the ethics of a rattlesnake. *No*, I'm not giving it to you yet, by Christ. I'm going to torture you a little more first. I'm going to make you *earn* this money, if I can. Listen, what about shining my shoes—do that for me, will you? They'll never get shined if you don't do it now." I pick up the shoes and ask him for the brush. I don't mind shining his shoes, not in the least. But that too seems to incense him. "You're going to shine them, are you? Well, by Jesus, that beats all hell. Listen, where's your pride—didn't you ever have any? And you're the guy that knows everything. It's amazing. You know so god-damned much that you have to shine your friend's shoes to worm a meal out of him. A fine pickle! Here, you

bastard, here's the brush! Shine the other pair too while
you're at it."

A pause. He's washing himself at the sink and humming
a bit. Suddenly, in a bright, cheerful tone—"How is it
out today, Henry? Is it sunny? Listen, I've got just the
place for you. What do you say to scallops and bacon with
a little tartar sauce on the side? It's a little joint down near
the inlet. A day like today is just the day for scallops and
bacon, eh what, Henry? Don't tell me you've got something to do . . . if I haul you down there you've got to
spend a little time with me, you know that, don't you?
Jesus, I wish I had your disposition. You just drift along,
from minute to minute. Sometimes I think you're a damned
sight better off than any of us, even if you are a stinking
son of a bitch and a traitor and a thief. When I'm with
you the day seems to pass like a dream. Listen, don't you
see what I mean when I say I've got to see you sometimes?
I go nuts being all by myself all the time. Why do I go
chasing around after cunt so much? Why do I play cards
all night? Why do I hang out with those bums from the
Point? I need to talk to someone, that's what."

A little later at the bay, sitting out over the water, with a
shot of rye in him and waiting for the sea food to be served
up. . . . "Life's not so bad if you can do what you want, eh
Henry? If I make a little dough I'm going to take a trip
around the world—and you're coming along with me. Yes,
though you don't deserve it, I'm going to spend some real
money on you one day. I want to see how you'd act if I
gave you plenty of rope. I'm going to *give* you the money,
see. . . . I won't pretend to lend it to you. We'll see
what'll happen to your fine ideas when you have some
dough in your pocket. Listen, when I was talking about
Plato the other day I meant to ask you something: I meant
to ask you if you ever read that yarn of his about Atlantis.
Did you? *You did?* Well, what do you think of it? Do
you think it was just a yarn, or do you think there might
have been a place like that once?"

I didn't dare to tell him that I suspected there were

hundreds and thousands of continents whose existence past or future we hadn't even begun to dream about, so I simply said I thought it quite possible indeed that such a place as Atlantis might once have been.

"Well, it doesn't matter much one way or the other, I suppose," he went on, "but I'll tell you what I think. I think there must have been a time like that once, a time when men were different. I can't believe that they always were the pigs they are now and have been for the last few thousand years. I think it's just possible that there was a time when men knew how to live, when they knew how to take it easy and to enjoy life. Do you know what drives me crazy? It's looking at my old man. Ever since he's retired he sits in front of the fire all day long and mopes. To sit there like a broken-down gorilla, that's what he slaved for all his life. Well shit, if I thought that was going to happen to me I'd blow my brains out now. Look around you . . . look at the people we know. . . . do you know one that's worth while? What's all the fuss about, I'd like to know? *We've got to live, they say. Why?* that's what I want to know. They'd all be a damned sight better off dead. They're all just so much manure. When the war broke out and I saw them go off to the trenches I said to myself *good,* maybe they'll come back with a little sense! A lot of them didn't come back, of course. But the others!—listen, do you suppose they got more *human,* more considerate? Not at all! They're all butchers at heart, and when they're up against it they squeal. They make me sick, the whole fucking lot of 'em. I see what they're like, bailing them out every day. I see it from both sides of the fence. On the other side it stinks even worse. Why, if I told you some of the things I knew about the judges who condemn these poor bastards you'd want to slug them. All you have to do is look at their faces. Yes sir, Henry, I'd like to think there was once a time when things were different. We haven't seen any real life—and we're not going to see any. This thing is going to last another few thousand years, if I know anything about it. You think I'm mercenary. You think I'm cuckoo to want to earn a lot of money, don't you? Well I'll tell you, I want to earn a little pile so that I can get my feet out of this muck. I'd go off and live with a nigger wench if I could get away from this atmosphere. I've worked my balls off trying to get where I am, which isn't very far. I don't believe in work any more than you do—I was trained that way, that's all. If I could put over a deal, if I could swindle a pile out of one of these dirty bastards I'm dealing with, I'd do it with a clear conscience. I know a little too much about the law, that's the trouble. But I'll fool them yet, you'll see. And when I put it over I'll put it over big. . . ."

Another shot of rye as the sea food's coming along and he starts in again. "I meant that about taking you on a trip with me. I'm thinking about it seriously. I suppose you'll tell me you've got a wife and a kid to look after. Listen when are you going to break off with that battle-ax of yours? Don't you know that you've got to ditch her?" He begins to laugh softly. "Ho! Ho! To think that I was the one who picked her out for you! Did I ever think you'd be chump enough to get hitched up to her? I thought I was recommending you a nice piece of tail and you, you poor slob, you marry her. Ho ho! Listen to me, Henry, while you've got a little sense left: don't let that sour-balled puss muck up your life for you, do you get me? I don't care what you do or where you go. I'd hate to see you leave town. . . . I'd miss you, I'm telling you that frankly, but Jesus, if you have to go to Africa, beat it, get out of her clutches, she's no good for you. Sometimes when I get hold of a good cunt I think to myself now there's something nice for Henry—and I have in mind to introduce her to you, and then of course I forget. But Jesus, man, there's thousands of cunts in the world you can get along with. To think that you had to pick on a mean bitch like that. . . . *Do you want more bacon?* You'd better eat what you want now, you know, there won't be any dough later. *Have another drink, eh?* Listen, if you

try to run away from me today I swear I'll never lend you
a cent. . . . What was I saying? Oh yeah, about that
screwy bitch you married. Listen, are you going to do it
or not? Every time I see you you tell me you're going to
run away, but you never do it. You don't think you're
supporting her, I hope? She don't *need* you, you sap, don't
you see that? She just wants to torture you. As for the
kid. . . . well, shit, if I were in your boots I'd drown it.
That sounds kind of mean, doesn't it, but you know what
I mean. You're not a father. I don't know what the hell
you are . . . I just know you're too goddamned good a
fellow to be wasting your life on them. Listen, why don't
you try to make something of yourself? You're young yet
and you make a good appearance. Go off somewhere, way
the hell off, and start all over again. If you need a little
money I'll raise it for you. It's like throwing it down a
sewer, I know, but I'll do it for you just the same. The
truth is, Henry, I like you a hell of a lot. I've taken more
from you than I would from anybody in the world. I
guess we have a lot in common, coming from the old
neighborhood. Funny I didn't know you in those days.
Shit, I'm getting sentimental. . . ."

The day wore on like that, with lots to eat and drink,
the sun out strong, a car to tote us around, cigars in between, dozing a little on the beach, studying the cunts
passing by, talking, laughing, singing a bit too—one of
many, many days I spent like that with MacGregor. Days
like that really seemed to make the wheel stop. On the
surface it was jolly and happy-go-lucky; time passing like
a sticky dream. But underneath it was fatalistic, premoni-
tory, leaving me the next day morbid and restless. I knew
very well I'd have to make a break some day; I knew
very well I was pissing my time away. But I knew also
that there was nothing I could do about it—*yet*. Something had to happen, something big, something that
would sweep me off my feet. All I needed was a push,
but it had to be some force outside my world that could
give me the right push, that I was certain of. I couldn't

eat my heart out, because it wasn't in my nature. All my life things had worked out all right—*in the end*. It wasn't in the cards for me to exert myself. Something had to be left to Providence—in my case a whole lot. Despite all the outward manifestations of misfortune or mismanagement I knew that I was born with a silver spoon in my mouth. And with a double crown, too. The external situation was bad, admitted—but what bothered me more was the internal situation. I was really afraid of myself, of my appetite, my curiosity, my flexibility, my permeability, my malleability, my geniality, my powers of adaptation. No situation in itself could frighten me: I somehow always saw myself sitting pretty, sitting inside a buttercup, as it were, and sipping the honey. Even if I were flung in jail I had a hunch I'd enjoy it. It was because I knew how not to resist, I suppose. Other people wore themselves out tugging and straining and pulling; my strategy was to float with the tide. What people did to me didn't bother me nearly so much as what they were doing to others or to themselves. I was really so damned well off inside that I had to take on the problems of the world. And that's why I was in a mess all the time. I wasn't synchronized with my own destiny, so to speak. I was trying to live out the world destiny. If I got home of an evening, for instance, and there was no food in the house, not even for the kid, I would turn right around and go looking for the food. But what I noticed about myself, and that was what puzzled me, was that no sooner outside and hustling for the grub than I was back at the *Weltanschauung* again. I didn't think of food for *us* exclusively, I thought of food in general, food in all its stages, everywhere in the world at that hour, and how it was gotten and how it was prepared and what people did if they didn't have it and how maybe there was a way to fix it so that everybody would have it when they wanted it and no more time wasted on such an idiotically simple problem. I felt sorry for the wife and kid, sure, but I also felt sorry for the Hottentots and the Australian bushmen, not to mention the starving Belgians and the Turks and the Armenians. I felt sorry for the human race, for the stupidity of man and his lack of imagination. Missing a meal wasn't so terrible—it was the ghastly emptiness of the street that disturbed me profoundly. All those bloody houses, one like another, and all so empty and cheerless looking. Fine paving stones under foot and asphalt in the middle of the street and beautifully-hideously-elegant brownstone stoops to walk up, and yet a guy could walk about all day and all night on this expensive material and be looking for a crust of bread. That's what got me. The incongruousness of it. If one could only dash out with a dinner bell and yell "Listen, listen, people, I'm a guy what's hungry. Who wants shoes shined? Who wants the garbage brought out? Who wants the drainpipes cleaned out?" If you could only go out in the street and put it to them clear like that. But no, you don't dare to open your trap. If you tell a guy in the street you're hungry you scare the shit out of him, he runs like hell. That's something I never understood. I don't understand it yet. The whole thing is so simple—you just say Yes when some one comes up to you. And if you can't say Yes you can take him by the arm and ask some other bird to help you out. Why you have to don a uniform and kill men you don't know, just to get that crust of bread, is a mystery to me. That's what I think about, more than about whose trap it's going down or how much it costs. Why should I give a fuck about what anything costs? I'm here to live, not to calculate. And that's just what the bastards don't want you to do—*to live!* They want you to spend your whole life adding up figures. That makes sense to them. That's reasonable. That's intelligent. If I were running the boat things wouldn't be so orderly perhaps, but it would be gayer, by Jesus! You wouldn't have to shit in your pants over trifles. Maybe there wouldn't be macadamized roads and streamlined cars and loudspeakers and gadgets of a million billion varieties, maybe there wouldn't even be glass in the windows, maybe you'd have to sleep on the ground, maybe there wouldn't be French cooking and Italian cooking and Chinese cooking, maybe people would kill each other when their patience was exhausted and maybe nobody would stop them because there wouldn't be any jails or any cops or judges, and there certainly wouldn't be any cabinet ministers or legislatures because there wouldn't be any goddamned laws to obey or disobey, and maybe it would take months and years to trek from place to place, but you wouldn't need a visa or a passport or a *carte d'identité* because you wouldn't be registered anywhere and you wouldn't bear a number and if you wanted to change your name every week you could do it because it wouldn't make any difference since you wouldn't own anything except what you could carry around with you and why would you want to own anything when everything would be free?

During this period when I was drifting from door to door, job to job, friend to friend, meal to meal, I did try nevertheless to rope off a little space for myself which might be an anchorage; it was more like a life buoy in the midst of a swift channel. To get within a mile of me was to hear a huge dolorous bell tolling. Nobody could see the anchorage—it was buried deep in the bottom of the channel. One saw me bobbing up and down on the surface, rocking gently sometimes or else swinging backwards and forwards agitatedly. What held me down safely was the big pigeonholed desk which I put in the parlor. This was the desk which had been in the old man's tailoring establishment for the last fifty years, which had given birth to many bills and many groans, which had housed strange souvenirs in its compartments, and which finally I had filched from him when he was ill and away from the establishment; and now it stood in the middle of the floor in our lugubrious parlor on the third floor of a respectable brownstone house in the dead center of the most respectable neighborhood in Brooklyn. I had to fight a tough battle to install it there, but I insisted that it be there in the midmost midst of the shebang. It was like putting a mastodon in the center of a dentist's office. But since the wife had no friends to visit her and since my friends didn't give a fuck if it were suspended from the chandelier, I kept it in the parlor and I put all the extra chairs we had around it in a big circle and then I sat down comfortably and I put my feet up on the desk and dreamed of what I would write if I could write. I had a spittoon alongside of the desk, a big brass one from the same establishment, and I would spit in it now and then to remind myself that it was there. All the pigeon-holes were empty and all the drawers were empty; there wasn't a thing on the desk or in it except a sheet of white paper on which I found it impossible to put so much as a pothook.

When I think of the titanic efforts I made to canalize the hot lava which was bubbling inside me, the efforts I repeated thousands of times to bring the funnel into place and capture *a* word, *a* phrase, I think inevitably of the men of the old stone age. A hundred thousand, two hundred thousand years, three hundred thousand years to arrive at the idea of the paleolith. A phantom struggle, because they weren't dreaming of such a thing as the paleolith. It came without effort, born of a second, a miracle you might say, except that everything which happens is miraculous. Things happen or they don't happen, that's all. Nothing is accomplished by sweat and struggle. Nearly everything which we call life is just insomnia, an agony because we've lost the habit of falling asleep. We don't know how to let go. We're like a Jack-in-the-box perched on top of a spring and the more we struggle the harder it is to get back in the box.

I think if I had been crazy I couldn't have hit upon a better scheme to consolidate my anchorage than to install this Neanderthal object in the middle of the parlor. With my feet on the desk, picking up the current, and my spinal column snugly socketed in a thick leather cushion, I was in an ideal relation to the flotsam and jetsam which was whirling about me, and which, because they were crazy and part of the flux, my friends were trying to convince me was life. I remember vividly the first contact with reality that I got through my feet, so to speak. The million words or so which I had written, mind you, well ordered, well connected, were as nothing to me—crude ciphers from the old stone age—because the contact was through the head and the head is a useless appendage unless you're anchored in midchannel deep in the mud. Everything I had written before was museum stuff, and most writing is still museum stuff and that's why it doesn't catch fire, doesn't inflame the world. I was only a mouthpiece for the ancestral race which was talking through me; even my dreams were not authentic, not bona fide Henry Miller dreams. To sit still and think one thought which would come up out of me, out of the life buoy, was a Herculean task. I didn't lack thoughts nor words nor the power of expression—I lacked something much more important: the lever which would shut off the juice. The bloody machine wouldn't stop, that was the difficulty. I was not only in the middle of the current but the current was running through me and I had no control over it whatever.

I remember the day I brought the machine to a dead stop and how the other mechanism, the one that was signed with my own initials and which I had made with my own hands and my own blood slowly began to function. I had gone to the theater nearby to see a vaudeville show; it was the matinee and I had a ticket for the balcony. Standing on line in the lobby, I already experienced a strange feeling of consistency. It was as though I were coagulating, becoming a recognizable consistent mass of jelly. It was like the ultimate stage in the healing of a wound. I was at the height of normality, which is a very abnormal condition. Cholera might come and blow its foul breath in my mouth—it wouldn't matter. I might bend over and kiss the ulcers of a leprous hand, and no harm could possibly come to me. There was not just a balance in this constant warfare between health and disease, which is all that most of us may hope for, but there was a plus integer in the blood which meant that, for a few moments at least, disease was completely routed. If one had the wisdom to take root in such a moment, one would never again be ill or unhappy or even die. But to leap to this conclusion is to make a jump which would take one back further than the old stone age. At that moment I wasn't even dreaming of taking root; I was experiencing for the first time in my life the meaning of the miraculous. I was so amazed when I heard my own cogs meshing that I was willing to die then and there for the privilege of the experience.

What happened was this. . . . As I passed the doorman holding the torn stub in my hand the lights were dimmed and the curtain went up. I stood a moment slightly dazed by the sudden darkness. As the curtain slowly rose I had the feeling that throughout the ages man had always been mysteriously stilled by this brief moment which preludes the spectacle. I could feel the curtain rising *in man.* And immediately I also realized that this was a symbol which was being presented to him endlessly in his sleep and that if he had been awake the players would never have taken the stage but he, Man, would have mounted the boards. I didn't think this thought—it was a realization, as I say, and so simple and overwhelmingly clear was it that the machine stopped dead instantly and I was standing in my own presence bathed in a luminous reality. I turned my eyes away from the stage and beheld the marble staircase which I should take to go to my seat in the balcony. I saw a man slowly mounting the steps, his hand laid across the balustrade. The man could have been myself, the old self which had been sleepwalking ever since I was born. My eye didn't take in the entire staircase, just the fews steps which the man had climbed or was climbing in the moment that I took it all in. The man never reached the top of the stairs and his hand was never removed from the marble balustrade.

I felt the curtain descend, and for another few moments I was behind the scenes moving amidst the sets, like the property man suddenly roused from his sleep and not sure whether he is still dreaming or looking at a dream which is being enacted on the stage. It was as fresh and green, as strangely new as the bread and cheese lands which the Biddenden maidens saw every day of their long life joined at the hips. I saw only that which was alive! the rest faded out in a penumbra. And it was in order to keep the world alive that I rushed home without waiting to see the performance and sat down to describe the little patch of staircase which is imperishable.

It was just about this time that the Dadaists were in full swing, to be followed shortly by the surrealists. I never heard of either group until some ten years later; I never read a French book and I never had a French idea. I was perhaps the unique Dadaist in America, and I didn't know it. I might just as well have been living in the jungles of the Amazon for all the contact I had with the outside world. Nobody understood what I was writing about or why I wrote that way. I was so lucid that they said I was daffy. I was describing the New World—unfortunately a little too soon because it had not yet been discovered and nobody could be persuaded that it existed. It was an ovarian world, still hidden away in the Fallopian tubes. Naturally nothing was clearly formulated: there was only the faint suggestion of a backbone visible, and certainly no arms or legs, no hair, no nails, no teeth. Sex was the last thing to be dreamed of; it was the world of Chronos and his ovicular progeny. It was the world of the iota, each iota being indispensable, frighteningly logical, and absolutely unpredictable. There was no such thing as *a thing*, because the concept "thing" was missing.

I say it was a New World I was describing, but like the New World which Columbus discovered it turned out to be a far older world than any we have known. I

saw beneath the superficial physiognomy of skin and
bone the indestructible world which man has always
carried within him; it was neither old nor new, really, but
the eternally true world which changes from moment to
moment. Everything I looked at was palimpsest and there
was no layer of writing too strange for me to decipher.
When my companions left me of an evening I would
often sit down and write to my friends the Australian
bushmen or the Mound Builders of the Mississippi Valley
or to the Igorots in the Philippines. I had to write English,
naturally, because it was the only language I spoke, but
between my language and the telegraphic code employed
by my bosom friends there was a world of difference.
Any primitive man would have understood me, any man
of archaic epochs would have understood me: only those
about me, that is to say, a continent of a hundred million
people, failed to understand my language. To write in-
telligibly for them I would have been obliged first of all
to kill something, secondly, to arrest time. I had just
made the realization that life is indestructible and that
there is no such thing as time, only the present. Did they
expect me to deny a truth which it had taken me all my
life to catch a glimpse of? They most certainly did. The
one thing they did not want to hear about was that life
is indestructible. Was not their precious new world reared
on the destruction of the innocent, on rape and plunder
and torture and devastation? Both continents had been
violated; both continents had been stripped and plundered of all that was precious—*in things*. No greater
humiliation, it seems to me, was meted out to any man
than to Montezuma; no race was ever more ruthlessly
wiped out than the American Indian; no land was ever
raped in the foul and bloody way that California was
raped by the gold diggers. I blush to think of our origins—
our hands are steeped in blood and crime. And there is
no letup to the slaughter and the pillage, as I discovered
at first hand traveling throughout the length and breadth
of the land. Down to the closest friend every man is a

potential murderer. Often it wasn't necessary to bring out the gun or the lasso or the branding iron—they had found subtler and more devilish ways of torturing and killing their own. For me the most excruciating agony was to have the word annihilated before it had even left my mouth. I learned, by bitter experience, to hold my tongue; I learned to sit in silence, and even smile, when actually I was foaming at the mouth. I learned to shake hands and say how do you do to all these innocent-looking fiends who were only waiting for me to sit down in order to suck my blood.

How was it possible, when I sat down in the parlor at my prehistoric desk, to use this code language of rape and murder? I was alone in this great hemisphere of violence, but I was not alone as far as the human race was concerned. I was lonely amidst a world of *things* lit up by phosphorescent flashes of cruelty. I was delirious with an energy which could not be unleashed except in the service of death and futility. I could not begin with a full statement—it would have meant the strait jacket or the electric chair. I was like a man who had been too long incarcerated in a dungeon—I had to feel my way slowly, falteringly, lest I stumble and be run over. I had to accustom myself gradually to the penalties which freedom involves. I had to grow a new epidermis which would protect me from this burning light in the sky.

The ovarian world is the product of a life rhythm. The moment a child is born it becomes part of a world in which there is not only the life rhythm but the death rhythm. The frantic desire to live, to live at any cost, is not a result of the life rhythm in us, but of the death rhythm. There is not only no need to keep alive at any price, but, if life is undesirable, it is absolutely wrong. This keeping oneself alive, out of a blind urge to defeat death, is in itself a means of sowing death. Every one who has not fully accepted life, who is not incrementing life, is helping to fill the world with death. To make the simplest gesture with the hand can convey the utmost sense of life; a word spoken with the whole being can give life. Activity in itself means nothing: it is often a sign of death. By simple external pressure, by force of surroundings and example, by the very climate which activity engenders, one can become part of a monstrous death machine, such as America, for example. What does a dynamo know of life, of peace, of reality? What does any individual American dynamo know of the wisdom and energy, of the life abundant and eternal possessed by a ragged beggar sitting under a tree in the act of meditation? What is *energy*? What is *life*? One has only to read the stupid twaddle of the scientific and philosophic textbooks to realize how less than nothing is the wisdom of these energetic Americans. Listen, they had me on the run, these crazy horsepower fiends; in order to break their insane rhythm, their death rhythm, I had to resort to a wave length which, until I found the proper sustenance in my own bowels, would at least nullify the rhythm they had set up. Certainly I did not need this grotesque, cumbersome, antediluvian desk which I had installed in the parlor; certainly I didn't need twelve empty chairs placed around it in a semicircle; I needed only elbow room in which to write and a thirteenth chair which would take me out of the zodiac they were using and put me in a heaven beyond heaven. But when you drive a man almost crazy and when, to his own surprise perhaps, he finds that he still has some resistance, some powers of his own, then you are apt to find such a man acting very much like a primitive being. Such a man is apt not only to become stubborn and dogged, but superstitious, a believer in magic and a practicer of magic. Such a man is beyond religion—it is his religiousness he is suffering from. Such a man becomes a monomaniac, bent on doing one thing only and that is to break the evil spell which has been put upon him. Such a man is beyond throwing bombs, beyond revolt; he wants to stop reacting, whether inertly or ferociously. This man, of all men on earth, wants the act to be a manifestation of life. If, in the realization of his terrible need, he begins to act regressively, to become unsocial, to stammer and stutter, to prove so utterly unadapted as to be incapable of earning a living, know that this man has found his way back to the womb and source of life and that tomorrow, instead of the contemptible object of ridicule which you have made of him, he will stand forth as a *man* in his own right and all the powers of the world will be of no avail against him.

Out of the crude cipher with which he communicates from his prehistoric desk with the archaic men of the world a new language builds up which cuts through the death language of the day like wireless through a storm. There is no magic in this wave length any more than there is magic in the womb. Men are lonely and out of communication with one another because all their inventions speak only of death. Death is the automaton which rules the world of activity. Death is silent, because it has no mouth. Death has never *expressed* anything. Death is wonderful too—*after life.* Only one like myself who has opened his mouth and spoken, only one who has said Yes, Yes, Yes, and again Yes! can open wide his arms to death and know no fear. Death as a reward, yes! Death as a result of fulfillment, yes! Death as a crown and shield, yes! But not death from the roots, isolating men, making them bitter and fearful and lonely, giving them fruitless energy, filling them with a will which can only say No! The first word any man writes when he has found himself, his own rhythm, which is the life rhythm, is Yes! Everything he writes thereafter is Yes, Yes, Yes—Yes in a thousand million ways. No dynamo, no matter how huge—not even a dynamo of a hundred million dead souls—can combat one man saying Yes!

The war was on and men were being slaughtered, one million, two million, five million, ten million, twenty million, finally a hundred million, then a billion, everybody, man, woman and child, down to the last one. "*No!*" they were shouting, "*No! they shall not pass!*" And yet everybody passed; everybody got a free pass, whether he shouted Yes or No. In the midst of this triumphant demonstration of spiritually destructive osmosis I sat with my feet planted on the big desk trying to communicate with Zeus the Father of Atlantis and with his lost progeny, ignorant of the fact that Apollinaire was to die the day before the Armistice in a military hospital, ignorant of the fact that in his "new writing" he had penned these indelible lines:

> Be forbearing when you compare us
> With those who were the perfection of order.
> We who everywhere seek adventure,
> We are not your enemies.
> We would give you vast and strange domains
> Where flowering mystery waits for him would pluck it.

Ignorant that in this same poem he had also written:

> Have compassion on us who are always fighting on the frontiers
> Of the boundless future,
> Compassion for our errors, compassion for our sins.

I was ignorant of the fact that there were men then living who went by the outlandish names of Blaise Cendrars, Jacques Vaché, Louis Aragon, Tristan Tzara, René Crevel, Henri de Montherlant, André Breton, Max Ernst, Georges Grosz; ignorant of the fact that on July 14, 1916, at the Saal Waag, in Zurich, the first Dada Manifesto had been proclaimed—"manifesto by Monsieur Antipyrine"—that in this strange document it was stated: "Dada is life without slippers or parallel . . . severe necessity without discipline or morality and we spit on humanity." Ignorant of the fact that the Dada Manifesto of 1918 contained these lines: "I am writing a manifesto and I want nothing, yet I say certain things, and I am against manifestoes as a matter of principle, as I am also against principles. . . . I write this manifesto to show that one may perform opposed actions together, in a single fresh respiration; I am against action; for continual contradiction, for affirmation also, I am neither for nor against and I do not explain for I hate good sense. . . .

There is a literature which does not reach the voracious mass. The work of creators, sprung from a real necessity on the part of the author, and for himself. Consciousness of a supreme egotism where the stars waste away. . . . Each page must explode, either with the profoundly serious and heavy, the whirlwind, dizziness, the new, the eternal, with the overwhelming hoax, with an enthusiasm for principles or with the mode of typography. On the one hand a staggering fleeing world, affianced to the jinglebells of the infernal gamut, on the other hand: *new beings. . . .*"

Thirty-two years later and I am still saying Yes! Yes, Monsieur Antipyrine! Yes, Monsieur Tristan Bustanoby Tzara! Yes, Monsieur Max Ernst Geburt! Yes! Monsieur René Crevel, now that you are dead by suicide, yes, the world is crazy, you were right. Yes, Monsiuer Blaise Cendrars, you were right to kill. Was it the day of the Armistice that you brought out your little book—*J'ai tué?* Yes, "keep on my lads, humanity. . . ." Yes, Jacques Vaché, quite right—"Art ought to be something funny and a trifle boring." Yes, my dear dead Vaché, how right you were and how funny and how boring and touching and tender and true: "It is of the essence of symbols to be symbolic." Say it again, from the other world! Have you a megaphone up there? Have you found all the arms and legs that were blown off during the mêlée? Can you put them together again? Do you remember the meeting at Nantes in 1916 with André Breton? Did you celebrate the birth of hysteria together? Had he told you, Breton, that there was only the marvelous and nothing but the marvelous and that the marvelous is always marvelous—and isn't it marvelous to hear it again, even though your ears are stopped? I want to include here, before passing on, a little portrait of you by Emile Bouvier for the benefit of my Brooklyn friends who may not have recognized me then but who will now, I am sure. . . .

" . . . he was not all crazy, and could explain his conduct when occasion required. His actions, none the less, were

as disconcerting as Jarry's worst eccentricities. For example, he was barely out of hospital when he hired himself out as a stevedore, and he thereafter passed his afternoons in unloading coal on the quays along the Loire.
In the evening, on the other hand, he would make the
rounds of the cafés and cinemas, dressed in the height of
fashion and with many variations of costume. What was
more, in time of war, he would strut forth sometimes
in the uniform of a lieutenant of hussars, sometimes in
that of an English officer, of an aviator or of a surgeon.
In civil life, he was quite as free and easy, thinking
nothing of introducing Breton under the name of André
Salmon, while he took unto himself, but quite without
vanity, the most wonderful titles and adventures. He
never said good morning nor good evening nor good-by,
and never took any notice of letters, except those from
his mother, when he had to ask for money. He did not
recognize his best friends from one day to another. . . ."

Do you recognize me, lads? Just a Brooklyn boy communicating with the red-haired albinos of the Zuni region. Making ready, with feet on the desk, to write
"strong works, works forever incomprehensible," as my
dead comrades were promising. These "strong works"—
would you recognize them if you saw them? Do you know
that of the millions who were killed not one death was necessary to produce "the strong work?" *New beings*, yes!
We have need of new beings still. We can do without the
telephone, without the automobile, without the high-
class bombers—but we can't do without new beings. If
Atlantis was submerged beneath the sea, if the Sphinx
and the Pyramids remain an eternal riddle, it is because
there were no more new beings being born. Stop the
machine a moment! Flash back! Flash back to 1914, to
the Kaiser sitting on his horse. Keep him sitting there
a moment with his withered arm clutching the bridle
rein. Look at his mustache! Look at his haughty air of
pride and arrogance! Look at his cannon fodder lined
up in strictest discipline, all ready to obey the word, to

get shot, to get disemboweled, to be burned in quick-lime. Hold it a moment, now, and look at the other side: the defenders of our great and glorious civilization, the men who will war to end war. Change their clothes, change their uniforms, change horses, change flags, change terrain. My, is that the Kaiser I see on a white horse? Are those the terrible Huns? And where is Big Bertha? Oh, I see—I thought it was pointing toward Notre-Dame? Humanity, me lads, humanity always marching in the van. . . . And the strong works we were speaking of? Where are the strong works? Call up the Western Union and dispatch a messenger fleet of foot —not a cripple or an octogenarian, but a young one! Ask him to find the great work and bring it back. We need it. We have a brand-new museum ready waiting to house it—and cellophane and the Dewey decimal system to file it. All we need is the name of the author. Even if he has no name, even if it is an anonymous work, we won't kick. Even if it has a little mustard gas in it we won't mind. Bring it back dead or alive—there's a twenty-five thous-and dollar reward for the man who fetches it.

And if they tell you that these things had to be, that things could not have happened otherwise, that France did her best and Germany her best and that little Liberia and little Ecuador and all the other allies also did their best, and that since the war everybody has been doing his best to patch things up or to forget, tell them that their best is not good enough, that we don't want to hear any more this logic of "doing the best one can," tell them we don't want the best of a bad bargain, we don't believe in bargains good or bad, nor in war memorials. We don't want to hear about the logic of events—or any kind of logic. "*Je ne parle pas logique,*" said Montherlant, "*je parle générosité.*" I don't think you heard it very well, since it was in French. I'll repeat it for you, in the Queen's own language: "I'm not talking logic, I'm talking gener-osity." That's bad English, as the Queen herself might speak it, but it's clear. *Generosity*—do you hear? You

never practice it, any of you, either in peace or in war.
You don't know the meaning of the word. You think to
supply guns and ammunition to the winning side is generosity; you think sending Red Cross nurses to the front,
or the Salvation Army, is generosity. You think a bonus
twenty years too late is generosity; you think a little pen-
sion and a wheel chair is generosity; you think if you give
a man his old job back it's generosity. You don't know
what the fucking word means, you bastards! To be generous is to say Yes before the man even opens his mouth.
To say Yes you have to be first a surrealist or a Dadaist,
because you have understood what it means to say No.
You can even say Yes and No at the same time, provided
you do more than is expected of you. Be a stevedore in
the daytime and a Beau Brummel in the nighttime. Wear
any uniform so long as it's not yours. When you write
your mother ask her to cough up a little dough so that
you may have a clean rag to wipe your ass with. Don't be
disturbed if you see your neighbor going after his wife
with a knife: he probably has good reason to go after
her, and if he kills her you may be sure he had the satis-
faction of knowing *why* he did it. If you're trying to
improve your mind, stop it! There's no improving the
mind. Look to your heart and gizzard—the brain is in
the heart.

Ah yes, if I had known then that these birds existed—
Cendrars, Vaché, Grosz, Ernst, Apollinaire—if I had
known that then, if I had known that in their own way
they were thinking exactly the same things as I was, I
think I'd have blown up. Yes, I think I'd have gone off
like a bomb. But I was ignorant. Ignorant of the fact
that almost fifty years previously a crazy Jew in South
America had given birth to such startlingly marvelous
phrases as "doubt's duck with the vermouth lips" or "I
have seen a fig eat an onager"—that about the same time
a Frenchman, who was only a boy, was saying: "Find
flowers that are chairs" . . . "my hunger is the black air's
bits" . . . "his heart, amber and spunk." Maybe at the same

time, or thereabouts, while Jarry was saying "in eating the
sound of moths," and Apollinaire repeating after him
"near a gentleman swallowing himself," and Breton murmuring softly "night's pedals move uninterruptedly,"
perhaps "in the air beautiful and black" which the lone
Jew had found under the Southern Cross another man,
also lonely and exiled and of Spanish origin, was preparing to put down on paper these memorable words: "I seek,
all in all, to console myself for my exile, for my exile from
eternity, for that *unearthing* (*destierro*) which I am fond
of referring to as my unheavening. . . . At present, I think
that the best way to write this novel is to tell how it
should be written. It is the novel of the novel, the creation
of creation. Or God of God, *Deus de Deo*." Had I known
he was going to add this, this which follows, I would
surely have gone off like a bomb. . . . "By being crazy
is understood losing one's reason. Reason, but not the
truth, for there are madmen who speak truths while
others keep silent. . . ." Speaking of these things, speaking of the war and the war dead, I cannot refrain from
mentioning that some twenty years later I ran across
this in French by a Frenchman. O miracles of miracles! *Il
faut le dire, il y a des cadavres que je ne respecte qu'à
moitié.* Yes, yes, and again yes! O, let us do some rash
thing—for the sheer pleasure of it! Let us do something
live and magnificent, even if destructive! Said the mad
cobbler: "All things are generated out of the grand
mystery, and proceed out of one degree into another.
Whatever goes forward in its degree, the same receives
no abominate."

Everywhere in all times the same ovarian world announcing itself. Yet also, parallel with these announce-
ments, these prophecies, these gynecological manifestoes,
parallel and contemporaneous with them new totem poles,
new taboos, new war dances. While into the air so black
and beautiful the brothers of man, the poets, the diggers
of the future, were spitting their magic lines, in this
same time, O profound and perplexing riddle, other men

were saying: "Won't you please come and take a job in our ammunition factory. We promise you the highest wages, the most sanitary and hygienic conditions. The work is so easy that even a child could do it." And if you had a sister, a wife, a mother, an aunt, as long as she could manipulate her hands, as long as she could prove that she had no bad habits, you were invited to bring her or them along to the ammunition works. If you were shy of soiling your hands they would explain to you very gently and intelligently just how these delicate mechanisms operated, what they did when they exploded, and why you must not waste even your garbage because . . . *et ipso facto e pluribus unum.* The thing that impressed me, going the rounds in search of work, was not so much that they made me vomit every day (assuming I had been lucky enough to put something into my guts), but that they always demanded to know if you were of good habits, if you were steady, if you were sober, if you were industrious, if you had ever worked before and if not why not. Even the garbage, which I had gotten the job of collecting for the municipality, was precious to them, the killers. Standing knee deep in the muck, the lowest of the low, a coolie, an outcast, still I was part of the death racket. I tried reading the *Inferno* at night, but it was in English and English is no language for a Catholic work. "Whatever enters in itself into its selfhood, viz., into its own lubet. . . ." *Lubet!* If I had had a word like that to conjure with then, how peacefully I might have gone about my garbage collecting! How sweet, in the night, when Dante is out of reach and the hands smell of muck and slime, to take unto oneself this word which in the Dutch means "lust" and in Latin "lubitum" or the divine *beneplacitum.* Standing knee deep in the garbage I said one day what Meister Eckhart is reported to have said long ago: "I truly have need of God, but God has need of me too." There was a job waiting for me in the slaughterhouse, a nice little job of sorting entrails, but I couldn't raise the fare to get to Chicago. I remained in Brooklyn, in my own palace of entrails, and turned round and round on the plinth of the labyrinth. I remained at home seeking the "germinal vesicle," "the dragon castle on the floor of the sea," "the Heavenly Heart," "the field of the square inch," "the house of the square foot," "the dark pass," "the space of former Heaven." I remained locked in, a prisoner of Forculus, god of the door, of Cardea, god of the hinge, and of Limentius, god of the threshold. I spoke only with their sisters, the three goddesses called Fear, Pallor and Fever. I saw no "Asian luxury," as had St. Augustine, or as he imagined he had. Nor did I see "the two twins born, so near together, that the second held the first by the heel." But I saw a street called Myrtle Avenue, which runs from Borough Hall to Fresh Pond Road, and down this street no saint ever walked (else it would have crumbled), down this street no miracle ever passed, nor any poet, nor any species of human genius, nor did any flower ever grow there, nor did the sun strike it squarely, nor did the rain ever wash it. For the genuine Inferno which I had to postpone for twenty years I give you Myrtle Avenue, one of the innumerable bridlepaths ridden by iron monsters which lead to the heart of America's emptiness. If you have only seen Essen or Manchester or Chicago or Levallois-Perret or Glasgow or Hoboken or Canarsie or Bayonne you have seen nothing of the magnificent emptiness of progress and enlightenment. Dear reader, you must see Myrtle Avenue before you die, if only to realize how far into the future Dante saw. You must believe me that on this street, neither in the houses which line it, nor the cobblestones which pave it, nor the elevated structure which cuts it atwain, neither in any creature that bears a name and lives thereon, neither in any animal, bird or insect passing through it to slaughter or already slaughtered, is there hope of "lubet," "sublimate" or "abominate." It is a street not of sorrow, for sorrow would be human and recognizable, but of sheer emptiness: it is emptier than the most extinct volcano, emptier than a vacuum, emptier than the word God in the mouth of an unbeliever.

I said I did not know a word of French then, and it is true, but I was just on the brink of making a great discovery, a discovery which would compensate for the emptiness of Myrtle Avenue and the whole American continent. I had almost reached the shore of that great French ocean which goes by the name of Elie Faure, an ocean which the French themselves had hardly navigated and which they had mistaken, it seems, for an inland sea. Reading him even in such a withered language as English has become I could see that this man who had described the glory of the human race on his cuff was Father Zeus of Atlantis whom I had been searching for. An ocean I called him, but he was also a world symphony. He was the first musician the French have produced; he was exalted and controlled, an anomaly, a Gallic Beethoven, a great physician of the soul, a giant lightning rod. He was also a sunflower turning with the sun, always drinking in the light, always radiant and blazing with vitality. He was neither an optimist nor a pessimist, any more than one can say that the ocean is beneficent or malevolent. He was a believer in the human race. He added a cubit to the race, by giving it back its dignity, its strength, its need of creation. He saw everything as creation, as solar joy. He didn't record it in orderly fashion, he recorded it musically. He was indifferent to the fact that the French have a tin ear—he was orchestrating for the whole world simultaneously. What was my amazement then, when some years later I arrived in France, to find that there were no monuments erected to him, no streets named after him. Worse, during eight whole years I never once heard a Frenchman mention his name. He had to die in order to be put in the pantheon of French deities—and how sickly must they look, his deific contemporaries, in the presence of this radiant sun! If he had not been a physician, and thus permitted to earn a livelihood, what might not have happened to him! Perhaps another able hand for the garbage trucks! The man who made the Egyptian frescoes come alive in all their flaming colors, this man could just as well have starved to death for all the public cared. But he was an ocean and the critics drowned in this ocean, and the editors and the publishers and the public too. It will take aeons for him to dry up, to evaporate. It will take about as long as for the French to acquire a musical ear.

If there had been no music I would have gone to the madhouse like Nijinsky. (It was just about this time that they discovered that Nijinsky was mad. He had been found giving his money away to the poor—always a bad sign!) My mind was filled with wonderful treasures, my taste was sharp and exigent, my muscles were in excellent condition, my appetite was strong, my wind sound. I had nothing to do except to improve myself, and I was going crazy with the improvements I made every day. Even if there were a job for me to fill I couldn't accept it, because what I needed was not work but a life more abundant. I couldn't waste time being a teacher, a lawyer, a physician, a politician or anything else that society had to offer. It was easier to accept menial jobs because it left my mind free. After I was fired from the garbage trucks I remember taking up with an Evangelist who seemed to have great confidence in me. I was a sort of usher, collector and private secretary. He brought to my attention the whole world of Indian philosophy. Evenings when I was free I would meet with my friends at the home of Ed Bauries who lived in an aristocratic section of Brooklyn. Ed Bauries was an eccentric pianist who couldn't read a note. He had a bosom pal called George Neumiller with whom he often played duets. Of the dozen or so who congregated at Ed Bauries' home nearly every one of us could play the piano. We were all between twenty-one and twenty-five at the time; we never brought any women along and we hardly ever mentioned the subject of woman during these sessions. We had plenty of beer to drink and a whole big house at our disposal, for it was in the summertime, when his folks were away, that we held our gatherings. Though there were a dozen other homes like this which I could speak of, I mention Ed Bauries' place because it was typical of something I have never encountered elsewhere in the world. Neither Ed Bauries himself nor any of his friends suspected the sort of books I was reading then nor the things which were occupying my mind. When I blew in I was greeted enthusiastically—as a clown. It was expected of me to start things going. There were about four pianos scattered throughout the big house, to say nothing of the celesta, the organ, guitars, mandolins, fiddles and what not. Ed Bauries was a nut, a very affable, sympathetic and generous one too. The sandwiches were always of the best, the beer plentiful, and if you wanted to stay the night he could fix you up on a divan just as pretty as you liked. Coming down the street—a big, wide street, somnolent, luxurious, a street altogether out of the world —I could hear the tinkle of the piano in the big parlor on the first floor. The windows were wide open and as I got into range I could see Al Burger or Connie Grimm sprawling in their big easy chairs, their feet on the window sill, and big beer mugs in their hands. Probably George Neumiller was at the piano, improvising, his shirt peeled off and a big cigar in his mouth. They were talking and laughing while George fooled around, searching for an opening. Soon as he hit a theme he would call for Ed and Ed would sit beside him, studying it out in his unprofessional way, then suddenly pouncing on the keys and giving tit for tat. Maybe when I'd walk in somebody would be trying to stand on his hands in the next room—there were three big rooms on the first floor which opened one on to the other and back of them was a garden, an enormous garden, with flowers, fruit trees, grape vines, statues, fountains and everything. Sometimes when it was too hot they brought the celesta or the little organ into the garden (and a keg of beer, naturally) and we'd sit around in the dark laughing and singing—until the neighbors forced us to stop. Sometimes the music was going on all through the house at once, on every floor. It was really crazy then, intoxicating, and if there had been women around it would have spoiled it. Sometimes it was like watching an endurance contest—Ed Bauries and George Neumiller at the grand piano, each trying to wear the other out, changing places without stopping, crossing hands, sometimes falling away to plain chopsticks, sometimes going like a Wurlitzer. And always something to laugh about all the time. Nobody asked what you did, what you thought about, and so forth. When you arrived at Ed Bauries' place you checked your identification marks. Nobody gave a fuck what size hat you wore or how much you paid for it. It was entertainment from the word go—and the sandwiches and the drinks were on the house. And when things got going, three or four pianos at once, the celesta, the organ, the mandolins, the guitars, beer running through the halls, the mantelpieces full of sandwiches and cigars, a breeze coming through from the garden, George Neumiller stripped to the waist and modulating like a fiend, it was better than any show I've ever seen put on and it didn't cost a cent. In fact, with the dressing and undressing that went on, I always came away with a little extra change and a pocketful of good cigars. I never saw any of them between times—only Monday nights throughout the summer, when Ed held open house.

Standing in the garden listening to the din I could scarcely believe that it was the same city. And if I had ever opened my trap and exposed my guts it would have been all over. Not one of these bozos amounted to anything, as the world reckons. They were just good eggs, children, fellows who liked music and who liked a good time. They liked it so much that sometimes we had to call the ambulance. Like the night Al Burger twisted his knee while showing us one of his stunts. Everybody so happy, so full of music, so lit up, that it took him an hour to persuade us he was really hurt. We try to carry him to a hospital but it's too far away and besides, it's such a good joke, that we drop him now and then and that makes him yell like a maniac. So finally we telephone for help from a police box, and the ambulance comes and the patrol wagon too. They take Al to the hospital and the rest of us to the hoosegow. And on the way we sing at the top of our lungs. And after we're bailed out we're still feeling good and the cops are feeling good too, and so we all adjourn to the basement where there's a cracked piano and we go on singing and playing. All this is like some period b.c. in history which ends not because there's a war but because even a joint like Ed Bauries' is not immune to the poison seeping in from the periphery. Because every street is becoming a Myrtle Avenue, because emptiness is filling the whole continent from the Atlantic to the Pacific. Because, after a certain time, you can't enter a single house throughout the length and breadth of the land and find a man standing on his hands singing. It just ain't done any more. And there ain't two pianos going at once anywhere, nor are there two men anywhere willing to play all night just for the fun of it. Two men who can play like Ed Bauries and George Neumiller are hired by the radio or the movies and only a thimbleful of their talent is used and the rest is thrown into the garbage can. Nobody knows, judging from public spectacles, what talent is disposable in the great American continent. Later on, and that's why I used to sit around on doorsteps in Tin Pan Alley, I would while away the afternoons listening to the professionals mugging it out. That was good too, but it was different. There was no fun in it, it was a perpetual rehearsal to bring in dollars and cents. Any man in America who had an ounce of humor in him was saving it up to put himself across. There were some wonderful nuts among them too, men I'll never forget, men who left no name behind them, and they were the best we produced. I remember an anonymous performer on the Keith circuit who was probably the craziest man in America, and perhaps he got fifty dollars a week for it. Three times a day, every day in the week, he came out and held the audience spellbound. He didn't have an act—he just improvised. He never repeated his jokes or

his stunts. He gave himself prodigally, and I don't think
he was a hop fiend either. He was one of those guys who
are born in the corn crakes and the energy and the joy in
him was so fierce that nothing could contain it. He could
play any instrument and dance any step and he could
invent a story on the spot and string it out till the bell
rang. He was not only satisfied to do his own act but he
would help the others out. He would stand in the wings
and wait for the right moment to break into the other
guy's act. He was the whole show and it was a show that
contained more therapy than the whole arsenal of modern
science. They ought to have paid a man like this the
wages which the President of the United States receives.
They ought to sack the President of the United States and
the whole Supreme Court and set up a man like this as
ruler. This man could cure any disease on the calendar.
He was the kind of guy, moreover, as would do it for
nothing, if you asked him to. This is the type of man which
empties the insane asylums. He doesn't propose a cure—
he makes everybody crazy. Between this solution and a
perpetual state of war, which is civilization, there is only
one other way out—and that is the road we will all take
eventually because everything else is doomed to failure.
The type that represents this one and only way bears a
head with six faces and eight eyes; the head is a revolving
lighthouse, and instead of a triple crown at the top, as
there might well be, there is a hole which ventilates what
few brains there are. There is very little brain, as I say, because there is very little baggage to carry about, because
living in full consciousness, the gray matter passes off into
light. This is the only type of man one can place above
the comedian; he neither laughs nor weeps, he is beyond
suffering. We don't recognize him yet because he is too
close to us, right under the skin, as a matter of fact. When
the comedian catches us in the guts this man, whose name
might be God, I suppose, if he had to use a name, speaks
up. When the whole human race is rocking with laughter,
'laughing so hard that it hurts, I mean, everybody then

has his foot on the path. In that moment everybody can just as well be God as anything else. In that moment you have the annihilation of dual, triple, quadruple and multiple consciousness, which is what makes the gray matter coil up in dead folds at the top of the skull. At that moment you can really feel the hole in the top of the head; you know that you once had an eye there and that this eye was capable of taking in everything at once. The eye is gone now, but when you laugh until the tears flow and your belly aches, you are really opening the skylight and ventilating the brains. Nobody can persuade you at that moment to take a gun and kill your enemy; neither can anybody persuade you to open a fat tome containing the metaphysical truths of the world and read it. If you know what freedom means, absolute freedom and not a relative freedom, then you must recognize that this is the nearest to it you will ever get. If I am against the condition of the world it is not because I am a moralist—it is because I want to laugh more. I don't say that God is one grand laugh: I say that you've got to laugh hard before you can get anywhere near God. My whole aim in life is to get near to God, that is, to get nearer to myself. That's why it doesn't matter to me what road I take. But music is very important. Music is a tonic for the pineal gland. Music isn't Bach or Beethoven; music is the can opener of the soul. It makes you terribly quiet inside, makes you aware that there's a roof to your being.

The stabbing horror of life is not contained in calamities and disasters, because these things wake one up and one gets very familiar and intimate with them and finally they become tame again . . . no, it is more like being in a hotel room in Hoboken, let us say, and just enough money in one's pocket for another meal. You are in a city that you never expect to be in again and you have only to pass the night in your hotel room, but it takes all the courage and pluck you possess to stay in that room. There must be a good reason why certain cities, certain places, inspire such loathing and dread. There must be some kind of perpetual murder going on in these places. The people are of the same race as you, they go about their business as people do anywhere, they build the same sort of house, no better, no worse, they have the same system of education, the same currency, the same newspapers— and yet they are absolutely different from the other people you know, and the whole atmosphere is different, and the rhythm is different and the tension is different. It's almost like looking at yourself in another incarnation. You know, with a most disturbing certitude, that what governs life is not money, not politics, not religion, not training, not race, not language, not customs, but something else, something you're trying to throttle all the time and which is really throttling you, because otherwise you wouldn't be terrified all of a sudden and wonder how you were going to escape. Some cities you don't even have to pass a night in—just an hour or two is enough to unnerve you. I think of Bayonne that way. I came on it in the night with a few addresses that had been given me. I had a brief case under my arm with a prospectus of the *Encyclopaedia Britannica*. I was supposed to go under cover of dark and sell the bloody encyclopedia to some poor devils who wanted to improve themselves. If I had been dropped off at Helsingfors I couldn't have felt more ill at ease than walking the streets of Bayonne. It wasn't an American city to me. It wasn't a city at all, but a huge octopus wriggling in the dark. The first door I came to looked so forbidding I didn't even bother to knock; I went like that to several addresses before I could summon the courage to knock. The first face I took a look at frightened the shit out of me. I don't mean timidity or embarrassment —I mean fear. It was the face of a hod carrier, an ignorant mick who would as lief fell you with an ax as spit in your eye. I pretended I had the wrong name and hurried on to the next address. Each time the door opened I saw another monster. And then I came at last to a poor simp who really wanted to improve himself and that broke me down. I felt truly ashamed of myself, of my country, my

race, my epoch. I had a devil of a time persuading him
not to buy the damned encyclopedia. He asked me innocently what then had brought me to his home—and without a minute's hesitation I told him an astounding lie, a lie
which was later to prove a great truth. I told him I was
only pretending to sell the encyclopedia in order to meet
people and write about them. That interested him enormously, even more than the encyclopedia. He wanted to
know what I would write about him, if I could say. It's
taken me twenty years to answer that question, but here
it is. If you would still like to know, John Doe of the
City of Bayonne, this is it. . . . I owe you a great deal
because after that lie I told you I left your house and I
tore up the prospectus furnished me by the *Encyclopaedia
Britannica* and I threw it in the gutter. I said to myself
I will never again go to people under false pretenses
even if it is to give them the Holy Bible. I will never
again sell anything, even if I have to starve. I am going
home now and I will sit down and really write about
people. And if anybody knocks at my door to sell me
something I will invite him in and say "why are you doing
this?" And if he says it is because he has to make a living
I will offer him what money I have and beg him once
again to think what he is doing. I want to prevent as
many men as possible from pretending that they have to
do this or that because they must earn a living. *It is not
true*. One can starve to death—it is much better. Every
man who voluntarily starves to death jams another cog
in the automatic process. I would rather see a man take
a gun and kill his neighbor, in order to get the food he
needs, than keep up the automatic process by pretending that he has to earn a living. That's what I want to say,
Mr. John Doe.

I pass on. Not the stabbing horror of disaster and calamity, I say, but the automatic throwback, the stark panorama of the soul's atavistic struggle. A bridge in North
Carolina, near the Tennessee border. Coming out of lush
tobacco fields, low cabins everywhere and the smell of

fresh wood burning. The day passed in a thick lake of waving green. Hardly a soul in sight. Then suddenly a clearing and I'm over a big gulch spanned by a rickety wooden bridge. This is the end of the world! How in God's name I got here and why I'm here I don't know. *How am I going to eat?* And if I ate the biggest meal imaginable I would still be sad, frightfully sad. I don't know where to go from here. This bridge is the end, the end of me, the end of my known world. This bridge is insanity: there is no reason why it should stand there and no reason why people should cross it. I refuse to budge another step, I balk at crossing that crazy bridge. Nearby is a low wall which I lie against trying to think what to do and where to go. I realize quietly what a terribly civilized person I am— the need I have for people, conversation, books, theater, music, cafés, drinks, and so forth. It's terrible to be civilized, because when you come to the end of the world you have nothing to support the terror of loneliness. To be civilized is to have complicated needs. And a man, when he is full blown, shouldn't need a thing. All day I had been moving through tobacco fields, and growing more and more uneasy. What have I to do with all this tobacco? What am I heading into? People everywhere are producing crops and goods for other people—and I am like a ghost sliding between all this unintelligible activity. I want to find some kind of work, but I don't want to be a part of this thing, this infernal automatic process. I pass through a town and I look at the newspaper telling what is happening in that town and its environs. It seems to me that *nothing* is happening, that the clock has stopped but that these poor devils are unaware of it. I have a strong intuition, moreover, that there is murder in the air. I can smell it. A few days back I passed the imaginary line which divides the North from the South. I wasn't aware of it until a darky came along driving a team; when he gets alongside of me he stands up in his seat and doffs his hat most respectfully. He had snow-white hair and a face of great dignity. That made me feel horrible: it made me realize that there are still slaves. This man had to tip his hat to me—because I was of the white race. Whereas I should have tipped my hat to him! I should have saluted him as a survivor of all the vile tortures the white men have inflicted on the black. I should have tipped my hat first, to let him know that I am not a part of this system, that I am begging forgiveness for all my white brethren who are too ignorant and cruel to make an honest overt gesture. Today I feel their eyes on me all the time; they watch from behind doors, from behind trees. All very quiet, very peaceful, seemingly. Nigger never say nuthin'. Nigger he hum all time. White man think nigger learn his place. Nigger learn nuthin'. Nigger wait. Nigger watch everything white man do. Nigger no say nuthin', no sir, no siree. BUT JUST THE SAME THE NIGGER IS KILLING THE WHITE MAN OFF! Every time the nigger looks at a white man he's putting a dagger through him. It's not the heat, it's not the hookworm, it's not the bad crops that's killing the South off—it's the nigger! The nigger is giving off a poison, whether he means to or not. The South is coked and doped with nigger poison.

Pass on. . . . Sitting outside a barber shop by the James River. I'll be here just ten minutes, while I take a load off my feet. There's a hotel and a few stores opposite me; it all tails off quickly, ends like it began—for no reason. From the bottom of my soul I pity the poor devils who are born and die here. There is no earthly reason why this place should exist. There is no reason why anybody should cross the street and get himself a shave and haircut, or even a sirloin steak. Men, buy yourselves a gun and kill each other off! Wipe this street out of my mind forever— it hasn't an ounce of meaning in it.

The same day, after nightfall. Still plugging on, digging deeper and deeper into the South. I'm coming away from a little town by a short road leading to the highway. Suddenly I hear footsteps behind me and soon a young man passes me on the trot, breathing heavily and cursing with all his might. I stand there a moment, wondering what it's all about. I hear another man coming on the trot; he's an older man and he's carrying a gun. He breathes fairly easy, and not a word out of his trap. Just as he comes in view the moon breaks through the clouds and I catch a good look at his face. He's a manhunter. I stand back as the others come up behind him. I'm trembling with fear. It's the sheriff, I hear a man say, and he's going to get him. Horrible. I move on toward the highway waiting to hear the shot that will end it all. I hear nothing—just this heavy breathing of the young man and the quick, eager steps of the mob following behind the sheriff. Just as I get near the main road a man steps out of the darkness and comes over to me very quietly. "Where yer goin', son?" he says, quiet like and almost tenderly. I stammer out something about the next town. "Better stay right here, son," he says. I didn't say another word. I let him take me back into town and hand me over like a thief. I lay on the floor with about fifty other blokes. I had a marvelous sexual dream which ended with the guillotine.

I plug on. . . . It's just as hard to go back as to go forward. I don't have the feeling of being an American citizen any more. The part of America I came from, where I had some rights, where I felt free, is so far behind me that it's beginning to get fuzzy in my memory. I feel as though someone's got a gun against my back all the time. Keep moving, is all I seem to hear. If a man talks to me I try not to seem too intelligent. I try to pretend that I am vitally interested in the crops, in the weather, in the elections. If I stand and stop they look at me, whites and blacks—they look me through and through as though I were juicy and edible. I've got to walk another thousand miles or so as though I had a deep purpose, as though I were really going somewhere. I've got to look sort of grateful, too, that nobody has yet taken a fancy to plug me. It's depressing and exhilarating at the same time. You're a marked man—and yet nobody pulls the trigger. They let you walk unmolested right into the Gulf of Mexico where you can drown yourself.

Yes sir, I reached the Gulf of Mexico and I walked right into it and drowned myself. I did it gratis. When they fished the corpse out they found it was marked F.O.B. Myrtle Avenue, Brooklyn; it was returned C.O.D. When I was asked later why I had killed myself I could only think to say—*because I wanted to electrify the cosmos!* I meant by that a very simple thing—The Delaware, Lackawanna and Western had been electrified, the Seaboard Air Line had been electrified, but the soul of man was still in the covered wagon stage. I was born in the midst of civilization and I accepted it very naturally —what else was there to do? But the joke was that nobody else was taking it seriously. I was the only man in the community who was truly civilized. There was no place for me—as yet. And yet the books I read, the music I heard assured me that there were other men in the world like myself. I had to go and drown myself in the Gulf of Mexico in order to have an excuse for continuing this pseudo-civilized existence. I had to delouse myself of my spiritual body, as it were.

When I woke up to the fact that as far as the scheme of things goes I was less than dirt I really became quite happy. I quickly lost all sense of responsibility. And if it weren't for the fact that my friends got tired of lending me money I might have gone on indefinitely pissing the time away. The world was like a museum to me; I saw nothing to do but eat into this marvelous chocolate layer cake which the men of the past had dumped on our hands. It annoyed everybody to see the way I enjoyed myself. Their logic was that art was very beautiful, oh yes, indeed, but you must work for a living and then you will find that you are too tired to think about art. But it was when I threatened to add a layer or two on my own account to this marvelous chocolate layer cake that they blew up on me. That was the finishing touch. That meant I was definitely crazy. First I was considered to be a useless

member of society; then for a time I was found to be a
reckless, happy-go-lucky corpse with a tremendous appetite; now I had become crazy. (*Listen, you bastard, you
find yourself a job . . . we're through with you!*) In a way
it was refreshing, this change of front. I could feel the
wind blowing through the corridors. At least "we" were
no longer becalmed. It was war, and as a corpse I was
just fresh enough to have a little fight left in me. War is
revivifying. War stirs the blood. It was in the midst of
the world war, which I had forgotten about, that this
change of heart took place. I got myself married overnight, to demonstrate to all and sundry that I didn't give
a fuck one way or the other. Getting married was O.K.
in their minds. I remember that, on the strength of the
announcement, I raised five bucks immediately. My friend
MacGregor paid for the license and even paid for the
shave and haircut which he insisted I go through with in
order to get married. They said you couldn't go without
being shaved; I didn't see any reason why you couldn't get
hitched up without a shave and haircut, but since it
didn't cost me anything I submitted to it. It was interesting to see how everybody was eager to contribute something to our maintenance. All of a sudden, just because I
had shown a bit of sense, they came flocking around us—
and couldn't they do this and couldn't they do that for us?
Of course the assumption was that now I would surely be
going to work, now I would see that life is serious
business. It never occurred to them that I might let my
wife work for me. I was really very decent to her in the
beginning. I wasn't a slave driver. All I asked for was carfare—to hunt for the mythical job—and a little pin money
for cigarettes, movies, et cetera. The important things,
such as books, music albums, gramophones, porterhouse
steaks and such like I found we could get on credit, now
that we were married. The installment plan had been invented expressly for guys like me. The down payment
was easy—the rest I left to Providence. One has to live,
they were always saying. Now, by God, that's what I said

to myself—*One has to live! Live first and pay afterwards.*
If I saw an overcoat I liked I went in and bought it. I
would buy it a little in advance of the season too, to show
that I was a serious-minded chap. Shit, I was a married
man and soon I would probably be a father—I was en-
titled to a winter overcoat at least, no? And when I had
the overcoat I thought of stout shoes to go with it—a pair
of thick cordovans such as I had wanted all my life but
never could afford. And when it grew bitter cold and I
was out looking for the job I used to get terribly hungry
sometimes—it's really healthy going out like that day
after day prowling about the city in rain and snow and
wind and hail—and so now and then I'd drop in to a
cosy tavern and order myself a juicy porterhouse steak
with onions and french fried potatoes. I took out life insurance and accident insurance too—it's important, when
you're married, to do things like that, so they told me.
Supposing I should drop dead one day—what then? I
remember the guy telling me that, in order to clinch his
argument. I had already told him I would sign up, but
he must have forgotten it. I had said, yes, immediately,
out of force of habit, but as I say, he had evidently overlooked it—or else it was against the code to sign a man
up until you had delivered the full sales talk. Anyway,
I was just getting ready to ask him how long it would
take before you could make a loan on the policy when
he popped the hypothetical question: *Supposing you
should drop dead one day—what then?* I guess he thought
I was a little off my nut the way I laughed at that. I
laughed until the tears rolled down my face. Finally he
said—"I don't see that I said anything so funny." "Well,"
I said, getting serious for a moment, "take a good look
at me. Now tell me, do you think I'm the sort of fellow
who gives a fuck what happens once he's dead?" He was
quite taken aback by this, apparently, because the next
thing he said was: "I don't think that's a very ethical
attitude, Mr. Miller. I'm sure you wouldn't want your
wife to . . ." "Listen," I said, "supposing I told you I

don't give a fuck what happens to my wife when I die—what then?" And since this seemed to injure his ethical susceptibilities still more I added for good measure—"As far as I'm concerned you don't have to pay the insurance when I croak—I'm only doing this to make you feel good. I'm trying to help the world along, don't you see? You've got to live, haven't you? Well, I'm just putting a little food in your mouth, that's all. If you have anything else to sell, trot it out. I buy anything that sounds good. I'm a buyer not a seller. I like to see people looking happy—that's why I buy things. Now listen, how much did you say that would come to per week? Fifty-seven cents? Fine. What's fifty-seven cents? You see that piano—that comes to about thirty-nine cents a week, I think. Look around you . . . everything you see costs so much a week. You say, *if I should die, what then?* Do you suppose I'm going to die on all these people? That would be a hell of a joke. No, I'd rather have them come and take the things away—if I can't pay for them, I mean. . . ." He was fidgeting about and there was a rather glassy stare in his eye, I thought. "Excuse me," I said, interrupting myself, "but wouldn't you like to have a little drink—to wet the policy?" He said he thought not, but I insisted, and besides, I hadn't signed the papers yet and my urine would have to be examined and approved of and all sorts of stamps and seals would have to be affixed—I knew all that crap by heart—so I thought we might have a little snifter first and in that way protract the serious business, because honestly, buying insurance or buying anything was a real pleasure to me and gave me the feeling that I was just like every other citizen, *a man, what!* and not a monkey. So I got out a bottle of sherry (which is all that was allowed me) and I poured out a generous glassful for him, thinking to myself that it was fine to see the sherry going because maybe the next time they'd buy something better for me. "I used to sell insurance too once upon a time," I said, raising the glass to my lips. "Sure, I can sell anything. The only thing is—I'm lazy.

Take a day like today—isn't it nicer to be indoors, reading a book or listening to the phonograph? Why should I go out and hustle for an insurance company? If I had been working today you wouldn't have caught me in—isn't that so? No, I think it's better to take it easy and help people out when they come along . . . like with you, for instance. It's much nicer to buy things than to sell them, don't you think? *If you have the money,* of course! In this house we don't need much money. As I was saying, the piano comes to about thirty-nine cents a week, or forty-two maybe, and the. . . ."

"Excuse me, Mr. Miller," he interrupted, "but don't you think we ought to get down to signing these papers?"

"Why, of course." I said cheerfully. "Did you bring them all with you? Which one do you think we ought to sign first? By the way, you haven't got a fountain pen you'd like to sell me, have you?"

"Just sign right here," he said, pretending to ignore my remarks. "And here, that's it. Now then, Mr. Miller, I think I'll say good day—and you'll be hearing from the company in a few days."

"Better make it sooner," I remarked, leading him to the door, "because I might change my mind and commit suicide."

"Why, of course, why yes, Mr. Miller, certainly we will. Good day now, good day!"

Of course the installment plan breaks down eventually, even if you're an assiduous buyer such as I was. I certainly did my best to keep the manufacturers and the advertising men of America busy, but they were disappointed in me it seems. Everybody was disappointed in me. But there was one man in particular who was more disappointed in me than anyone and that was a man who had really made an effort to befriend me and whom I had let down. I think of him and the way he took me on as his assistant—so readily and graciously—because later, when I was hiring and firing like a forty-two horse caliber revolver, I was betrayed right and left myself, but by that time I had become so inoculated that it didn't matter a damn. But this man had gone out of his way to show me that he believed in me. He was the editor of a catalogue for a great mail order house. It was an enormous compendium of horseshit which was put out once a year and which took the whole year to make ready. I hadn't the slightest idea what it was all about and why I dropped into his office that day I don't know, unless it was because I wanted to get warm, as I had been knocking about the docks all day trying to get a job as a checker or some damned thing. It was cosy in his office and I made him a long speech so as to get thawed out. I didn't know what job to ask for—just a job, I said. He was a sensitive man and very kindhearted. He seemed to guess that I was a writer, or wanted to be a writer, because soon he was asking me what I liked to read and what was my opinion of this writer and that writer. It just happened that I had a list of books in my pocket—books I was searching for at the public library—and so I brought it out and showed it to him. "Great Scott!" he exclaimed, "do you really read these books?" I modestly shook my head in the affirmative, and then as often happened to me when I was touched off by some silly remark like that, I began to talk about Hamsun's *Mysteries* which I had just been reading. From then on the man was like putty in my hands. When he asked me if I would like to be his assistant he apologized for offering me such a lowly position; he said I could take my time learning the ins and outs of the job, he was sure it would be a cinch for me. And then he asked me if he couldn't lend me some money, out of his own pocket, until I got paid. Before I could say yes or no he had fished out a twenty-dollar bill and thrust it in my hand. Naturally I was touched. I was ready to work like a son of a bitch for him. Assistant editor—it sounded quite good, especially to the creditors in the neighborhood. And for a while I was so happy to be eating roast beef and chicken and tenderloins of pork that I pretended I liked the job. Actually it was difficult for me to keep awake. What I had to learn I had learned in a week's time. And after that? After that I saw myself doing penal servitude for life. In order to make the best of it I whiled away the time writing stories and essays and long letters to my friends. Perhaps they thought I was writing up new ideas for the company, because for quite a while nobody paid any attention to me. I thought it was a wonderful job. I had almost the whole day to myself, for my writing, having learned to dispose of the company's work in about an hour's time. I was so enthusiastic about my own private work that I gave orders to my underlings not to disturb me except at stipulated moments. I was sailing along like a breeze, the company paying me regularly and the slave drivers doing the work I had mapped out for them, when one day, just when I am in the midst of an important essay on *The Anti-Christ,* a man whom I had never seen before walks up to my desk, bends over my shoulder, and in a sarcastic tone of voice begins to read aloud what I had just written. I didn't need to inquire who he was or what he was up to—the only thought in my head was, and that I repeated to myself frantically—*Will I get an extra week's pay?* When it came time to bid good-by to my benefactor I felt a little ashamed of myself, particularly when he said, right off the bat like—"I tried to get you an extra week's pay but they wouldn't hear of it. I wish there was something I could do for you—you're only standing in your own way, you know. To tell you the truth, I still have the greatest faith in you—but I'm afraid you're going to have a hard time of it, for a while. You don't fit in anywhere. Some day you'll make a great writer, I feel sure of it. Well, excuse me," he added, shaking hands with me warmly, "I've got to see the boss. Good luck to you!"

I felt a bit cut up about the incident. I wished it had been possible to prove to him then and there that his faith was justified. I wished I could have justified myself before the whole world at that moment: I would have jumped off the Brooklyn Bridge if it would have con-

vinced people that I wasn't a heartless son of a bitch. I
had a heart as big as a whale, as I was soon to prove, but
nobody was examining into my heart. Everybody was
being let down hard—not only the installment companies,
but the landlord, the butcher, the baker, the gas, water
and electricity devils, *everybody*. If only I could get to
believe in this business of work! To save my life I couldn't
see it. I could only see that people were working their balls
off because they didn't know any better. I thought of the
speech I had made which won me the job. In some ways
I was very much like Herr Nagel myself. No telling from
minute to minute what I would do. No knowing whether
I was a monster or a saint. Like so many wonderful men
of our time, Herr Nagel was a desperate man—and it was
this very desperation which made him such a likable chap.
Hamsun didn't know what to make of this character
himself: he knew he existed, and he knew that there was
something more to him than a mere buffoon and a mysti-
fier. I think he loved Herr Nagel more than any other
character he created. And why? Because Herr Nagel was
the unacknowledged saint which every artist is—the
man who is ridiculed because his solutions, which are
truly profound, seem too simple for the world. No man
wants to be an artist—he is driven to it because the world
refuses to recognize his proper leadership. Work meant
nothing to me, because the real work to be done was
being evaded. People regarded me as lazy and shift-
less, but on the contrary I was an exceedingly active
individual. Even if it was just hunting for a piece of
tail, that was something, and well worth while, especially if compared to other forms of activity—such as
making buttons or turning screws, or even removing ap-
pendixes. And why did people listen to me so readily
when I applied for a job? Why did they find me entertaining? For the reason, no doubt, that I had always spent
my time profitably. I brought them gifts—from my hours
at the public library, from my idle ramblings through the
streets, from my intimate experiences with women, from

my afternoons at the burlesque, from my visits to the
museum and the art galleries. Had I been a dud, just a
poor honest bugger who wanted to work his balls off for
so much a week, they wouldn't have offered me the jobs
they did, nor would they have handed me cigars or taken
me to lunch or lent me money, as they frequently did.
I must have had something to offer which perhaps un-
knowingly they prized beyond horsepower or techni-
cal ability. I didn't know myself what it was, because I
had neither pride, nor vanity, nor envy. About the big
issues I was clear, but confronted by the petty details
of life I was bewildered. I had to witness this same bewilderment on a colossal scale before I could grasp what
it was all about. Ordinary men are often quicker in
sizing up the practical situation: their ego is commensu-
rate with the demands made upon it: the world is not
very different from what they imagine it to be. But a man
who is completely out of step with the rest of the world
is either suffering from a colossal inflation of his ego
or else the ego is so submerged as to be practically non-
existent. Herr Nagel had to dive off the deep end in
search of his true ego; his existence was a mystery, to
himself and to everyone else. I couldn't afford to leave
things hanging in suspense that way—the mystery was
too intriguing. Even if I had to rub myself like a cat
against every human being I encountered, I was going to
get to the bottom of it. Rub long enough and hard
enough and the spark will come!

The hibernation of animals, the suspension of life
practiced by certain low forms of life, the marvelous
vitality of the bedbug which lies in wait endlessly behind the wallpaper, the trance of the Yogi, the catalepsy
of the pathologic individual, the mystic's union with
the cosmos, the immortality of cellular life, all these
things the artist learns in order to awaken the world
at the propitious moment. The artist belongs to the X
root race of man; he is the spiritual microbe, as it were,
which carries over from one root race to another. He is

not crushed by misfortune, because he is not a part of the physical, racial scheme of things. His appearance is always synchronous with catastrophe and dissolution; he is the cyclical being which lives in the epicycle. The experience which he acquires is never used for personal ends; it serves the larger purpose to which he is geared. Nothing is lost on him, however trifling. If he is interrupted for twenty-five years in the reading of a book he can go on from the page where he left off as though nothing had happened in between. Everything that happens in between, which is "life" to most people, is merely an interruption in his forward round. The eternality of his work, when he expresses himself, is merely the reflection of the automatism of life in which he is obliged to lie dormant, a sleeper on the back of sleep, waiting for the signal which will announce the moment of birth. This is the big issue, and this was always clear to me, even when I denied it. The dissatisfaction which drives one on from one word to another, one creation to another, is simply a protest against the futility of postponement. The more awake one becomes, as artistic microbe, the less desire one has to do anything. Fully awake, everything is just and there is no need to come out of the trance. Action, as expressed in creating a work of art, is a concession to the automatic principle of death. Drowning myself in the Gulf of Mexico I was able to partake of an active life which would permit the real self to hibernate until I was ripe to be born. I understood it perfectly, though I acted blindly and confusedly. I swam back into the stream of human activity until I got to the source of all action and there I muscled in, calling myself personnel director of a telegraph company, and allowed the tide of humanity to wash over me like great white-capped breakers. All this active life, preceding the final act of desperation, led me from doubt to doubt, blinding me more and more to the real self which, like a continent choked with the evidences of a great and thriving civilization, had already sunk beneath the surface of the sea.

The colossal ego was submerged, and what people observed moving frantically above the surface was the periscope of the soul searching for its target. Everything that came within range had to be destroyed, if I were ever to rise again and ride the waves. This monster which rose now and then to fix its target with deadly aim, which dove again and roved and plundered ceaselessly would, when the time came, rise for the last time to reveal itself as an ark, would gather unto itself a pair of each kind and at last, when the floods abated, would settle down on the summit of a lofty mountain peak thence to open wide its doors and return to the world what had been preserved from the catastrophe.

If I shudder now and then, when I think of my active life, if I have nightmares, possibly it is because I think of all the men I robbed and murdered in my day sleep. I did everything which my nature bade me to do. Nature is eternally whispering in one's ear—"if you would survive you must kill!" Being human, you kill not like the animal but automatically, and the killing is disguised and its ramifications are endless, so that you kill without even thinking about it, you kill without need. The men who are the most honored are the greatest killers. They believe that they are serving their fellowmen, and they are sincere in believing so; but they are heartless murderers and at moments, when they come awake, they realize their crimes and perform frantic, quixotic acts of goodness in order to expiate their guilt. The goodness of man stinks more than the evil which is in him, for the goodness is not yet acknowledged, not an affirmation of the conscious self. Being pushed over the precipice, it is easy at the last moment to surrender all one's possessions, to turn and extend a last embrace to all who are left behind. How are we to stop the blind rush? How are we to stop the automatic process, each one pushing the other over the precipice?

As I sat at my desk, over which I had put up a sign reading "Do not abandon all hope ye who enter here!"—

as I sat there saying Yes, No, Yes, No, I realized, with a despair that was turning to white frenzy, that I was a puppet in whose hands society had placed a Gatling gun. If I performed a good deed it was no different, ultimately, than if I had performed a bad deed. I was like an equals sign through which the algebraic swarm of humanity was passing. I was a rather important, active equals sign, like a general in time of war, but no matter how competent I were to become I could never change into a plus or a minus sign. Nor could anyone else, as far as I could determine. Our whole life was built up on this principle of equation. The integers had become symbols which were shuffled about in the interests of death. Pity, despair, passion, hope, courage—these were the temporal refractions caused by looking at equations from varying angles. To stop the endless juggling by turning one's back on it, or by facing it squarely and writing about it, would be no help either. In a hall of mirrors there is no way to turn your back on yourself. *I will not do this. I will do some other thing!* Very good. But can you do nothing at all? Can you stop thinking about not doing anything? Can you stop dead, and without thinking, radiate the truth which you know? That was the idea which lodged in the back of my head and which burned and burned, and perhaps when I was most expansive, most radiant with energy, most sympathetic, most willing, helpful, sincere, good, it was this fixed idea which was shining through, and automatically I was saying—"why, don't mention it. . . . nothing at all, I assure you. . . . no, please don't thank me, it's nothing," etc. etc. From firing the gun so many hundreds of times a day perhaps I didn't even notice the detonations any more; perhaps I thought I was opening pigeon traps and filling the sky with milky white fowl. Did you ever see a synthetic monster on the screen, a Frankenstein realized in flesh and blood? Can you imagine how he might be trained to pull a trigger and see pigeons flying at the same time? Frankenstein is not a myth: Frankenstein is a very real creation born of the personal experience of a sensitive human being. The monster is always more real when it does not assume the proportions of flesh and blood. The monster of the screen is nothing compared to the monster of the imagination; even the existent pathologic monsters who find their way into the police station are but feeble demonstrations of the monstrous reality which the pathologist lives with. But to be the monster and the pathologist at the same time—that is reserved for certain species of men who, disguised as artists, are supremely aware that sleep is an even greater danger than insomnia. In order not to fall asleep, in order not to become victims of that insomnia which is called "living," they resort to the drug of putting words together endlessly. This is *not* an automatic process, they say, because there is always present the illusion that they can stop it at will. But they cannot stop; they have only succeeded in creating an illusion, which is perhaps a feeble something, but it is far from being wide awake and neither active nor inactive. *I wanted to be wide awake without talking or writing about it, in order to accept life absolutely.* I mentioned the archaic men in the remote places of the world with whom I was communicating frequently. Why did I think these "savages" more capable of understanding me than the men and women who surrounded me? Was I crazy to believe such a thing? I don't think so in the least. These "savages" are the degenerate remnants of earlier races of man who, I believe, must have had a greater hold on reality. The immortality of the race is constantly before our eyes in these specimens of the past who linger on in withered splendor. Whether the human race is immortal or not is not my concern, but the vitality of the race does mean something to me, and that it should be active or dormant means even more. As the vitality of the new race banks down the vitality of the old races manifests itself to the waking mind with greater and greater significance. The vitality of the old races lingers on even in death, but the vitality of the new race which is about to die seems already nonexistent. *If a man were taking a swarming hive of bees to the river to drown them. . . .* That was the image I carried about in me. If only I were the man, and not the bee! In some vague, inexplicable way I knew that I *was* the man, that I would not be drowned in the hive, like the others. Always, when we came forward in a group, I was signaled to stand apart; from birth I was favored that way, and, no matter what tribulations I went through, I knew they were not fatal or lasting. Also, another strange thing took place in me whenever I was called to stand forth. I knew that I was superior to the man who was summoning me! The tremendous humility which I practiced was not hypocritical but a condition provoked by the realization of the fateful character of the situation. The intelligence which I possessed, even as a stripling, frightened me; it was the intelligence of a "savage," which is always superior to that of civilized men in that it is more adequate to the exigencies of circumstance. It is a *life* intelligence, even though life has seemingly passed them by. I felt almost as if I had been shot forward into a round of existence which for the rest of mankind had not yet attained its full rhythm. I was obliged to mark time if I were to remain with them and not be shunted off to another sphere of existence. On the other hand, I was in many ways lower than the human beings about me. It was as though I had come out of the fires of hell not entirely purged. I had still a tail and a pair of horns, and when my passions were aroused I breathed a sulphurous poison which was annihilating. I was always called a "lucky devil." The good that happened to me was called "luck," and the evil was always regarded as a result of my shortcomings. Rather, as the fruit of my blindness. Rarely did anyone ever spot the evil in me! I was as adroit, in this respect, as the devil himself. But that I was frequently blind, everybody could see that. And at such times I was left alone, shunned, like the devil himself. Then I left the world, returned to the fires of hell—voluntarily. These comings and goings are as real to me, more real, in fact, than anything that happened in between. The friends who think they know me know nothing about me for the reason that the real me changed hands countless times. Neither the men who thanked me, nor the men who cursed me, knew with whom they were dealing. Nobody ever got on to a solid footing with me, because I was constantly liquidating my personality. I was keeping what is called the "personality" in abeyance for the moment when, leaving it to coagulate, it would adopt a proper human rhythm. I was hiding my face until the moment when I would find myself in step with the world. All this was, of course, a mistake. Even the role of artist is worth adopting, while marking time. Action is important, even if it entails futile activity. One should not say Yes, No, Yes, No, even seated in the highest place. One should not be drowned in the human tidal wave, even for the sake of becoming a Master. One must beat with his own rhythm—at any price. I accumulated thousands of years of experience in a few short years, but the experience was wasted because I had no need of it. I had already been crucified and marked by the cross; I had been born free of the need to suffer—and yet I knew no other way to struggle forward than to repeat the drama. All my intelligence was against it. Suffering is futile, my intelligence told me over and over, but I went on suffering *voluntarily*. Suffering has never taught me a thing; for others it may still be necessary, but for me it is nothing more than an algebraic demonstration of spiritual inadaptability. The whole drama which the man of today is acting out through suffering does not exist for me: it never did, actually. All my Calvaries were rosy crucifixions, pseudo-tragedies to keep the fires of hell burning brightly for the real sinners who are in danger of being forgotten.

Another thing . . . the mystery which enveloped my behavior grew deeper the nearer I came to the circle of uterine relatives. The mother from whose loins I sprang was a complete stranger to me. To begin with, after giving birth to me she gave birth to my sister, whom I usually refer to as my brother. My sister was a sort of harmless monster, an angel who had been given the body of an idiot. It gave me a strange feeling, as a boy, to be growing up and developing side by side with this being who was doomed to remain all her life a mental dwarf. It was impossible to be a brother to her because it was impossible to regard this atavistic hulk of a body as a "sister." She would have functioned perfectly, I imagine, among the Australian primitives. She might even have been raised to power and eminence among them, for, as I said, she was the essence of goodness, she knew no evil. But so far as living the civilized life goes she was helpless; she not only had no desire to kill but she had no desire to thrive at the expense of others. She was incapacitated for work, because even if they had been able to train her to make caps for high explosives, for example, she might absent-mindedly throw her wages in the river on the way home or she might give them to a beggar in the street. Often in my presence she was whipped like a dog for having performed some beautiful act of grace in her absent-mindedness, as they called it. Nothing was worse, I learned as a child, than to do a good deed without reason. I had received the same punishment as my sister, in the beginning, because I too had a habit of giving things away, especially new things which had just been given me. I had even received a beating once, at the age of five, for having advised my mother to cut a wart off her finger. She had asked me what to do about it one day and, with my limited knowledge of medicine, I told her to cut it off with the scissors, which she did, like an idiot. A few days later she got blood poisoning and then she got hold of me and she said—"you told me to cut it off, didn't you?" and she gave me a sound thrashing. From that day on I knew that I was born in the wrong household. From that day on I learned like lightning. Talk about adaptation! By the time I was ten I had lived out the whole theory of evolution. And there I was, evolv-

ing through all the phases of animal life and yet chained
to this creature called my "sister" who was evidently a
primitive being and who would never, even at the age
of ninety, arrive at a comprehension of the alphabet. Instead of growing up like a stalwart tree I began to lean to
one side, in complete defiance of the law of gravity.
Instead of shooting out limbs and leaves I grew windows
and turrets. The whole being, as it grew, was turning into
stone, and the higher I shot up the more I defied the law
of gravity. I was a phenomenon in the midst of the landscape, but one which attracted people and elicited praise.
If the mother who bore us had only made another effort
perhaps a marvelous white buffalo might have been born
and the three of us might have been permanently installed in a museum and protected for life. The conversations which took place between the leaning tower of Pisa,
the whipping post, the snoring machine and the ptero-
dactyl in human flesh were, to say the least, a bit queer.
Anything might be the subject of conversation—a bread
crumb which the "sister" had overlooked in brushing the
tablecloth or Joseph's coat of many colors which, in the
old man's tailoring brain, might have been either double-
breasted or cutaway or frock. If I came from the ice
pond, where I had been skating all afternoon, the important thing was not the ozone which I had breathed
free of charge, nor the geometric convolutions which were
strengthening my muscles, but the little spot of rust under
the clamps which, if not rubbed off immediately, might
deteriorate the whole skate and bring about the dissolution
of some pragmatic value which was incomprehensible to
my prodigal turn of thought. This little rust spot, to take a
trifling example, might entrain the most hallucinating results. Perhaps the "sister," in searching for the kerosene
can, might overturn the jar of prunes which were being
stewed and thus endanger all our lives by robbing us of
the required calories in the morrow's meal. A severe beating would have to be given, not in anger, because that
would disturb the digestive apparatus, but silently and

efficiently, as a chemist would beat up the white of an egg in preparation for a minor analysis. But the "sister," not understanding the prophylactic nature of the punishment, would give vent to the most bloodcurdling screams and this would so affect the old man that he would go out for a walk and return two or three hours later blind drunk and, what was worse, scratching a little paint off the rolling doors in his blind staggers. The little piece of paint that had been chipped off would bring on a battle royal which was very bad for my dream life, because in my dream life I frequently changed places with my sister, accepting the tortures inflicted upon her and nourishing them with my supersensitive brain. It was in these dreams, always accompanied by the sound of glass breaking, of shrieks, curses, groans and sobs, that I gathered an unformulated knowledge of the ancient mysteries, of the rites of initiation, of the transmigration of souls and so on. It might begin with a scene from real life—the sister standing by the blackboard in the kitchen, the mother towering over her with a ruler, saying two and two makes how much? and the sister screaming *five.* Bang! *no, seven,* Bang! *no, thirteen, eighteen, twenty!* I would be sitting at the table, doing my lessons, just as in real life during these scenes, when by a slight twist or squirm, perhaps as I saw the ruler come down on the sister's face, suddenly I would be in another realm where glass was unknown, as it was unknown to the Kickapoos or the Lenni-Lenape. The faces of those about me were familiar —they were my uterine relatives who, for some mysterious reason, failed to recognize me in this new *ambiance.* They were garbed in black and the color of their skin was ash gray, like that of the Tibetan devils. They were all fitted out with knives and other instruments of torture: they belonged to the caste of sacrificial butchers. I seemed to have absolute liberty and the authority of a god, and yet by some capricious turn of events the end would be that I'd be lying on the sacrificial block and one of my charming uterine relatives would be bending over

me with a gleaming knife to cut out my heart. In sweat
and terror I would begin to recite "my lessons" in a high,
screaming voice, faster and faster, as I felt the knife
searching for my heart. Two and two is four, five and
five is ten, earth, air, fire, water, Monday, Tuesday,
Wednesday, hydrogen, oxygen, nitrogen, Meocene, Pleo-
cene, Eocene, the Father, the Son, the Holy Ghost, Asia,
Africa, Europe, Australia, red, blue, yellow, the sorrel,
the persimmon, the pawpaw, the catalpa . . . *faster and
faster* . . . Odin, Wotan, Parsifal, King Alfred, Frederick
the Great, the Hanseatic League, the Battle of Hastings,
Thermopylae, 1492, 1776, 1812, Admiral Farragut, Pic-
kett's charge, The Light Brigade, we are gathered here
today, the Lord is my shepherd, I shall not, one and indivisible, no, 16, no, 27, help! murder! police!—and yelling louder and louder and going faster and faster I go
completely off my nut and there is no more pain, no more
terror, even though they are piercing me everywhere with
knives. Suddenly I am absolutely calm and the body
which is lying on the block, which they are still gouging
with glee and ecstasy, feels nothing because I, the owner
of it, have escaped. I have become a tower of stone
which leans over the scene and watches with scientific
interest. I have only to succumb to the law of gravity and
I will fall on them and obliterate them. But I do not succumb to the law of gravity because I am too fascinated
by the horror of it all. I am so fascinated, in fact, that I
grow more and more windows. And as the light penetrates
the stone interior of my being I can feel that my roots,
which are in the earth, are alive and that I shall one day
be able to remove myself at will from this trance in which
I am fixed.

So much for the dream, in which I am helplessly
rooted. But in actuality, when the dear uterine relatives
come, I am as free as a bird and darting to and fro
like a magnetic needle. If they ask me a question I give
them five answers, each of which is better than the other;
if they ask me to play a waltz I play a double-breasted

sonata for the left hand; if they ask me to help myself
to another leg of chicken I clean up the plate, dressing
and all; if they urge me to go out and play in the street
I go out and in my enthusiasm I cut my cousin's head
open with a tin can; if they threaten to give me a thrashing I say go to it, I don't mind! If they pat me on the head
for my good progress at school I spit on the floor to show
that I have still something to learn. I do everything they
wish me to do *plus*. If they wish me to be quiet and say
nothing I become as quiet as a rock: I don't hear when
they speak to me, I don't move when I'm touched, I
don't cry when I'm pinched, I don't budge when I'm
pushed. If they complain that I'm stubborn I become as
pliant and yielding as rubber. If they wish me to get
fatigued so that I will not display too much energy I let
them give me all kinds of work to do and I do the jobs
so thoroughly that I collapse on the floor finally like a
sack of wheat. If they wish me to be reasonable I become
ultra-reasonable, which drives them crazy. If they wish
me to obey I obey to the letter, which causes endless
confusion. And all this because the molecular life of
brother-and-sister is incompatible with the atomic
weights which have been allotted us. Because she doesn't
grow at all I grow like a mushroom; because she has no
personality I become a colossus; because she is free of
evil I become a thirty-two-branched candelabra of evil;
because she demands nothing of anyone I demand everything; because she inspires ridicule everywhere I inspire
fear and respect; because she is humiliated and tortured
I wreak vengeance upon everyone, friend and foe alike;
because she is helpless I make myself all-powerful. The
gigantism from which I suffered was simply the result
of an effort to wipe out the little stain of rust which had
attached itself to the family skate, so to speak. That
little stain of rust under the clamps made me a champion
skater. It made me skate so fast and furiously that even
when the ice had melted I was still skating, skating
through mud, through asphalt, through brooks and rivers

and melon patches and theories of economics and so forth. I could skate through hell, I was that fast and nimble.

But all this fancy skating was of no use—Father Cox-cox, the pan-American Noah, was always calling me back to the Ark. Every time I stopped skating there was a cataclysm—the earth opened up and swallowed me. I was a brother to every man and at the same time a traitor to myself. I made the most astounding sacrifices, only to find that they were of no value. Of what use was it to prove that I could be what was expected of me when I did not want to be any of these things? Every time you come to the limit of what is demanded of you, you are faced with the same problem—to be yourself! And with the first step you make in this direction you realize that there is neither plus nor minus; you throw the skates away and swim. There is no suffering any more because there is nothing which can threaten your security. And there is no desire to be of help to others even, because why rob them of a privilege which must be earned? Life stretches out from moment to moment in stupendous infinitude. Nothing can be more real than what you suppose it to be. Whatever you think the cosmos to be it is and it could not possibly be anything else as long as you are you and I am I. You live in the fruits of your action and your action is the harvest of your thought. Thought and action are one, because swimming you are in it and of it, and *it* is everything you desire it to be, no more, no less. Every stroke counts for eternity. The heating and cooling system is one system, and Cancer is separated from Capricorn only by an imaginary line. You don't become ecstatic and you are not plunged into violent grief; you don't pray for rain, neither do you dance a jig. You live like a happy rock in the midst of the ocean: you are fixed while everything about you is in turbulent motion. You are fixed in a reality which permits the thought that nothing is fixed, that even the happiest and mightiest rock will one day be utterly dissolved and fluid as the ocean from which it was born.

This is the musical life which I was approaching by first skating like a maniac through all the vestibules and corridors which lead from the outer to the inner. My struggles never brought me near it, nor did my furious activity, nor my rubbing elbows with humanity. All that was simply a movement from vector to vector in a circle which, however the perimeter expanded, remained withal parallel to the realm I speak of. The wheel of destiny can be transcended at any moment because at every point of its surface it touches the real world and only a spark of illumination is necessary to bring about the miraculous, to transform the skater to a swimmer and the swimmer to a rock. The rock is merely an image of the act which stops the futile rotation of the wheel and plunges the being into full consciousness. And full consciousness is indeed like an inexhaustible ocean which gives itself to sun and moon and also *includes* the sun and moon. Everything which is is born out of the limitless ocean of light —even the night.

Sometimes, in the ceaseless revolutions of the wheel, I caught a glimpse of the nature of the jump which it was necessary to make. To jump clear of the clockwork—that was the liberating thought. To be something more, something *different*, than the most brilliant maniac of the earth! The story of man on earth bored me. Conquest, even the conquest of evil, bored me. To radiate goodness is marvelous, because it is tonic, invigorating, vitalizing. But just *to be* is still more marvelous, because it is endless and requires no demonstration. To be is music, which is a profanation of silence in the interest of silence, and therefore beyond good and evil. Music is the manifestation of action without activity. It is the pure act of creation swimming on its own bosom. Music neither goads nor defends, neither seeks nor explains. Music is the noiseless sound made by the swimmer in the ocean of consciousness. It is a reward which can only be given by oneself. It is the gift of the god which one is because he has ceased thinking about God. It is an augur of the god which every one will become in due time, when all that *is* will *be* beyond imagination.

CODA

Not long ago I was walking the streets of New York. Dear old Broadway. It was night and the sky was an Oriental blue, as blue as the gold in the ceiling of the *Pagode*, rue de Babylone, when the machine starts clicking. I was passing exactly below the place where we first met. I stood there a moment looking up at the red lights in the windows. The music sounded as it always sounded—light, peppery, enchanting. I was alone and there were millions of people around me. It came over me, as I stood there, that I wasn't thinking of her any more; I was thinking of this book which I am writing, and the book had become more important to me than her, than all that had happened to us. Will this book be the truth, the whole truth, and nothing but the truth, so help me God? Plunging into the crowd again I wrestled with this question of "truth." For years I have been trying to tell this story and always the question of truth has weighed upon me like a nightmare. Time and again I have related to others the circumstances of our life, and I have always told the truth. But the truth can also be a lie. The truth is not enough. Truth is only the core of a totality which is inexhaustible.

I remember that the first time we were ever separated this idea of totality seized me by the hair. She pretended, when she left me, or maybe she believed it herself, that it was necessary for our welfare. I knew in my heart that she was trying to be free of me, but I was too cowardly to admit it to myself. But when I realized that she could do without me, even for a limited time, the truth which I had tried to shut out began to grow with alarming rapidity. It was more painful than anything I had ever experienced before, but it was also healing. When I was completely emptied, when the loneliness had reached such a point that it could not be sharpened any further, I suddenly felt that, to go on living, this intolerable truth had to be incorporated into something greater than the frame of personal misfortune. I felt that I had made an imperceptible switch into another realm, a realm of tougher, more elastic fiber, which the most horrible truth was powerless to destroy. I sat down to write her a letter telling her that I was so miserable over the thought of losing her that I had decided to begin a book about her, a book which would immortalize her. It would be a book, I said, such as no one had ever seen before. I rambled on ecstatically, and in the midst of it I suddenly broke off to ask myself why I was so happy.

Passing beneath the dance hall, thinking again of this book, I realized suddenly that our life had come to an end: I realized that the book I was planning was nothing more than a tomb in which to bury her—and the me which had belonged to her. That was some time ago, and ever since I have been trying to write it. Why is it so difficult? Why? Because the idea of an "end" is intolerable to me.

Truth lies in this knowledge of the end which is ruthless and remorseless. We can know the truth and accept it, or we can refuse the knowledge of it and neither die nor be born again. In this manner it is possible to live forever, a negative life as solid and complete, or as dispersed and fragmentary, as the atom. And if we pursue this road far enough, even this atomic eternity can yield to nothingness and the universe itself fall apart.

For years now I have been trying to tell this story; each time I have started out I have chosen a different route. I am like an explorer who, wishing to circumnavigate the globe, deems it unnecessary to carry even a compass.

Moreover, from dreaming over it so long, the story itself
has come to resemble a vast, fortified city, and I who
dream it over and over, am outside the city, a wanderer,
arriving before one gate after another too exhausted to
enter. And as with the wanderer, this city in which my
story is situated eludes me perpetually. Always in sight
it nevertheless remains unattainable, a sort of ghostly
citadel floating in the clouds. From the soaring, crenelated
battlements flocks of huge white geese swoop down in
steady, wedge-shaped formation. With the tips of their
blue-white wings they brush the dreams that dazzle my
vision. My feet move confusedly; no sooner do I gain
a foothold than I am lost again. I wander aimlessly, trying
to gain a solid, unshakable foothold whence I can com-
mand a view of my life, but behind me there lies only a
welter of crisscrossed tracks, a groping, confused, en-
circling, the spasmodic gambit of the chicken whose head
has just been lopped off.

Whenever I try to explain to myself the peculiar pattern which my life has taken, when I reach back to the
first cause, as it were, I think inevitably of the girl I first
loved. It seems to me that everything dates from that
aborted affair. A strange, masochistic affair it was, ridiculous and tragic at the same time. Perhaps I had the
pleasure of kissing her two or three times, the sort of
kiss one reserves for a goddess. Perhaps I saw her alone
several times. Certainly she could never have dreamed that
for over a year I walked past her home every night hoping to catch a glimpse of her at the window. Every night
after dinner I would get up from the table and take the
long route which led to her home. She was never at the
window when I passed and I never had the courage to
stand in front of the house and wait. Back and forth I
passed, back and forth, but never hide nor hair of her.
Why didn't I write her? Why didn't I call her up? Once I
remember summoning enough pluck to invite her to the
theater. I arrived at her home with a bunch of violets,
the first and only time I ever bought flowers for a woman.

As we were leaving the theater the violets dropped from her corsage, and in my confusion I stepped on them. I begged her to leave them there, but she insisted on gathering them up. I was thinking how awkward I was—it was only long afterwards that I recalled the smile she had given me as she stooped down to pick up the violets.

It was a complete fiasco. In the end I ran away. Actually I was running away from another woman, but the day before leaving town I decided to see her once again. It was midafternoon and she came out to talk to me in the street, in the little areaway which was fenced off. She was already engaged to another man; she pretended to be happy about it but I could see, blind as I was, that she wasn't as happy as she pretended to be. If I had only said the word I am sure she would have dropped the other fellow; perhaps she would even have gone away with me. I preferred to punish myself. I said good-by nonchalantly and I went down the street like a dead man. The next morning I was bound for the Coast, determined to start a new life.

The new life was also a fiasco. I ended up on a ranch in Chula Vista, the most miserable man that ever walked the earth. There was this girl I loved and there was the other woman, for whom I felt only a profound pity. I had been living with her for two years, this other woman, but it seemed like a lifetime. I was twenty-one and she admitted to be thirty-six. Every time I looked at her I said to myself—when I am thirty she will be forty-five, when I am forty she will be fifty-five, when I am fifty she will be sixty-five. She had fine wrinkles under the eyes, laughing wrinkles, but wrinkles just the same. When I kissed her they were magnified a dozen times. She laughed easily, but her eyes were sad, terribly sad. They were Armenian eyes. Her hair, which had been red once, was now a peroxide blonde. Otherwise she was adorable—a Venusian body, a Venusian soul, loyal, lovable, grateful, everything a woman should be, *except that she was fifteen years older*. The fifteen years' difference drove me crazy.

When I went out with her I thought only—how will it be ten years hence? Or else, what age does she seem to have now? Do I look old enough for her? Once we got back to the house it was all right. Climbing the stairs I would run my finger up her crotch, which used to make her whinny like a horse. If her son, who was almost my age, were in bed we would close the doors and lock ourselves in the kitchen. She'd lie on the narrow kitchen table and I'd slough it into her. It was marvelous. And what made it more marvelous was that with each performance I would say to myself—*This is the last time . . . tomorrow I will beat it!* And then, since she was the janitress, I would go down to the cellar and roll the ash barrels out for her. In the morning, when the son had left for work, I would climb up to the roof and air the bedding. Both she and the son had T.B. . . . Sometimes there were no table bouts. Sometimes the hopelessness of it all got me by the throat and I would put on my things and go for a walk. Now and then I forgot to return. And when I did that I was more miserable than ever, because I knew that she would be waiting for me with those large sorrowful eyes. I'd go back to her like a man who had a sacred duty to perform. I'd lie down on the bed and let her caress me; I'd study the wrinkles under her eyes and the roots of her hair which were turning red. Lying there like that, I would often think about the other one, the one I loved, would wonder if she were lying down for it too, or. . . Those long walks I took three hundred and sixty-five days of the year!—I would go over them in my mind lying beside the other woman. How many times since have I relived these walks! The dreariest, bleakest, ugliest streets man ever created. In anguish I relive these walks, these streets, these first smashed hopes. The window is there, but no Melisande; the garden too is there, but no sheen of gold. Pass and repass, the window always vacant. The evening star hangs low; Tristan appears, then Fidelio, and then Oberon. The hydra-headed dog barks with all his mouths and though there are no swamps I hear the frogs croaking every-where. Same houses, same car lines, same everything. She is hiding behind the curtain, she is waiting for me to pass, she is doing this or doing that. . . . *but she is not there, never, never, never.* Is it a grand opera or is it a hurdy-gurdy playing? It is Amato bursting his golden lung; it is the *Rubaiyat*, it is Mount Everest, it is a moonless night, it is a sob at dawn, it is a boy making believe, it is Puss in the Boot, it is Mauna Loa, it is fox or astrakhan, it is of no stuff and no time, it is endless and it begins over and over, under the heart, in the back of the throat, in the soles of the feet, and why not just once, just once, for the love of Christ, just a shadow or a rustle of the curtain, or a breath on the windowpane, something once, if only a lie, something to stop the pain, to stop this walking up and down, up and down. . . . Walking home-ward. Same houses, same lampposts, same everything. I walk past my own home, past the cemetery, past the gas tanks, past the car barns, past the reservoir, out into the open country. I sit beside the road with my head in my hands and sob. Poor bugger that I am, I can't contract my heart enough to burst the veins. I would like to suffo-cate with grief but instead I give birth to a rock.

Meanwhile the other one is waiting. I can see her again as she sat on the low stoop waiting for me, her eyes large and dolorous, her face pale and trembling with eagerness. *Pity* I always thought it was brought me back, but now as I walk toward her and see the look in her eyes I don't know any more what it is, only that we will go inside and lie together and she will get up half weeping, half laugh-ing, and she will grow very silent and watch me, study me as I move about, and never ask me what is torturing me, never, never, because that is the one thing she fears, the one thing she dreads to know. *I don't love you!* Can't she hear me screaming it? *I don't love you!* Over and over I yell it, with lips tight, with hatred in my heart, with despair, with hopeless rage. But the words never leave my lips. I look at her and I am tongue-tied.

I can't do it. . . . Time, time, endless time on our hands and nothing to fill it but lies.

Well, I don't want to rehearse the whole of my life leading up to the fatal moment—it is too long and too painful. Besides, did my life really lead up to this culminating moment? I doubt it. I think there were innumerable moments when I had the chance to make a beginning, but I lacked the strength and the faith. On the evening in question I deliberately walked out on myself: I walked right out of the old life and into the new. There wasn't the slightest effort involved. I was thirty then. I had a wife and child and what is called a "responsible" position. These are the facts and facts mean nothing. The truth is my desire was so great it became a reality. At such a moment what a man *does* is of no great importance, it's what he *is* that counts. It's at such a moment that a man becomes an angel. That is precisely what happened to me: *I became an angel.* It is not the purity of an angel which is so valuable, as the fact it can fly. An angel can break the pattern anywhere at any moment and find its heaven; it has the power to descend into the lowest matter and to extricate itself at will. The night in question I understood it perfectly. I was pure and inhuman, I was detached, I had wings. I was depossessed of the past and I had no concern about the future. I was beyond ecstasy. When I left the office I folded my wings and hid them beneath my coat.

The dance hall was just opposite the side entrance of the theater where I used to sit in the afternoons instead of looking for work. It was a street of theaters and I used to sit there for hours at a time dreaming the most violent dreams. The whole theatrical life of New York was concentrated in that one street, so it seemed. It was Broadway, it was success, fame, glitter, paint, the asbestos curtain and the hole in the curtain. Sitting on the steps of the theater I used to stare at the dance hall opposite, at the string of red lanterns which even in the summer afternoons were lit up. In every window there was a spinning ventilator which seemed to waft the music into the street, where it was broken by the jangled din of traffic. Opposite the other side of the dance hall was a comfort station and here too I used to sit now and then, hoping either to make a woman or make a touch. Above the comfort station, on the street level, was a kiosk with foreign papers and magazines; the very sight of these papers, of the strange languages in which they were printed, was sufficient to dislocate me for the day.

Without the slightest premeditation I climbed the stairs to the dance hall, went directly to the little window of the booth where Nick, the Greek, sat with a roll of tickets in front of him. Like the urinal below and the steps of the theater, this hand of the Greek now seems to me a separate and detached thing—the enormous hairy hand of an ogre borrowed from some horrible Scandinavian fairy tale. It was the hand which spoke to me always, the hand which said "Miss Mara will not be here tonight," or "Yes, Miss Mara is coming late tonight." It was this hand which I dreamt of as a child when I slept in the bedroom with the barred window. In my fevered sleep suddenly this window would light up, to reveal the ogre clutching at the bars. Night after night the hairy monster visited me, clutching at the bars and gnashing its teeth. I would awake in a cold sweat, the house dark, the room absolutely silent.

Standing at the edge of the dance floor I notice her coming toward me; she is coming with sails spread, the large full face beautifully balanced on the long, columnar neck. I see a woman perhaps eighteen, perhaps thirty, with blue-black hair and a large white face, a full white face in which the eyes shine brilliantly. She has on a tailored blue suit of duveteen. I remember distinctly now the fullness of her body, and that her hair was fine and straight, parted on the side, like a man's. I remember the smile she gave me—knowing, mysterious, fugitive—a smile that sprang up suddenly, like a puff of wind.

The whole being was concentrated in the face. I could

have taken just the head and walked home with it; I could have put it beside me at night, on a pillow, and made love to it. The mouth and the eyes, when they opened up, the whole being glowed from them. There was an illumination which came from some unknown source, from a center hidden deep in the earth. I could think of nothing but the face, the strange, womblike quality of the smile, the engulfing immediacy of it. The smile was so painfully swift and fleeting that it was like the flash of a knife. This smile, this face, was borne aloft on a long white neck, the sturdy, swanlike neck of the medium—and of the lost and the damned.

I stand on the corner under the red lights, waiting for her to come down. It is about two in the morning and she is signing off. I am standing on Broadway with a flower in my buttonhole, feeling absolutely clean and alone. Almost the whole evening we have been talking about Strindberg, about a character of his named Henriette. I listened with such tense alertness that I fell into a trance. It was as if, with the opening phrase, we had started on a race—in opposite directions. Henriette! Almost immediately the name was mentioned she began to talk about herself, without ever quite losing hold of Henriette. Henriette was attached to her by a long, invisible string which she manipulated imperceptibly with one finger, like the street hawker who stands a little removed from the black cloth on the sidewalk, apparently indifferent to the little mechanism which is jiggling on the cloth, but betraying himself by the spasmodic movement of the little finger to which the black thread is attached. Henriette is me, my real self, she seemed to be saying. She wanted me to believe that Henriette was really the incarnation of evil. She said it so naturally, so innocently, with an almost sub-human candor—how was I to believe that she meant it? I could only smile as though to show her I was convinced.

Suddenly I feel her coming. I turn my head. Yes, there she is coming full on, the sails spread, the eyes glowing. For the first time I see now what a carriage she has.

She comes forward like a bird, a human bird wrapped in a soft fur. The engine is going full steam: I want to shout, to give a blast that will make the whole world cock its ears. What a walk! It's not a walk, it's a glide. Tall, stately, full-bodied, self-possessed, she cuts the smoke and jazz and red-light glow like the queen mother of all the slippery Babylonian whores. On the corner of Broadway just opposite the comfort station, this is happening. Broadway—it's her realm. This is Broadway, this is New York, this is America. She's America on foot, winged and sexed. She is the lubet, the abominate and the sublimate—with a dash of hydrochloric acid, nitroglycerin, laudanum and powdered onyx. Opulence she has, and magnificence; it's America right or wrong, and the ocean on either side. For the first time in my life the whole continent hits me full force, hits me between the eyes. This is America, buffaloes or no buffaloes, America the emery wheel of hope and disillusionment. Whatever made America made her, bone, blood, muscle, eyeball, gait, rhythm, poise, confidence, brass and hollow gut. She's almost on top of me, the full face gleaming like calcium. The big soft fur is slipping from her shoulder. She doesn't notice it. She doesn't seem to care if her clothes should drop off. She doesn't give a fuck about anything. It's America moving like a streak of lightning toward the glass warehouse of red-blooded hysteria. Amurrica, fur or no fur, shoes or no shoes. Amurrica C.O.D. *And scram, you bastards, before we plug you!* It's got me in the guts, I'm quaking. Something's coming to me and there's no dodging it. She's coming head on, through the plate glass window. If she would only stop a second, if she would only let me be for just one moment. But no, not a single moment does she grant me. Swift, ruthless, imperious, like Fate itself she is on me, a sword cutting me through and through. . . .

She has me by the hand, she holds it tight. I walk beside her without fear. Inside me the stars are twinkling;

inside me a great blue vault where a moment ago the engines were pounding furiously.

One can wait a whole lifetime for a moment like this. The woman whom you never hoped to meet now sits before you, and she talks and looks exactly like the person you dreamed about. But strangest of all is that you never realized before that you had dreamed about her. Your whole past is like a long sleep which would have been forgotten had there been no dream. And the dream too might have been forgotten had there been no memory, but remembrance is there in the blood and the blood is like an ocean in which everything is washed away but that which is new and more substantial even than life: REALITY.

We are seated in a little booth in the Chinese restaurant across the way. Out of the corner of my eye I catch the flicker of the illuminated letters running up and down the sky. She is still talking about Henriette, or maybe it is about herself. Her little black bonnet, her bag and fur are lying beside her on the bench. Every few minutes she lights a fresh cigarette which burns away as she talks. There is no beginning nor end; it spurts out of her like a flame and consumes everything within reach. No knowing how or where she began. Suddenly she is in the midst of a long narrative, a fresh one, but it is always the same. Her talk is as formless as dream: there are no grooves, no walls, no exits, no stops. I have the feeling of being drowned in a deep mesh of words, of crawling painfully back to the top of the net, of looking into her eyes and trying to find there some reflection of the significance of her words—but I can find nothing, nothing except my own image wavering in a bottomless well. Though she speaks of nothing but herself I am unable to form the slightest image of her being. She leans forward, with elbows on the table, and her words inundate me; wave after wave rolling over me and yet nothing builds up inside me, nothing that I can seize with my mind. She's telling me about her father, about the strange life they led at the edge of Sherwood Forest where she was born, or at least she *was* telling me about this, but now it's about Henriette again, or is it Dostoevski?—I'm not sure —but anyway, suddenly I realize that she's not talking about any of these any more but about a man who took her home one night and as they stood on the stoop saying good-night he suddenly reached down and pulled up her dress. She pauses a moment as though to reassure me that this is what she means to talk about. I look at her bewilderedly. I can't imagine by what route we got to this point. *What man?* What had he been saying to her? I let her continue, thinking that she will probably come back to it, but no, she's ahead of me again and now it seems the man, *this* man, is already dead, a suicide, and she is trying to make me understand that it was an awful blow to her, but what she really seems to convey is that she is proud of the fact that she drove a man to suicide. I can't picture the man as dead; I can only think of him as he stood on her stoop lifting her dress, a man without a name but alive and perpetually fixed in the act of bending down to lift up her dress. There is another man who was her father and I see him with a string of race horses, or sometimes in a little inn just outside Vienna; rather I see him on the roof of the inn flying kites to while the time away. And between this man who was her father and the man with whom she was madly in love I can make no separation. He is someone in her life about whom she would rather not talk, but just the same she comes back to him all the time, and though I'm not sure that it was *not* the man who lifted up her dress neither am I sure that it wasn't the man who committed suicide. Perhaps it's the man whom she started to talk about when we sat down to eat. Just as we were sitting down I remember now that she began to talk rather hectically about a man whom she had just seen entering the cafeteria. She even mentioned his name, but I forgot it immediately. But I remember her saying that she had lived with him and that he had done something which she didn't like—she didn't say what—and so she had walked out on him, left him flat, without a word of explanation. And then, just as we were entering the chop suey joint, they ran into each other and she was still trembling over it as we sat down in the little booth. . . . For one long moment I have the most uneasy sensation. Maybe every word she uttered was a lie! Not an ordinary lie, no, something worse, something indescribable. Only sometimes the truth comes out like that too, especially if you think you're never going to see the person again. Sometimes you can tell a perfect stranger what you would never dare reveal to your most intimate friend. It's like going to sleep in the midst of a party; you become so interested in yourself that you go to sleep. And when you're sound asleep you begin to talk to someone, someone who was in the same room with you all the time and therefore understands everything even though you begin in the middle of a sentence. And perhaps this other person goes to sleep also, or was always asleep, and that's why it was so easy to encounter him, and if he doesn't say anything to disturb you then you know that what you are saying is real and true and that you are wide-awake and there is no other reality except this being wide-awake asleep. Never before have I been so wide-awake and so sound asleep at the same time. If the ogre in my dreams had really pushed the bars aside and taken me by the hand I would have been frightened to death and consequently now dead, that is, forever asleep and therefore always at large, and nothing would be strange any more, nor untrue, even if what happened did not happen. What happened must have happened long ago, in the night undoubtedly. And what is now happening is also happening long ago, in the night, and this is no more true than the dream of the ogre and the bars which would not give, except that now the bars are broken and she whom I feared has me by the hand and there is no difference between that which I feared and what is, because I was asleep and now I am wide-awake asleep and there is nothing more to fear, nor to expect, nor to hope for, but just this which is and which knows no end.

She wants to go. To go. . . . Again her haunch, that slippery glide as when she came down from the dance hall and moved into me. Again her words . . . "suddenly for no reason at all, he bent down and lifted up my dress." She's slipping the fur around her neck; the little black bonnet sets her face off like a cameo. The round, full face, with Slavic cheekbones. How could I dream this, never having seen it? How could I know that she would rise like this, close and full, the face full white and blooming like a magnolia? I tremble as the fullness of her thigh brushes me. She seems even a little taller than I, though she is not. It's the way she holds her chin. She doesn't notice where she's walking. She walks *over* things, on, on, with eyes wide open and staring into space. No past, no future. Even the present seems dubious. The self seems to have left her, and the body rushes forward, the neck full and taut, white as the face, full like the face. The talk goes on, in that low, throaty voice. No beginning, no end. I'm aware not of time nor the passing of time, but of time-lessness. She's got the little womb in the throat hooked up to the big womb in the pelvis. The cab is at the curb and she is still chewing the cosmological chaff of the outer ego. I pick up the speaking tube and connect with the double uterus. Hello, hello, are you there? Let's go! Let's get on with it—cabs, boats, trains, naphtha launches; beaches, bedbugs, highways, byways, ruins; relics, old world, new world, pier, jetty; the high forceps, the swinging trapeze, the ditch, the delta, the alligators, the crocodiles, talk, talk, and more talk; then roads again and more dust in the eyes, more rainbows, more cloudbursts, more breakfast foods, more creams, more lotions. And when all the roads have been traversed and there is left only the dust of our frantic feet there will still remain the memory of your large full face so white, and the wide mouth with fresh lips parted, the teeth chalk white and each one perfect, and in this remembrance nothing can possibly change because this, like your teeth, is perfect. . . .

It is Sunday, the first Sunday of my new life, and I am wearing the dog collar you fastened around my neck. A new life stretches before me. It begins with the day of rest. I lie back on a broad green leaf and I watch the sun bursting in your womb. What a clabber and clatter it makes! All this expressly for me, what? If only you had a million suns in you! If only I could lie here forever enjoying the celestial fireworks!

I lie suspended over the surface of the moon. The world is in a womblike trance: the inner and the outer ego are in equilibrium. You promised me so much that if I never come out of this it will make no difference. It seems to me that it is exactly 25,960 years since I have been asleep in the black womb of sex. It seems to me that I slept perhaps 365 years too many. But at any rate I am now in the right house, among the sixes, and what lies behind me is well and what lies ahead is well. You come to me disguised as Venus, but you are Lilith, and I know it. My whole life is in the balance; I will enjoy the luxury of this for one day. Tomorrow I shall tip the scales. Tomorrow the equilibrium will be finished; if I ever find it again it will be in the blood and not in the stars. It is well that you promise me so much. I need to be promised nearly everything, for I have lived in the shadow of the sun too long. I want light and chastity—and a solar fire in the guts. I want to be deceived and disillusioned so that I may complete the upper triangle and not be continually flying off the planet into space. I believe everything you tell me, but I know also that it will all turn out differently. I take you as a star and a trap, as a stone to tip the scales, as a judge that is blindfolded, as a hole to fall into, as a path to walk, as a cross and an arrow. Up to the present I traveled the opposite way of the sun; henceforth I travel two ways, as sun and as moon. Henceforth I take on two sexes, two hemispheres, two skies, two sets of everything. Henceforth I shall be double-jointed and double-sexed. Everything that happens will happen twice. I shall be as a visitor to this earth, partaking of its blessings and carrying off its gifts. I shall neither serve nor be served. I shall seek the end in myself.

I look out again at the sun—my first full gaze. It is blood-red and men are walking about on the rooftops. Everything above the horizon is clear to me. It is like Easter Sunday. Death is behind me and birth too. I am going to live now among the life maladies. I am going to live the spiritual life of the pygmy, the secret life of the little man in the wilderness of the bush. Inner and outer have changed places. Equilibrium is no longer the goal —the scales must be destroyed. Let me hear you promise again all those sunny things you carry inside you. Let me try to believe for one day, while I rest in the open, that the sun brings good tidings. Let me rot in splendor while the sun bursts in your womb. I believe all your lies implicitly. I take you as the personification of evil, as the destroyer of the soul, as the maharanee of the night. Tack your womb up on my wall, so that I may remember you. We must get going. Tomorrow, tomorrow. . . .

September, 1938
Villa Seurat, Paris

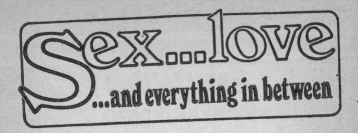

Sex...love
...and everything in between

Available at your bookstore or use this coupon.